TRADITIONAL SAMPLERS

TRADITIONAL SAMPLERS

SARAH DON

◆

While you my dear your needlework attend
Observe the counsel of a faithful friend
And strive an inward ornament to gain
Or all your needlework will prove in vain.

VIKING

To Betty, Jobo, Bewick, Nellie and Sasha

(frontispiece)
A Spanish sampler showing a large number of geometric
border patterns worked mostly in satin stitch; other stitches
used are hem, back, diagonal chevron, four-sided and outline stitches, with bullion knots. It is signed Gertrudes de
Cpayso and dated 1729. The materials are silk on linen and
the work measures 36 × 26½in (91.4 × 67cm) *(Victoria
and Albert Museum, London)*

First published in 1986 by Viking Penguin Inc.
40 West 23rd Street, New York, N.Y. 10010, USA
Published simultaneously in Canada by
Penguin Books Canada Limited

ISBN 0–670–80732–X
Library of Congress Catalog Card Number 85–41068 (CIP Data Available)

Printed in Great Britain

Contents

Introduction

Like all traditional crafts, sampler-making has only been successful when it has served a purpose or fulfilled a need. Some of the most beautiful samplers are those made before the advent of printed patterns, when patterns and motifs were embroidered onto fabric to provide a useful record for future use. Later, samplers were used as practice pieces; on them the embroiderer would experiment with different stitches, colours and threads, and work out designs for other, more major, works. By the eighteenth century, samplers were the means by which young girls learnt the skills of needlework; later, in schools, they became useful exercises for teaching, for example, mathematical tables and geography. Poor children in schools and orphanages were taught only the most basic skills and worked row upon row of alphabets and numerals onto their samplers. It was hoped that these children would eventually obtain employment in service, having become proficient in the marking of linen, darning and mending.

When samplers were worked for their decorative value alone, standards deteriorated rapidly. The advent of the craze for Berlin woolwork during the Victorian era heralded the decline of the sampler, both throughout Europe and, later on, in America.

Sampler-making today is gaining in popularity and samplers are being made both by serious students of embroidery and by needlewomen who consider their craft a hobby. Sampler-making will survive so long as the finished works serve some real purpose, whether as practice pieces for beginners, notebooks for students or commemorative pieces depicting an historical occasion or a family tree.

This book has been written in the hope that it may promote and encourage the art of sampler-making, and prove a useful source of reference. There are traditional patterns and motifs from samplers over the last five centuries which have successfully survived many fashions and trends and, I believe, remain valid designs for working onto textiles today.

The complete samplers are intended for beginners and for those who may lack the confidence to design their own work. I am sure that after working one of the projects here, you will have gained sufficient skills and confidence to attempt working some of your own ideas. Try experimenting with colours, threads and fabrics. The materials and colours given with each project are intended as a rough guide and do not have to be followed slavishly. The same applies where there is text included in the work: use the text of your own choice — perhaps a favourite verse or a dedication.

I have tried to cover samplers from many different periods, including pieces from the Victorian era, whitework, blackwork, a number of alphabets, a multiplication table and a rebus sampler showing the story of Noah's Ark. The range of complexity of the samplers and of the skill required is also as wide as possible and I hope I have catered for all abilities.

I should like to encourage all embroiderers to explore the possibilities of further education through the various guilds and institutions that exist; a brief list of these is given, together with their addresses, at the end of the book. There is also a list of relevant publications in the bibliography; those that are possible sources of patterns and motifs are marked with an asterisk.

A very famous English sampler, worked by Jane Bostocke in 1598 to celebrate the birth of her daughter, Alice. A very large number of border patterns and all-over repeat patterns have been worked, together with a lion, a deer, a dog and a tiger standing over a daisy pattern border. Some of these patterns have been included in the project for the blackwork sampler. The threads used for the sampler are metal threads and silk on linen, with the inclusion of pearls and beads. The stitches used include back, satin, chain, ladder buttonhole, detached buttonhole, cross, arrowhead, interlacing, pattern couching, coral and two-sided Italian cross stitches with speckling, bullion and French knots. This sampler measures 17 × 15in (43 × 38cm) *(Victoria and Albert Museum, London)*

Note: When working with the charts and colour photographs the colours of the threads may not match exactly with the colours shown in the photographs, due to variations in printing and changes in dye lots for the threads. The latter can cause differences noticeable easily by eye.

1
Samplers through the Ages

Early Samplers

The word exampler or sampler is derived from the French *examplair*, meaning a kind of model or pattern to work by, copy or imitate. The Latin word *exemplum*, meaning a copy, pattern or model, was, by the sixteenth century, spelt *saumpler, sampler* or *exampler*.

The earliest surviving samplers are those worked in double running stitch and pattern darning; they were recovered from Egyptian burial grounds and are probably medieval. European embroideries were almost certainly influenced by the patterns on these works which had designs based on the ancient lozenge, S and X forms worked in running stitch.

As a result of the Renaissance movement, there was a strong revival of European interest in all forms of decoration in the late fifteenth and early sixteenth centuries. Many women took to the art of needlework to decorate not only personal attire, but also furnishings around the home. It was a most pleasurable pastime but a costly one; silk, gold and silver threads, beads and even tiny seed pearls were all expensive materials, so the craft was restricted to rich, often titled, ladies.

At this time there were no printed patterns available for needleworkers; patterns were passed from hand to hand, many slowly filtering through the Continent from the Middle East. This process was accelerated by the sudden increase in travel and foreign activity at this time.

An English sampler of the first half of the seventeenth century with numerous spot motifs and geometric patterns in a very large number of stitches including plaited braid, rococo, tent, back, crosslet, Algerian eye, interlacing, long-armed cross, Hungarian, Florentine, Roumanian, guilloche and chain stitches, with buttonhole wheels and laid and couched work. The threads used are silver, silver-gilt and silk on linen and the piece measures only 20½ × 12in (52 × 30.5cm). The patterns include diaper designs filled with acorns and floral motifs, knot patterns and repeating motifs. A number of small creatures have also been included — a frog, a caterpillar, duck and fish, together with various butterflies. This example illustrates the way in which these early samplers were used as notebooks and practice pieces *(Victoria and Albert Museum, London)*

The recording of patterns and motifs on fabric for future use was an essential task and resulted in the creation of the sampler. New patterns and stitches were avidly collected and exchanged among friends and were immediately added to the sampler before they could be forgotten. They were placed in a random or haphazard way over the cloth to fill every vacant space, hence the name random or spot sampler. These pieces were excellent practice grounds too, with the needleworker jotting down new stitches and experimenting with colours and threads, perhaps before proceeding to a more major work.

English sixteenth-century samplers were always worked on a linen ground with silk threads, although some examples also used gold and silver threads and seed pearls. The shape was narrow — 6-9in (15-23cm) wide and up to 24in (61cm) long, the length being determined by the loom width of the woven cloth.

The work on these samplers is so well executed that it is believed to be that of adult and expert needlewomen. Numerous geometric patterns were worked; excellent use was made of silk and metal threads; and many different stitches resulted in stunningly beautiful designs. Along with these patterns was worked a large range of spot motifs — a huge variety of flowers and animals from domestic animals such as dogs, horses, hares and swans to exotic creatures such as peacocks, lions and leopards. Any spaces occurring between these were filled with smaller creatures such as birds and insects, caterpillars, fish, snakes, frogs and butterflies. Some of the many stitches used were Hungarian, Florentine, tent, cross, long-armed cross, two-sided Italian cross, rice, running, double running, Algerian eye and buttonhole stitches.

Twenty different colours might be used on one piece of embroidery and these were tried out first on the worker's sampler. Popular colour schemes at the time were in different shades of blue, green, yellow, orange, brown and red, with an even larger number of shades being created by twisting together strands of two different colours. The resulting samplers would be highly treasured possessions, so much so that they were often bequeathed by will or mentioned in royal inventories.

The demand for printed patterns for needlework

was eventually exploited commercially and the first printed pattern book arrived in 1523, printed in Augsburg, Germany, by Johann Sibmacher. Similar books then appeared from French and Italian presses and finally in England from 1587. One pattern book, published in 1587 under the title *Singolari e Nuovi Disegni* and designed by Federico Vincioli, was to influence samplers in the sixteenth and seventeenth centuries. (The book has been reprinted as *Renaissance Patterns for Lace, Embroidery and Needlepoint*.) Italian work of the time showed a strong Islamic influence and was distinguished by its strongly geometric and elaborate floral borders. Pattern books were not commonly available and samplers continued to be made as reference sheets and practice pieces.

In England at this time, one of the most effective types of embroidery was blackwork. This technique used a single thread of black silk worked in double running stitch on a white or cream linen ground, and was to remain popular well into the seventeenth century. It was worked on clothes, chiefly cuffs and collars, in an extremely effective way. Double running stitch was particularly useful for this purpose as it had no wrong side, being worked twice along the design, first in one direction and then back again. Catherine of Aragon arrived in England from Spain in 1501 and the introduction of blackwork into Britain is popularly attributed to her, although examples had existed before her arrival. The patterns used for blackwork do have strong Moorish influences and geometric patterns worked in back stitch had been traditional in Spain for centuries. I am sure, however, that Catherine's arrival in England did promote the popularity of blackwork, and one of the names by which the running stitch became known was Spanish stitch. It was also given the name Holbein, because the painter of that name regularly had sitters wearing clothes decorated with blackwork embroidery.

Patterns originally printed for lacemaking during the Renaissance period showed linear designs which were eagerly and easily adapted for blackwork. With the increased circulation of engraved illustrations, designs such as those for formal gardens and knot gardens were also an inspiration. They were particularly suitable for blackwork, but also provided ideas for other types of embroidery; many beautiful pieces inspired by gardens and garden designs have been worked.

Few samplers from the sixteenth century have survived, and the signing and dating of samplers during this period was not common. The earliest dated surviving sampler was made by Jane Bostocke (p6). It was discovered as recently as 1960 and is one of the most famous samplers in the Victoria and Albert Museum in London. It was probably worked as a gift for Jane's daughter and she has included the inscription:

A sampler from the middle of the seventeenth century upon which have been worked a number of floral motifs and geometric patterns which I find particularly fascinating. These all-over repeating patterns are fairly simple and could easily be adapted for use today. The threads used are silver, silver-gilt and silk on linen, the stitches are eye, plaited braid, Florentine, Hungarian, cross, crosslet, long-armed cross, tent, Roumanian, rococo, gobelin, interlacing and drawn-fabric stitches. The sampler measures 20 × 8in (51 × 20cm) *(Victoria and Albert Museum, London)*

ALICE:LEE:WAS:BORNE:THE:23:OF:
NOVEMBER:BEING:TWESDAY:IN:
THE:AFTER:NOONE:1556.

The sampler is worked in red, brown, blue and white silks and includes black beads, seed pearls and metal threads, using back, satin, chain, two-sided Italian, cross, buttonhole and coral stitches and French knots. Some of the patterns (and the alphabet) on this sampler are used in the Blackwork Sampler (17).

During Elizabeth I's reign in England, trade with the East and the New World gave a terrific impetus to all the arts. The arrival of new materials and ideas from abroad began the exciting developments which led traditional English embroidery into the seventeenth century, now known as the golden age of sampler-making.

Seventeenth-century Samplers

In the seventeenth century, samplers were comparatively numerous and some of the most beautiful and

This distinctive Mexican sampler from the late eighteenth or nineteenth century contains a number of realistically worked motifs including birds, flowers, a butterfly or moth, a rather lovely rabbit and what appears to be a poodle carrying a basket of flowers. Silver-gilt thread and pure silk are worked on linen, with the inclusion of spangles. Long and short, satin and stem stitches with French knots are used and the sampler measures 12 × 15½in (30.5 × 39cm) *(Victoria and Albert Museum, London)*

imaginative pieces ever made come from the UK. At the beginning of this century, most were still being made as records and practice pieces for patterns, motifs and stitches. The designs and colour schemes were quite exquisite and the standards of stitchery and technique were very high.

Samplers produced in Germany at this time were either worked using a very simple floral border to surround a number of small geometric motifs placed at random, or included alphabets and border patterns as well as a number of motifs, again randomly placed.

The motifs included the instruments of the Passion, birds, animals, fruit trees and castles. The samplers were similar to those being made in England: long and narrow in shape and mostly worked in cross stitch in a number of colours.

Dutch samplers from this time were very like their German counterparts in the choice of subjects depicted and general layout, but they were distinguished by their shape — they were either square or wider than they were long.

It would seem that Spanish and Mexican samplers were being made in the sixteenth and seventeenth centuries, though very few have survived. Using brightly coloured silks of a number of different colours on white linen, they were given rather elaborate treatment. Satin stitch was predominantly used for the geometric motifs and patterns, with alphabets and verses appearing rarely. Spanish samplers were square or rectangular and frequently signed and dated. Mexican samplers were usually rectangular with motifs such as animals and birds placed at random.

French samplers were square or broader than they were long and were worked almost entirely in cross stitch. Italian samplers were also wider than they were long, but included the use of other stitches such as feather, double running, satin and chain stitches.

In England, during Charles I's reign, there was a tremendous increase in the wealth of society; much of this money was spent on elegant refinements and large quantities of household linens and furnishings. Ladies found the skill of needlework to be a highly desirable asset and used embroidery to decorate these furnishings and items of attire.

The number of pattern books in circulation increased. These included the famous *A schole-house for the needle*, by Richard Shorleyker, published in 1624. The following lines are from the poem 'The Needle's Excellency' by John Taylor. This was later also the title for a book, the twelfth edition of which was published in London in 1632; it consisted of needlework patterns originally published in Germany in 1597 under the title *Schön Neues Modelbuch*, by Johann Sibmacher.

Here Practice and Invention may be free,
And as a Squirrell skips from tree to tree,
So maids may (from their Mistresses, or their Mother)
Learne to leave one worke, and to learne an other,
For here they may make choyce of which is which,
And skip from worke to worke, from stitch to stitch,
Until, in time, delightfull practice shall
(with profit) make them perfect in them all.

In the early part of the century, samplers continued to be worked by adult needlewomen and were still in the form of the spot or random samplers of the sixteenth century, recognisable by their long and narrow shape. These samplers were particularly colourful and imaginative. Animals, both real and mythological, birds and flowers were worked in very fine tent stitch with a high degree of shading. The designs of this period strongly reflect the current fashions of the time. A wide range of fauna and flowers appears, with the Tudor rose being the favourite. Roses were the national emblems of the Tudor kings and appear on samplers as red and white flowers, usually in full face rather than in bud; both single and double varieties were depicted. Carnations, pansies, tulips, lions and stags appear regularly, along with snails, caterpillars, butterflies and fish. Favourite fruits were pineapples, figs, grapes and strawberries. Animals were to become increasingly popular towards the latter half of the century. The earliest recorded human figures on a sampler appear on a piece dated 1630. Samplers of this time were rarely signed in full and only a few included the initials of the needleworker.

The band sampler was popular in this century and consisted of tightly packed rows of border patterns with hardly a space left unworked and using a wide variety of stitches. Most of the linen used for these samplers was imported and was still very costly; hence the obvious need to economise with fabric. The threads used were silk, gold and silver, with beads, seed pearls and sequins incorporated into the designs.

The bands of patterning had both geometrical and floral designs and, as with the spot samplers, used roses, carnations and strawberries in repeating border patterns. Another popular motif worked into border patterns was the acorn. This was shown both on its own and with the oak leaf; although it appears on many samplers from this century, it was to disappear completely by the beginning of the eighteenth century.

Patterns outlined with running stitch were still popular but, over the years, workers began to fill them in with coloured silks and metal threads, using a number of different stitches.

Assisi work, which originated in northern Italy, was often included on these samplers for a few rows, or in deep borders at the edges of linens. Popular motifs worked and repeated across borders were birds, rosettes, stars, hearts and heraldic animals. They were sewn using a number of different stitches including cross stitch, tent, single-faggot and plaited-braid. Older pieces used outlines of back stitch, buttonhole or whipping stitch.

'Boxers' were representations of the human form and were usually worked in back stitch or running stitch; later on they were filled in with coloured silks, usually in satin stitch. These figures are often depicted carrying what could be a heart shape, an acorn or perhaps a flower. In modern days they have been given the name 'boxers' because of their stance. One

An English band sampler of the mid-seventeenth century which has a number of motifs worked in double running stitch and wide floral bands of patterning. The motifs include a lion and a unicorn; charts for the strawberry plant and a number of the smaller floral motifs are given in the blackwork project on page 116. The materials used for the band sampler are silk on linen, in double running, stem, Montenegrin, cross, Algerian eye, outline and detached filling stitches. The sampler measures 18 × 7½in (45.5 × 19cm) *(Victoria and Albert Museum, London)*

explanation for their significance is that they are lovers exchanging gifts. A large flowering plant appearing between the figures is said to have originated as a female figure holding a gift (a sprig of foliage), which, through many translations and repeated copying, has been modified to the shape and form of a bush. Boxers have also been referred to as Renaissance cupids or as early versions of Adam and Eve.

Bands of more complicated whitework and openwork would often appear at the bottom of these samplers. Perhaps this kind of work was left to last, by which time the worker might have gained enough skill and expertise to execute the techniques proficiently.

Whitework is the name given to all types of embroidery on white linen worked with white thread, and the simplest forms are designs of block satin stitch, double running stitch and detached buttonhole bars. Cut and drawn work is more difficult. Geometric and floral designs are worked on a framework of threads which is first prepared by drawing out and cutting threads from a piece of linen and replacing them with diagonal threads. More complicated pieces included designs which depicted the human figure; Adam and Eve and mermaids were popular subjects.

The fashion for whitework was probably stimulated by the craze for lace which seemed to decorate every item of attire at this time. Whitework was a way of achieving a similar effect more quickly and was used for modest decoration on edges and hems. Denmark was the home of some rather beautiful pieces of whitework, as too was Sweden. During the period when only the nobility were permitted to wear lace, ordinary Danish women used whitework to decorate items of clothing.

Samplers worked solely in cutwork are in a much smaller group. One such piece which can be seen in the London Museum shows the arms of Queen Elizabeth I, which suggests that this type of work was current at the beginning of this century. The earliest signed and dated cutwork sampler was worked in 1634.

In England, during the early years of the reign of Charles I, the art of needlework became a well-established part of the school curriculum, with samplers being used to familiarise young children with the many different embroidery and lacework techniques.

By the mid-seventeenth century, alphabets were included in samplers, along with signatures at the bottom of the work. The neat rows of patterning and the inclusion of these alphabets were an indication that sampler-making was becoming more and more significant as a school exercise for children.

As printed patterns for needlework and designs printed on embroidery canvas became more readily available, the use of the sampler as a record was virtually over; but children's samplers were still meant

13

An Italian whitework sampler of the mid-seventeenth century which is signed Gvllia Piccolomini. A number of intricate and rather lovely geometric patterns have been worked in cut and drawn-thread work, using linen on linen. A female figure has been included in the bottom left-hand corner. Cut and drawn-thread work samplers were also being worked at this time in England, with the patterns tending more towards those based on floral designs. This sampler measures 32 × 18in (81 × 46cm) *(Victoria and Albert Museum, London)*

as practice pieces for the different stitches and as notebooks of patterns for future use. Alphabets were needed for marking linen, and spot motifs would be used for smaller items such as purses and pincushions. Some lovely examples of whitework and cutwork were being worked by children and still had practical uses up to the middle of the seventeenth century. By this time, the borders worked on samplers had become over-fussy and large and would have been far too elaborate to work on household linen.

The children's work was of a very high standard and used remarkably varied techniques. The samplers were a credit to the thoroughness of the teachers' instruction and the teacher's name was often included in the finished piece.

From about 1650 onwards, short, pious, moral and religious inscriptions were often added. Utility was now obviously a secondary consideration and samplers had become purely beginners' exercises in fine needlework. The teaching of needlework in schools was encouraged by the Protestant ethic which considered it an excellent way of discouraging idleness in young girls aged between eight and eleven years. The eighteenth-century dictionary definition by Samuel Johnson of the word 'sampler' was 'a piece worked by young girls for improvement'. This was the mood in which sampler-making entered the eighteenth century.

Eighteenth-century Samplers

Embroidery in general at this time continued to flourish, being strongly influenced by the many exotic textiles imported from India, China and Persia. Unfortunately, however, the standard of sampler-making was to deteriorate rapidly from now on, with samplers being worked by children as young as five years. It is not really surprising that the new-found embroidery techniques and fashions being worked by adult needlewomen did not appear on these children's samplers. The children used far fewer stitches, and much brighter colours.

In Germany during the eighteenth century, another type of sampler was being worked using just one or two colours. Black thread was worked on a cream ground using cross stitch, or red was used on a white ground with a variety of stitches, including satin, hem and eyelet stitches.

The shape of samplers was also changing. In England they were shorter and wider, taking on the proportions of a picture. Samplers had lost their need for utility and could now be classed as needlework pictures. They were intended to be ornamental and the finished work would be displayed in the home by proud parents as a record of their child's achievement at school.

English samplers consisted of stylised borders surrounding rows of alphabets and numerals, a lengthy piece of text or a short verse or inscription. Spaces were filled with symmetrically placed motifs, birds, small animals, flowers and trees. There were trees in every shape and size, with the conical tree the most popular. These motifs were often worked in pairs and were sparsely arranged around the sampler; the need to economise with fabric had apparently disappeared. The choice and arrangement of subject matter was very carefully thought out, in order to make a successful, well-ordered and balanced picture. Samplers of this century and the next were in complete contrast to the random spot and band samplers of earlier centuries which owed much of their beauty to the fact that their working was an essential art.

Nearly all samplers were now made by schoolchildren but the importance of needlework in schools had become secondary; the samplers were merely vehicles for instruction, primarily of religious and moral teachings and also for lessons on geography, English and mathematics. The most popular needlework exercises were almanacs, mathematical tables and maps, as well as the usual numbers and letters. The art of darning was learnt by children and darned samplers were popular in Germany, Holland and England. They were worked on rather fine material, such as muslin, using subtle colours, and counted-thread work.

Today these samplers give us a fascinating insight into the social history of the time. Although no longer works of art, they are still achievements in their own right, to be wondered at and admired. They possess a very special kind of charm, especially when we realise that children of such tender age endured the long and tedious task of stitching row upon row of alphabets, hymns and lengthy passages of religious and moralistic text (including the Lord's Prayer, the Ten Commandments and the Apostles' Creed).

In the latter half of this century, these inscriptions were generally replaced by shorter verses, though in the same tone. Those most commonly used were from the writings of Philip Doddridge, John Wesley and Dr Isaac Watts, whose book of *Divine and Moral Songs for Children* was addressed to 'all that are concerned in the education of children . . . whatever may conduce to give the minds of children a relish for virtue and religion. . . .' One of Dr Watts's verses which appeared on a sampler read:

Virtue's the chiefest beauty of the mind
The greatest ornament of mankind
Virtue's our safeguard and our guiding star
That stirs up reason when senses err.

The mortality rate of children at this time was very high and the religious population seemed to be pre-occupied, almost obsessed, with the subject of death. The generally pessimistic and gloomy outlook on life was reflected in the verses used:

Our life is never at a stand
'Tis like a fading flower
Death is always near at hand
Comes nearer every hour.

Another verse on the same subject worked on a sampler was even shorter and more to the point:

When I am dead and worms me eat
Here you shall see my name complete.

The materials used at this time varied. Linen was still popular and in the first half of this century a fine woollen canvas called tammy cloth was much in vogue. This was susceptible to moths and did not remain popular for long. Needless to say, few pieces worked on this cloth have survived. Cotton was used occasionally at the end of this century, and satin was regularly used for map samplers. Satin could be bought with the map's outline already printed or hand-drawn onto it. Maps were also worked on fine silk gauze or tiffany, a fine muslin-like material.

The threads popularly used were still silk and linen, and later in the century, wool and cotton. Metallic threads were now very rarely used. Chenille was occasionally worked on map samplers; black silk and human hair added an air of sentimentality on mourning samplers. One such sampler bore the following inscription:

Heavenly Love
Christ's Arms Do Still Stand Open To Receive
All Weary Prodigals That Sin Do Leave
For Them He Left His Father's Blest Abode
Made Son Of Man To Make Man Son Of God
To Cure Their Wounds He Lives Elixir Bled
And Died A Death To Rise Them From The Dead.

This Work Was Done With The Hair of Mr Thomas Vickery
By Elizabeth, His Daughter, 1782.

In the middle of the eighteenth century, a relatively small number of stitches were being used, including cross stitch, Algerian eye, double running stitch and four-sided stitch; by the end of the century, cross stitch became the sole survivor of what was once an enormous repertoire of stitches used on samplers — it is often described as the sampler stitch.

The obsession with learning and stitching the alphabet which had begun in the seventeenth century, continued right through the eighteenth century, and finally receded in the early part of the nineteenth century. The simplicity and legibility of the letters were most important, and they were usually worked in cross stitch and Algerian eye. Very occasionally, elaborate initial letters appeared, worked in various stitches.

Many samplers showed the old alphabet, from which J and U were omitted, with I and V being used in their place. Q was often the same as P, but reversed. Z was often omitted altogether as a letter not much in use. Alphabets were usually laid out in rows, being worked across the sampler and divided by lines of border patterns varying in design, size and complexity.

Letters were occasionally worked in pairs — AA, BB, CC etc — using different stitches for the first and second letters. The capital and lower-case letters were also worked in pairs — Aa, Bb, etc. In most samplers, though, the capitals were worked first, with the lower-case letters being set out underneath. Spaces at the ends of rows were often filled in with small patterns or motifs — hearts, crowns and so on. If the sewer was feeling lazy, letters were missed out altogether, especially if the last few letters of the alphabet did not fit into the final line.

In Germany, alphabets were given extremely elaborate treatment using several colours and a number of different stitches. The same is true of samplers from Holland and Denmark, though to a lesser extent. Crowns and coronets, which often appeared on Dutch and German samplers, also featured on English pieces, because they were used in the linen-marking process. Each rank of nobility was denoted by its own distinctive coronet which would have been embroidered onto the linen above the owner's initials and the date on which the linen was acquired. Hearts, which were worked onto Central European samplers, did not often appear on English ones, although little flying cupids were quite popular.

English samplers with complex bands of patterning, including those with figures of boxers, did not die out until after the middle of this century along with any cut and drawn whitework. Very simple patterns worked in cross stitch appeared in the rows between alphabets; the older band patterns had become much simplified and were used as borders around the whole sampler. Printed cottons from India had influenced some of these patterns, which were now freer, more flowing and worked in brighter colours. Floral patterns were worked with more curving lines as opposed to the rather angular and geometric band-sampler patterns. The choice of patterns was probably determined by the teacher, as were the verses used, with a number of favourites appearing time and time again. Popular border patterns which appeared regularly such as the strawberry, rosebud and carnation designs, showed little variation or distortion over the years.

Some of the most charming samplers from England at this time were those made by the few very young children who were allowed to work their own ideas. They showed great imagination and originality, some working their own homes and members of their families, though they were rarely identified as such. Many samplers were worked in honour and gratitude to parents, thanking them for their care and guidance or for the child's education. The following two verses are typical of those which would be worked:

Dear mother I am young and cannot show
Such work as I unto your goodness owe
Be pleased to smile on this my small endeavour
I'll strive to learn and be obedient forever.

Oh smile on those whose liberal care
Provides for our instruction here;
And let our conduct ever prove
We're grateful for their generous love.

Houses and landscaped rural scenes, found on European samplers from earlier times, were increasingly occupying the lower halves of English samplers and would include shepherds and shepherdesses, dovecotes and windmills, animals, urns and vases. Forts and ships appeared sometimes, but were featured more on Dutch samplers. The people depicted on the rigging of these sailing ships are thought to represent members of the embroiderer's own family.

Other European samplers of the eighteenth century consisted mainly of a number of different motifs placed at random around the cloth and the subjects depicted might include the emblems of the Passion, flowers, trees and furniture. French samplers sometimes had a verse contained by a shield or cartouche. The subjects typical of Dutch and German samplers were dogs, deer and trees as well as many religious scenes. These included the return of the spies from Canaan, and Adam and Eve. Adam and Eve also became quite common on English samplers by the latter half of this century. They were usually shown beneath the Tree of Knowledge laden with apples and often with the serpent, itself a popular motif. The snake could be seen as a symbol either of evil, or of the Resurrection (because it shed its skin to emerge anew). Sometimes Adam and Eve would appear naked, and sometimes fully clothed. This verse is typical of the kind which would accompany these figures:

This charming little sampler of the mid-eighteenth century is signed Hannah Haynes and has cutwork with hollie point insertions. The cutwork is surrounded by a border of large flowers which are worked in satin, cross, rococo and back stitches with French knots. The background to this floral border has used satin stitch in a rather interesting way and there is a fascinating textural quality to the whole piece. The materials are silk and linen on linen and the sampler measures 8 × 8in (20 × 20cm) *(Victoria and Albert Museum, London)*

Adam and Eve whilst innocent
In paradise were placed
But soon the serpent by his wiles
The happy pair disgraced.

This following verse was a rather more compassionate one:

Adam alone in paradise did grieve
And thought Eden a desert without Eve
Until God, pitying his lonesome state
Crown'd all his wishes with a lovely mate
Then why should men think mean or slight her
That could not live in paradise without her.

Rebus samplers are those where words in a piece of text are replaced by a picture; they are quite rare. The story of Noah's ark lent itself well to this treatment: the words 'dove', 'ark' etc would be replaced by a pictorial rendering of a dove and an ark.

More popular were acrostic samplers where the first letter of the first word on each line, read vertically, spelt out a short message or the name of a person. The favourite acrostic was that of Christ, but quite often they were worked as memorial samplers.

Other favourite classroom exercises were almanacs, multiplication tables and tables for pounds, shillings and pence — though they could not always be relied upon to be correct. These were usually worked in cross stitch, perhaps with a pictorial scene below and with a patterned border around the whole.

From about 1770, map samplers became very popular and were worked in large numbers. The most common maps were those showing England and Wales, with just a part of Scotland and Ireland. Some, of particular interest, show local areas, and others a single county. Some map samplers covered two whole hemispheres — the Old and the New Worlds. France, Spain and Ireland were among the single countries worked. In America, children produced three dimensional globes of the world rather than maps. These map samplers were considered an excellent way of teaching geography to the children and although most were horribly inaccurate, because the children copied and drew the outlines themselves, their making was a reflection of the growing public interest in foreign travel and affairs.

Sometimes countries were outlined with chenille thread, and the lettering was usually worked in cross stitch or Algerian eye. The maps were worked on fine linen, silk gauze or taffeta and were often oval in shape, surrounded by a garland and bows or flowers. On maps of Britain, a wreath or scroll containing the maker's name and the date on which the piece was completed was placed in the North Sea. Most included the points of the compass and, very occasionally, a scale or lines of latitude.

Nineteenth-century Samplers

In England, rigid standards of morality and decency were to dominate in the reign of Queen Victoria and the majority of the population were very poor. There was a high demand for child labour and most young children of the poorer classes managed to earn a little extra money working down the coal mines and in the fields.

Before the invention of the sewing machine, in the first half of this century, many women and children worked with their needles in poverty and hunger, both in urban slums and in country villages:

Work, work, work
Seam and gusset and band,
Band and gusset, and seam,
Till over the buttons I fall asleep
And sew them on in a dream.

Thomas Hood: 'The Song of the Shirt'

Children as young as four years old spent all day in the tiny cramped rooms of the lace schools. They wound bobbins and helped their elders to sew lace; although conditions must have been terribly hard, this work was probably preferred to labouring in the coal mines.

Education at this time was sorely neglected, and until the introduction of state schools later in the century, the only form of education for poor children came from Sunday schools, charity schools and orphanages. Children who did attend these schools were not taught reading and writing; apart from moral instruction and Bible reading, they were taught only spinning, knitting and sewing. Girls who learnt to sew and darn then had the chance to find work in service with a family and although it was poorly paid work, it must have seemed much more comfortable than working in one of the factories and mills that were the backbone of the Victorian economy.

Most clothes at this time were made, altered and repaired at home and the obsession with marking every single item of clothing and household linen continued. There was plenty of sewing for the ladies' maid whilst the lady of the house busied herself with the management of her servants, good works, religion and childbearing. Ladies of the Victorian era spent most of their leisure time in the genteel art of embellishing and decorating every sort of household furnishing with needlework.

Charity samplers were developed to supply the children with the skills required for their future occupation. They were very plain and densely packed with hardly an inch left unworked, and the standard of work was generally very high. They were worked either on linen or a coarse-mesh canvas and the thread was usually wool, occasionally silk. More often than not they were in a single colour, either red or black — a characteristic of some earlier German samplers.

This sampler was worked by M. A. Tipper and includes the following inscription:

M A Tipper
New Orphan House
North Wing
Ashley Down
Bristol
1868.
(The 6 was later changed to 0, to make the sampler seem earlier)

M. A. Tipper was born on 16 September 1852 and was admitted to the orphanage in 1863, aged eleven years. This piece shows the purely functional purpose of samplers, to teach children the basic skills of sewing alphabets and numerals for marking linen. Nevertheless, this sampler must have been quite a feat, taking many hours to complete. The alphabets, numerals and border patterns are densely worked, showing strict economy of space and fabric *(Fitzwilliam Museum, Cambridge)*

This cushion was one of three samplers which are thought to have been worked in 1879 by Annie Parker, a prisoner at the Clerkenwell House of Correction. Annie (who served over 400 separate sentences for drunkenness) worked this sampler in human hair, presumably the only material to hand. The cushion has been worked using cross stitch and is decorated with a crocheted cotton-lace edging *(Black Museum, New Scotland Yard, London, by permission of the Commissioner of the Metropolitan Police)*

The stitches that the children were required to master included: back, buttonhole, chain, darning, herringbone, marking, basting, overcast and oellit stitches. As well as the usual rows of alphabets (up to twenty different versions might be worked on one sampler), and bands of simple patterning, the now statutory religious or moralistic text was worked, sometimes with a small Bible or crucifix in the centre. The upright alphabet was the most common; the sloping version also appeared and was used for marking fine linen. Each sampler was marked with both the name and address of the worker, and the date on which it was completed, along with a number which is thought to have been the child's identification number at the school or orphanage.

Schools often took in plain work, usually darning or repairing worn linen. The profits were to help fund the schools, but the children were probably considered cheap labour. Hannah More, who established the Mendip schools in the late eighteenth century, said: 'My plan of instruction is extremely simple and limited. They learn on weekdays such coarse works as may fit them for servants. I allow of no writing for the poor. . . .' Hannah even composed a series of moral tales and verses specially for the children.

The three Brontë sisters all produced samplers that were typical of this time and convey well the atmosphere of the times. The sisters were ten, eleven and thirteen years old and the samplers were sewn around the year 1830. They show a total lack of ornament and consist of lengthy pieces of religious text surrounded by very simple borders, worked in dark green silk on a rough textured canvas.

Later on in this century state schools were introduced and they too limited their curriculum to religion, good moral precepts and needlework. The children learnt only plain sewing, not fancy embroidery techniques. This work included different kinds of seams, making buttonholes, darning and inserting cuffs and collars. School manuals produced during this century stressed the importance of women learning needlework so that they could obtain work in service. The following words appeared in the preface to *Plain Needlework in all its branches,* published in 1849 for use in the National Industrial School of the Holy Trinity, at Finchley, London.

> [The necessity for women to have] a practical acquaintance with needlework. . . . As regards plain needlework especially, this is more particularly the case with reference to females in humble life, whether with a view to domestic neatness and economy, or to profitable occupation in a pecuniary light.

In America, this acquaintance with needlework was also considered a most important part of a young girl's upbringing and was taught in schools across the country. American sampler-making developed rapidly and is discussed separately later in the book.

Apart from the very plain samplers, there were also those which did include motifs. These motifs, though, had become stereotyped and over-simplified and were arranged around the sampler in such a way that perfect symmetry was the paramount consideration. Animals, birds, flowers and trees were all perfectly balanced and often placed in pairs. The number of motifs in use was far fewer than in the eighteenth century and there was much less variety. Where houses and gardens were worked, they were very simply treated and all were worked in bold and rather garish colours.

The following quotation comes from a work by Sophia F. Caulfeild and Blanche C. Saward, under the heading 'To Make A Sampler':

> Take some Mosaic Canvas, of the finest make, and woven so that each thread is at equal distance apart. Cut this 18 inches wide and 20 inches long, and measure off a border all round of 4 inches. For the border, half an inch from the edge, draw out threads in a pattern to the depth

(cont on p24)

The top sampler was made by Emily Jane Brontë in March 1829 when she was eleven years old. The large amount of religious text which is surrounded by a Greek-key border must have been very boring to work and is typical of samplers from this time. It is worked with green-black silk on canvas and is similar to those worked by Emily's sisters *(Brontë Society, Brontë Parsonage, Haworth, West Yorkshire)*

Anne Brontë's sampler, dated Nov 28 1828. There are a few very simple border patterns and two alphabets with short pieces of religious text worked on rough canvas. It is a rather sombre piece, reflective of the sad times in the three sisters' lives. Charlotte Brontë's sampler is almost identical to this one of Anne's *(Brontë Society, Brontë Parsonage, Haworth, West Yorkshire)*

KNOW THYSELF ALL WISDOM CENTRES THERE.

PENCE

d	s
12 are	1 0
20	1 8
24	2 0
30	2 6
36	3 0
40	3 4
48	4 0
50	4 2
60	5 0
70	5 10
72	6 0
80	6 8
84	7 0
90	7 6
96	8 0

SHILLINGS

s	£ s
20 are	1 0
30	1 10
40	2 0
50	2 10
60	3 0
70	3 10
80	4 0
90	4 10
100	5 0
110	5 10
120	6 0
130	6 10
140	7 0
150	7 10
160	8 0

Lifes but a span mans longest years
Are nothing Lord to thee
When fix'd in glory he appears
What splendid vanity

Worked with Mifs E Geoghegan.

E Sherwin.
Aged 11 years,
1835

(opposite) English sampler showing a table of pounds, shillings and pence worked in 1835 by E. Sherwin, aged eleven (with the help of Miss E. Geoghegan). It uses eyelet and cross stitches, and a typical Greek-key border *(Brooklyn Museum, New York)*

(above) This type of mid-nineteenth century woolwork sampler was usually worked by professionals for display. The materials are silver thread, wool and silk on linen, and beads. Cross, Hungarian, satin, Florentine and brick stitches are used, with laid and couched work. It is 4in (10cm) by 10ft 1¼in (3m 3cm). The mainly geometric border and repeating patterns make good creative use of the different stitches *(Victorian and Albert Museum, London)*

of half an inch, and work over these with coloured silk; then work a conventional scroll pattern, in shades of several colours, and in tent stitch, to fill up the remaining 3 inches of the border. Divide the centre of the sampler into three sections. In the top section work a figure design. [In the old samplers this was generally a sacred subject, such as Adam and Eve before the Tree of Knowledge.] In the centre section work an alphabet in capital letters, and in the bottom an appropriate verse, the name of the worker, and the date.

All the decorative arts, including embroidery, deteriorated rapidly in this century, and became overelaborate. From the 1830s onwards, embroidery was taken over by a passion for Berlin woolwork, a craze which spread through both Europe and America. The technique employed wool in rather bright and garish colours worked on double canvas in a wide variety of different geometric and floral patterns and using a large number of stitches.

Berlin wools, or zephyr yarns, were spun at Gotha in Germany and then dyed in Berlin. The patterns for this work also came from Berlin and the first printed patterns on graph paper were published in 1804–5 by a man named Philipson. These were imported to England in large numbers and by 1840, over 14,000 designs had been produced.

During the first half of the nineteenth century, great improvements had been made in the science of dyeing and after an English chemist called Henry Perkins had accidentally discovered a new dye which was to be called mauve, great use was made of new and exciting colours such as magenta and violet. The new Berlin wools were much softer than the previous hard, twisted worsted yarns and the colours were a great deal faster. The huge variety of different colours which was now available meant that a high degree of shading could be achieved, thereby giving more realistic renderings of the subjects being worked. Complete scenes were highly three-dimensional and the technique was rather like painting by numbers — indeed favourite paintings were often copied in great detail. Other threads such as silk and gold, and occasionally beads, were incorporated into the designs, so highlighting particular areas.

In England, the subjects most commonly worked were whole scenes or vignettes of domestic pets, and portraits of the royal family; Queen Victoria's King Charles spaniel, Dash, was a very popular subject. Floral and geometric motifs and patterns were also very popular and were used to furnish all sorts of household items including footstools, curtain ties, firescreens, cushions and even bell pulls.

By the end of the nineteenth century, children's samplers showed obvious influences from this craze for Berlin woolwork and included subjects similar to those currently being worked in wool by adult needle-

women. Floral bouquets, landscaped scenes and family pets were all being worked, with rather crude attempts at the realistic shading which was characteristic of Berlin woolwork.

A very wide variety of canvas stitches was being employed, including Hungarian, Florentine, brick, a number of different cross stitches, Leviathan stitch and perspective stitch. There were many types of canvas available at this time. Berlin canvas was very fine, needed no grounding, and was available in black, white and pearl white, the last being the most expensive type. Penelope was a canvas which had groups of four threads (usually canvas for Berlin work had threads in pairs). German canvas was the least expensive and every tenth thread was yellow in order to make counting easier.

There is a group of Berlin woolwork samplers which were made at this time. These are long strips of canvas with blocks of floral and geometric patterns, often with simple border patterns appearing in between each. These were worked using many of the stitches popular at the time and are similar to the seventeenth-century band samplers. For a short time at least, samplers had regained their original purpose: it is believed that these Berlin woolwork samplers were intended as some kind of reference sheet, either for the needleworker's own use, or for resale in needlework shops for the amateur to copy.

Slowly, Berlin woolwork fell from favour and came under particular criticism from the Church and its architects who were taking an interest in embroidery; the work was considered purely an exercise in copying skills. In England, at the time of the Arts and Crafts Movement, William Morris and others were attempting to bring about a revival in the art of embroidery, but with little effect. These were days when machines were producing remarkable results in the field of textiles. Isaac Singer had produced the first successful sewing machine, and the first embroidery machine, which was invented in 1828, had been developed to produce rather sophisticated effects. Needlewomen were no longer attempting to create major works and did not see the need to learn the art of stitchery. Now this need had disappeared, the skills used for working fine embroidery were sorely neglected.

Happily, the art of embroidery is today experiencing a strong revival, with large numbers of embroiderers working in both traditional and contemporary styles. Samplers survive as beginners' pieces and as experimental grounds for more expert workers.

(*opposite*) Celebration of a Child's Birthday (p60)
(*overleaf, left*) Multicoloured Alphabets in Wool (p62); Spaniel (p64); (*right*) Adam and Eve (p66); Red and Green Alphabets (p68); Red Alphabets (p71)

ABCDEFGHIJKLMNOPQR
STUVWXYZ1234567890
abcdefghijklmnopqrstuvwxy
z.

Oliver Von Born 16 Jan. 1981 x

1984

2
Samplers around the World

Sampler-making has played an important role in women's lives throughout history, and strong sampler-making traditions developed in a large number of countries around the world. These include France, Italy, Spain and the Spanish colonies, Mexico, Belgium, Scandinavia and Switzerland, with Britain, Germany, Holland and America holding the strongest traditions.

Each country retained its own national characteristics although there was much interplay of designs and patterns throughout Europe. The art of sampler-making crossed the Atlantic with the Pilgrim Fathers to the New World where it grew and flourished. In each country, sampler-making followed similar developments through the centuries and underwent the same processes of gradual decline which accelerated from the mid-nineteenth century onwards, when samplers had lost their original purpose.

America
Samplers and the art of sampler-making came to America with the early settlers and most colonial women took their needlework very seriously. Mothers took great pride in their work and taught their daughters the art of stitching. The resulting samplers were hung in the parlour as proof of the daughter's ability to produce fine needlework. Darning, mending and marking were still important tasks in the home and girls were not considered marriageable until they had mastered the art of stitchery.

From the diary of Anna Green Winslow, written in 1771 and containing a record of a Boston school, comes the following account of a girl's duties for one day (9 March).

A very snowy day. I have been a very good girl today about my work however . . . in the first place I sew'd on the bosom of uncle's shirt, mended two pairs of gloves, mended for the wash two handkerchiefs (one cambrick), sewed on half a border of a lawn apron of aunt's, read part of the XXIst chapter of Exodus and a story in the Mother's gift.

Original samplers, ideas and designs were brought to America from the old country and the first samplers made there reflected the national characteristics of the embroiderer's homeland. After 1750, there developed a distinctly American flavour to sampler-making. There was great imagination and flair in design, and the use of stitches, colours and different threads produced lively and distinctive works. Samplers became far less formal and symmetrical than British ones of the time.

The fabric used was usually unbleached linen, but light brown, bottle-green, grey and black were also used. Tiffany was also used until the early nineteenth century when linsey-woolsey (a mixture of flax and wool) became popular. Tammy was not as common as in Britain. Silk was by far the most popular thread, followed by wool and linen. In the eighteenth century, American sampler-makers made good, creative use of metal threads and spangles and worked pearl-stitched edgings and blackwork borders, though these slowly died out in the nineteenth century. Pattern-darning was often used to fill in backgrounds and through the clever use of simple stitches and colour, landscaped scenes appeared highly three-dimensional. Samplers were mounted and often framed, with silk-ribbon borders which were ruched, pleated or quilled; in some regions, gold braid or white satin damask was used.

Samplers in the second half of the eighteenth century generally consisted of a small square in which a verse or inscription was worked, surrounded by a very wide border which formed the major part of the work and was intended to be the main feature. Inside this border would be a landscaped scene with figures, trees, perhaps a dog, some sheep and winged cherubs. Large floral designs were often included, possibly worked up the sides of the border and with the sky at the top. Cross-band samplers were still being made around 1800, but were being replaced by the more pictorial types. The wide variety of stitches worked also diminished in the late eighteenth century and, as elsewhere in the world, cross stitch became the most popular stitch on samplers. A small number of lacework samplers were made in the late eighteenth century, especially in Philadelphia. These differed from the English pieces of the seventeenth century in

(opposite) American Fort and Animals (p70)

that they used pictorial designs rather than bands of patterning.

Mid-nineteenth-century Jewish samplers are instantly recognisable by the Hebrew alphabet and religious symbols, such as the spies of Canaan.

A group of samplers made in Pennsylvania by girls of German or Dutch ancestry are very different in character from other samplers being made in America. They were worked mostly in cross stitch and consisted of a roughly arranged collection of motifs. There were no borders, although the samplers were sometimes framed with silk ribbon. Among the different motifs worked were pairs of peacocks, flowers in vases, pointed stars, hearts and coronets, which were all similar to those appearing on European samplers.

Along with many other art forms, American samplers of the 1800s show the spirit of republicanism: many patriotic themes and emblems were worked onto them, including the American eagle with its wings outstretched. After the War of Independence, women's education had improved, although needlework still featured strongly in the school curriculum.

As in Britain, sampler-making was prominent in American educational establishments and both plain and fancy needlework were taught. Poor children learnt plain work and worked samplers of alphabets and numerals. The more adventurous pictorial pieces were made at fashionable ladies' seminaries and were intended to be framed. The very best samplers were worked by girls aged between twelve and sixteen years from the Boston area.

Reputations of schools were founded almost entirely on the standard, originality and style of the samplers being worked there, with each school developing its own individual characteristics of sampler design. These were largely decided by individual teachers, many of whom came from Britain.

Mrs Leah Meguier ran a school in Pennsylvania in the early nineteenth century, which produced very beautiful and imaginative samplers. They were often divided into as many as twenty-two 1in (2.5cm) squares, each containing a different motif or geometric pattern, including birds, flowers, butterflies, hearts and baskets of eggs. In the middle would be a scene which would include one or two figures, often a woman holding flowers. Weeping willows, often found in the area, were also popular. A few squares at the bottom would include an inscription or verse and quite often the name of the teacher was included. The following lines are typical of Pennsylvania verses:

> This work of mine my friends may have
> When I am dead and in my grave
> This I did to let you see
> What care my parents took of me.

Faces and figures in pictorial scenes were usually hand-painted and sequins were often used for further embellishment. The finished work was quite often framed with silk ribbon and gold lace.

Another well-known school was in Providence, Rhode Island, and was known as the Balch Academy. It was run by Miss Balch between 1785 and 1799 and took in both day and boarding girls. The samplers produced here had the major portion of the work as a landscaped scene, usually featuring large public buildings, often inside grand pillars. They were often heavily decorated with borders of large flowers growing out of urns and vases. Short inscriptions or verses were also included and the following are typical:

> Honour and renown will be the ingenious crown.

> May spotless innocence and truth
> my every action guide
> and guard my inexperienced youth
> from arrogance and pride.

The stitches used were cross, stem, satin and rococo. Pattern-darning, which was usually diagonal, was often used to fill in backgrounds and was a main characteristic of the work from this school.

Westtown was a boarding school in Chester county which opened in 1799 and was supervised by the Quakers or the Society of Friends. It was one of the most distinguished seminaries in the country. The Quaker approach to education was sober and strict, and this was reflected in the samplers that were made there. Both boys and girls attended, but only the girls were taught the art of needlework; they learnt plain sewing such as mending, marking and darning. Later on, they were allowed to work samplers and globes. Map samplers were rare in America, probably due to the size of the country.

The earliest samplers worked at this school were very simple, often with vines and leaves worked into borders around alphabets and a few simple motifs. Coloured silks were used but, more often than not, samplers were worked in just black silk on linen. As in Britain, moral sentiments were expressed but here they were in the form of poems. Occasionally, more proficient workers were allowed to sew views of the school on samplers which would be framed, but in general this more adventurous work was frowned upon.

Like European blackwork samplers, this piece has been worked mostly in double running stitch. It is a Turkish sampler from the eighteenth or nineteenth century worked in silk on linen and measures 26 × 16½in (66 × 42cm). There are a large number of motifs which include many buildings, flowers and plants, all with a strong Eastern flavour. There are a few border patterns, but no animals *(Victoria and Albert Museum, London)*

In the nineteenth century, samplers depicting family records or registers became very popular and remind us of how high the rate of infant mortality was, and of the strain that childbirth put on women bearing large numbers of children. Men often remarried two or three times. Some of these registers were in very plain work with a simple informative text surrounded by narrow borders. Others received much more elaborate treatment. The text was often worked inside an arch supported by columns and decorated with floral wreaths. Others were designed in the form of genealogical trees, with names and dates being worked inside fruits hanging from the branches.

Samplers were made in large numbers at the beginning of the nineteenth century but over the years the numbers and the standard of workmanship were to decline. By the mid-nineteenth century, samplers were being worked in wool and on a coarse canvas. These featured alphabets and numerals and were probably made by young girls. The craze for Berlin woolwork had effects on American embroidery in much the same way as in Britain, and the great age of the American sampler was now over.

Germany

From Germany, where the early publication of the first pattern books showed that the art of embroidery was well established, came great numbers of samplers.

A German sampler dated 1618 is thought to be the earliest dated example from the Continent, though there is evidence to suggest that samplers were being worked in Germany in the sixteenth century. Another early German sampler dated 1704 was made in Dölbeln, in Saxony, and consists of six various border patterns, two alphabets, numerals and a collection of small motifs near the bottom of the sampler, which include animals, flowers, birds and crowns. A small cartouche includes the initials of the worker and the whole is worked in cross stitch. The shape of this sampler is long and narrow and is similar to that of English seventeenth-century samplers. Samplers from Germany almost always include the initials of the worker and the date, although they are not often fully signed.

The shape of German samplers gradually became squarer, although they were occasionally rectangular; they were generally smaller than English samplers. There was no careful arrangement of motifs and alphabets in the early specimens, which usually included an alphabet, a number of designs and motifs scattered around the work.

Longer samplers of the eighteenth century were arranged more methodically, with lines of alphabets at the top, larger subjects in the middle and border patterns along the bottom. Those in the middle would often be religious scenes, which were very popular on German samplers of this period. These included representations of the crucifixion and the emblems of the Passion — the crown of thorns, sponge, hourglass, pincers, dice, cock, scourge, ladder, nails and hammer. Adam and Eve beneath the Tree of Knowledge and the serpent were also popular.

German samplers made at the beginning of the eighteenth century show a close resemblance to British samplers made in the first half of the century, being worked in cross stitch with motifs arranged symmetrically on the fabric. Borders were worked with various flowers, fruit and animals incorporated into the design, including roses, lilies, pinks, grapes, pears, deer and birds.

Alphabets were very popular and were worked in roman or rather ornate gothic styles. Short inscriptions or mottoes of a religious nature were preferred to text and verses. Houses and domestic scenes were not very common, but in the nineteenth century they did appear along with town gates, village scenes, furniture and animals, including lions, deer and parrots.

The finished sampler was usually mounted and edged with silk ribbon, often with the elaborate ruching also popular with American sampler-workers. It would be regarded as an heirloom to be kept in the family.

The repertoire of stitches used on German samplers was far more limited than on English ones; the earliest pieces were worked entirely in cross stitch, with the introduction of a few more stitches later on in the eighteenth century. Darning samplers were worked in Germany from very early times and were much more popular there than in England.

The early pieces showed restraint in the choice of colours, but after the middle of the nineteenth century, with the advances made in the production of aniline dyes, a very large selection of colours became available. The area of Vierlande near Hamburg developed characteristic samples which used just black thread on white linen.

Early samplers were worked on unbleached linen using silk or linen thread. As in Britain, tammy cloth came into fashion in the early nineteenth century and was available in narrow widths specially produced for sampler-making. Towards the end of the nineteenth century, samplers produced in schools were worked on a coarse canvas whilst others, which were probably worked at home, were sewn on cotton cambric.

The sampler was to remain the most popular way of teaching needlework to children in Germany, until the school curriculum was changed after the end of World War I and sampler-making was banned.

Holland

Dutch samplers are quite different in character from German examples, the shape generally being broader.

Another major distinction is that they are worked across the fabric, with the selvedges appearing at the sides of the sampler rather than at the top and the bottom. They are usually signed with the worker's initials and the date. Dutch samplers were produced in large numbers and included a huge variety of alphabets, designs and motifs, most of which had some religious significance. There was, however, an absence of any religious text or verses. Another strong characteristic of Dutch samplers are the very elaborately treated alphabets and numerals which were often worked in two or more colours and stitches.

The design and arrangement of these samplers are definitely patchy, with all sorts of motifs being loosely scattered around the material in a random fashion. Many of the subjects are religious and include the spies of Canaan, the now ubiquitous Adam and Eve, the five wise and five foolish virgins, many forms of the Tree of Life and the Virgin and Child, crosses and the sacred heart. Christ was depicted with the woman of Samaria at the well.

Cartouches and garlands are also included to contain dates and initials. Ships, mermaids, windmills and human figures are also quite popular. Other motifs range from buildings such as churches and houses, to household furniture, fruits, flowers, animals, birds and geometric motifs. A book published recently, *Embroidery Motifs from Dutch Samplers,* shows hundreds of designs, patterns, motifs and alphabets, and lists many of the meanings and translations which they are given. Dutch samplers were mainly worked in cross stitch but also made use of back stitch, bird's eye stitch and an open kind of satin stitch.

This Italian sampler was worked by Virginia Rocchi in the mid-nineteenth century. A pretty bouquet of flowers is worked in the centre; the alphabets are worked in cross stitch and Algerian eye. The border has been worked in a number of flowing floral patterns. The materials are silk on linen, and the sampler measures 13¾ × 20in (35 × 51cm) *(Victoria and Albert Museum, London)*

Some motifs appearing regularly on British samplers of the late seventeenth century were taken originally from Dutch samplers. I have noticed two designs in particular which originated from Holland and appear time and again on English samplers. These are a little scene with a stag seated underneath two trees and another with buildings which look like a chapel or school. The latter design has been used on the multiplication table project included in this book.

Spain

Spanish samplers were usually rather large and could be square or long in shape. They were generally sewn in silk, using striking colours in a very effective way. The material was almost entirely covered with a large variety of border patterns; as many as thirty different designs might be worked on one sampler. The patterns were totally geometric.

Early samplers were worked almost entirely in satin stitch, although cross and back stitches were occasionally used. Some Spanish samplers contained cut and drawn work. A very few pieces contained alphabets and these samplers, although rarely dated, were often signed in full. There are many Spanish samplers executed entirely in counted-thread work in one colour only, usually black. This was Spanish blackwork, a technique which became very popular in England.

Turkish and Moroccan samplers, which can be seen at the Victoria and Albert Museum in London, show patterns used for household linen; on one Moroccan sampler of the late eighteenth or early nineteenth century appear a number of borders which belong to European embroideries and pattern books of the first half of the sixteenth century.

Italy

Italy is the home of some very beautiful lacework. Italian cutwork and lacework were both great influences on Britain and the rest of Europe during the sixteenth and seventeenth centuries. Italian samplers of the seventeenth century contained lovely examples of cut and drawn work, with border patterns incorporating religious motifs which included the crucifixion and the symbols of the Passion. Italy also produced coloured samplers. A typical example from around 1800 was nearly square in shape and included alphabets and numerals, crosses, trees, figures and animals, and the fourteen emblems of the Passion.

France

Although the sampler does not seem to have been very popular in France, judging from the very few examples that have survived French samplers are beautifully fine. They were often worked on fine muslin and to a very high standard.

Most samplers were made by girls in convent schools and were perhaps practice pieces for skills to be employed in working ecclesiastical embroideries. The subjects were mainly religious and not usually pictorial. Many varied and subtle floral designs and borders were worked, some of which were much admired and copied on English pieces. These samplers did not include text or verses, and few workers gave their ages.

Other Countries

Swiss samplers displayed some very fine work but lacked vitality; whilst Belgium samplers closely resembled those from Germany, a much greater variety of stitches was used. Scandinavian samplers were usually worked on fine muslin and there are some lovely examples of Scandinavian drawn-thread work. In Denmark, when only the nobility were allowed to wear lace, other women developed a particular kind of embroidery that produced lacy effects. It was worked on cheesecloth initially, and later on fine muslin.

In India, where Anglo-Indian mothers taught their daughters the art of sampler-making and where some schooling existed in seminaries at Calcutta, samplers were worked under strong oriental influences. When combined with the European style, these influences produced some rather interesting and unique pieces.

An unsigned Danish sampler dated 1751. This more organised sampler has two figures in a landscaped scene surrounded by squares of patterning, which is again bordered by an arrangement of flowers and leaves. In the centre of the larger flowers appear some intriguing faces. The materials are silver-gilt thread, silk and wool on linen and the stitches include cross, tent, rococo, chain, eye, crosslet, brick and Florentine stitches, with padded and laid couched work. It measures 30½ × 26in (76 × 66cm) *(Victoria and Albert Museum, London)*

3

Symbols and Verses

Many art historians who have studied the symbolism of motifs appearing on decorative art forms have arrived at different conclusions. The mythology of ancient peoples from around the world, together with the use of motifs as heraldic emblems and religious symbols, naturally leads to some confusion in interpretation. Most motifs will have some kind of religious significance as well as being derived from ancient legends or folklore; some are simply renditions of everyday items and have no particular meaning. I have included here a few of the most popular interpretations of the many different birds, beasts, fruits, flowers and trees which are depicted on samplers through the centuries and from around the world.

Flowers

The rose is often called the flower of love, beauty and joy and it was a very early pagan symbol signifying earthly love. It was also a symbol of Venus, of Dionysus and of Bacchus, and became the flower of divine love when seen with the Virgin Mary. Five roses on a bush are said to represent the blood of the martyrs. In the Middle Ages, the rose was a symbol of the mystic vision, of courtly love and of the female pudenda. Because of its popularity in English gardens of the time, the rose became the national emblem of the Tudor kings and has appeared frequently on English samplers.

The carnation originated in the Far East and its name was derived from the Latin *carnis,* meaning flesh (the first carnation was flesh coloured). It is supposed to represent maternal love, and, when connected with the Virgin Mary, it has similar meanings to the rose.

The tulip, often called the symbol of perfect love, originated in the East. A Persian legend tells of how a young man, rejected by the girl he loved, cried in the desert. When his tears fell to the ground they turned into tulips. The tulip shape is similar to that of the chalice and also has a religious significance.

A lily is said to have sprung up where Eve dropped a tear on leaving Eden, and the white Madonna lily is said to have been yellow when the Virgin Mary stooped to pick it up. It is known as the flower of heaven, symbolising purity or chastity, and is some-times thought to represent the Redeemer or the saints and the kingdom of heaven. In some eastern countries it is a symbol of fertility. It is sometimes thought that the fleur-de-lys was derived from the lily and that this was further stylised into the Prince of Wales' feathers, although these two designs could well have been inspired by the iris.

Both the violet and the daisy are said to be the flowers of humility, while the marigold represents obedience and is one of the flowers of the sun. The honeysuckle represents enduring faith, and, as a garden flower, is supposed to have power to avert the evil eye. It was a firm favourite with the Tudors.

The cowslip, or herb peter, is said to symbolise the keys of Saint Peter; the columbine is said to symbolise the Holy Spirit as it closely resembles the shape of a dove. The pansy, or love-in-idleness, with its three faces in the sacred trefoil shape, represents the Holy Trinity, as its Latin name, *Herba tri iatis,* suggests.

Fruits

The Latin word for apple, *malum,* also means evil, to denote Christianity's forbidden fruit. In folklore, the apple was offered as a gift, a declaration of love. It was also the symbol of love and fertility because of its beauty and sweetness. The pear also appears regularly on samplers and embroideries and is sometimes considered more likely than the apple to have been the forbidden fruit.

Grapes have a strong religious significance and represent the blood of Jesus. A bunch of grapes being carried by the spies of Canaan is often seen on samplers through the centuries. The cherry is considered to be another of the fruits of heaven. The strawberry represents perfect righteousness, as it is considered the perfect fruit, having no stones or pips. The leaves have a shape similar to the sacred trefoil, giving the strawberry religious significance. The white flowers are said to indicate innocence and purity.

Ancient Hebrews used the pomegranate embroidered on religious garments and the fruit was said to have inspired the design of Solomon's crown. It has been considered the emblem of the Christian Church and its religious meaning is hope of eternal life. It was used as a heraldic emblem in the sixteenth century and appeared regularly on samplers of this time. It also features in Chinese poetry and in the Near East its abundance of seeds symbolises fertility. In Greek legend, Ceres' daughter Persephone had to spend half of every year underground because she ate one pomegranate seed while in Hades.

Trees

The Tree of Knowledge was the tree heavily laden with the fruit of the knowledge of good and evil, which ultimately led to the Fall. It is commonly depicted on samplers with the clad or unclad figures of Adam and Eve, and often with the serpent.

The Tree of Life has, through the ages, been depicted in many different ways. In Egypt, the gods are said to have lived in its branches and survived on its fruit — 'the bread of life'. In Persia, the Tree of Life bore all the seeds for living plants, to be scattered by the birds which are often depicted around the tree. In ancient Hindu writings the tree is considered a divine mother and a bearer of life: the progress and growth of a tree planted after the birth of a baby is said to determine that of the child. The Tree of the Universe was believed to have been an ash tree and was the symbol of the Universe.

The weeping willow tree appears regularly on later samplers, being especially popular with American sampler-makers. It is traditionally the tree of sorrow. The olive has religious significance, representing peace and good will. The oak tree has played an important role in British mythology since its popularity with the druids, and was further promoted by Charles II who hid in an oak tree when fleeing from the government's army. It appeared often as a heraldic emblem, and both acorns and oak leaves were worked into patterns on samplers.

Birds, Animals and Insects

Dove: A symbol of the Holy Ghost, representing mercy and peace; a dove with a letter in its beak is a messenger of love.
Duck: Marital fidelity.
Unicorn: A symbol of chastity and purity; also a sign of the Redeemer.
Goose: Watchfulness and stupidity.
Cock: A symbol of Christ, and of watchfulness and penitence.
Hare: Faintheartedness, timidity and flight.
Hart: Gentleness and pride.

Dog: Watchfulness and fidelity.
Cat: Idleness and coquetry.
Stork: Parental love.
Parrot: Talkativeness and gossip.
Peacock: Vanity, immortality and eternal life.
Tortoise: Strength.
Snake: Reward and wickedness.
Falcon: Pride and nobility.
Butterfly: Joy, pleasure and immortality.
Swan: The bird of love, a symbol of a good death. In German mythology it is the creature of the sun, the bringer of light and life.
Lion: Strength and steadfastness.
Monkey: The devil, the antithesis of the Virgin.
Owl: Sometimes represents the devil and avarice; alternatively it can represent wisdom and learning due to its connections with Athena the goddess of wisdom.
Squirrel: Mischief.
Horse: A symbol of the sun, male potency and fertility; also pride, speed and ardour.
Bee: A symbol of chastity.

Verses

Apart from the many pieces of religious text that were included on later samplers, a very large number of verses were also worked. They prove a fascinating insight into the social history of the time. We can read of the great importance placed on needlework and of the Victorians' obsession with the subject of death. Many verses were highly moralistic, others expounded on the woman's role, and although these may seem rather amusing, I am sure that at the time they were seriously meant. The verses for children are quite charming and could still be worked today. Those concerning needlework and for parents are also still relevant. A sampler that has been worked specially to celebrate an occasion or dedicated to a particular person is of very great value. A verse or piece of text included in a sampler together with as much information as possible (your name, the date and where it was made etc) will add special interest to the piece, creating something that will be treasured for a very long time.

The following verses are just a few of the more interesting ones that I have seen worked on samplers; I hope some of them will be worked again, although you may wish to use another favourite piece of text that would be relevant to a particular sampler.

To Parents

This work of mine my friends may have
When I am dead and in my grave
This I did to let you see
What care my parents took of me.

On this Fair Canvas does my needle write
With Love and Duty both this I indite
And in these lines dear Parent I impart
The tender feelings of a Grateful Heart.

My mother hatherto hath don her best to make
me a work woman as well as the rest
Anne Iater is my name and England is my nation
and south work is my dwelling place and
Christ is my salvation

Dear mother I am young and cannot show
Such work as I unto your goodness owe
Be pleased to smile on this my small endeavour
I'll strive to learn and be obedient forever.

Many daughters have done virtuously
But thou excellest them all.

Lord thou wast pleased to bestow on me a Mother truly
kind,
Whose constant care was to instil good precepts on my
mind:
And plant the seeds of virtue in my young and tender
breast.
Ere thou didst snatch her from my sight with thee to be
at rest.
Grant me O Lord thy constant aid to thy holy will.
That a tender Mothers pious wish may be in me fulfilled.

Oh smile on those whose liberal care
Provides for our instruction here;
And let our conduct ever prove
We're grateful for their generous love.

Next unto God dear parents I address
Myself to you in humble thankfulness
For all your care and charge on me bestowed
The means of learning unto me allowed
Go on I pray and let me still pursue
Those golden arts the friendless never knew

Verses for Children

The trees were green,
The sun was hot,
Sometimes I worked,
And sometimes not.
Seven years my age,
My name Jane Grey,
and often much,
Too fond of play.

Angels are happy clothed with wings
But our new Cloaths are dangerous things
The child well drest had need to be aware
Lest her fine raiment prove a snare
But happy children they whose dress
Is the redeemer's righteousness
Ere long in glory they shall shine
Rob'd in that raiment all divine

Jesus permit thy gracious name to stand
As the first effort of an infant hand
And while her fingers on the canvas move
Incline her tender heart to seek thy love
With thy dear children let her have a part.

Dear child delay no time
But with all speed amend
The longer thou dost live
The nearer to thy end
Oh child most dear
Incline thy ear
And hearken to God's voice.

Sweet it is to see a child
Tender, merciful and mild
Eveready to perform
Acts of kindness to a worm.

Poetic

I am like the lonesome dove
That mourns its absent mate
From hill to hill from vale to vale
Its sorrows to relate
But Caanaane land is just before
Sweet spring is coming on
A few more beating winds and rains
And winter will be gone

Catch the sunshine, don't be grieving
O'er that darksome billow there
Life's a sea of stormy billows,
We must meet them everywhere.
Pass right through them, do not tarry
Overcome the heaving tide,
There's a sparkling gleam of sunshine
Waiting on the other side.

A Woman's Role

Adam alone in Paradise did grieve
And thought Eden a desert without Eve
Until God, pitying his lonesome state
Crown'd all his wishes with a lovely mate
Then why should men think mean or slight her
That could not live in Paradise without her.

A silent and loving woman is a gift of the Lord and there
is nothing so much worth as a mind well instructed.

She who is truly polite knows how to
contradict with respect and please without
adulation, is equally remote from insipid
complaisance and low familiarity.

One did commend to me a WIFE both fair and young
That had French Spanish and Italian Tongue
I thanked him kindly and told him I loved none such
For I thought one tongue for a Wife too much
What love ye not the Learned, Yes as my life
A Learned Scholar but not a Learned Wife.

With cheerful mind we yield to men
The higher honours of the pen
The needles our great care,
In this we chiefly wish to shine
How far the art's already mine
This Sampler does declare.

Religious Verses

.... is my name
America is my nation
.... is my dwelling place
And Christ is my salvation.

See how the lilies flourish white and fair
See how the ravens fed from heaven are,
Then ne'er distrust the God for cloth and bread
Whilst lilies flourish and the ravens fed.

Seek to be good instead of great and
Sing my makers praise.

The Holy Feast of Easter was injoined
To bring Christ's Ressurrection to our mind.
Rise then from Sin as He did from the Grave
That by His Merrits he Your Souls may save.

How blest are they who in their Prime
the paths of truth have early trod,
Who yield the first fruits of their time
And consecrate their youth to God.

Concerning Needlework

In the glad morn of blooming youth
These various threads I drew,
And now behold this finished piece
Lies glorious to the view.
So when bright youth shall charm no more
And age shall chill my blood,
May I review my life and say,
Behold my works are good.

In reading this if any faults you see
Mend them yourself and find no fault in me.

.... worked this in great speed
And left it here for you to read.

When I was young
And in my prime
Here you may see
How I spent my time.

Of female arts in usefulness
The needle far exceeds the rest,
In ornament there's no device
Affords adorning half so nice.

How blest the Maid whom circling years improve
Her God the object of her warmest love
Whose active years successive as they glide
The Book, the Needle and the Pen divide.

On Virtues

Learn little maid, each useful art
Which may adorn thy youth.
Learn to improve thy tender heart
In virtue, Grace and truth.
Shun every vice with studied care
Each female folly flee
That every grace that crowns the fair
May all attend on thee.

Vain is alike the joy we seek,
And vain what we possess,
Unless harmonious Reason tunes
The passions into peace.
To temper'd wishes just desires,
Is happiness confin'd,
And, deaf to folly's call, attends
The music of my mind.

Humility I'd recommend
Good nature, too, with ease,
Be generous, good and kind to all,
You'll never fail to please.

The bird which soars on highest wing
Builds on the ground her lowly nest;
And she that doth most sweetly sing
Sings in the shade when all things rest.
In lark and nightingale we see
What honour hath humility.

Contented with my humble state I
will pass my peaceful days

If I am right, Oh teach my heart
Still in the right to stay,
If I am wrong, thy grace impart
To find that better way.

When wealth to virtuous hands is given
It blesses like the dews of heav'n
Like heav'n it hears the orphan's cries
And wipes the tears from widows eyes.

Health Seems a Cherub Most Divinely bright,
More Soft than Air, More gay than Morning Light,
Hail, blooming Goddess, thou propitious power,
Whose blessings Mortals Next to Life implore,
Such Graces in your Heavenly Eyes appear
That Cottages are Courts, when you are there.

On Friendship

In prosperity friends are plenty
In adversity not one in twenty.

Declare thy secret thought to none,
For fear of shame and sorrow.
For he that is your friend to-day
May be the foe to-morrow.

Return the kindness that you do receive
As far as your ability gives leave
Keep such company as you may improve
or that may improve you

Be you unto others kind and true
As you'd have others be to you,
And never do or say to men
What'er you would not take again

Tell me ye knowing and discerning few
Where I may find a friend both firm and true
Who dares stand by me when in deep distress
And this his love and friendship most express.

Words of Caution

Learn to contemn all praise betimes
For flattery is the Nurse of Crimes
With early Virtue plant thy Breast
The Specious Arts of Vice detest
Regard the world with cautious eye
Nor raise your expectations high
See that the balanced scale be such
You neither fear nor hope too much

With soothing wiles he won my easy heart
He sigh'd and vow'd, but oh he feigned the smart;
Sure of all friends the blackest we can find
Are those ingrates who stab our peace of mind

Sweetly blooms the rose of May
Glitt'ring with the tears of morn
So insideous smiles betray
While they hide the treacherous thorn

What is the blooming tincture of the skin
To peace of mind and harmony within?
What is the bright sparkling of the finest eye,
To the soft soothing of a calm reply?
Can comeliness of form, or shape, or air,
With comeliness of words or deeds compare?
No — Those at first the unwary heart may gain,
But these — these only, can the heart retain.
And you, ye fair with cautious arm
'Gainst Man's perfidious Arts,
For Youth and Beauty vainly charm
When virtue once departs

Short Moralistic Lines

My time at school well spent
I never shall repent

A house divided against itself can't stand

'Tis education forms the common mind;
Just as the twig is bent the tree's inclined.

Zeal in a good cause will merit applause.

To wisdom's counsel lend an ear,
true godliness to gain.

That which will not make a pot may make a pot lid

He who spends all he gets is on the road to want.

A small hole will sink a great ship.

Time cut them all
Both great and small.

A diligent Scholar is an ornament to a School

Concerning Death

When I can read my title clear
to mansions in the skies,
I'll bid farewell to every fear
And wipe my weeping eyes.

Fragrant the rose, but it fades in time
The violet sweet, but quickly past the prime
White lillies hang their heads and soon decay
And whiter snow in minutes melts away
Such and so with'ring are our early joys
Which time or sickness speedily destroys.

No longer I follow a sound
No longer a dream I pursue
O happiness now to be found
Unobtainable treasure Adieu.

Our life is never at a stand
'Tis like a fading flower
Death which is always near at hand
Comes nearer every hour

When I am dead and worms me eat
Here you shall see my name complete.

There is an hour when I must die
Nor can I tell how soon twill come
A thousand children young as I
Are called by death to hear their doom.

Redeem the mispent time thats past
And live each day as it were thy last
And of thy talents take great care
For thy last day thyself prepare

The rising morning can't assure
That we shall end the day
For death stands ready at the door
To take our lives away.

Ye friends of my heart
Ere from you I depart
This hope to my breast is most near
If again we shall meet
In this rural retreat
May we meet as we part with a tear.

May no marble bestow
The splendour of woe
Which the children vanity rear
No fiction of fame
Shall blazon my name
All I ask is a wish is a tear.

Lillies blended with the rose
Now no more adorn her face
Nor her Cheek with Blushes glow
Adding Charms to every grace.

O may I seize the transient hour
Improve each moment as it flies
Life a short summer man a flower
He dies Alas how soon he dies.

Mother dear weep not for me
When in this yard my grave you see
My time was short and blest was he
That called me to eternity

When spring appears, when violets grow,
And shed a rich perfume,
How soon the fragrance breathes its last
How short lived is the bloom?

4
Making a Sampler

Most types of embroidery need the support of some kind of frame whilst they are being worked, as this prevents distortion and helps to achieve neater stitchery. All the projects should be worked on one of the types of frame described below.

Hoops

These are two rings, usually of wood, in between which the fabric is sandwiched. The outer ring is then tightened by a small screw and the fabric is held taut. The hoop must be larger than the intended embroidery. Hoops are available in a number of sizes, the largest being of a heavier weight and quite sturdy. Hoops are preferred for small pieces of embroidery on lightweight fabrics.

Frames

There are a number of different kinds, the best being those which are square and large enough to take the complete embroidery without the need for rolling up the work. Some frames with floor stands are available.

Needles

Only blunt-ended needles should be used for counted-thread work; sharp-ended needles will pierce both the threads of the fabric and any embroidered threads already worked. This will mean distorted stitches which will not lie neatly. The size of the needle used should relate to the size of the threads, the thread count and the thickness of the thread to be worked.

Scissors

Embroidery scissors are fine and sharp. Dressmaking scissors should be used for cutting the fabric, but dressmaker's 'unpickers' should never be used. Scissors intended for embroidery or dressmaking should never be used for cutting paper, as this will blunt them.

Fabric

All the fabrics I have used for the projects are sold specially for counted-thread work and are commonly available in needlework shops and large department stores with a fabric department. Fabric is sold labelled with the number of holes (threads) to the square inch or centimetre — this is the thread count and varies greatly. The fewer the number of holes to the square inch or centimetre, the larger a piece of counted-thread embroidery will be. There are many different sorts of fabrics available, made in different yarns, with different finishes, textures and colours; these factors, together with the thread count, are all important when designing an embroidery.

Plain-weave Fabric

This is usually tightly woven with a smooth surface and a single weave; some varieties are available on which it is possible to count the threads for counted-thread embroidery. The number of threads for the warp and the weft will not usually be the same on plain-weave fabrics.

Evenweave Fabric

This is also fabric with a plain, single weave, but the number of threads for the warp and the weft are the same. The texture is open and the threads are easily counted. Popular types available are fine white and coloured linens, cambric, Glenshee and Glamis.

Hardanger

This differs from the evenweave fabrics in that it has pairs of threads intersecting. I have found this most effective for blackwork embroidery as the threads are very easy to count and the fabric remains firm, keeping its shape better than a single-weave fabric. Hardanger is available in a number of colours.

Binca

Like hardanger, this is another multiweave fabric, usually with interlaced groups of four threads.

Canvas

This is the name given to any kind of fabric in which the threads are tightly spun and woven with a space between them. It comes in different qualities, colours and widths, and the thread count varies. Canvas can be bought in a single or a double mesh. A locked-weave canvas has two weft yarns twisted together with the warp, which greatly reduces distortion and is much preferred. It is always wise to work on good-quality canvas — it is not only easier to work on but also produces much better results. Synthetic canvases should be avoided. Canvas is sold in white, bleached white, and a number of darker colours.

Threads

There is an enormous variety of threads available for embroidery purposes. I have used some of the most popular ones for the projects in this book.

Stranded Cottons

Anchor Stranded Cottons and DMC Stranded Cottons are both well-known brands consisting of six strands of cotton twisted together loosely which can be separated into groups of the required number, so giving different thicknesses. They are available in an enormous range of colours.

Coton Perlé

This is available in a number of brands and a large range of colours. It is a twisted two-ply thread with a high sheen.

Coton à Broder

This is a single (or three-strand) thread made by Coats and is equivalent to about two strands of the above stranded cottons. It is available in a fairly large number of colours.

Bella Donna

This is a silky thread made from 100 per cent viscose and comes in a number of colours. It has a high sheen and can produce some lovely effects with different stitches. It is, however, difficult to work and very slippery, the ends tending to fluff up rather quickly.

Wool

Wools are available in a number of qualities and weights. Generally, the larger the thread count, the thicker the yarn should be. There are two types of wool used for embroidery: those which are intended to be worked whole and those which are made up of a number of strands which can be separated into either a single strand, or several strands.

All embroidery wools are worsted yarns, which means that they are made with wool of a long staple and spun with plenty of twist. The staples or hairs of the wool are spun in one direction. To avoid damaging the yarn, it must be threaded so that the wool is pulled through the canvas in the direction in which it was spun.

The thickness of the yarn or the number of strands which are used should remain constant unless otherwise stated. Different brands of yarn all vary in thickness, so it is advisable to work a whole embroidery using colours from just one particular brand of wool.

Different dyes affect wool in various ways and you may find that the thickness of certain colours varies. If the yarn is not of a sufficient thickness to cover the ground properly, an extra strand may have to be included.

Tension Guide

The following guide is intended to help you find the correct thickness of thread to use with the many different weights of fabric which are available. The information given is based on the assumption that the principal stitches to be used are either cross or tent stitches.

The figures given here are approximate, and as all embroiderers work at different tensions it is wise to experiment with the threads and fabrics before beginning a piece of embroidery. Try a small test area of stitching using both cross and tent stitches. You will then be able to judge whether or not the thread is of the correct thickness for the fabric you are using. The resulting stitches must not be bulky or difficult to work, nor must they be too thin. When working with wool on canvas, the stitches must cover the ground sufficiently.

Evenweave Lightweight Fabrics

For a thread count of 18 to 22 holes to 1in (2.5cm): coton perlé.
20 to 23 holes to 1in (2.5cm): four strands of stranded cotton.
24 to 30 holes to 1in (2.5cm): three strands of stranded cotton.
27 to 40 holes to 1in (2.5cm): two strands of stranded cotton.
24 to 28 holes to 1in (2.5cm): coton à broder.
All these figures are for working cross stitch over two threads.

Canvas

For a thread count of 7 to 9 pairs of threads to 1in (2.5cm): Coats Tapisserie Wool, using cross stitch, over one pair of threads.
14 to 18 holes to 1in (2.5cm) (single mesh): Coats Tapisserie Wool, using cross stitch, over two threads.
12 holes to 1in (2.5cm) (single mesh): Coats Tapisserie Wool using tent stitch, over a single thread.
12 to 14 pairs of threads to 1in (2.5cm): two strands of embroidery wool using tent stitch over one pair of threads.

Size and Preparation of Fabric

If you are following the instructions for one of the projects in this book, you will need fabric at least 8in (20cm) larger on all four sides than the completed sampler. If you are designing your own, you need to calculate the size of the intended work and then add

(cont on p49)

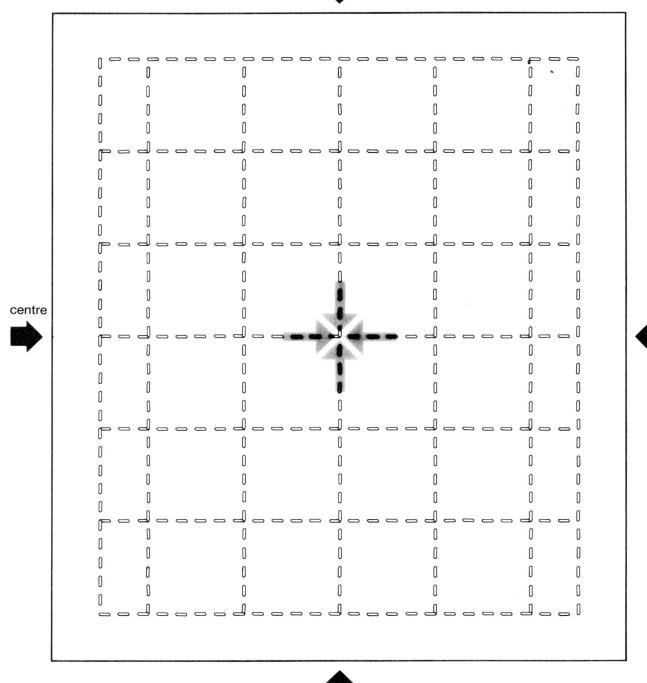

centre

Fig 1   Guidelines. Lines of tacking outline the total area to be worked, indicate the centre of the sampler, and divide the piece into squares of 20/25 stitches

(*opposite*) Trees, Flowers and Birds (p77)
(*overleaf*) Alphabets and Border Patterns (p85); Wedding Celebration (p76)

webbing on rollers at top and bottom

fabric

match up centres of fabric and webbing

Fig 2 Mounting fabric onto a frame

the extra 8in (20cm) all round. To do this you need to know the thread count, that is, the number of threads per inch (2.5cm) of the fabric. Work out the number of stitches horizontally across the sampler, and also from top to bottom. Multiply the number of stitches across the work by the number of threads over which you intend to work each stitch (in cross stitch this is generally two). This will give you the number of threads to be worked over. Divide this figure by the thread count and this will give you the total width in inches or centimetres. Repeat these calculations for the length of the sampler.

Before cutting the fabric to the required size, remember that the selvedges are generally placed at the sides of the sampler. This is especially important when working with fabrics that are not of an even weave, that is, when the number of threads to the inch (2.5cm) is not the same across both the warp and the weft.

When cutting the fabric, you may find it easier to pull a whole length of thread from the fabric along the line you intend to cut.

Guidelines (see page 44)
Before starting a sampler it is advisable to work guidelines of tacking stitches in a brightly coloured thread. These act as very useful markers to help with the correct positioning of the designs and motifs. They are vital when working lines of text, as they help prevent the lettering from wandering from the correct lines of threads. Guidelines can be worked above and below lines of lettering and if you follow these very carefully they will prove a great help.

(*opposite*) Child Holding a Rabbit (p84)

Before mounting the fabric onto the frame, find the centre of the fabric by folding it in half both lengthwise and across the width. Where the two folds meet, work a small stitch — this marks the centre. The first guidelines should be for the length down and the width across the centre of the fabric. Count very carefully, working from the centre out. Further guidelines may be worked to form a grid across the fabric. Pencil in on the chart corresponding lines, perhaps twenty or twenty-five squares apart. Finish with a line all around the outer limit of the proposed sampler. Remember that each square on the chart represents one stitch and not one thread or hole. When you have finished, it is wise to check again that your lines are in exactly the right place — any mistakes will lead to a great deal of confusion.

Mounting Fabric onto an Embroidery Frame
This method should not be used for those frames which require a portion of the work to be rolled up; a square frame large enough to take the whole area to be worked without the need for rolling up is preferred.

After working tacking-stitch guidelines, fold over 1in (2.5cm) on all sides and hem lightly. With the selvedges at the sides, sew webbing tape along both sides. For heavier canvas it is not necessary to hem the edges or to use webbing. The edges can simply be sealed with a heavy tape.

Now sew the top of the fabric to the webbing on the top arm of the frame, making sure that the centres of the fabric and the frame are matched up. Repeat this for the bottom of the fabric and the frame. Assemble the complete frame, rolling up any excess fabric at the

49

Fig 3   Mounting fabric in a hoop. The larger ring is placed on top of the right side of the fabric, and the smaller ring is placed underneath

top and the bottom. With strong thread, lace through the webbing at the sides of the fabric and around the sides of the frame. The lacing should be pulled tightly enough to stretch the fabric across the frame, and the top and bottom of the frame should be adjusted to stretch the fabric vertically. The fabric should now be firmly and evenly stretched on the frame. From time to time as the sampler progresses, it will be necessary to adjust both the lacing and the frame to ensure that the fabric remains properly stretched.

Mounting Fabric onto a Hoop
The hoop used should be large enough to take the whole area to be worked; it should never be placed *over* stitching. The inner hoop can be covered with white bias binding which will help to stop the fabric from slipping and prevent it from being distorted. Wrap the tape around the edges of the hoop, covering it completely. Place the fabric in position over the inner hoop. Loosen the screw on the outer hoop and place over the fabric and the inner hoop. Tighten the screw slightly and adjust the fabric, making sure that it is in position and that it is square. Continue to tighten the screw until the two hoops are locked together, ensuring that the fabric is stretched firmly across the hoop.

Preparing the Threads
The length of the thread to be used should not be longer than 18in (46cm); anything longer may twist and tangle. Wool may start wearing thin, cottons will lose any sheen they may have and the textures of threads such as coton perlé, gold and silver, may suffer.

Wool
Wool is spun in one direction, with the staples or individual hairs being twisted from one end. The wool should be pulled through the fabric in the same direction as it was spun so as not to pull the staples the wrong way. You can feel this by running your finger and thumb up and down the thread.

Stranded wool should be stripped, the strands separated and the required number placed together.

Stranded Cottons
These too should be stripped into individual strands and the required numbers put together.

Using the Charts
There are no definite rules about where to start. In my experience each sampler is different. If there is a piece of text or an alphabet to be included it would be wise to work that first; otherwise begin with the focal point of the sampler, or the largest motif to be worked. I usually sew the border last. The guidelines marked on the

charts should be used to achieve the correct placing of the different motifs and designs. You might find it helpful to shade over lightly with a pencil the areas on the charts that have been worked.

Each square on the chart represents one stitch and not one thread or hole. A symbol inside a square represents a stitch worked in a particular colour, which is indicated in the colour key given with each project. An empty square, unless otherwise stated, represents unworked ground. Areas representing satin stitch may be shaded on the charts, and unless otherwise stated a stitch is worked into every hole and over the number of threads shown on the chart. In some projects you will need to work closely with charts and colour photographs to match stitches and colours, and there is certainly scope for using your own ideas/ colours etc. It would be wise for beginners to start with those projects using only one stitch throughout (eg Projects 1, 2 and 3).

Working in Ends
Work the first stroke of the first stitch to emerge at the front of the work, leaving a length of about 3in (7.5cm) spare at the back of the work. Begin working the stitches and at the same time hold the thread remaining at the back of the work in such a position that it is covered by the reverse strokes of the stitches being worked, so weaving it into the under side of the work. Do this for about ½in (1cm) and then cut away the excess. When you wish to finish the thread, you can use the same method to secure both the end of one thread and the beginning of the next. Ends of threads can be woven into the reverse of existing stitches, though you may feel that this distorts the front of the stitches. This distortion should not happen if a blunt-ended needle is used, because the threads will not be pierced by the needle.

Stitching
When working a group or solid area of stitches, remember that the needle should be brought up to the front of the work through unworked ground, and down through holes where stitches have already been worked. This rule should be followed wherever possible and with a little forethought and planning, stitching should be straightforward.

If your thread develops a lot of twist as you work, let the needle and the thread hang freely from your work, so allowing the thread to untwist. Other problems may be caused by using too great a length of thread.

If your stitching seems lumpy and uneven, the thread may be too thick — see page 43 for a guide to thread thicknesses and weights of fabrics. Correct mounting of the fabric onto the frame or hoop is also an important factor.

Borders and Turning Corners
If you are designing your own sampler, always plan your design on graph paper first, making careful calculations as to how many stitches your design will require.

Draw the border pattern onto the graph paper, beginning at the very centre of one side of the sampler. Work to the top, stopping at a suitable distance away from the sides of the work.

Fig 4   How to turn a corner in a border

There are several different ways of treating the corners of borders. The most common is to turn the 90° angle in mirror fashion. Hold a flat-edged mirror (one that is not bevelled and not in a frame) vertically to the graph paper, at 45° to the line of border patterning. The mirror should be touching the paper exactly where you wish to turn the border. Now look into the mirror and you will see your border pattern reversed in the mirror and travelling across the top of the planned sampler, forming a perfectly symmetrical turn in the pattern. By moving the mirror backwards and forwards, you will see the endless possible variations of turning the border at different points along the repeat of the pattern.

By placing the whole border a little higher or lower, you can also alter the width and length of the sampler until it suits the design as a whole or enables you to fit in the necessary motifs, alphabets etc.

The corners of border patterns do not necessarily have to be symmetrical, but it is important to end up with a well-balanced design. The Wedding Celebration project (8) has a border of flowers which is not perfectly symmetrical but looks right. The Multiplication Table (13) has patterned squares at the corners where the border pattern finishes. The small Rabbit sampler (19) has a bow in one corner.

Lettering and Text

The arrangement of lettering on a sampler can seem daunting, but it only needs a little time and patience. You will need to chart out the letters and text onto graph paper first, having decided upon the exact words you wish to include; do not forget the punctuation marks.

There are several tricks which can be used to make lettering fit neatly into an area. The spaces between each word can be shortened or lengthened, or you can change a particular word to another shorter or longer word with the same meaning; for example, 'worked', 'sewn' and 'embroidered' all mean the same. Names can be worked in full, using just initials or with initial and surname: Sarah Don, S.D. or S. Don. Dates and numerals can also be in words or figures, but try to remain consistent in the use of initials or numerals throughout the work.

Small symbols or short pieces of simple border patterns can be worked at the ends of rows of lettering to fill up any spaces that are left. Crowns and hearts have been traditionally used for this purpose. A tiny pattern or motif can be used instead of spacing in between each word.

The use of tacking stitches as guidelines is most important; these are placed at the top and bottom of the lines of text to prevent them from 'wandering'.

If you are familiar with the style of the alphabet you are using, you can work out how long and over how many stitches and threads a word or number of words will be. Count the number of stitches for each letter of each word. Allow another stitch between each letter of each word and (generally) four stitches between each word. The total will give you the number of stitches which a line of text will cover, and, depending on how many threads your stitches are worked over, the number of threads.

Simple lines of border patterns or satin stitch can be used to divide lines of text, and can take the place of punctuation marks. Words can be in capitals or in lower case, or the first letter of each word can be in capitals and the remainder in lower case. Script can also be used.

Complete sets of alphabets and numerals are given after the projects, page 135. They are numbered for easy reference, and each project has information on which sets to use where relevant.

Golden Rules of Embroidery

There are many strict rules to be followed when working a piece of embroidery. The following rules were definitely not made to be broken!

Never use an 'unpicker' to cut through stitches that have to be unpicked.
Never start a new thread with a knot to secure the end.

Do not press counted-thread embroidery — it will be completely flattened and lifeless.
Do not fold your work; always store it flat and never in coloured tissues. Use white, acid-free tissue paper.
The needle must never be left in the fabric; in time it will distort the fabric and may rust, leaving a nasty stain.
Do not leave the work rolled up on a frame for any length of time — loosen the roller or hoop until you are ready to start working again.

Mounting and Framing

Having removed the finished sampler from the frame or hoop, make sure that all the edges are neatly hemmed with a border of not more than 4in (10cm) outside the finished edges of the stitched area. Carefully measure across and down the embroidered area of the work at the widest points. Cut a piece of very thick strong card ½-1in (12-25mm) larger all round than this, making sure that it is perfectly square. A large set square will be necessary. The extra card will partly disappear into the picture frame. If more space is preferred around the work, allow the appropriate measurement on the edges when measuring the card.

Cut a double layer of muslin 1½-2in (3.5-5cm) larger than the card. Stretch this firmly over the card and secure to the back with masking tape. Place the embroidery over the card and the muslin using pins to hold the work at the back of the card. The pins can be adjusted as you place the work squarely onto the card. The fabric should be slightly stretched over the card to prevent wrinkles and folds.

The work now has to be laced together across the back of the work by means of strong thread. Start at the centre of the width of the work. Thread a long length of strong thread onto a tapestry needle and secure at the centre of one of the sides of hemmed edge. Take it over to the other side at the centre and catch at the edge by passing the needle through just once. Return to the first side and repeat 1in (2.5cm) further up the side. Repeat this process until the top of the card has been reached. Leave the thread loose. Repeat this process for the lower half of the sampler, and then again for the length of the sampler. The ends of the thread are now gently tightened until there is no slack, and fastened off. Any pins used to hold the work in place at the back of the work can now be removed. Your work should be sitting square on the card, ready for framing.

It is always wise to choose a professional framer who is familiar with the framing of textiles. Your work should be delivered to the framers ready mounted onto muslin and card. The most important consideration is that the glass should not touch the embroidery. The type of frame should be chosen carefully and most framers will be able to advise you on this. The Royal

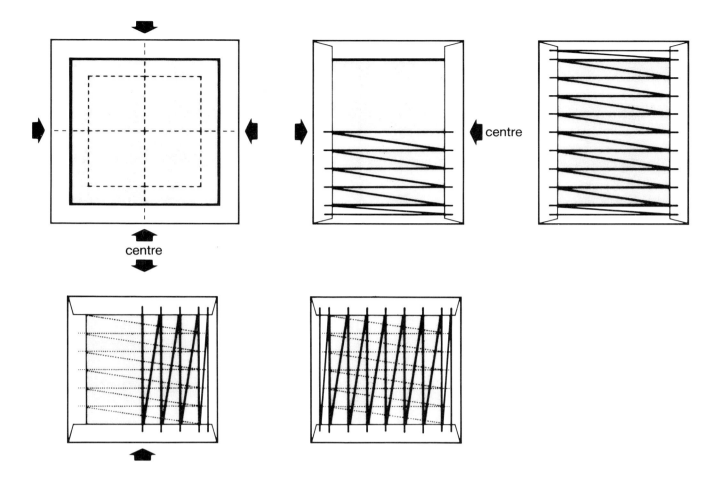

School of Needlework provides a service for mounting embroideries ready for framing and also undertakes cleaning and restoration work. The School can also advise you on the choice of picture framers. I have used Terry Burns Picture Framers at the Royal Academy of Arts in London, who are experienced in this kind of work.

Cleaning and Restoration

Samplers and other types of embroidery should never be placed in direct sunlight or under strong artificial lights. They should also be kept out of direct heat from radiators and fires; the dry atmosphere, fumes and dust particles will, over time, cause irreparable damage, even when the work is framed and behind glass.

Modern samplers can be washed if the fabric and threads that have been used are known to be colour-fast. Use a mild liquid detergent in lukewarm water. Do not wring or squeeze the article; just moving it about gently in the water will be sufficient, but do not leave it to soak. Make sure that it has been thoroughly rinsed before laying it out to dry flat on a white towel (do not dry over a radiator). Pressing should be avoided but should you feel this is necessary, take care

Fig 5   Mounting embroidery onto card

to press only the unworked ground around the stitching.

I do not advise any method of cleaning for old textiles or those that have threads which are not colour-fast; instead, I refer the reader to the following publications:

Finch, K., and Putnam, G., *Caring for Textiles* (Barrie and Jenkins, 1977)
Mailand, H.F., *Consideration for the Care of Textiles and Costumes* (Indianapolis Museum of Art, 1978)
Leene, J.E., *Textile Conservation* (Butterworth, 1972)

There are a small number of firms specialising in the cleaning and restoration of textiles including the Royal School of Needlework, who will undertake work of this kind. Museums with large collections of textiles are also willing to give advice on this subject and the Victoria and Albert Museum in London will advise and help with the dating and identification of older individual pieces of needlework.

5
Stitches

In the following section I have described all the stitches used for the projects in this book. When working the different projects, follow the instructions on the stitches used for the number of threads to be worked over, etc. Some of the stitches I have used are also known by different names, so it would be wise to read through these instructions first before embarking on a project, to avoid confusion.

Plain Cross Stitch

Plain cross stitch consists of two diagonal strokes. The first stroke of each stitch must always be worked in the same direction. When a line or group of stitches are to be worked, I find it best to work the first stroke of all the stitches across one row and then to return back along the row, working the second stroke of the stitches. The next row of stitches is then worked. The work will be neater if the needle is brought up through unworked ground to the right side of the work and down again to the back of the work through a hole shared with a stitch already worked.

Fig 6   Plain cross stitch

Long-armed Cross Stitch

This is just one variation of cross stitch and is worked in a continuous line or row. It consists of two diagonal strokes; the first is the same as for plain cross stitch but the second return stroke is longer.

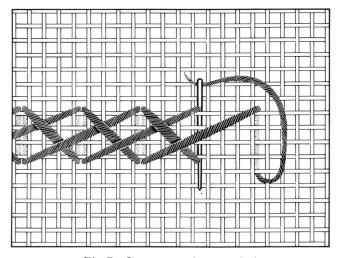

Fig 7   Long-armed cross stitch

Satin Stitch

This is a straight stitch and can be worked vertically, horizontally or diagonally. It is usually worked into every hole and over a number of threads, so covering the fabric well. This is not always the case, and the charts show exactly where the stitches are worked and over how many threads.

Fig 8   Satin stitch

Fig 9   Satin stitch arranged in diamonds

Satin stitch is also used to form different geometric patterns such as triangles and diamonds and herringbone (figs 9-11) which can be used as borders or all-over patterns.

Satin Stitch Trailing
This is satin stitch worked as described above, but over a length of thread or number of threads, which gives a slightly raised, padded effect.

Algerian Eye
This is a stitch using eight or sixteen strokes which occupy a square and radiate from a centre hole. The thread should be pulled through the fabric with a certain degree of tension, so that the centre hole is visible when the stitch is finished; but take care not to distort the shape of the square. Algerian eye is often outlined with back stitch (fig 14).

Fig 10   Satin stitch arranged in a chevron pattern

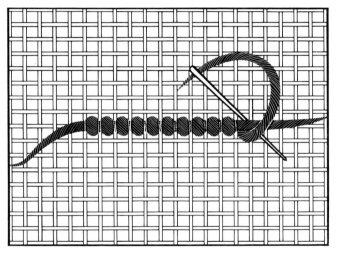

Fig 12   Satin stitch trailing

Fig 11   Satin stitch arranged in triangles

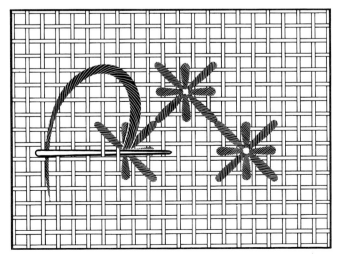

Fig 13   Algerian eye, worked over four by four threads

Fig 14   Algerian eye, worked over eight by eight threads outlined with back stitch.

Fig 17   One-quarter eyelet worked over four by four threads (top) and five by five threads (bottom)

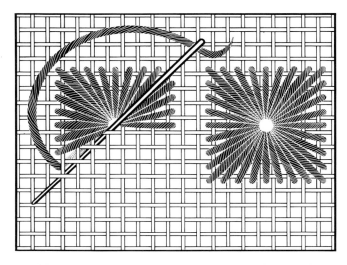

Fig 15   Eyelet worked over eight by eight threads

Fig 18   Diamond eyelet

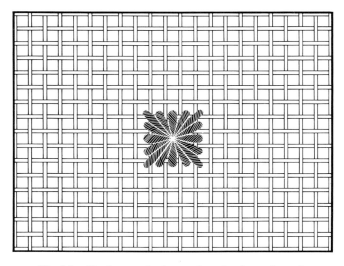

Fig 16   Eyelet worked over four by four threads

Eyelet

This is very similar to Algerian eye, but there are twice as many strokes so that the finished eyelet has a more solid appearance. One quarter of an eyelet can be used on its own or repeated to form an all-over pattern (see fig 17). It can also be used as a 'diamond' eyelet (fig 18).

Tent (Brick or Continental) Stitch

I have used this stitch for the lettering on many of the samplers in this book and for a few of the motifs. It consists of a diagonal stroke which is always worked in the same direction. On the right side of the work it covers just one thread of the fabric and is worked diagonally. On the wrong side of the embroidery it is worked over at least two threads of the fabric and diagonally.

Fig 19   Tent stitch

Fig 21   Back stitch

Fig 20   Double running stitch

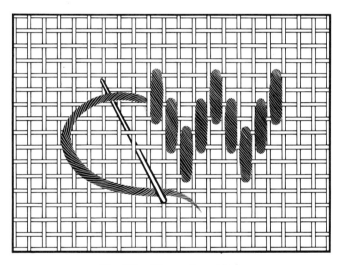

Fig 22   Florentine stitch

When tent stitch is used for lettering a little forethought is required in order to start and end at a place where the strokes of the stitch can be worked as described above. The reverse stroke of the stitch must be worked diagonally and over more than one thread of the fabric.

Double Running Stitch

This is the stitch popularly used for blackwork. It is composed by working straight stitches with spaces between them in one direction and then completing the missing stitches on the way back. This stitch is usually used to outline patterns and designs. Should you find double running stitch difficult to work on a complicated design, you can use back stitch instead.

Back Stitch

This is also a straight stitch and is worked with one stroke on the right side of the fabric.

Florentine Stitch

Florentine is a pattern of straight stitches which can be of the same or varying lengths, using a number of colours. Innumerable different patterns are possible. Tent and cross are a few of the other stitches which are used to create Florentine patterns, but the stitch shown in fig 22 is the stitch referred to as Florentine stitch for the projects in this book.

French Knots

These are made by wrapping the thread around the needle twice, very close to the fabric. The thread is then gently pulled against the needle until it is taut, and the needle is inserted into the fabric two holes from where it emerged; it is then pulled through both the loops on the needle and the fabric.

I have used French knots scattered around the border of the Wedding Celebration sampler (8). They can be used close together to fill an area, producing a textured surface. The thicker the thread, the larger the knot; in counted-thread work, the knots will often need to be worked in thread thicker than that used for the other stitches.

Square Stitch

This uses straight stitches to surround a square. The thread should be pulled fairly firmly on each stroke so that the threads of the fabric are pulled together and the finished stitches form an open, lacy effect.

Fig 23   French knot

Fig 24   Square stitch

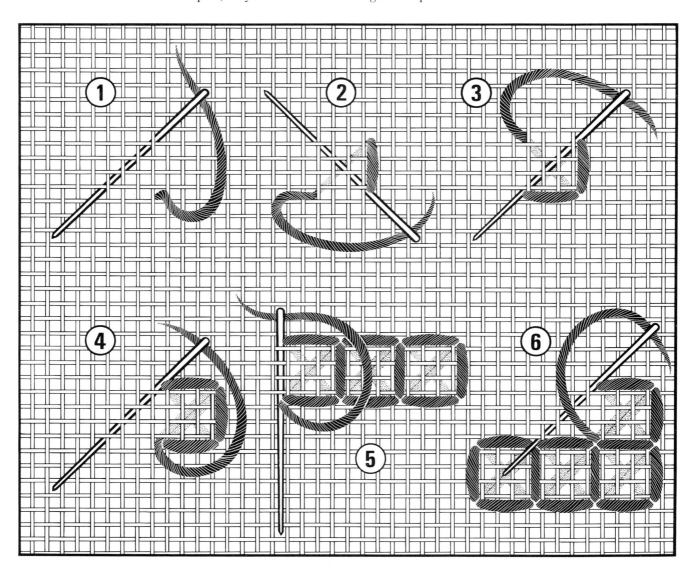

Projects

1
Celebration of a Child's Birthday

(colour photograph page 25)

This design has been worked from a sampler in the Tunbridge Wells Museum in Kent, England. I have worked it in stranded cottons on cream-coloured hardanger fabric, in colours close to the original. There are two cherubs blowing trumpets, two birds and a rather crudely designed but charming pot of flowers in the centre. If the name you wish to include at the bottom is rather longer than the one shown, the surname could be omitted, or the border could be lengthened by working two more whole repeats of the patterns to allow for another line of text underneath.

Fabric
Cream-coloured hardanger fabric, sixteen pairs of threads to 1in (2.5cm). The finished work measures 5½ × 8in (14 × 20cm). When buying your fabric, allow an extra 8in (20cm) on every side.

Thread
Anchor Mouline Stranded Cotton.

Stitch (see Chapter 5)
Cross stitch throughout; three strands are worked over one pair of threads. Each symbol on the chart represents one cross stitch worked in the colour indicated by the colour key.

Colour Key
O	red	042	× 1 skein
X	pink	038	× 1 skein
●	pink	066	× 1 skein
Z	green	0214	× 1 skein
C	beige	0347	× 1 skein
/	brown	360	× 1 skein
•	blue	0850	× 1 skein

All amounts are approximate.

Alphabets and Numerals
Complete sets of the alphabets and numerals are given after the projects. See Alphabet 5 and Numerals 3.

2
Multicoloured Alphabets in Wool

(colour photograph page 26)

This design was inspired by a sampler in the collection of Mrs Pamela Morgan. Her sampler was worked in wool on canvas using many different colours, and is signed 'Ethel Minnie Sedgewick aged 8 years'. The original measures 11 × 15in (28 × 38cm). I have kept the design and colours of this sampler very close to the original, changing a few of the colours which on the original have faded badly, and tidying up some of the border patterns. I have worked the name and date of birth of my son, but you could work your own name and the date on which you completed the sampler. This is a good sampler for beginners to work, as it is simple and uncomplicated but the result is quite charming. Try working it in different colours of your own choice, perhaps using up oddments.

Fabric

Dark-coloured, double-mesh canvas, ten pairs of threads to 1in (2.5cm). The finished work measures 12½ × 15½in (30.5 × 39cm). When buying your fabric, allow an extra 8in (20cm) on every side.

Thread

Coats Tapisserie Wool.

Stitch (see Chapter 5)

Cross stitch throughout, worked over one pair of threads. Each symbol on the chart represents one cross stitch worked in the colour indicated by the colour key.

Colour Key

O	red	045	× 2 skeins
//	blue	0506	× 1 skein
=	pink	068	× 1 skein
+	grey	0398	× 1 skein
Z	yellow	0734	× 1 skein
C	olive	0268	× 1 skein
✳	brown	0418	× 1 skein
—	purple	0869	× 1 skein
•	green	0269	× 1 skein
/	green	0266	× 1 skein
S	green	0842	× 1 skein
X	green	0215	× 1 skein
>	green	0858	× 1 skein
V	green	0506	× 1 skein
⋇	pink	0661	× 1 skein
●	rust	0351	× 1 skein
∧	pink	0895	× 1 skein

All amounts are approximate.

3

Spaniel

(colour photograph page 26)

This design has been taken from a sampler owned by Mr and Mrs Goodwin which is in wool on good-quality sacking! It was worked by a ship's carpenter, H. Baldwin, around 1900. As with all the pieces I have been able to study closely, the original colours have faded, some much more so than others. They were originally very bright and gaudy, but now, with time, they have turned into lovely muted shades, adding much charm and character to the work. I have kept the colours close to those of the original as it appears now. The sampler is worked in wool on double canvas using tent stitch. I have included the year in which it was worked; you could also include your name or initials, using an alphabet from those given.

Fabric
Double-mesh canvas, twelve double threads to 1in (2.5cm). The finished sampler measures 13 × 9in (33 × 23cm). When buying your fabric, allow an extra 8in (20cm) on every side.

Thread
Coats Tapisserie Wool.

Stitch (see Chapter 5)
Tent stitch throughout, worked over one double thread. Each symbol on the chart represents one tent stitch worked in the colour indicated by the colour key.

Colour Key
✱	rust	0741	× 1 skein
+	pink	3166	× 1 skein
Z	beige	0904	× 1 skein
●	brown	0420	× 1 skein
/	sand	0713	× 1 skein
X	green	0859	× 1 skein
ℓ	olive	0269	× 1 skein
•	black	0403	× 4 skeins
∩	brown	0378	× 1 skein
O	white	0390	× 2 skeins
■	pink	0503	× 1 skein
S	cream	0388	× 1 skein

All amounts are approximate.

Numerals
Numerals 12.

4
Adam and Eve

(colour photograph page 27)

This is a Dutch version of Adam and Eve, which I have surrounded with a delicate border of carnations taken from a small hold-all in the Victoria and Albert Museum, London. The hold-all was made in the mid-eighteenth century using silks on linen in cross stitch. I have used the colours from this hold-all, which are rather muted but very pretty. Adam and Eve stand holding hands under the Tree of Knowledge, which is laden with apples. The serpent is also included, along with two rather over-sized birds!

Fabric
Beige evenweave fabric, 27 holes to 1in (2.5cm). The finished sampler measures 8¾ × 10½in (22 × 26.5cm). When buying your fabric, allow an extra 8in (20cm) on every side.

Thread
Coats Coton à Broder.

Stitches (see Chapter 5)
Satin stitch trailing for the lines making the square frame; the thread is used whole over two threads of the fabric and stitched over one whole thread.

All remaining symbols represent cross stitch in the colour indicated by the key; use the thread whole over two threads.

Colour Key
X   green   0260 × 2 skeins
/   pink   8960 × 2 skeins
O   red   0340 × 1 skein
●   blue   0128 × 1 skein
◢   yellow   0298 × 1 skein

All amounts are approximate.

Alphabet
Alphabet 11.

5

Red and Green Alphabets

(colour photograph page 27)

These alphabets and border patterns appear on an American sampler sewn by Elizabeth Lawson and dated 1833. It also shows a number of names and initials, including 'Alexander Thompson American Consul' underneath the American Eagle. I have rearranged some of the alphabets and border patterns into a smaller design using simple basic stitches in the hope that it will appeal to beginners. The first alphabet is in cross stitch, the second is in back stitch and one of the lines of simple border patterns is in eyelets. Colours of your own choice can be substituted for those used here; you could put together any odds and ends you may have to make a large range of colours.

Fabric
White linen evenweave, 26 holes to 1in (2.5cm). The finished sampler measures 7 × 9¼in (17.5 × 23.5cm). When buying your fabric, allow an extra 8in (20cm) on all sides.

Thread
Anchor Mouline Stranded Cotton.

Stitches (see Chapter 5)
Back stitch indicated by solid line; two strands are worked over two threads. This is used for the second alphabet; refer to photograph for colours.

Eyelet (indicated by large star symbol); two strands are worked. The finished eyelet occupies a square of four by four threads. This is used in red for the decoration under the sixth row of letters.

All remaining symbols represent cross stitch in the colour indicated by the key; three strands worked over two threads.

Colour Key
X red   0341 × 1 skein
• pink   0339 × 1 skein
O olive   0856 × 1 skein
/ green   0924 × 1 skein

All amounts are approximate.

Alphabet and Numerals
Alphabet 6, Numerals 7.

6

American Fort and Animals

(colour photograph page 28, chart pages 72-3)

The designs used for this sampler have been taken from a lovely American sampler worked by nine-year-old Sophia Ellis; it is dated 8 February 1785. She used a large number of religious and secular motifs worked in cross and satin stitches. There are also two alphabets and a set of numerals, together with the words, 'health is a jewel dropped from heaven which money cannot buy the life of . . . peace and pleasant harmony'.

I have included a number of the motifs and designs from the original and worked the sampler in colours as true as possible to those used by Sophia Ellis. The year in which the work is completed is included; you could include your name or an inscription — choose an alphabet from those shown.

Fabric
White evenweave linen, 26 holes to 1in (2.5cm). The finished sampler measures 12½ × 13in (31.5 × 33cm). When buying your fabric, allow an extra 8in (20cm) on every side.

Thread
Anchor Mouline Stranded Cotton; DMC Fil Or (gold thread).

Stitches (see Chapter 5)
Areas of satin stitch are shown by solid lines; three strands of cotton are worked over the number of threads indicated on the chart. Gold thread is used doubled. Refer to photograph for colours.

Back stitch is shown by broken lines; two strands of cotton are worked in black over two threads. Areas within the broken lines to be filled in with satin stitch; refer to photograph for colours.

Satin stitch trailing indicated by thick solid line; three strands of cotton are worked into every hole, over two threads, and stitched over a three-strand length of cotton. This is used for the top row only, in grey.

All remaining symbols represent cross stitch in the colour indicated by the key; two strands worked over two threads. Gold thread is used doubled over two threads.

Colour Key
Anchor Mouline Stranded Cotton:

V	blue	0167	× 2 skeins
O	green	0216	× 2 skeins
●	green	0218	× 2 skeins
·	pink	06	× 1 skein
Z	yellow	0311	× 1 skein (fort, satin stitch)
∩	pink	0895	× 1 skein
S	grey	975	× 1 skein
/	red	0896	× 1 skein
X	black	0403	× 1 skein
✻	DMC Fil Or (gold thread)		× 2 reels

All amounts are approximate.

Numerals
Numerals 3.

7
Red Alphabets

(colour photograph page 27, chart pages 74-5)

This sampler has been put together using alphabets from old pattern books in my collection, which I believe to have been printed in Germany. The alphabet at the top is worked in two shades of red and the second is in script. Underneath I have included the words:

> Sarah Don is my name
> And with my needle
> I wrought the same.

The stitches used for this sampler are very fine and it would not be an easy project for a beginner to work. I have seen a similar piece made up into a small cushion edged with a wide frill of lace, which was very effective.

Fabric
White linen evenweave, 26 holes to 1in (2.5cm). The finished sampler measures 9 × 6¼in (23 × 15.5cm). When buying your fabric, allow an extra 8in (20cm) on every side.

Thread
Coats Coton à Broder

Stitch (see Chapter 5)
Tent stitch throughout worked over a single thread, except for the heart which is in back stitch. Each symbol represents one stitch in the colour indicated by the key.

Colour Key
/   red   019 × 1 skein
•   dark red   044 × 1 skein

All amounts are approximate.

Alphabets and Numerals
Alphabets 10 and 11, Numerals 12.

American Fort and Animals

Colour Key

Anchor Mouline Stranded Cotton

V	blue	0167
O	green	0216
●	green	0218
•	pink	06
Z	yellow	0311
∩	pink	0895
S	grey	975
/	red	0896
X	black	0403
✻	DMC Fil Or (gold thread)	

Red Alphabets
Colour Key
/ red
• dark red

8
Wedding Celebration

(colour photograph page 47, chart pages 78-9)

This sampler is to celebrate a wedding and includes a large amount of text giving details about the couple, their families and the wedding itself. I have used an attractive Dutch alphabet for the text with two cherubs and a heart underneath. This is framed by a Dutch floral border of tulips, roses and carnations, dotted with tiny French knots. I have used the colours which featured in the flowers and the bridesmaids' dresses at the wedding, and have included some silver thread.

For this sampler, you will have to plan the text, making sure that the names and dates are all correct, and then chart carefully the full text into the area for the central section. Remember that each square on the chart represents one stitch and two threads of the fabric. Spaces at the ends of the lines of text can be filled with a motif from those shown with the alphabets. The heart and cherubs can be omitted if you wish to use the whole central space for text.

Fabric
Cream linen evenweave, 28 holes to 1in (2.5cm). The finished sampler measures 13½ × 16½in (34 × 42cm). When buying your fabric, allow an extra 8in (20cm) on every side.

Thread
Anchor Mouline Stranded Cotton.
DMC Fil Argent à Broder (silver thread).

Stitches (see Chapter 5)
Satin stitch for silver triangles; the silver thread is used double (three strands if cotton used).
Satin stitch trailing for straight lines; three strands are worked into every hole over two threads and are stitched over a three-strand length of stranded cotton (see photograph for colours).
French knots; these are worked last, sprinkled around the border in all the colours used, including silver. They are not marked on the chart. The cotton is used with three strands and the silver thread is used double. All remaining symbols represent cross stitch in the colour indicated by the key; two strands worked over two threads.

Colour Key
Anchor Mouline Stranded Cotton:

/	pink	0969	× 1 skein
●	pink	0970	× 1 skein
•	pink	0893	× 1 skein
	purple	0870	× 1 skein (text)
▲	purple	095	× 1 skein
O	purple	0111	× 2 skeins
∩	purple	097	× 1 skein
	purple	096	× 1 skein (text)
	purple	099	× 2 skeins (text)
✳	yellow	0362	× 1 skein
V	brown	0359	× 1 skein
X	green	0861	× 1 skein
Z	orange	010	× 1 skein
	DMC Fil Argent à Broder (silver thread)		

All amounts are approximate.

Alphabets and Numerals
Alphabet 17, Numerals 18.

9
Trees, Flowers and Birds

(colour photograph page 45, chart pages 80-3)

This sampler is based on one in my own collection, which is worked with silks on linen in cross stitch. It bears the words, 'Elizabeth Miles' work Bishop's Lydeard September 1848', and measures 13 × 12in (33 × 30.5cm). The design is perfectly symmetrical, with alphabets, stylised trees, pots of flowers and birds carefully placed around the cloth. It is very typical of samplers from the mid-nineteenth century which were intended to be purely decorative needlework pictures to be hung with pride on the wall.

The design has been copied faithfully from the original but the finished sampler is rather larger. I have included my name, the town I live in and the date on which the sampler was completed.

Fabric

Cream-coloured evenweave fabric, 26 holes to 1in (2.5cm). The finished sampler measures 22½ × 21in (57 × 53cm). When buying your fabric, allow an extra 8in (20cm) on every side.

Thread

Anchor Mouline Stranded Cotton.

Stitch (see Chapter 5)

Cross stitch throughout; two strands are worked over two threads. Each symbol on the chart represents one stitch in the colour indicated by the key.

Colour Key

X	green	0862	× 2 skeins
/	gold	0308	× 2 skeins
O	olive	0846	× 2 skeins
✳	brown	0888	× 2 skeins
●	green	0845	× 1 skein
•	brown	0393	× 1 skein
C	beige	0887	× 1 skein
∩	beige	0373	× 2 skeins
S	brown	0369	× 1 skein

All amounts are approximate.

Wedding celebration

Colour Key
Anchor Mouline Stranded Cotton:

/	pink	0969	O	purple	0111	V	brown	0359
●	pink	0970	∩	purple	097	X	green	0861
·	pink	0893		purple	096	Z	orange	010
	purple	0870		purple	099		DMC Fil Argent à Broder
▲	purple	095	✳	yellow	0362		(silver thread)

Trees, Flowers and Birds

Colour Key

X	green	0862	● green	0845
/	gold	0308	• brown	0393
O	olive	0846	C beige	0887
✳	brown	0888	∩ beige	0373
			S brown	0369

82

10
Child Holding a Rabbit

(colour photograph page 48, chart pages 86-7)

This is a design taken from a woolwork sampler in my own collection, which is worked on a light-coloured canvas in wools which are now rather faded. On the original, the child's purple trousers have faded to blue and beige. This is a very pretty though modest sampler, the attempt at shading showing the trend for more realistic designs; the use of colour is typical of this type of sampler from the Victorian period. It was worked by a little girl called Alice Mitchell, aged eight. I have copied the original quite faithfully, although my design works out a little larger.

Fabric
Cream double canvas, nine pairs of threads to 1in (2.5cm). The finished sampler measures 19 × 21in (48 × 53cm). When buying your fabric, allow an extra 8in (20cm) on every side.

Thread
Coats Tapisserie Wool.

Stitch (see Chapter 5)
Cross stitch throughout, worked over one pair of threads. Each symbol represents one stitch in the colour indicated by the key.

Alphabets and Numerals
Alphabets 5 and 6, Numerals 7.

Colour Key

Symbol	Colour	Code	Amount
ℓ	brown	0351	× 1 skein
△	brown	0358	× 1 skein
I	brown	0380	× 1 skein
U	beige	0373	× 1 skein
⊿	stone	0388	× 1 skein
Q	brown	0845	× 1 skein
y	olive	0424	× 1 skein
●	white	0725	× 1 skein
X	blue	0506	× 3 skeins
//	green	0264	× 1 skein
h	pink	0503	× 1 skein
▢	pink	0069	× 1 skein
/	pink	0037	× 3 skeins
₆	blue	0139	× 1 skein
∞	black	0360	× 1 skein
b	blue	0145	× 1 skein
—	brown	0903	× 1 skein
※	beige	0390	× 1 skein
O	green	0842	× 3 skeins
∩	yellow	3230	× 1 skein
Z and ▲	pink	3098	× 1 skein
S and ∽	grey	0397	× 1 skein
+	white	0441	× 1 skein
✕	grey	0401	× 1 skein
C	purple	099	× 1 skein
L	purple	095	× 1 skein
V	purple	097	× 1 skein
✳	red	045	× 1 skein
•	pink	0336	× 1 skein
t	beige	0570	× 1 skein
ؘ	brown	0420	× 1 skein

All amounts are approximate.

11
Alphabets and Border Patterns

(colour photograph page 46, chart pages 88-93)

This sampler includes a large number of my favourite alphabets, border patterns and crowns which have been taken from samplers dating from the last four centuries and from around the world. I have tried not to repeat these designs elsewhere in the book and they are meant as a source of patterns for you to use when designing your own samplers. Try experimenting with different colours and stitches. My initials and the year in which I completed the sampler are included.

The first alphabet, which is Dutch, is given rather elaborate treatment. It is worked in cross stitch with a pattern worked in back stitch in a contrasting colour around the edges of the letters. The second alphabet is worked in Algerian eye and the third, worked in cross stitch, came from a German pattern book in my own collection. The border patterns underneath include some old favourites which were popularly used — rosebud, honeysuckle, strawberry, tulip and carnation. The large floral pattern at the bottom is taken from a pattern book by Peter Quentel printed in the sixteenth century. The cartouche containing the date is taken from an English sampler in my own collection, dated 1826; I have seen many versions of this on samplers from England and Holland.

Fabric
Natural Glenshee evenweave linen, 29 holes to 1in (2.5cm). The finished sampler measures 20 × 25in (53 × 71cm). When buying your fabric, allow an extra 8in (20cm) on every side.

Thread
Anchor Mouline Stranded Cotton

Stitches (see Chapter 5)
Back stitch (indicated by broken or solid line with no symbol); two strands are worked over two threads (see photograph for colour).
Algerian eye (indicated by large star symbol); two strands are worked so that the finished stitch occupies a square of four by four threads (see photograph for colour).
Satin stitch (solid line with colour symbol inside); two strands are worked into every hole over the number of threads indicated on the chart.
All remaining symbols represent cross stitch in the colour indicated by the key; two strands worked over two threads.

Colour and Stitch Key

Symbol	Colour	Code	Amount
/	blue	0161	× 2 skeins
∧ and ∨	blue	0851	× 2 skeins
●	red	011	× 2 skeins
*	olive	0845	× 2 skeins
X	green	216	× 2 skeins
Z	yellow	297	× 2 skeins
O	pink	9	× 2 skeins
----□	back stitch (see photograph for colour)		
❈◇❈	satin stitch (colour indicated by symbols)		
✳	Algerian eye (see photograph for colour)		

All amounts are approximate.

Alphabet and Numerals
Alphabet 11, Numerals 12.

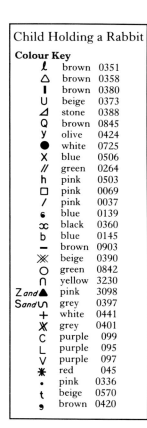

Child Holding a Rabbit

Colour Key

ℓ	brown	0351
△	brown	0358
I	brown	0380
U	beige	0373
◿	stone	0388
Q	brown	0845
y	olive	0424
●	white	0725
X	blue	0506
//	green	0264
h	pink	0503
□	pink	0069
/	pink	0037
ϭ	blue	0139
∝	black	0360
b	blue	0145
—	brown	0903
※	beige	0390
O	green	0842
∩	yellow	3230
Z and ▲	pink	3098
S and ᔕ	grey	0397
+	white	0441
✕	grey	0401
C	purple	099
L	purple	095
V	purple	097
✳	red	045
•	pink	0336
t	beige	0570
໑	brown	0420

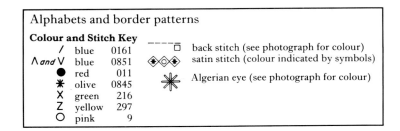

Alphabets and border patterns

Colour and Stitch Key

Symbol	Colour	Number
/	blue	0161
∧ and ∨	blue	0851
●	red	011
✳	olive	0845
X	green	216
Z	yellow	297
○	pink	9

- – – – ▫ back stitch (see photograph for colour)
- ◈◇◈ satin stitch (colour indicated by symbols)
- ✳ Algerian eye (see photograph for colour)

Alphabets and border patterns

Colour and Stitch Key

/	blue	0161
∧ and V	blue	0851
●	red	011
✳	olive	0845
X	green	216
Z	yellow	297
O	pink	9

- - - - ▯ back stitch (see photograph for colour)

◈◈◈ satin stitch (colour indicated by symbols)

✳ Algerian eye (see photograph for colour)

Alphabets and border patterns

Colour and Stitch Key

/	blue	0161	
∧ and ∨	blue	0851	
●	red	011	
✳	olive	0845	
X	green	216	
Z	yellow	297	
O	pink	9	

- - - - ▭ back stitch (see photograph for colour)

✳◇✳ satin stitch (colour indicated by symbols)

✳ Algerian eye (see photograph for colour)

93

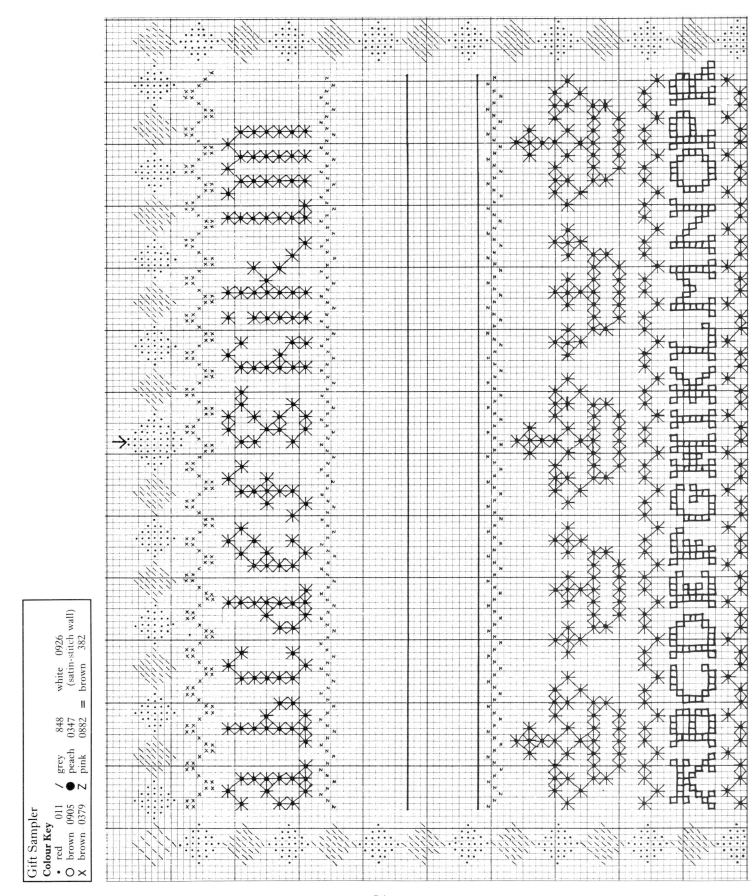

Gift Sampler
Colour Key
· red   011   / grey   848   white   0926
O brown 0905   ● peach   0347   (satin-stitch wall)
X brown 0379   Z pink   0882   = brown   382

94

12

Gift Sampler

(colour photograph page 98, chart pages 94-5)

The alphabets used here were taken from an English sampler dated 1733. Border patterns from other English pieces of about the same time have also been incorporated into the design, together with Dutch cats and rabbits. I worked this particular sampler for two young friends of mine who each have a cat and a rabbit as pets. You may like to work a different group of motifs into this area. The different alphabets are worked in eyelet, cross stitch and satin stitch trailing. The brick pattern is worked using satin stitch in between rows of satin stitch trailing. The areas left blank on the charts are for your own text, and there are guidelines to help with positioning (do not stitch lines).

Fabric
Soft cream linen evenweave, 27 holes to 1in (2.5cm). The finished sampler measures 10¼ × 14½in (26 × 37cm). When buying your fabric, allow an extra 8in (20cm) on every side.

Thread
Anchor Mouline Stranded Cotton.

Stitches (see Chapter 5)
Satin stitch for second alphabet and wall; three strands are worked over two threads unless otherwise shown on chart (see photograph for colours).

Eyelet (indicated by large star symbol); three strands are worked over two threads. The completed stitch occupied a square of four by four threads (see photograph for colour).

Satin stitch trailing for horizontal lines; three strands are worked over two threads, over a length of three strands of cotton (see photograph for colours).

Back stitch in black has been used for the rabbit's ears. All remaining symbols represent cross stitch in the colour indicated by the key; three strands worked over two threads.

Colour Key
•	red	011	× 2 skeins
O	brown	0905	× 2 skeins
X	brown	0379	× 1 skein
/	grey	848	× 2 skeins
●	peach	0347	× 1 skein
Z	pink	0882	× 1 skein
	white	0926	× 1 skein (satin-stitch wall)
=	brown	382	× 1 skein

All amounts are approximate.

Alphabets and Numerals
Alphabets 5, 8, 9, 25 and 27,
Numerals 26.

(opposite) Multiplication Table (p101); Busy Bee (p108); Valentine (p106)
(overleaf) Gift Sampler (p96); Noah's Ark (p109)

MULTIPLICATION·TABLE·S·DON·8

1	2	3	4	5	6	7	8	9	10	11	12
2	4	6	8	10	12	14	16	18	20	22	24
3	6	9	12	15	18	21	24	27	30	33	36
4	8	12	16	20	24	28	32	36	40	44	48
5	10	15	20	25	30	35	40	45	50	55	60
6	12	18	24	30	36	42	48	54	60	66	72
7	14	21	28	35	42	49	56	63	70	77	84
8	16	24	32	40	48	56	64	72	80	88	96
9	18	27	36	45	54	63	72	81	90	99	108
10	20	30	40	50	60	70	80	90	100	110	120
11	22	33	44	55	66	77	88	99	110	121	132
12	24	36	48	60	72	84	96	108	120	132	144

1951

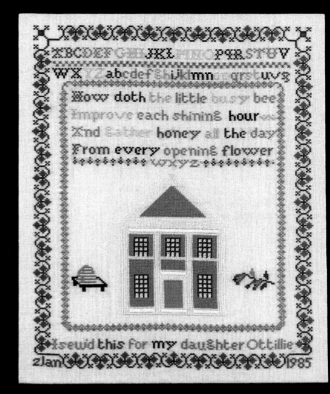

ABCDEF GHI JKL MNOP QR STUV
WX YZ abcdef ghijklmn opqrstuvz

How doth the little busy bee
Improve each shining hour
And gather honey all the day
From every opening flower
✦✦✦✦✦ wxyz ✦✦✦✦✦

I sewid this for my daughter Ottillie
2 Jan 1985

♥ BERNARD.

1984

Noah sent forth a 🕊 out
of the that
came to him again in the eve
-ning with an olive 🍃 that
she had plucked in her 🕊 so

Noah knew that the Waters
were abated from the earth.

Sarah Don 1785

13
Multiplication Table

(colour photograph page 97, chart pages 102-5)

These tables were often worked by children as popular school exercises, though they were not always correct. I have worked mine with a typically English honeysuckle border and included a Dutch landscaped scene at the bottom. This scene has been worked by English sampler-makers several times, in various degrees of complexity and using different colours. I have also worked two garlands of flowers in which you can work dates or initials. The table could be worked on its own and surrounded just by the border given here or with one of your own choice. (See page 51 for advice on turning the corners of borders.)

Fabric
Cream Danish linen evenweave, thirty holes to 1in (2.5cm). The finished sampler measures 16¼ × 17¼in (41 × 44cm). When buying your fabric, allow an extra 8in (20cm) on every side.

Thread
DMC Stranded Cotton.

Stitch (see Chapter 5)
Cross stitch throughout; two strands are worked over two threads. Each symbol represents one cross stitch in the colour indicated by the key.

Colour Key

X	blue	926	× 2 skeins
h	red	3350	× 3 skeins
/	blue	930	× 1 skein
C	yellow	743	× 1 skein
✳	red	315	× 2 skeins
V	pink	950	× 1 skein
●	olive	3012	× 2 skeins
O	green	730	× 1 skein
+	pink	407	× 1 skein
t	green	859	× 1 skein
•	brown	938	× 1 skein
S	blue	501	× 1 skein
L	green	956	× 1 skein
Z	brown	379	× 1 skein

All amounts are approximate.

Alphabet
Alphabet 4.

(opposite) Blackwork Sampler (p116)

Multiplication Table

Colour Key

X	blue	926	✳	red	315	t	green	859
h	red	3350	V	pink	950	•	brown	938
/	blue	930	●	olive	3012	S	blue	501
C	yellow	743	O	green	730	L	green	956
			+	pink	407	Z	brown	379

Multiplication Table

Colour Key

X	blue	926	✱	red	315	t green 859
h	red	3350	V	pink	950	• brown 938
/	blue	930	●	olive	3012	S blue 501
C	yellow	743	O	green	730	L green 956
			+	pink	407	Z brown 379

14
Valentine

(colour photograph page 97)

Samplers were often made and given as tokens of affection. This one is similar in style to the Valentines made around the turn of the century, and often exchanged between soldiers and their wives/girlfriends during World War I. The colours are my own choice, although the motifs are traditionally used on samplers. All of them have different symbolic meanings; you could use appropriate motifs of your own choice (see pages 36-7, on symbolism). The lettering has been taken from an old German pattern book.

Fabric
White linen evenweave, 28 holes to 1in (2.5cm). The finished sampler measures 8½ × 4¼in (21.5 × 11cm). When buying your fabric, allow an extra 8in (20cm) on every side.

Thread
Coats Coton à Broder.

Stitches (see Chapter 5)
Motifs C-E and lettering: tent stitch, worked over a single thread.
Motifs A and B: white satin stitch outlined in red back stitch (dotted line), worked over the number of threads shown on the chart.
All remaining symbols represent cross stitch worked over two threads in colours indicated by key.

Colour Key
/	yellow	298 × 1 skein	
✱	red	47 × 1 skein	
O	green	262 × 1 skein	
•	purple	101 × 1 skein	(and text)
●	white	396 × 1 skein	

Alphabets and Numerals
Alphabets 15, Numerals 16.

15

Busy Bee

(colour photograph page 97, chart pages 110-11)

This sampler is based on one from the second half of the nineteenth century which bears the name of St Mary's National Girls' School but is not signed or dated. It shows a pretty pink building representing the school, with alphabets, lines of Biblical text, a basket of fruit, flowers and a tree. The whole is surrounded by a strawberry border — a very popular design which appeared time and again without much variation in either style or colour.

The sampler was unfinished; the space around the building was probably meant to be filled with a number of different motifs. I rather like the space fairly empty and have included only a beehive and flowers in the design to complement the poem which I have used to replace the Biblical text. You may wish to fill in the area with some of your favourite motifs. The colours I have used are close to those used in the original. At the bottom there is an inscription dedicating the work to one of my daughters; space permitting, you can substitute the inscription of your choice. The date on which I completed the sampler is worked into the bottom corners of the border, the day and the month in the left-hand corner, the year in the right-hand corner. If there is not enough room for the month in letters, it can be worked in numerals.

Fabric
Off-white linen evenweave, 27 holes to 1in (2.5cm). The finished sampler measures 13¾ × 17½in (35 × 44.5cm). When buying your fabric, allow an extra 8in (20cm) on every side.

Thread
Anchor Mouline Stranded Cotton.

Stitches (see Chapter 5)
House: satin stitch (white horizontal and vertical 'frame'); three strands are worked into every hole and over six threads. The rest of the house is in tent stitch; all six strands worked over two threads.

Eyelet (for decoration between alphabets); use three strands of dark blue. The finished eyelet occupies a square of four by four threads.

All remaining symbols represent cross stitch in the colour indicated by key; three strands worked over two threads.

Colour Key

Symbol	Colour	Code	Amount
X	green	0878	× 3 skeins
•	red	013	× 3 skeins
●	pink	0895	× 3 skeins
O	pink	6	× 1 skein
/	blue	0145	× 2 skeins
S	blue	158	× 1 skein
✳	yellow	0307	× 1 skein
C	brown	382	× 1 skein
//	white	01	× 3 skeins

All amounts are approximate.

Numerals
Numerals 30.

16
Noah's Ark

(colour photograph page 99, chart pages 112-13)

Rebus samplers such as this were made in the eighteenth century as one of many school needlework exercises; rebuses were, however, rather rare. The story of Noah's ark lends itself well to this kind of treatment, as would many classical stories and nursery rhymes. The words that are missing from the text are replaced by pictures, in this case dove, ark, leaf and beak.

I have used the same text and lettering as in a sampler made in 1793 by ten-year-old Elizabeth Bullocks. The ark, doves and the border are different, and I have included a rising sun at the bottom.

Fabric
White linen evenweave fabric, 26 holes to 1in (2.5cm). The finished sampler measures 12 × 15in (30.5 × 38cm). When buying your fabric, allow an extra 8in (20cm) on every side.

Thread
Anchor Mouline Stranded Cotton.

Stitches (see Chapter 5)
Areas of satin stitch shown within lines; three strands are worked over the number of threads indicated on the chart (see photograph for colours). Satin stitch is used freehand for leaves and sun's rays.

All remaining symbols represent cross stitch in the colour indicated by the key; three strands worked over two threads.

Colour Key

X	blue	0152	× 2 skeins
C	yellow	311	× 1 skein (satin-stitch sun)
/	green	0267	× 1 skein
✳	green	0269	× 1 skein
O	green	0261	× 1 skein
•	white	01	× 1 skein
V	rust	5975	× 1 skein (satin-stitch ark)
Z	pink	0892	× 1 skein
●	brown	944	× 1 skein
■	blue	0976	× 2 skeins (satin-stitch sea and border)

All amounts are approximate.

Alphabets and Numerals
Alphabets 20 and 22, Numerals 10.

Busy Bee
Colour Key
X green 0878
· red 013
● pink 0895
○ pink 6
/ blue 0145
S blue 158
✳ yellow 0307
C brown 382
// white 01

Noah's Ark
Colour Key
X	blue	0152	
C	yellow	311	(satin-stitch sun)
/	green	0267	
✱	green	0269	
O	green	0261	
•	white	01	
V	rust	5975	(satin-stitch ark)
Z	pink	0892	
●	brown	944	
■	blue	0976	(satin-stitch sea and border)

Deer motif (see p116)

Daisy motif (see p 116)

Blackwork Sampler

17
Blackwork Sampler

(colour photograph page 100, chart pages 114-15)

This is a collection of traditional sixteenth- and seventeenth-century blackwork motifs, symbols, borders and all-over repeat patterns, densely packed so as to include as many different designs as possible. The sampler can be worked as it is, or patterns or motifs used for your own design. It is intended as a reference piece. Black thread was traditional, but occasionally, paler more muted colours were used in shades of brown, green, blue and red. Later, blackwork designs were embellished with filling stitches and later still, richer fillings were used, incorporating metal threads, beads and seed pearls. 'Boxers' like the ones used in this sampler were filled with satin stitch, hence clothing them, perhaps out of modesty.

After working some designs in double running stitch you may be inspired to experiment with colours, filling stitches, beads and metal threads. Using stranded cottons will allow you to have different thicknesses of the thread to give plenty of variation in density and texture. This sampler includes the traditional 'boxers', a lion, various insects, birds, fish, a pineapple, flowers and a number of borders and repeat patterns.

Note: A close, evenweave fabric is essential for this technique, as is a blunt needle of the correct size. Too large a needle will distort the woven threads, too small a needle will pierce and damage the individual threads, which will then not lie neatly.

Fabric
White hardanger, twenty-two double threads to 1in (2.5cm). The finished sampler measures 12 × 18in (30 × 45.5cm). When buying your fabric, allow an extra 8in (20cm) on every side.

Thread
Coats Coton à Broder.

Stitches (see Chapter 5)
Double running stitch worked over two double threads, *or* back stitch worked over two double threads.
Deer and daisy motifs: cross stitch (cross symbol on chart), worked over one double thread, with satin stitch for heads of daisies.

Colour Key
black 0403 × 4 skeins (approx)

Alphabets and Numerals
Alphabet 5, Numerals 18.

(left) Deer and daisy motifs

(opposite) Quaker Seminary (p121); Rabbit (p124)
(overleaf) Family Tree (p125); Lamb of God (p128)

Peter Worrell
Son of
Frank & Florence
Worrell

Kathleen Houghton
Daughter of
Ronald & Amy Alice
Houghton

Married in the Year
1949

Their Children in

Rotation of Birth

Josephine May
Born Aug 9 1950

Amanda Caroline
Born Dec. 9 1957

Sarah Jane
Born Aug. 10 1951

Victoria Frances
Born Dec. 13 1961

Bridget Elizabeth
Born April. 30 1954

deceased
Kathleen ~ 1971
Joseph ~ 1973

Grandchildren

Joseph Don
Emily Don
Karen and
Deborah Melhuish
Oliver Don

Ottilie Don
Adam Caisley
Ben Grinter
Aimee Grinter
Kathleen Caisley

1984.

My God inscribe my name
There let me fill some humble place
Beneath the slaughtered Lamb
In thy fair Book of life Divine

18

Quaker Seminary

(colour photograph page 117, chart pages 122-3)

This sampler is based on one in the collection of the Embroiderers' Guild. It is thought to be a representation of a Quaker seminary and was worked by a boy, Richard Harrison; it is dated 'May 1 1740'. It is very bright and colourful, with an attractive, geometric-patterned border. The house is depicted in fine detail in contrast to the more crudely designed flowers and trees. I have followed the design quite closely but have shortened the tall, striped border across the top which you may prefer to extend.

Fabric
Cream single-mesh canvas, 10 holes to 1in (2.5cm). The finished sampler measures 24 × 16in (61 × 40.5cm). When buying your fabric, allow an extra 8in (20cm) on every side.

Thread
Anchor Tapisserie Wool.

Stitch (see Chapter 5)
Cross stitch throughout, worked over two threads. Each symbol represents one stitch in the colour indicated by the key.

Colour Key

X	red	0412 ×	11	skeins
•	pink	068 ×	4	skeins
S	pink	0336 ×	3	skeins
/	blue	0139 ×	1	skein
✳	blue	145 ×	2	skeins
+	green	0269 ×	2	skeins
=	brown	0379 ×	2	skeins
●	yellow	0311 ×	8	skeins
◿	white	0386 ×	7	skeins
//	grey	0981 ×	2	skeins
C	yellow	0500 ×	1	skein
O	blue	0851 ×	2	skeins
V	green	0842 ×	2	skeins
Z	brown	0985 ×	2	skeins
∩	brown	0360 ×	1	skein

All amounts are approximate.

Alphabets and Numerals
Alphabet 13, Numerals 14.

(opposite) Whitework Sampler (p132)

Quaker Seminary
Colour Key

X	red	0412
•	pink	068
S	pink	0336
/	blue	0139
*	blue	145
+	green	0269
=	brown	0379
●	yellow	0311
△	white	0386
//	grey	0981
C	yellow	0500
O	blue	0851
V	green	0842
Z	brown	0985
∩	brown	0360

19
Rabbit

(colour photograph page 117)

This charming little rabbit is just one of many motifs on a large Dutch sampler worked in silks. I thought it would be perfect for a child to sew, and have worked it in wool on canvas, using tent stitch. It is surrounded by a leafy border and a bow. The year in which it was worked is included at the bottom.

Fabric
Single mesh canvas, 12 holes to 1in (2.5cm). This sampler measures 5 × 5in (12.5 × 12.5cm). When buying your fabric, allow an extra 8in (20cm) on every side.

Thread
Coats Tapisserie Wool.

Stitch (see Chapter 5)
Tent stitch throughout, worked over a single thread.

Colour Key
•	cream	0384	× 1 skein
X	blue	0163	× 1 skein
O	green	0424	× 1 skein
C	beige	0421	× 1 skein
/	pink	0503	× 1 skein
●	black	0403	× 1 skein
Z	pale pink	037	× 1 skein
✳	brown	0987	× 1 skein

All amounts are approximate.

Numerals
Numerals 12.

20
Family Tree

(colour photograph page 118, chart pages 126-7)

This family tree is taken from a very famous sampler worked by S. Stearn in about 1830 and now at the Victoria and Albert Museum, London. The original is worked in silk on linen using cross and tent stitches and is rather fine. I have adapted the design, rearranging the motifs slightly to accommodate a little more text for the names of grandchildren.

Should you wish to work this sampler, you will have to work out the text exactly to fit into the available space. Carefully plan the text onto the chart for the central section making sure that names and dates are all correct. It is possible to extend or shorten the box containing the names of the grandchildren, by moving the top line of the box up or down. Dates can be written in either words or figures, depending on how much room you have. Names can either be in full, or christian names can be replaced by initials. With a little time and patience spent on planning and careful counting, it should be possible for you to work this family tree for your own family's history. A complete alphabet and set of numerals for this sampler are given on page 135. (See page 52 for further instructions on working lettering.)

Fabric
Off-white linen evenweave, 26 holes to 1in (2.5cm). The finished sampler measures 11 × 16in (28 × 40.5cm). When buying your fabric, allow an extra 8in (20cm) on every side.

Thread
Anchor Mouline Stranded Cotton.

Stitches (see Chapter 5)
Cross stitch; three strands are worked over two threads in colour indicated by key.
Lettering: tent stitch in dark brown; two strands are worked over one thread.

Colour Key

●	red	045	× 2 skeins
○	red	042	× 2 skeins
/	pink	039	× 2 skeins
C	pink	038	× 2 skeins
∩	green	0212	× 2 skeins
X	olive	0845	× 2 skeins
*	yellow	0888	× 1 skein
V	brown	0905	× 2 skeins (plus lettering)
t	pink	06	× 1 skein
Z	pink	24	× 1 skein
//	off-white	0852	× 2 skeins
•	white	02	× 1 skein
△	yellow	305	× 1 skein
U	brown	889	× 1 skein
L	brown	370	× 1 skein
+	beige	887	× 1 skein

All amounts are approximate.

Alphabets and Numerals
Alphabets 1 and 2, Numerals 3.

Family Tree

Colour Key

●	red	045	t	pink	06
○	red	042	Z	pink	24
/	pink	039	//	off-white	0852
C	pink	038	•	white	02
∩	green	0212	△	yellow	305
X	olive	0845	U	brown	889
✳	yellow	0888	L	brown	370
V	brown	0905	+	beige	887

21
Lamb of God

(colour photograph page 119, chart pages 130-1)

This sampler is a very extravagant and experimental exercise in the use of simple stitches and colour. Cross, satin, straight stitches and eyelets are all used to create a very large number of patterns and textures, each one being different. The work is framed by a gold border with the inscription:

> In thy book of life divine
> May God inscribe my name
> There let me fill some humble place
> Beneath the slaughtered lamb.

These words were taken from the last four lines of a verse worked on a sampler made by Sarah Mitchell in 1822. The central section is a Dutch motif of the Lamb of God, a symbol representing Christ as the lamb led to slaughter. The lamb appears here with blood streaming from its chest.

Each section has been given a reference letter so it can be described individually. (NB Some of the panels do not match exactly with the colour photograph.)

The Chart (section by section)
A: Worked in diamond eyelet in the colours indicated by the symbols (see colour key).
B and O: Satin-stitch triangles worked in the colours indicated by the symbols (see colour key).
C: Florentine stitch worked in reds and yellows, following the pattern in the detailed diagram.
D: One quarter of an eyelet stitch worked in the colours indicated by the symbols.
E and H: Satin stitch in herringbone pattern using the colours indicated by the symbols.
F: This is worked in cross stitch, using colours indicated by the symbols.
G: Diamond eyelet using the colours indicated by the symbols.
I: Algerian eye is worked in the colours indicated by the symbols and outlined with back stitch in gold thread.
J: Satin stitch worked in the colours indicated by the symbols.
K and R: Florentine stitch using reds, greens and yellows, following the pattern in the chart.
L: Eyelet worked in the colours indicated by the symbols.

M: Satin-stitch diamonds worked in the colours indicated by the symbols.
N: Cross stitch: each symbol represents one stitch worked in the colours indicated by the symbols.
P: A satin-stitch pattern worked in the colours indicated by the symbols. The direction of the stitches is shown on the detailed diagram.
Q: Satin-stitch 'bricks' worked in the colours indicated by the symbols. See detailed diagram.
S: The symbols represent cross-stitch triangles on the lower part, with satin-stitch triangles above.
T: The central square is worked entirely in cross stitch with each symbol representing one stitch in the colour indicated in the colour key.
Border: cross stitch for the dividing lines between sections; and long-armed cross stitch.
Scale: Each square on the large chart (p130) represents two threads of the fabric. The three smaller charts (p129) show details of some of the stitches and use one square for one thread of the fabric.

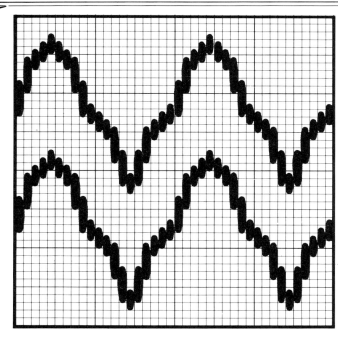

Block C of Lamb of God

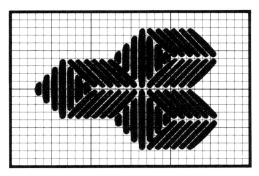

Block P of Lamb of God

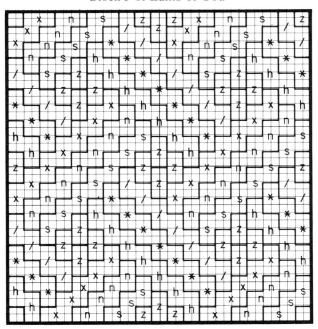

Block Q of Lamb of God

Fabric
Evenweave linen, 28 holes to 1in (2.5cm). The finished sampler measures 12¼ × 13¾in (31 × 35cm). When buying your fabric, allow an extra 8in (20cm) on every side.

Thread
Coats Coton à Broder.
DMC Fil Or (gold thread).

Stitches (see Chapter 5)
Cross stitch, worked over two threads.
Satin stitch.
Florentine stitch.
Back stitch.
Eyelet.
Diamond eyelet.
Algerian eye.
Long-armed cross stitch.
All stitches are worked over the number of threads shown on the chart.
Additional charts given for sections C, Q and P have one square representing just one thread of the fabric.

Colour Key
O	DMC Fil Or (gold thread) × 4 reels		
	Coats Coton à Broder:		
X	green	0245	× 1 skein
∩	green	0239	× 2 skeins
+	black	0403	× 1 skein
✱	red	019	× 1 skein
/	red	044	× 2 skeins
h	red	46	× 1 skein
Z	yellow	0298	× 1 skein
•	blue	0134	× 3 skeins
∧	blue	0169	× 1 skein
S	cream	0386	× 2 skeins
//	blue	978	× 1 skein
●	blue	128	× 1 skein

All amounts are approximate.

Alphabets and Numerals
Alphabets 21 and 22, Numerals 12.

Lamb of God

Colour Key

Symbol	Colour	Code
O	DMC Fil Or (gold thread)	

Coats Coton à Broder:

Symbol	Colour	Code
X	green	0245
∩	green	0239
+	black	0403
✱	red	019
/	red	044
h	red	46
Z	yellow	0298
•	blue	0134
∧	blue	0169
S	cream	0386
//	blue	978
●	blue	128

The Chart (section by section)

A: Worked in diamond eyelet in the colours indicated by the symbols (see colour key).

B and O: Satin-stitch triangles worked in the colours indicated by the symbols (see colour key).

C: Florentine stitch worked in reds and yellows, following the pattern in the detailed diagram.

D: One quarter of an eyelet stitch worked in the colours indicated by the symbols.

E and H: Satin stitch in herringbone pattern using the colours indicated by the symbols.

F: This is worked in cross stitch, using colours indicated by the symbols.

G: Diamond eyelet using the colours indicated by the symbols.

I: Algerian eye is worked in the colours indicated by the symbols and outlined with back stitch in gold thread.

J: Satin stitch worked in the colours indicated by the symbols.

K and R: Florentine stitch using reds, greens and yellows, following the pattern in the chart.

L: Eyelet worked in the colours indicated by the symbols.

A	B	C	D
R			E
Q		T	F
P			G
O	M	K	H
N	S L	J	I

M: Satin-stitch diamonds worked in the colours indicated by the symbols.

N: Cross stitch: each symbol represents one stitch worked in the colours indicated by the symbols.

P: A satin-stitch pattern worked in the colours indicated by the symbols. The direction of the stitches is shown on the detailed diagram.

Q: Satin-stitch 'bricks' worked in the colours indicated by the symbols. See detailed diagram.

S: The symbols represent cross-stitch triangles on the lower part, with satin-stitch triangles above.

T: The central square is worked entirely in cross stitch with each symbol representing one stitch in the colour indicated in the colour key.

Border: cross stitch for the dividing lines between sections; and long-armed cross stitch.

Scale: Each square on the large chart (p130) represents two threads of the fabric. The three smaller charts (p129) show details of some of the stitches and use one square for one thread of the fabric.

22
Whitework Sampler

(colour photograph page 120, chart pages 133-4)

Whitework is the name given to embroidery worked in white thread on a white ground. This sampler uses a small number of basic embroidery stitches to illustrate a few of the simpler patterns which were used for such work. It is intended as a practice piece for beginners who may then wish to embark on a more ambitious project. The most prominent stitch used for whitework is satin or flat stitch, which also dominates this sampler (worked in the direction shown by the arrows). The patterns worked here include the popular carnation, acorns, hearts and a number of geometric patterns. Initials and the year in which the piece is worked are included at the bottom using Algerian eye.

The thread I have used is a very pretty one, but a little slippery and rather difficult to work. It can be substituted for other threads; three strands of stranded cotton would work well on the fabric recommended here.

NB   Only one half of the sampler is given on the chart. Information on which stitch to use is also given on the chart.

Fabric
White linen evenweave, 26 holes to 1in (2.5cm). The finished sampler measures 6½ × 12in (15.5 × 30.5cm). When buying your fabric, allow an extra 8in (20cm) on every side.

Thread
Three skeins of Bella Donna high-gloss twist thread in cream, no. 1012. This is used halved throughout and over the number of threads indicated on the chart.

Stitches (see Chapter 5)
Satin stitch (direction of working is indicated by arrows).
Algerian eye.
Cross stitch.
Long-armed cross stitch.
Square stitch.

Alphabet and Numerals
Alphabet and Numerals 23.

back stitch

Satin stitch

long-armed cross

satin stitch and
Algerian eye

square stitch

satin stitch

long-armed cross

satin stitch

Algerian eye

satin stitch

long-armed cross

satin stitch

2 rows cross
stitch

satin stitch

2 rows square
stitch

satin stitch and
Algerian eye

cross stitch

text in
Algerian eye

long-armed cross

eyelet or
Algerian eye

satin stitch or back stitch

1

2

3

4

5

6

7

8

9

10

eyelet or Algerian eye

19

20

21

22

23

24

25

26

27

28 ABCDEFGHIJKLMNO PQRSTVWXYZ 12345678910

back stitch or satin stitch

29

cross stitch and back stitch

30

Embroidery Courses

There are a very large number of different courses on embroidery held at schools and colleges throughout the UK, covering every possible technique and application of the craft. They range from the more serious three-year City and Guilds courses to short courses of day or evening classes. Anyone considering further education in the field of embroidery should contact their local education authority for a list of schools and colleges which will supply prospectuses for the various courses held.

The two very famous educational establishments for embroidery are the Royal School of Needlework, 25 Prince's Gate, London, and the Embroiderers' Guild, Hampton Court Palace, East Molesey, Surrey. The Royal School of Needlework was first established in 1872 and was formed with the wish both to improve the standard of art in embroidery and to create employment. Twenty young ladies were employed here in the first year, a figure which had increased to 150 by 1903. Embroideries worked at the School were exhibited all around the world, many royal commissions were undertaken and historical embroideries were cleaned, repaired and restored. Classes have been held here for over a hundred years on ecclesiastical, secular and ceremonial embroidery. Today the Royal School is still responsible for the coronation robes and many regimental commissions, and the restoration of historical pieces continues. The School holds a large number of different courses, many of which are sponsored by the Inner London Education Authority. Private classes are also given and new apprentices are accepted every year for a two-year diploma course with the aim of supplying the workroom with new embroiderers. Visitors are welcome at the School by arrangement and Friends of the School receive a regular newsletter and have access to the School's library.

The Embroiderers' Guild is now housed at Hampton Court Palace. It is an educational charity set up in 1906 with the aim of promoting the craft of embroidery to the highest possible standards. Guild members can participate in the many classes, lectures and workshops held at the Hampton Court apartment and have access to the library and study folios containing samples of embroidery, slides, photographs, notes and bibliographies. The Guild owns a large collection of historical and modern embroideries and organises frequent exhibitions.

USA

The Embroiderers' Guild of America, like the Embroiderers' Guild in Britain, is a non-profit making, educational organisation which began in 1958 and now has chapters throughout America. The address for information is 6 East 45th Street, Room 1501, New York 10017.

Another non-profit making organisation founded to 'promote high quality in the art of embroidery' is the National Standards Council of American Embroiderers. Enquiries should be addressed to the membership secretary, National Standards Council of American Embroiderers, 223 NW 12th Street, Pendleton, Oregon 97801.

Canada

Contact the Canadian Embroiderers' Guild, 434 Village Green Avenue, London, Ontario.

Australia

For information on the Australian Embroiderers' Guild, write to the secretary of the Embroiderers' Guild New South Wales, Beaumont Street, 167 Elizabeth Street, Sydney, NSW 2000.

New Zealand

The address of the Association of New Zealand Embroiderers' Guilds is PO Box 37198, Parwell, Auckland.

Museums and Collections

Many of the museums in the following list have excellent study facilities, and students are made welcome. Special arrangements have to be made with museum staff for the study of reserve collections.

UK and Eire

The American Museum in Britain, Claverton Manor, Bath
Blaise Castle House Museum, Bristol
Bristol City Museum, Bristol
The Bodleian Library, Oxford
The British Museum, Museum of Mankind, London
Camphill Museum, Glasgow
Dorset County Museum, Dorchester
The Embroiderers' Guild, Hampton Court Palace, East
   Molesey
Fitzwilliam Museum, Cambridge
Gawthorpe Hall, Padiham, near Preston
Glasgow's Museums and Art Galleries, Camphill Museum,
   Glasgow
Guildford Museum, Guildford
The Lady Lever Art Gallery, Port Sunlight, Merseyside
Lancaster City Council Museum, Lancaster
Museum of English Rural Life, Reading
The National Museum of Ireland, Dublin
The National Museum of Wales, St Fagan's, Cardiff
Nottingham Museum of Costume and Textiles, Nottingham
Royal School of Needlework, London
Royal Scottish Museum, Edinburgh
Ruskin Museum, Coniston, Cumbria
Strangers' Hall Museum, Norwich
The Suffolk Collection, Ranger's House, London

Tunbridge Wells Museum, Tunbridge Wells
Ulster Folk Museum, Holywood, County Down
Victoria and Albert Museum, London
William Morris Gallery, London

The AA Guide to Stately Homes, Museums, Castles and Gardens in Britain gives a comprehensive list of museums in Britain, dates and times of opening, addresses and phone numbers.

USA

Brooklyn Museum, New York
Cooper-Hewitt Museum of Design (Smithsonian Institution), New York
The Daughters of the American Revolution Museum,
   Washington DC
Denver Art Museum, Colorado
Essex Institute, Salem, Massachusetts
Helen L. Allen Collection, University of Wisconsin, Madison
Henry Francis du Pont Winterhur Museum, Winterhur,
   Delaware
Indian Service Museum, Browning, Montana
Metropolitan Museum of Art, New York
Museum of American Folk Art, New York
Museum of Art, Rhode Island School of Design
Museum of the City of New York, New York
The Museum of Fine Arts, Boston
Philadelphia Museum of Art, Philadelphia
Pilgrim Society, Plymouth, Massachusetts
William Penn Memorial Museum, Harrisburg, Pennsylvania
Williamsburg Museum, Virginia

Suppliers

The threads used for the projects in this book are made either by Coats or DMC and are widely available in both the United Kingdom and the USA from many department stores and specialist needlework shops. I have included here a list of mail-order suppliers, in case you have any difficulty in obtaining the required materials. The shops listed may also be able to help you to find the right fabrics.

UK
Coats Threads
The following shops operate a mail-order service within the United Kingdom and hold complete ranges of the Coats threads used in this book.

A. & J. Franklin and Sons
13a Botolphs Street
Colchester
Essex

*Harrods,
Art Needlework Dept
Knightsbridge
London SW1

Jenners Ltd
Needlework Dept
Princes Street
Edinburgh

Needleneeds
Beauchamp Place
London SW1

The Richmond Art Centre
181 City Road
Cardiff
Glamorgan
CF2 3JB

*So Simple Ltd
192 Petts Wood Road
Petts Wood
Orpington
Kent BR5 1LG

Woolfayre Ltd
120 High Street
Northallerton
North Yorkshire
D17 8PQ

U-Duit
7 Church Street
Ripley
Derbyshire
DE5 3BU

*These shops also operate a mail-order service to overseas residents.

DMC Threads
The following shops operate a mail-order service within the United Kingdom and hold the complete range of DMC threads. Dunlicraft, the distributors for these threads, will supply a complete list of stockists on request.

Aldertons
1-3 Swan Lane
Norwich

Aurelia
762-4 Christchurch Road
Bournemouth
Dorset

Bella Craft Shop
Marston Road
Stafford
Staffordshire

Fayre Fabrics
56 Market Place
Inverurie
Aberdeenshire

John Lewis
St James Centre
Edinburgh

Lalla Thomas Ltd
413 Abergele Road
Old Colwyn
Clwyd

Lurgan Fobel Centre
43 High Street
Lurgan
Co Armagh

Newport Handicrafts
Upper St James Street
Newport
Isle of Wight

Southern Handicrafts
25 Kensington Gardens
Brighton
Sussex

Templetons
Mill Street
Ayrshire

The Craftworkshop
89 St Nicholas Market
Bristol
Avon

The Hobby House
3-4 Little Castle Street
Truro
Cornwall

Lady Jayne Fabrics
40 Mill Street
Ballymena
Co Antrim

Liberty's
Regent Street
London W1

The Model and Craft Centre
260 Dewsbury Road
Wakefield
Yorkshire

Russells
Castle Street
Carlisle
Cumbria

Suzicraft
5 Crampers Field
Counden
Coventry

Westbrook Crafts
127 Canterbury Road
Westbrook
Margate
Kent

USA
Coats threads used for the projects in this book are sold in many shops throughout the USA, but if you have any problems in finding them, write to: J. & P. Coats (UK) Limited, National Distribution Centre, 39 Durham Street, Glasgow G41 1BS. They will inform you of your nearest stockist or mail-order supplier.

DMC threads are also available in the USA and a list of suppliers can be obtained from the DMC Corporation, 107 Trumble Street, Elizabeth, New Jersey 07026.

Bibliography

An asterisk indicates possible source of patterns and motifs.

Ashton, Sir Arthur, *Samplers* (Medici Society, London and Boston, 1926)

Beck, T., *Embroidered Gardens* (Angus and Robertson, London, 1979)

*Bolton, E. S. and Coe, E. J., *American Samplers* (The National Society of the Colonial Dames of America: Massachusetts Branch, 1921, reprinted by Dover, New York, 1921)

Bridgeman, H., and Drury, E., *Needlework: an Illustrated History* (Paddington Press, New York and London, 1978)

*Christie, A. G. I., *Samplers and Stitches* (B. T. Batsford, London, 1921, reprinted 1985)

Churchill Bath, V., *Needlework in America: History, Designs and Techniques* (Mills and Boon, London, 1979)

Clabburn, P., *Samplers* (Shire Publications, Aylesbury, 1977)

*Colby, A., *Samplers* (B. T. Batsford, London, 1964, reprinted 1984)

Digby, G. W., *Elizabethan Embroidery* (Faber and Faber, London, 1963)

*Dreesman, C., *Samplers for Today* (Van Nostrand Reinhold, New York, 1972)

*Drysdale, R., *The Art of Blackwork Embroidery* (Mills and Boon, London, 1975)

Edwards, J., *The first of Joan Edwards' small books on the history of embroidery: Berlin Work* (Bayford Books, Dorking, 1980)

Edwards, J., *The fifth of Joan Edwards' small books on the history of embroidery: Samplermaking* (Bayford Books, Dorking, 1983)

Embroiderers' Guild, The, *Needlework School,* (Windward, QED Publishing, London, 1984)

*Fawdry, M., and Brown, D., *The Book of Samplers* (Lutterworth Press, Guildford and London, 1980)

*Geddes, E., and McNeill, M., *Blackwork Embroidery* (Dover, New York, 1976)

*Gierl, I., *Cross Stitch Patterns* (B. T. Batsford, London, 1977)

Gombrich, E. H., *The Sense of Order* (Phaidon, Oxford, 1979)

*Gostelow, Mary, *Blackwork* (B. T. Batsford, London, 1976, reprinted 1985)

*Gostelow, M., *The Cross Stitch Book* (B. T. Batsford, London, 1982)

Haig, E., *The Floral Symbolism of the Great Masters* (Kegan Paul and Co, London, 1913)

Horner, M. M., *The Story of Samplers* (Philadelphia Museum of Art, Philadelphia, 1963)

*Huish, M., *Samplers and Tapestry Embroideries* (Longmans Green, London, 1913, reprinted by Dover, New York, 1970)

Jones, M. E., *British Samplers* (Pen in Hand, Oxford, 1948)

*Kay, D., *Sew a Sampler* (Adam and Charles Black, London, 1979)

Kendrick, A. F., *English Needlework* (Adam and Charles Black, London, 1933)

King, D., *Samplers* (Victoria and Albert Museum, Her Majesty's Stationery Office, London, 1960)

Krueger, G., *A Gallery of American Samplers: The Theodore H. Kapnek Collection* (E. P. Dutton, 1978)

Krueger, G., *New England Samplers to 1840* (Old Sturbridge Village, Sturbridge, Massachusetts, 1978)

Levey, M., *Discovering Embroidery of the 19th Century* (Shire Publications, Aylesbury, 1971)

*Lewis, F., *Needlepoint Samplers* (Cassell, London, 1981)

*Meulenbelt-Nieuwburg, A., *Embroidery Motifs from Dutch Samplers* (B. T. Batsford, London, 1974, reprinted 1984)

Oddy, R., *Samplers in the Guildford Museum* (Guildford Museum, Dorking, 1951)

*Paige-Burns, H., and Thorne-Thomson, K., *American Cross Stitch* (Van Nostrand Reinhold, New York, 1974)

Payne, F. G., *Samplers and Embroideries in the National Museum of Wales* (The National Museum of Wales, Cardiff, 1939)

*Procter, M. G., *Victorian Canvas Work: Berlin Woolwork* (B. T. Batsford, London, 1972)

.Schiffer, M. B., *Historical Needlework of Pennsylvania* (Charles Scribner and Sons, New York, 1968)

*Sebba, A., *Five Centuries of a Gentle Craft* (Weidenfeld and Nicolson, London, 1979)

Swift, G., *The Batsford Encyclopaedia of Embroidery Techniques* (B. T. Batsford, London, 1984)

Synge, L., *Antique Needlework* (Blandford Press, Poole, 1982)

Victoria and Albert Museum, *English Samplers* (Her Majesty's Stationery Office, London, 1947)

Victoria and Albert Museum, *The Needle's Excellency: a Travelling Exhibition* (Her Majesty's Stationery Office, London, 1973)

*Vinciolo, F., *Singuliers et nouveaux pourtraits*, 1587 (unabridged facsimile published by Dover, New York, 1971)

Wade, V., *The Basic Stitches of Embroidery* (Victoria and

Albert Museum, Her Majesty's Stationery Office, London, 1966)

Wandel, G., *Klassiske Korssting* (Politikens Forlag, Copenhagen, 1971)

*Weiss, R., *Victorian Alphabets, Monograms and Names for Needleworkers* (Dover, New York, 1974)

Magazines

Embroidery, published quarterly by the Embroiderers' Guild, East Molesey, Surrey.

Counted Thread, a quarterly publication of the Counted Thread Society, 3305 South Newport Street, Denver, Colorado 80224, USA.

Flying Needle, published by the National Standards Council, 223 NW 12th Street, Pendleton, Oregon 97801, USA.

Needle Arts, published by the Embroiderers' Guild of America, 6 East 45th Street, Room 1501, New York 10017, USA.

The Needlework Times, available from Suite 1405, North Michigan Avenue, Chicago, Illinois 60602, USA.

Symed Korssting from Denmark and *Ariadne Kruissteken* from Holland.
I have seen these two magazines on sale in some specialist needlework shops in England.

Index

ENDPAPERS: Evening shower breaking up over the Sheenjek River

Had this on our
coffee table for a
month + were sorely
tempted to keep it. But
we bought it for you —
happy anniversary, +
many, many more to come!
love,
Joan + John

Earth and the Great Weather
THE BROOKS RANGE

Glorious it is to see

The caribou flocking down from the forests

And beginning

Their wandering to the north.

Timidly they watch

For the pitfalls of man.

Glorious it is to see

The great herds from the forests

Spreading out over plains of white.

Glorious to see.

    Yayai—ya—yiya.

Glorious it is to see
Early summer's short-haired caribou
Beginning to wander.
Glorious to see them trot
To and fro
Across the promontories,
Seeking a crossing place.
      Yai—ya—yiya.

Glorious it is
To see the great musk oxen
Gathering in herds.
The little dogs they watch for
When they gather in herds
Glorious to see.
      Yai—ya—yiya.

JOHN MILTON: *Foothills and mist*

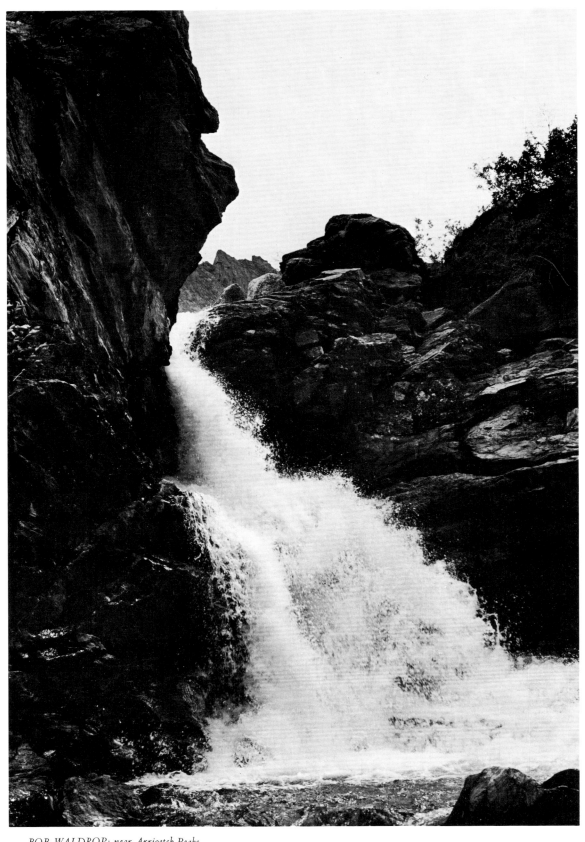

BOB WALDROP: near Arrigetch Peaks

Glorious it is
To see young women
Gathering in little groups
And paying visits in the houses—
Then all at once the men
Do so want to be manly,
While the girls simply
Think of some little lie.
  Yayai—ya—yiya.

Glorious it is
To see long-haired winter caribou
Returning to the forests.
Fearfully they watch
For the little people,
While the herd follows the ebb-mark of the sea
With a storm of clattering hooves.
Glorious it is
When wandering time is come.
    Yayai—ya—yiya.
              —Netsit

DONALD AITKEN: *Caribou, Arctic Coastal Plain*

JOHN MILTON: Romanzof Mountains

The great sea
Has set me adrift
It moves me like the weed in a great river
Earth and the great weather
Move me,
Have carried me away
And move my inward parts with joy.

—OSARQAQ

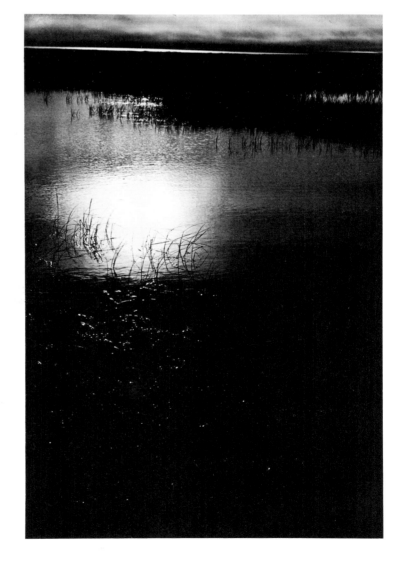

JOHN MILTON: *Wetlands, Arctic Plain*

Earth and the Great Weather:

foreword by David Brower

introduction by John P. Milton

photographs by Pete Martin, Wilbur Mills,
John P. Milton, Gilbert Staender, and others

with selections from Lois Crisler, Robert Marshall, Nalungiaq,
Netsit, Knud Rasmussen, David Roberts,
Vilhjálmur Stefansson, Tatilgak, and others

by Kenneth Brower

THE BROOKS RANGE

FRIENDS OF THE EARTH ◉ SAN FRANCISCO, NEW YORK, LONDON, PARIS

A CONTINUUM BOOK / THE SEABURY PRESS NEW YORK

ACKNOWLEDGMENTS

We are thankful, first, to the men who helped us on the trip through the Brooks Range that began this book: Averill Thayer of the U.S. Fish and Wildlife Service, Neil Allen and Harold Kaueolook of Kaktovik. Second, to the Alaskans whose advice and opinion helped shape our introductory arguments: James Hemming of the Alaska Department of Fish and Game, David Klein and Peter C. Lent of the Alaska Cooperative Wildlife Research Unit, Richard Gordon of Juneau, Pete Martin and Art Davidson of Anchorage, and to the Alaska Field Office of the National Park Service. Finally, to those in the lower forty-eight who helped on the last leg: Wilbur Mills, George Marshall, Robert Brower, James Turner, Noel Izett, Nelson Graburn, and the Friends of the Earth San Francisco staff.

We are grateful for permission to reprint excerpts from these:

The University of Alaska, Department of Anthropology and Geography, College, Alaska: *Kobuk River People,* by J. L. Giddings, 1961.

The University of California Press, Berkeley: *Alaska Wilderness,* by Robert Marshall, 1970.

Harper and Row, New York: *Arctic Wild,* by Lois Crisler, 1958.

The heirs of Knud Rasmussen: *The Netsilik Eskimos,* copyright 1931; *Intellectual Culture of the Copper Eskimos,* copyright 1932; *The Mackenzie Eskimos,* copyright 1942.

Alfred A. Knopf, Inc., New York: *Ancient Men of the Arctic,* by J. Louis Giddings.

Little, Brown and Company, Boston: *The People of the Deer,* by Farley Mowat, 1952.

The Macmillan Company, New York: *My Life with the Eskimo,* by Vilhjálmur Stefansson, copyright 1913 (copyright renewed 1941 by Vilhjálmur Stefansson).

McClelland and Stewart, Toronto: *Eskimo Sculpture/Sculpture Esquimaude,* by George Swinton, copyright 1965.

Julian Messner, Inc., New York: *I Sailed with Rasmussen,* by Peter Freuchen, 1958.

Random House, Inc., New York: *The Selected Poetry of Robinson Jeffers,* by Robinson Jeffers, copyright 1934, renewed by Donnan Jeffers and Garth Jeffers.

Routledge and Kegan Paul, Ltd., London: *The People of the Polar North,* by Knud Rasmussen, copyright 1908.

The University of Washington Press, Seattle: *Eskimo Childhood and Interpersonal Relationships,* by Margaret Lantis, 1960.

All Eskimo poetry and quotations in this book were recorded and translated by Knud Rasmussen, with the exception of the story on the caribou of the moon, recorded by Vilhjálmur Stefansson, and the Kobuk River narrative, recorded by J. Louis Giddings.

The juxtaposition of quotations from Herodotus and John Ross that begins chapter 4, "Explorers," is the work of Edmund Carpenter in *Anerca,* J. M. Dent and Sons, Ltd.

All the line drawings in this book are from a single engraved walrus tusk. Walrus-tusk art of this school, sold to whaling men during a twenty-year period at the turn of the century, was a short-lived industry among Eskimos from the Bering Strait to Point Barrow.

This Friends of the Earth/Seabury Press printing contains corrections of minor errors but no substantive changes in text, photographs, or other illustrations. For current information about what is happening in the earth's wild places, write Friends of the Earth, San Francisco.

JOHN MILTON: Overflow ice, Sheenjek Valley

CONTENTS

FIFTY-NINE COLOR PLATES

Foreword

HEADED toward the Pole on the direct route from Copenhagen to Anchorage, we watched the sun set for the first time that day at four in the afternoon and flew north into night. The captain announced our estimated time of arrival and I divided the distance by the hours and wrote on the airline map the times we would pass over principal points of interest. The map bore historical notes about the famous explorers and the successive dates on which their various expeditions got nearer and nearer the point from which everything else on earth was south. Before the light was gone on the last bleak land passing seven miles below us, a strong feeling of admiration for the explorers welled within me. For a quickly passing moment I wished I could have been there with them then.

I remembered my first polar-route flight, made memorable by what I was reading as I traveled across Greenland's icy mountains, over Baffin Island and its own great mountains, then across Hudson's Bay with a sweeping view north, whenever the cloud cover permitted, of the last great wilderness in North America. Loren Eiseley's *The Immense Journey* and the brilliance of his narrative of man's encounter with time alternated with the brilliance, out the starboard window, of the north country where man had looked hard at the limiting cold and had broken through that limit with his wits and his spirit.

But now I was reading what *The Economist* had to say about oil exploration in the Arctic and, once in that mood, began clipping what *The Times*, *The Observer*, and the *Financial Times* were saying about oil spills to add to my extensive collection on what tanker pilots didn't know about staying afloat. I was happy to have the stewardess change the subject by offering me a cocktail. Long before dinner it had got quite dark, and as we sped about nine miles per minute above the scene of arduous exploring long ago, I put on my headset and the movie began.

What the movie was I don't remember, because my headset was already off. I had glanced at my watch, saw that it was time to look below for the lights of Spitzbergen, and there they were. Far more diverting was the light in the sky, a display of the aurora borealis. My first view of an aurora was in 1939, when I saw it from the Sierra Nevada. In 1955 I saw one from Ellensburg, Washington; Kenneth Brower, then eleven, would not believe it was an aurora. For fifteen years I never saw it again. But here was a bold white light arched broadly over us, changing to a thin profile as we flew beneath its arch. There

were not many passengers, so I could switch from port to starboard windows at will and did often, fascinated by the phenomenon. No one else seemed aware of it except a Japanese opposite me who kept his head to the window, a pillow alongside to exclude extraneous light. We exchanged glances of appreciation. "Isn't the captain going to announce this display?" I asked the stewardess, still excited by what I had seen only twice before in fifty-eight years. "No," she said, "the passengers would be annoyed to have the movie interrupted."

Later she woke those who wished to know when we were directly over the North Pole and I looked out again. The aurora was gone. The clouds concealing the Arctic Ocean were lit only by starlight. As dawn broke in the south, the cloud cover thinned and strange patterns emerged, a lacework of new leads and old in the ice pack. Ice patterns changed to polygons; permafrost was under the snow and our crossing of the Arctic Ocean was over. An airstrip showed faintly, Prudhoe Bay, I thought, but we passed too high and fast for me to spot landmarks I had seen there on the ground two months before, when the tundra world was green and the oil companies were showing conservationists their Prudhoe camp. We had learned about drilling pads, berms, life below zero, the care and feeding of tundra, the search for exotic grasses to heal scars. An Eskimo antilitter crew was out on the nearby tundra with big plastic bags. We learned that the oil company's ecologist thought caribou liked the pads and berms and would not be disturbed in their migration by the above-ground portions of the 800-mile proposed pipeline. We could marvel at the technology that allowed man to find oil in this icy desert and bring it to the surface. It was rather frightening to stand on a platform partway up a rig and watch an expert team slap pipe into the ground in a bit-changing operation. The rig, tower, platform, cables, winch drums, and engine shuddered and shrieked in violent surges and smashing stops that seemed about to tear the place apart. I resolved not to use gasoline again if it took this much trouble to get it.

If the technology for getting at the oil and bringing it to the surface was impressive, the technology for getting it to market was not. Looking at the miles of four-foot Japanese pipe piled on site, I worried about the rush to get it there before enough was known about whether it would work or whether, if it worked, the Alaskan environment could keep on working within range of it. I worried about the determination to get the oil out and used up fast, about the stubborn refusal to understand the long-term consequences of short-time exploitation.

I was worrying all over again now as our North Pole flight sped us toward the Brooks Range. I conjured up disjointed paragraphs of a letter I would send, were I Chairman of the Board of Atlantic Richfield or of British Petroleum, chief developers of Arctic Slope oil, to my directors and stockholders. It would explain how the company, out of corporate responsibility, must pause for breath in its dash for oil until a whole series of facts were in that were not yet available to anyone. The pause would cost everybody money; but if it were a pause that would help people live longer, part of the cost ought to be recoverable. The company was leading in a more rational approach to keeping the planet a tolerable one than corporations had previously thought necessary. The company did not think that the environmental crisis was a figment. Would the stockholders therefore be helpful and patient with the corporation in its deliberate choice to forego profits that might risk the environment excessively. And would stockholders who sincerely felt that costs to the corporation were more important than costs to the earth please sell their stock to someone who felt differently. A professional worrier could conceive the letter. But could a chairman send it, or a stockholder like it?

Alpenglow was now lighting the summits of the Brooks Range. Whether it was dawn or twilight, it would not reach the North Slope for months yet. Ahead, the sun broke the world's rim to the south of us and climbed feebly into a flaming sky as we flew over the tapestry of meanders of the Yukon. Shortly past Mount McKinley we started letting down. Ten hours out of Copenhagen we landed in Anchorage at two in the afternoon, two hours before we had departed Denmark, and half an hour later the sun set in the south for the second time that day; night came again and stayed this time. The show was over.

Crossing several meridians at jet speed is always upsetting. Being benighted twice in one day was more than my sidereal clock could handle. Another kind of double twilight, however, was far more disturbing, the twilight for exploration and for wilderness. The speed and ease of my travel took the exploration out of it and off the planet. I could ask, as Aldo Leopold did, "Of what avail are forty freedoms without a blank spot on the map?" The early explorers had earned a chance to see the blank spots of the far north but my fellow passengers and I had not. We could select from eight stereo channels as we looked down at where the blank spots had been.

Concurrently twilight was descending on wilderness. Just three years before my flights, Kenneth Brower, John

Milton, and Steve Pearson were soaking up the Brooks Range wilderness experience that *Earth and the Great Weather* has much to say about. Three people had only themselves to depend upon, no source of resupply, unknown mountains, nameless valleys, rivers of stone, seas of grass, the ultimate wilderness. In three short years the oil stampede had put a civilized stamp on an area the size of Massachusetts in the remotest part of the North Slope. The civilizing had only begun to run its course. There is tension in the fabric of wilderness and when it is cut it withdraws fast and far. The 800-mile pipeline, cut across the ultimate wilderness, was to be the second civilizing step in a series of no one could predict how many more steps. Already Ken, John, and Steve were deprived of knowing again the wildness they had known. Their route had lost the beyondness that counted very much. Where would their sons look for a chance to know wildness. "To be precious, the heritage of wilderness must be open only to those who can earn it again for themselves," Garrett Hardin has said. "The rest, since they cannot gain the genuine treasure by their own efforts, must relinquish the shadow of it." He quotes Goethe's "We must earn again for ourselves what we have inherited."

Earn it where? In whatever vestige of wilderness is left after this generation of brief tenants has glutted itself on conveniences, including a plethora of energy, no matter what it costs all who are to follow? Do the oil seekers and users intend to leave anything unspoiled? The extractors, seemingly the most efficient international organization yet put together, plan to double their all-time drain in the next decade, and to do so come what may and from wherever it may—the Arctic, western Pacific, continental shelf off Southeast Asia, the Middle East, South America, Algeria, the Gulf, Santa Barbara. The possibility of slowing the mad race, and of sparing a resource six hundred million years in the making and 60 years in the using, and of using it for purposes oil alone can serve, seems not to have entered any system of government's mind.

The oil people, finders and users, are the primary targets here because they are best organized of all in the unintended war to eradicate wilderness from the earth. They have plenty of company. Surely they must be on the verge of sensing that a planet too well oiled will, like a cormorant, die. Or are they? "The connection between the ability of civilization to protect wildness and the ability of civilization to survive is not so tenuous as we might wish," I said twelve years ago. "The kind of thinking that motivates the grab for what's left at the bottom of the barrel—the pitiful fragment of resources in the remaining wilderness—is the kind of thinking that has lost this country friends it cannot afford to lose." I said this at the North American Wildlife Conference in New York City. Between then and now mankind has used up as much oil as in all the preceeding years, and the United States has gone far toward losing every friend it had. No one is proposing to send us another statue at the moment. And in March 1971 another North American Wildlife Conference, in Portland, was hearing an industry-dominated panel argue long, oblivious to alternative routes and schedules for development, that the oil should be hurried to market across the last great wilderness within U.S. borders and also across some of the most seismically active terrain within those borders or anyone else's. The oil-company representatives on the panel echoed the view of the Department of the Interior in its draft statement about the impact of North Slope oil development upon the environment: yes, there would probably be some damage, but demands for energy required forging ahead. National security would somehow be served. How depletion would serve national security was not explained; one who would strengthen the nation by using up its oil, a Friends of the Earth advertisement suggested, would probably burn his firewood before winter.

And when the final depletion comes, what kind of ghosts do we want in the Arctic or Northwest Passage ecosystems—still one of the greatest wildernesses on the planet? Voicing the concern of fellow Eskimos, "spirited pure lovers of that land who depend upon that land for a living," Willy Willoya puts a more cogent question: "When will the Caucasions let us rest and live peacefully? Where is the god they worship, when they destroy all our human rights and privileges? Where is the liberty and justice they proclaim to the entire world? Where are the wise, the strong and the brave amongst the Americans who would be good to their brothers and their lands? And to the creatures and the islands and the waters and the meadows and the tundra and the caves and the mountains that are our home?"

Wilderness, in the days of popular concern about total environment and degradation, has had too quiet a voice speaking in its behalf. Pollution has been easier to herald because its impact is in nostrils, eyes, and genes everywhere. If what wilderness we have left is to serve its highest purpose—being there for itself and its indigenous life forms, being there as the outside to a world that is otherwise a cage, being there for its wholeness, its beauty, its truth—then those who understand it must speak again as lucidly and as persuasively as did Aldo Leopold, Robert Marshall, and Howard Zahnizer. Nancy Newhall, put it beautifully thirteen years ago: "Wilderness holds answers to questions man has not yet learned how to ask." Physicists are peculiarly mindful of natural law and one of them, J. H. Rush, made the point just as tellingly: "When man obliterates wilderness, he repudiates the evolutionary force that put him on this planet. In a deeply terrifying sense, man is on his own." With no answers to the questions he would one day be wise enough to pose.

With no further effort at all, by merely letting our present momentum sweep us on with it, we can grind through the world's last wilderness by 1984 at the latest. Just the undisciplined dash for energy can by itself obliterate wilderness. So dash on then, find the energy, and spend it! But what to do for an encore? The recoverable fossil fuels will be gone. The feasible damsites will all have been built upon and will before too long be silted in. We will have run out of ways—once we find any—to dilute atomic waste from fission and will realize that fusion is better left in Pandora's box, remembering what came out last time we opened it. We will have endangered the oxygen sink of the atmosphere by probing the earth's fossil fires in geothermal experimentation. So we will use less energy, not more. We will return to ways of getting by with the energy the sun gives us each day instead of exploding and spilling our way through the energy capital the earth took four billion years to acquire.

Do we return to those ways while the world still has wilderness in it, or do we postpone the inevitable turning until we have severed outright and irrevocably those unbroken living connections to the beginning of life that the wilderness has so far preserved? Do we really want to repudiate the evolutionary force? These are questions a rational man should not have much trouble answering if he paused to think them through.

Charles Burnham warned against making little plans; they lack the power, he said, to inspire men's admiration or support. So why not a big plan? Blessed as we are with more data than were ever collected before, and confronted with an improving technology that might better serve us than direct us, we should prepare a plan not for a decade or a century, but a bolder plan to last a millenium, with option to renew.

A big, long-ranging plan of that order could lead to self-fulfilling predictions that are agreeable instead of the kind we have been getting lately. At a time when we see too many things wrong on the land and going wrong in the sea, why not contemplate a thousand good years instead of concocting sedatives for 1984?

Unconventional though the thought may be, the United States could make it clear that we should like to see international leadership rotate peacefully a few times in the course of this thousand years. Such a relaxed attitude might give mankind, and the other mutually dependent creatures in the environment man is part of, a better chance at the succeeding thousand-year period. Perhaps we should not plan for a period beyond that, even though bristlecone pines do.

It is not the example of the bristlecone, however, that suggests a plan of this magnitude. It is the nuclear dilemma, the strange, self-centered behavior that allows us to deposit high-level radioactive waste (a term from the AEC's Honeybucket Glossary) in the global ecosystem, waste that some one hundred billion future men must take meticulous care of in order that a multitude of us today may enjoy our own brief pass at the planet with all the conveniences we are accustomed. to. This waste is the dirtiest garbage of all. Forgetting its thermal pollution ("enrichment") for the moment, we know it is mutagenic, teratogenic, and damnably long-lived. We have already produced a great deal of it and this productivity is proliferating while we watch—or better, while we read ads calling it clean and look the other way. Our children must know where we left it and keep away. So must theirs, and *theirs*, by oral tradition if all others means fail. All this for at least a thousand years, with no fail-safe technique devised yet for the warehousing, no one putting up bond, no one prepared to write the insurance, no long-lasting Directions for Survivors chiseled in stone tablets, but with plenty of people willing to sell and install the machinery and merchandise the electrical power, and with all hands in the first, second, and third worlds eager to buy it without limit and without asking what it really costs.

The least we can do, if morality and ethics are still in our fiber, is to plan a thousand years of amenities for our progeny while they mind our nuclear garbage.

So a thousand good years, and an aim. Mere survival is not enough in the world we seek. Our institutions need to accommodate an optimistic vision of man's future, to believe that if the golden rule is all right in religions, it should not be avoided in life.

A thousand-year plan for oil, with particular respect to the immediate foreground in Alaska, would recognize the contribution of those who discovered the North Slope oil resource, appropriately cover the costs they cannot cover, reward them, pay the state for storage underground, then record the oil reserve as part of the inventory to be budgeted to last a thousand years. The Plan would contemplate that oil may one day serve a more important purpose than fueling automobiles and supersonic transports. Precipitate exploitation would be discouraged and

extravagant use would be prohibited. Studies of potential dangers of removing and transporting the oil in and across fragile ecosystems would be exhaustive and not an exercise in salvage ecology. The costs of perfecting spill-proof transportation would be met and development would await the meeting, the oil remaining safely stored underground until then, *in situ*. Whatever the costs were would be passed on to the user, who has always paid the costs anyway although he has not always known it. If this materially raises the price, that increase in itself would make economically feasible the development of more efficient oil-using devices. We would pollute far less because pollution would be too wasteful and too expensive. This would be a residual advantage and a welcome one, since the Plan would not only expect oil to be available for a millenium, but also would expect the air to remain breatheable for the duration.

Applied to people, the Plan would celebrate and hold hard to the diversity that makes them strong, beautiful, and interesting.

Applied to land use it would obliterate laissez-faire.

In forestry, it would eradicate monoculture.

In agriculture, it would stop decimating organic diversity three billion years in the making.

It would recognize that if population continues to grow at the present rate, mankind will outweigh the earth and there are better things to do with both.

Applied to pace, the Plan would encourage people to slow down and live, to take time to look for the real show, heeding Robinson Jeffers:

> But look how noble the world is.
> The lonely-flowing waters, the secret-keeping stones,
> The flowing sky.

No one ought to have too little courage to try, for what is the alternative? Begun soon, the Thousand-Year Plan should have rewards along the way. It should keep alive an orchestration of living things more beautiful than we now know, and perhaps even more beautiful than any of us remembers.

Any of us, that is, except those who have known what Kenneth Brower and his friends remember in what this book has to say. There is a bit of requiem in it already, and we can be grateful that it is a beautiful requiem. We are more grateful that the world still has most of this ultimate wilderness still living, and there lies within man the power to let it stay that way.

DAVID R. BROWER

Berkeley, California
March 25, 1971

INTRODUCTION

VERY LITTLE is known about the ecology of the Arctic. We do know that it is made up of unusually fragile ecosystems. The discovery of oil in the Arctic has made it imperative that we study and understand this fragility. Like all natural ecosystems, the Arctic Ocean, the tundra, and the adjoining arctic mountains are open, dynamic systems, each of them composed of many organisms that have evolved adaptations and interdependencies with one another, with climate and geology.

Of the factors that have affected the Arctic and the life in it, low temperature is of prime importance. The extreme cold that prevails most of the year has determined the life styles of the Arctic's plants and animals and made for the formation of relatively simple communities. One consequence of the long season of cold is perennially frozen ground, or permafrost. Permafrost underlies much of northern Alaska and most of the Arctic, and it has important limiting effects on plants. Subsurface ice wedges, polygonal fractured ground, frost scars, hummocks, and pingos (giant frost heaves) all limit the frequency and distribution of arctic vegetation. Just south of Point Barrow, Alaska, permafrost depths have been measured to 1330 feet. Further inland, where the moderating influence of the Arctic Ocean is reduced, permafrost depths of more than 2000 feet have been found. Much of this frozen material has been so for thousands of years. The permafrost prevents downward movement of water through the soil, and produces wet, boggy land surfaces and abundant ponds and lakes wherever the land is not well drained.

Of critical importance to plant life, and therefore to animals, is the seasonal summer thawing of the "active layer" of the tundra surface. Soil thawing on the Arctic Slope may vary from a few inches to a half a dozen feet deep. Owing to the insulating effect of peat and its overlying mat of vegetation, boggy soils thaw more slowly, to a lesser depth, and then refreeze more slowly, than do dry upland soils. Plant community types seem to be closely related to depth of thaw and the moisture content of the soil.

Another consequence of arctic cold has been the repeated glaciation of arctic regions. The land has only recently emerged from under ice. Successional processes continue today in the arctic tundra and must have a profound impact on vegetation, but we know very little about them.

In addition, the amount of precipitation is quite low, usually totalling between four and eight inches annually. Indeed, if subjected to the yearly temperature regimes of more southerly climes, the Arctic would be a desert. Nevertheless, because of the low evaporation rates of northern zones and underlying permafrost conditions, the arctic tundra and mountains are usually quite moist or wet during the short summer. For the remainder of the year, most moisture is held frozen and static.

But the Arctic is not always cold. At Point Barrow the average annual temperature is 10°F, with the lowest winter temperature in the minus 50°F range, but summer temperatures are often quite high, usually averaging 40°F in the interior plains. And summer temperatures close to the earth's surface, where the tundra vegetation grows and most small animals live, are often much higher than this. From June through August the very long daylight hours of low-angle sun cause a burst of plant productivity. Solar energy, captured through photosynthesis by plants, provides food for thousands of migratory and resident birds, various insects, several fish species and a variety of year-round resident mammals—lemming, vole, marmot, arctic ground squirrel, arctic hare, beaver, red squirrel, porcupine, musk ox, moose, Dall sheep, and caribou. In turn, these herbivorous animals are food for red and arctic fox, wolf, coyote, martin, wolverine, otter, mink, weasel, shrew, lynx, black bear, grizzly bear, polar bear, and predacious bird species like snowy owl, jaeger, and gyrfalcon. Some of these animals, the red squirrel for example, inhabit only the South Slope's forested valleys; others, like the polar bear, are restricted to tundra or Arctic Ocean. Most of these species are found in both environments, either as migrants or as permanent residents.

From southern valleys of the Brooks Range, the black spruce and white spruce forests (taiga) typical of interior Alaska extend long fingers of dark green up toward the high passes of the Range. The mountains are the major barrier separating the taiga forests from the treeless expanse of foothills and coastal plains to the north. This causes a sharp distinction between taiga and tundra, in contrast to the gradual transition between these biomes typical of Canada's flat, sweeping Northwest Territories.

The diversity of plant species living under the severe limiting conditions of the tundra is less than that of the taiga. South of the Arctic Divide in the Brooks Range, the spruce forest contains many other plants as well. Dwarf birch, willow, alder, sheep laurel, labrador tea and a small rhododendron are common shrubs associated with this open, rather scattered spruce woods. Some spruce trees, though small in size, are quite old. Along the upper Sheenjek River, Olaus Murie found one white spruce ten inches in diameter (eight inches up from the base) that was 298 years old. In other parts of these southern valleys, pure or mixed strands of willow, alder and poplar often follow stream courses; extensive areas of dwarf shrubs (dwarf birch and willow mixed with cushions of various mosses and lichens) and tussock grass also are common. Wetter areas usually are typical muskeg terrain made up of soggy mosses, sedge meadows, and scrubby heath. Alpine regions tend to be dry with much bare, exposed ground, and prostrate, cushiony mats of lichen, mosses, several ferns, and dwarfed species of *Cassiope, Vaccinium, Salix,* and various other small plants.

North of the Arctic Divide the forest disappears almost entirely, save for a few sheltered pockets of tall willow, poplar, or alder. The severity of the land increases. The tundra biome is dominated by small, compact, stunted vegetation structured to resist environmental extremes of cold, dessication, lack of light, and abrasion from wind-blown sand and snow. Although the number of plant species is low (only about one hundred vascular plants), they occur in highly complex communities adapted to a multitude of microenvironmental conditions. Day length, temperature, light, precipitation, slope, soil texture, drainage, permafrost conditions, animal browsing, exposure, and duration of snow cover are only some of the factors influencing the way the plant communities form. Herbaceous perennials and low shrubs are common. Cushions, tussocks, rosettes, and prostrate woody shrubs are the usual adaptations to the area's harsh constraints. Sedges, lichens, mosses, flowering grasses and herbs, and flattened shrubs are most abundant.

In all these plant communities productive growth occurs in the short time between snowmelt (normally in June) and the onset of fall (usually in late August). Most plants first use their stored root reserves as energy sources to quickly put forth leaves in spring; then during the maximum period of available solar energy they send down much of this newly-captured food energy to their roots and seeds for next year's growth needs.

Tundra vegetation supports large numbers of small herbivorous mammals, as well as birds, insects, and large mammals. The arctic ground squirrel; tundra, singing, and red-backed voles; hoary marmot; and collared and brown lemmings are all typical of the Alaskan tundra and are well adapted to its rigors. The growth of fur, fat, and feathers helps many animals to survive the extremes of cold, particularly larger animals. The small mammals adapt by hibernation or by feeding under the snow cover, which protects them from both cold and most predators.

Perhaps the best known small mammal of the tundra ecosystem is the brown lemming. As with other vegetarian creatures inhabiting these cold plains and barren slopes, its population regularly builds up to very high levels until its food supply is exhausted. The stress of crowding during this period may also contribute to increased disease and deteriorating behavior patterns. The lemmings' migration outward from the centers of super-abundance are a circumpolar phenomenon. Large numbers of predacious birds and mammals gather to follow and feast on lemmings as they move, until the rodent population crashes, at which point, the predators' own populations decline abruptly. Snowy owls, jaegers, weasels, shrews, and arctic fox numbers are particularly susceptible to regular decline following cyclic lemming population crashes.

The tendency in ecosystems toward lower numbers of species under severe limiting conditions is well-illustrated by the low animal and plant diversity of the tundra. Nevertheless, it is fascinating to observe that large numbers of birds migrate to northern Alaska and Canada during the brief flush of high summer productivity. A surge of vegetative growth is stimulated by the almost continuous incoming solar energy, and the birds make use of it. One hundred and seventy-one bird species have been identified north of the Arctic Divide in Alaska. Literally millions of waterfowl migrate through or nest in this vast area. In the 23,000 square mile Arctic Coastal Plain of Alaska an estimated 50,000 white-fronted geese come to nest. Approximately 150,000 old-squaw ducks also summer in this region. Pintail, black brant, greater scaup, surf scoters, red-breasted mergansers, and four species of eider are common migrants. Lapland longspurs, snow buntings, plover, sandpipers, loons, and ptarmigan are also relatively abundant as are various sparrows, other longspurs, gulls, and terns. Jaegers, snowy owls, short-eared owls, rough-legged hawks, golden eagles, peregrine falcons, and gyrfalcons hunt the coastal plain and among the mountains. Many depend upon the mountain isolation for nesting sites.

Of all these birds, perhaps the most completely adapted

to the year-round rigors of tundra life is the ptarmigan. In summer it forages on berries and shoots, camouflaged by its brown and white plumage. In winter it feeds largely on willow buds, protected then by feathers of solid white and able to walk easily on the snow because of the heavy growth of feathers on its feet.

The commonest large herbivorous land mammal of northern Alaska is the caribou. The caribou migrate great distances because food is insufficient in any small area to sustain the often large herds. Migration over large land areas assures food support for substantial numbers of caribou while helping to prevent overgrazing and habitat destruction of any particular region. Predators (like the wolf) that depend upon such migratory herbivores usually become great wanderers themselves.

Over the past quarter of a century, increasing scientific attention has gone into studying the behavior and ecology of arctic caribou. There appear to be two important north Alaskan populations of this animal. One, the Arctic Herd, is thought to contain 300,000 individuals. The Arctic Herd winters in the southern valleys of the Brooks Range west of Anaktuvuk Pass. In the forests there they are sheltered from some of the extreme conditions of the Arctic Slope and find rich mats of lichen to feed upon. Sometime during the spring, this herd moves north through various passes to the central Arctic Plain, where the calves are born. The caribou remains, usually scattered in small bands, north of the Brooks Range through the summer.

The second important population, the Porcupine Herd, numbers about 140,000 and winters in the forested valleys draining south from the Brooks Range into the Porcupine River. Part of the herd winters along the Firth River and other valleys of the northwestern Yukon Territory just east of the Arctic National Wildlife Range. Like the Arctic Herd, the Porcupine Herd also summers and calves on the North Slope, but usually farther eastward, in the foothills and coastal plains east of the Colville River. This is precisely the area now facing development for road, oil-rig, and pipeline construction.

There seems to be some mixing between both herd populations during the summer, and some scattered caribou are known to winter along the coast of the Arctic Ocean. Nevertheless, the calving and wintering grounds for the two groups seem to have been well separated during the years they have been studied. A great deal more work is needed to determine whether both herds are discrete populations or whether considerable mixing takes place in some years (particularly during the calving period).

For caribou, summer is a period of intense harassment by mosquitoes and other insects. Insect attacks are particularly difficult for the bulls during the summer-growth stage of their sensitive, blood-filled antlers. In order to escape this aggravation, many seek windswept hills and ridges where the wind sweeps the air of flies and mosquitoes; other caribou seek the coast, attracted by the cooler summer temperatures, wind, and new plant growth for feeding. Whole groups of animals sometimes escape insects by immersing themselves in lakes, rivers and even in salty coastal waters.

In the fall, the scattered clusters of caribou band together into large concentrations and begin their migrations south. During this time the antlers of the bulls harden; soon they enter their rut and engage in mating and combat until late fall, burning up their large reserves of back fat.

Aside from the wolf and numerous parasites, the caribou has few natural enemies. An occasional sick or young individual is pulled down by grizzly, wolverine, or lynx, but man is the single most important predator. As many as 20,000 caribou are taken from arctic herds each year by native Alaskans, and a very few killed by sportsmen. The herds appear able to sustain this level of harvest, but any substantially increased hunting pressure could pose problems. Current oil-related developments, in particular new road and airplane access and increased use of snow machines for hunting, could be trouble for caribou populations. Any human disturbance of the calving grounds or degradation of the delicate coastal tundra will have a severely disruptive impact on the herds. Blockage of migration routes by pipelines could also create problems. Careless helicopter operations are already causing difficulties on the North Slope. Caribou run from helicopters, whether the harassment is accidental or deliberate. Robert Belous writes that, "A healthy caribou running in panic for two or three miles becomes, in the words of a noted zoologist, 'a death candidate.' A winter-starved pregnant female who has just completed a 200-mile migration lasts only about half a mile before aborting or dying."

Less common in the Brooks Range than the caribou is the moose. This largest member of the deer family has always been numerous in the southern valleys of the Range, but until about thirty years ago had never been reported on the North Slope. At that time the Eskimos of the region did not have a word for moose. Since then, the improbable-looking animal has spread north along the Colville River all the way to the arctic coast, and east and west into the foothills and adjacent coastal plain. No one knows why this has happened. Because the moose's primary food is willow, flood plains and river bottoms are its preferred habitat. After man, the wolf is its main predator. Relatively little disturbance of the moose is anticipated from oil activities, although use of river-edge gravel for road and pipeline construction would deplete part of its willow habitat.

My first view of Dall sheep was in the upper Sheenjek River of the Brooks Range. Climbing up into a high, heavily glaciated basin, I was startled when several rocks clattered down a high cliff and steep talus slope nearby. Looking up, I saw seven sheep gracefully ascending the precipice high above me, their white bodies flowing up the cliff with the smooth, liquid coordination of dancers. For the remainder of my time in the mountains they were almost constant, though distant and reserved, companions.

Wolves and grizzlies kill an occasional Dall sheep, but starvation, accidental death by avalanche or in falls from cliffs, and human hunting are probably far more important causes of death. Dall sheep are almost entirely creatures of high ridges and slopes where they feed on lichens, mosses, grasses, and other herbaceous growth. In winter enough plant food for their survival is exposed by winds, and in summer life is easy. Sometimes sheep will move down into valley bottoms for winter feeding, but generally they are found the year round on grassy, gentle slopes that have steep cliffs nearby as refuge from predators. Beautifully adapted to an alpine life, they are able to utilize energy, stored in alpine plants, that is inaccessible to other large herbivores. The Dall sheep occupies a spectacular niche in Brooks Range ecology.

The only other large herbivore found on the open tundra plains is the musk ox. Small herds were still encountered on the Arctic Slope through the early 1800's, but soon thereafter they disappeared (probably owing to increased Eskimo hunting pressure). During the winter of 1968-9, fifty males from Nunivak Island were released on the North Slope; more such transplants are planned to help re-establish a population in this region. Major natural populations are now restricted to northern Canada and Greenland, with successful transplant populations established in Norway (as well as on Nunivak Island). At one time this shaggy animal was circumpolar in its distribution, and during the period of massive Pleistocene glaciation it ranged as far south as France. Perhaps it can now re-occupy a substantial bit of its old terrain.

The musk ox is the only arctic animal with a happy experience of modern man. Many arctic species are now threatened directly by hunting, trapping, and poisoning programs, and indirectly by destruction of habitat and pollution. The carnivores are particularly sensitive to such pressures.

Organic matter stored by green plants supplies the primary food energy available to all animal life. Organic nutrients may be recycled in ecosystems and passed through food chains with relatively little loss, but the flow of energy always involves loss to living systems. As energy is transferred from one organism to another, a considerable portion is lost to the ecosystem as dissipated heat. At each level of transfer, there is less potential energy for any animal to utilize. The nearer in a food chain an animal population is to direct utilization of plant energy, therefore, the more food energy is available to it. As a consequence, animals in the tundra whose diet is composed of plants (herbivores), generally have a large population mass (biomass). Carnivores that feed on these herbivores capture less energy and therefore have less biomass. Finally, those carnivores that feed on other carnivores have the smallest biomass and capture the least energy.

Because carnivores are at the very top of tundra food chains, they are sensitive to disturbances at all levels of the ecosystem. They are most vulnerable to overall environmental degradation, and in the simplified tundra ecosystem their problem is intensified. Because carnivores often also compete with man, the greatest predator of all, their survival is endangered in an even more direct way. In northern Alaska, the wolf, polar bear, grizzly bear, wolverine, gyrfalcon, and peregrine falcon are seriously threatened.

The wolf in particular exemplifies the irrational hatred man can have for a successfully competing carnivore. For many thousands of years, caribou, sheep, moose, musk oxen, and other herbivores, and arctic wolves, have co-existed without the wolf wiping his prey species out. Wolves in fact are important to the continued survival of many herbivores, through their testing of the strength and endurance of these animals. Wolves remove unhealthy animals that might otherwise spread sickness, selecting in favor of the more genetically vigorous and culling out the old. Wolf predation helps caribou maintain their population within the carrying capacity of the environment, preventing overpopulation, range damage, and starvation.

For this service we have poisoned wolves with a wide variety of toxic baits; placed bounties on their heads; trapped, then clubbed or shot them; run them to exhaustion with airplanes, then shotgunned them. We have virtually eliminated wolves from the contiguous United States, and until this year were well on the way to wiping them out in Alaska, their final American refuge: The State of Alaska should be commended for finally removing its wolf bounty, and for attempting to halt all killing of the animal throughout the Brooks Range provinces.

The grizzly bear is found in sparse, dispersed populations throughout the Arctic. Although nominally given some seasonal protection as a trophy animal, the rapid invasion of the Brooks Range and Coastal Plain by pipelines and associated roads and camps poses a serious threat to grizzlies. The bears of the region live in a highly exposed environment that provides little cover from hunters. With easier, more extensive, and cheaper access, hunting, if uncontrolled, will rapidly increase. More bears will be killed as "threats" as they are attracted to the camp dumps that may soon spread across arctic Alaska. Industry managers usually have little control over their contractors and sub-contractors, who are often now killing bears and wolverines under the guise of camp protection. The growing use of snow machines by Eskimo hunters is also ominous for both grizzly and wolverine populations. Protection for both is needed quickly.

Two handsome birds of prey, the gyrfalcon and peregrine falcon, nest in the crags of the highest Brooks Range and tend to use the same sites repeatedly for years. If roads, planes, helicopters, tundra buggies, and snow vehicles begin to penetrate these mountains more frequently, disturbance of nesting will follow. This disturbance, in combination with lowered nesting success caused by pesticide intake, may already have badly hurt falcon populations. In eastern North America, the peregrine falcon has just become extinct because of pesticides. A more direct problem is the illegal but flourishing trade in birds for falconry. Eyries are raided and the young falcons sold for as much as $1,000 each in lands as distant as Iran. The cumulative impact of all such pressures on arctic birds of prey could well be catastrophic.

The polar bear is found on the ice pack off the Alaskan coast and occasionally comes ashore, particularly when the ice drifts in to land. The animals tend to move north with the retreating ice in summer, then south again as winter winds begin to hasten the formation of new ice. Seals are their main food. The bears are superb stalkers and usually hunt seals where they collect along open leads in the ice, or wait for them to rise at breathing holes. The polar bear is a circumpolar creature. Whether the species is composed of discrete populations or whether the bears drift from region to region on a truly circumpolar scale remains to be known. One major denning area for the Canadian–Alaskan Arctic has been located on Banks Island and adjacent Canadian islands. Such denning areas are in particular need of complete protection and sanctuary.

The International Union for the Conservation of Nature (IUCN) has already listed the polar bear in its Red Data Book of the world's rare and endangered species. In 1968 the IUCN sponsored a highly successful international meeting of experts from the USSR, Canada, Norway, Denmark and the USA, to work together on designing a truly international research and conservation program for the species. Such a program is urgently needed. Serious shifts in the nature and intensity of polar bear hunting have occurred in the last decades. Before then, almost all hunting was done in traditional style by Eskimo hunters who stalked the animal by dog team and on foot out over the ice pack. Since then, aboriginal hunting has been almost completely replaced by the trophy hunting of white hunters who hire light aircraft equipped with skis to seek out and run down the bears on the pack ice. Cornered and exhausted, the animals are then shot—often without the sportsmen even leaving the plane. Last year more than 300 polar bears were shot from Alaska, with most of the hunting (some of it illegal) done out of bases in Barrow, Kotzebue, Point Hope, and Teller. Each hunt costs several thousand dollars, a price only the wealthiest white "sportsmen" can afford.

Because of the international concern that the species is near extinction, some restrictions on sport hunting have been initiated in Alaska. A total sport hunting ban is in effect in the USSR and Canada. Alaska could do as well. Currently, intensive research into reproduction, population size, patterns of migration and denning, and food habits is underway on an international scale. The polar bear symbolizes the interconnected, circumpolar nature of arctic environments. Like the fish, whales, and seals of arctic waters, the polar bears of the arctic ice travel freely between nations. No country can claim them as its own. Our success in relations with polar bears will have important implications for the future integrity of the polar regions and their interrelated ecosystems. In Antarctica, nations have cooperatively moved to recognize the ecological wholeness and management needs of an entire polar continent. We should do as well for the other pole.

But no motivation has the power to rend nature like greed, and no fluid has the power to stir man's greed like oil. Perhaps we have waited too long to successfully initiate unselfish international action in the Arctic. If action is to come, it must come quickly.

*   *   *

My main conclusion from seven months of thinking about Prudhoe Bay is that neither science nor government was—or is —prepared for discovery of oil in the Arctic. Science cannot predict the quantitative effects of the industry's disturbance of arctic soils and vegetation on biological communities, nor can science estimate the economic and social costs of these disturbances.

—ROBERT WEEDEN

It is hard to imagine a worse place for the discovery of oil than arctic Alaska. For an oil company genuinely concerned with protection of the environment, the dilemma faced there must seem designed by the devil. There is no way to extract oil, no technique to turn to, that does not involve great unknowns and possible catastrophe for the arctic ecosystem. The probable impacts of arctic oil development on Alaska and the adjacent seas are only just beginning to come into focus. The first troubles, strangely, have been social. When the Alaskan Statehood Act was passed in 1958, 103 million acres were made available for withdrawal from federal domain. The first two million acres chosen included much of the potentially oil-rich Arctic Coastal Plain. This land included traditional native fishing and hunting grounds and even some villages. The withdrawal was accomplished before the Eskimos knew what was happening to them, through the convenient device of publishing a legal notice in a newspaper little known to Native peoples. Since no claimants showed up, the State took the land. When Alaska's aboriginal peoples (one fifth of the state population) learned what had happened to the lands they had always considered theirs, they banded together to protest to Congress. Their case is still being "worked out."

In the meantime, vast acreage around Prudhoe Bay has been leased to several oil companies; Atlantic Richfield (Arco), Humble, and British Petroleum have the major stakes. The reserves at Prudhoe are now very conservatively estimated at fifteen billion barrels. Other estimates of the region's oil potential run as high as 100 billion barrels. For perspective, until now the world's largest known oil field has been in Kuwait, with estimated reserves of 60 billion barrels. Alaska's oil—whatever the exact amount—represents enormous potential revenues for the state government.

Prior to the initial strike on March 13, 1968, by Arco, there was no road or railroad across the Brooks Range, and heavy ship transport by sea to the area had always been blocked by arctic ice. Now, a little less than two years later, more than 30 wells have been drilled (an average well can produce 10,000 barrels a day), and 110 are planned for completion by 1973. A rough winter road, the "Walter Hickel Highway" has been slashed 400 miles from Fairbanks through Anaktuvuk Pass to the North Slope. Another road and an 800-mile-long, 48-inch pipeline are planned (the pipe has already arrived in Alaska). This pipeline and road would cut across another part of the Brooks Range, connecting the oilfields with a port being built at Valdez. Feasibility studies on a natural gas pipeline are also underway. This third development corridor would slice southeast across the tundra, through the mountains just south of the Arctic Wildlife Range, then pass across Canada. Finally, farther west, the state is pushing for a railroad from Fairbanks up into the beautiful southwestern Brooks Range region. This area (near Bornite) has rich copper deposits that industry is eager to exploit.

Aside from the future environmental problems awaiting this vast investment of oil industry capital and planning, there are grave technological problems presented by permafrost. In July of 1970 I flew over the Arctic Plain. Below me was a vast, calm sea of tundra that eventually washed up against the snowy peaks of the Brooks Range. No unnatural mark flawed the expanse of wild terrain; only the intricate patterns of tundra ponds, polygons, willow-edged streams, and occasional river bluffs.

The plane neared an old oil survey camp, and looking down I saw a broad, water-filled scar running across the smooth tundra below. This was the result of some long-forgotten ride on one of those small, tank-like weasels used as cross-country transport throughout northern Alaska. Its passage had crushed the vegetation, allowing the permafrost to thaw, and starting erosion. A pipeline, with its accompanying construction roads and maintenance airports, threatens far more damaging disturbances of permafrost equilibrium and almost certainly would trigger serious erosion. Until Friends of the Earth, the Wilderness Society, and the Environmental Defense Fund won a U.S. District Court injunction halting pipeline haul-road construction for the inadequate attention its planners paid to environmental impacts, the oil companies were willing to move hastily ahead. The injunction barred the federal government from giving the Trans-Alaskan Pipeline System (TAPS) a right-of-way permit for the haul road. The injunction was an important warning to the oil industry against its traditional neglect of environment; it was also a precedent for requiring pre-development analysis for the prevention of ecological degradation on federal lands throughout the Nation.

Adequate environmental engineering for development in permafrost terrain will require much more planning time and a considerably higher cost than similar developments in warmer environments. That the pipe will be filled with hot oil at a temperature of 176°F complicates the engineering problem. If the pipe is buried six feet deep, such temperatures would thaw "a cylindrical region twenty to thirty feet in diameter in typical permafrost materials," reports Arthur Lachenbruch in a study for the U.S. Geological Survey. He also indicates that insulation would only increase oil temperatures and not reduce soil thawing. Under some conditions, Lachenbruch writes, the whole thawed area could flow like molasses, causing the uphill part of the pipe to lie in a deep trench while at the downhill end millions of cubic feet of mud would spew over the tundra. Virtually nothing is known about how to harmonize oil development with the many terrestrial processes unique to tundra ecosystems.

Another difficulty is the vertical wedges of ice that regularly spear through many Alaskan soils. The pipeline could easily thaw these ice wedges and lose its support in hundreds of places along the projected route. Lachenbruch writes that, "in typical ice wedge terrain, conditions which might exceed the stress of the pipeline could occur on the average of once every mile. . . ." Along much of its route the pipeline will follow streams and rivers. Several dozen rivers and more than one hundred streams will be crossed. Should either elevated or buried pipelines break, large quantities of oil could quickly pour into such streams and rivers and out across the tundra. If close to the coast, the oil could reach the biologically productive coastal margins. The shock of a sudden oil pollution on the fish, birds and mammals utilizing these areas could be catastrophic.

In the southern half of Alaska, for several hundred miles before the pipeline reaches Valdez, earthquakes are relatively common. Three major earthquake zones must be crossed by the line. What happens if there is another quake of the magnitude that devastated Anchorage in 1964? A similar threat is the possibility of landslides and landslip in mountainous areas after the equilibrium of hill slopes is disrupted by construction activities. A large slide could burst the hot line. A single fracture from any cause could release up to 20,000 barrels of oil before the spill is halted. According to the time and the place of the rupture, the ecological consequences could be devastating.

The probable impact of any refining done at Prudhoe, Fairbanks, or Anchorage has been ignored. Winter "ice fog" inversions are common in Alaska and could be expected to hold in air pollution, which then could build up to serious levels. Any sulfur dioxide released could have a disastrous impact on the base of the tundra food chain: lichens. These small plants are extremely susceptible to even low levels of sulfur-dioxide pollution. If they were destroyed, most of the tundra food chain would be seriously affected, from lemming to caribou to wolf.

Doubtless the oil companies, in their own self interest, will take every possible engineering precaution to prevent oil from spilling. Nevertheless, their past poor record in safer environments, when considered with the extreme hazards of off-shore drilling, marine transport, and pipe-line transport under arctic conditions, all indicate that if the oil development proceeds it is certain to do environmental damage.

Much gravel from rivers is already being used for oil-well pads and road construction at Prudhoe. A great deal more would be needed for the pipelines and associated maintenance roads. The effect on fish populations of taking this gravel, which they use for spawning, is unknown. Coastal beaches, dunes, and islands are also threatened by gravel mining. These sites are very important nesting areas for numerous birds and mammals, and should be carefully protected from development. Some engineers have discussed elevating the pipeline to minimize permafrost thaw. If the pipeline is an elevated affair, what will this do to migratory patterns of caribou and wolf? The projected lines run right through important caribou calving grounds. And what are the implications of increased access and hunting via the roads for already threatened species—the wolverine, wolf, peregrine falcon, and gyrfalcon?

One of the most serious threats to the Brooks Range wilderness would be from the vastly increased mineral exploration and mining activities possible from the pipeline access roads. A huge new virgin territory would be made vulnerable. Large numbers of vacation cottage developments, particularly around lakes, would also become much more feasible for subdivision. What impact would this have on the pristine feel of the country? Thousands of men with mobile weasels and snow machines pouring out into the fragile tundra from the new access roads could initiate wide-scale erosion as well as increased disturbance and hunting of animals.

Litter, a problem in the Arctic as it is nowhere else, might become commonplace. Robert Weeden writes of the North Slope's Naval Petroleum Reserve Number 4: "I once heard it said that of the thousands of oil drums left in Pet 4 twenty years ago, half still hold water; the other half have been shot at. Apocryphal or not, that comment illustrates the dismaying longevity of discarded objects in the arctic environment. Orange peelings last months, paper lasts years, wood scraps last decades, and metal and plastic is almost immortal in the cold, dry northern climate. Furthermore, there probably isn't any other landscape in the world, except for warm deserts, so poorly designed for hiding debris." The very spaciousness that gives the tundra its beauty draws the eye quickly to any visual pollution.

Such problems cannot be avoided simply by shipping the oil out by sea in huge surface or submarine tankers. In 1969 Humble Oil sent a giant tanker, the *Manhattan*, up the eastern coast of North America and through the North-west Passage. The purpose was to demonstrate the practicality of bringing out oil this way. The *Manhattan* suffered a severe gash in its bow that would have caused a serious spill—had the tanker been full of oil. The ship-crushing characteristics of the arctic ice are well known. It would take only one crushed or gashed 250,000 ton supertanker to create a super-spill and super environmental catastrophe. Should such a tanker spill occur, or should the oil lines that will run out under the shallow arctic seas break, or should offshore drilling be begun and the inevitable blowout follow, the resulting ocean pollution could make the problems of Santa Barbara or the *Torrey Canyon* look mild. Our almost total ignorance of the ecology, oceanography, and ice characteristics of the Arctic Ocean make such a prospect deeply frightening.

Between Alaska's Point Barrow and Canada's Banks Island, the Arctic Ocean is known as the Beaufort Sea. This Sea is shallow for many miles out from the shoreline but quickly deepens beyond the continental shelf. Tidal changes here are minor—less than a foot—and a year-round current usually moves from east to west along the coast. During winter, the sea is locked firm in ice; while the short summer lasts, an ice-free zone from a few miles to three dozen miles wide opens along shore. Even then, chill winds from the north can blow the ice pack back against the coast. It is in this narrow lead of open water that any marine oil spill would be concentrated, prevented by the ice from dispersing.

In comparison to more southerly waters, the Beaufort Sea is relatively low in biological productivity. Its marine ecosystems, like those of the adjoining land, have fewer species. Nevertheless, about fifty kinds of fish and numerous plankton swim here. During the summer season of continuous light, phytoplankton multiply prodigiously, contributing energy to numerous small fish and several species of whale. In turn, the fish are eaten by bearded, ringed, and ribbon seals, by birds, and by larger fish and toothed whales. At the top of this food chain is the polar bear, which feeds largely on seal, and the killer whale. Very little is known about this ecosystem, but it is probable that any major oil blowout, spill or leak, would have an effect vastly more disruptive than in any of the world's more temperate ecosystems. Low water temperatures, minimal wave action, and relatively few microorganisms available to break down the oil would probably combine to make any pollution unusually persistent. The simplicity of these cold-water ecosystems make them especially vulnerable to such contamination. Marine plankton, if adversely affected, could topple the entire food chain.

The millions of migrating waterfowl that feed in or rest on these seas could be the most afflicted of all, should an oil catastrophe occur during spring, summer, or fall. The estimated one million adult eider ducks, 300,000 old-squaw, and many other species such as brant, move through or summer in this region. A single oil slick, if on the wrong patch of water at the wrong time, could have calamitous effects on these birds. The fact that any spill or blowout would most probably occur in the narrow coastal lead, and tend to be confined there, only increases the danger, for this is the very zone most heavily used by the seabirds. Similarly, oil slicks could easily foul the fragile beaches of the coast. These narrow strips along the shore are vital to many nesting birds, to foxes, and other animals. Oil pollution of the many freshwater lakes used by bird populations also could pose environmental hazards.

If the *Manhattan* had a pilot in her bow who shouted out obstacles, his cries would be a catalogue of dangers. If the Trans-Alaska Pipeline had a conductor who announced whistle stops, he would sound like a prophet of doom: Earthquake, ice wedge, landslip, erosion. He would see everything but attacks by Indians, and if the Native land claims are not settled, perhaps that too. The proposed pipeline is a chain of risks connecting an almost certainly polluted Beaufort Sea, to an inevitably polluted bay at Valdez—one of the most beautiful bays in Alaska, where you now can catch salmon from the pier, but where tankers may soon pump out their ballasts. Still, the items in this catalogue of dangers, the links in this chain of risks, are only parts of a larger trouble.

For me, and for substantial numbers of people who feel the same way, the most important issue at stake in arctic oil development is an intangible—the integrity of North America's largest, and one of its most beautiful, wildernesses. Pipelines, roads, oil rigs, mining camps, weasel tractors, litter, ports, tankers, airports—all will degrade the wholeness of the last whole North American place. For us, the central issue is the destruction of beauty, of wide, unbroken spaces, of that quality—more fragile even than the tundra—that is wildness.

Man's technology has given him the power to embark on an unprecedented biospheric experiment: the simplification, control, and conversion of the biosphere into more human protoplasm. The history of mankind can be read as the progressive acquisition of more and more of the Earth's energy and raw materials. At the current frenetic pace of technological growth, this accelerating absorption of biospheric resources may be beyond anyone's capability to alter it. If this is true, then our species is in fatal trouble.

As arctic oil development proceeds, no one in any position of power is asking: "Is it really necessary?" No one is suggesting that we leave arctic oil as a reserve, to wait the day we really need it. Nor are environmental implications beyond the Arctic Coast and Brooks Range being given much attention. At a time when fossil-fueled urban air pollution is one of the most serious threats to our well-being, what contribution to the degradation of our national health will arctic oil provide? At a time when marine oil-tanker spills and leaks are causing massive degradation of the world's coasts, estuaries, and oceans, how much more such pollution can we expect from accidents with arctic oil? At a time when fossil, atomic, and hydroelectric power sources all loom as serious environmental specters, what would the billions planned to be spent on arctic oil achieve if invested in developing clean, efficient, environmentally non-consumptive energy alternatives, and the establishment of an ecologically sound national energy policy? The fuel cell and solar power are two such ecologically viable alternatives already feasible for many applications where fossil fuels are still used. At a time when urban blight, pollution, racial strife, poverty, and global starvation are screaming facts of human life, what might the planned investment in arctic oil mean if allocated directly to solving these problems. No one knows. Nor is anyone planning on finding out.

No one in power is considering alternatives. Many Alaskan Natives would prefer a development on their own, rather than on Western, precepts. In the current oil boom aboriginal values—the virtues of hunting, fishing, cultural freedom, and self-determination—seem to carry no weight. White culture is only asking the native peoples for their price—not for alternative directions affecting themselves and their land. There is still no adequate means for allowing native peoples to evolve their own priorities. Those Natives who value wilderness and its resources have little chance to create their own future, a future likely to be in better harmony with the processes of the earth.

The biosphere, and the many delicately-balanced yet dynamic ecosystems that make it up, is an open system: its energy comes from the sun. We, and the other animals that join us on this planet's journey through space and time, live by the grace of green plants and the photosynthesis that gives us food and breathable air. Should the biosphere begin to break down as a result of our leeching it, we will crash much as lemming populations crash in the Arctic. But lemmings do it regularly, every four years or so—we have no practice ourselves at cyclic recovery. As they have before, the cockroach, the ant, and the tortoise, meek creatures less specialized, with ambitions less grand than our own, will inherit the Earth. But we still have the choice: to opt for beauty over ugliness, diversity over impoverishment, harmony over domination, life over death. As a former traveler in the Brooks Range, I hope we will.

Washington, D.C.
July 1970   —JOHN P. MILTON

A PROPOSAL

ARCTIC ALASKA remains a vast and unknown land. In our present ignorance about what is there, any system of parks and reserves we might design is certain to overlook something—an unsurpassed national park, perhaps, a waterfowl refuge, a wild river. We do know enough to be sure that no system of reserves—short of that proposed by Robert Marshall: a single great wilderness area embracing all northern Alaska—will be adequate protection. The irregular and unboundaried wanderings of the great caribou herds, for one thing, are too wide for any reserve with fixed boundaries. We will need to let the caribou vote on them. A comprehensive protection plan, enlisting the cooperative effort of all the land-management agencies now operating in Alaska (agencies now often working at cross purposes) will be necessary outside reserve limits if our last great wilderness is not to be lost a bite at a time.

The finest remaining wilderness under the U.S. flag, so far designated as such, is the Arctic National Wildlife Range. It is now the only wilderness preserve of any kind

SOME PROPOSED RESERVATIONS AND DEVELOPMENT IN THE BROOKS RANGE OF NORTHERN ALASKA

North of the Arctic Circle, an area larger than the state of California, where "we will need to let the caribou vote."

-- - Proposed reserve boundaries
⌒ Proposed wild rivers
⇔ Proposed pipeline route

═══ "Hickel Highway"
········ Route of 1967 crossing
Scale: The map is 800 miles wide.

Map prepared by James M. Cutter; data from Richard J. Gordon and others, 1970.

in the Arctic. The entire area should be managed solely for wilderness. Selected lakes and gravel bars should be chosen as air access points—this is Alaska and it isn't easy to walk in. Beyond that, minimal facilities for aerial and ground patrols are allowable, but that is all. At present, surface oil and mineral exploration is permitted, so long as no surface vehicles are used. This activity has greatly increased in recent years, until it now begins to threaten the integrity of the area. Wilbur Mills, perhaps the leading advocate of this preserve since the death of Olaus Murie, reports that buildings are thrown together haphazardly and debris discarded widely. The magnitude of permanent damage is so far minor. The preserve has been closed to oil leasing and pipeline construction. As Secretary of the Interior, Walter J. Hickel promised to keep it that way.

The Arctic Wildlife Range will come up for Wilderness Act hearings in 1971 or '72. Conservationists should

be ready to fight for wilderness classification. The Bureau of Sport Fisheries and Wildlife, which manages the Range, will need support.

The preserve does not encompass the entire range of the Porcupine Herd of 140,000 caribou. Cooperative agreements between land and wildlife agencies will be needed to give the herd protection wherever it roams outside the Range, particularly on the calving grounds. Part of the range of the Porcupine Herd lies in the Yukon Territory of Canada. The Yukon Conservation Society, headed by John Lammers, proposes a Canadian counterpart to the Arctic Wildlife Range. Included would be the caribou range east to Blow River, as well as the Old Crow Flats, a major waterfowl breeding ground just inside the tree line. Tom Barry, the Canadian Wildlife Service biologist who has helped establish a number of outstanding though as yet little-publicized waterfowl sanctuaries in the Canadian Arctic, has highest hopes of gaining protection for the

Old Crow Flats segment, on which the Canadian Wildlife Service has already gained a degree of regulatory power over oil exploration. (In March of 1970 the Canadian government shut down a drilling operation on the Old Crow Flats because of the industry's indiscriminate practices.) Park planners within Canada's Department of Indian Affairs and Northern Development have recommended that the northern panhandle of Yukon Territories, adjacent to the Arctic Wildlife Range, be set aside as Canada's first tundra park. So the chances of our having what in effect would be an international tundra park are looking up.

A complex of state and federal wildlife refuges should be established in northern Alaska to complement the Arctic Wildlife Range. Most important is the calving grounds of the Arctic Herd of caribou, the largest herd of animals on the continent, with 300,000 members. The major concentration at calving time (late spring) is in an extensive region of tundra foothills in the western Arctic, in the vicinity of Lookout Ridge and the Utukok River. University of Alaska biologist Peter Lent has studied the region intensively and recommends that a 2700-square-mile tract be set aside. The Alaska Fish and Game Department would like to see this area selected by the State's Natural Resources Department from federal land, then given over to them for management.

Along the nearby coast, conservationists propose a national wildlife refuge in the area of Cape Thompson and the Kukpuk River. Northern Alaska's largest seabird colony breeds each summer on the cliffs. I myself have seen and been impressed by the sizeable concentrations of eiders and other arctic water birds in the sheltered Kukpuk estuary. Musk oxen have recently been reintroduced here, as in the Arctic Wildlife Range. Project Chariot, the abortive plan to blast an atomic harbor in the Cape Thompson area, brought forth the most intensive biological research project ever carried out in the American Arctic. Continuity of research now becomes possible there, and the Cape Thompson–Kukpuk region should be protected as a permanent scientific study area, as well as an attractive meeting of hills and sea. The Cape Thompson coast fits Corey Ford's translation of the name Alaska: "where the sea breaks its back against the mountains."

A major oil find is quite likely in the region of the proposed Utukok and Cape Thompson–Kukpuk reserves, perhaps near the Kukpowruk River. While time for orderly planning still remains, the State should work out a cooperative plan with the Bureau of Land Management and the Bureau of Sport Fisheries and Wildlife to protect from unnecessary disturbance and habitat destruction the entire spring and summer range of this greatest new-world herd of land mammals. The largest concentrations of caribou in America range between the Utukok calving grounds and the upper Kukpuk and Kukpowruk. An area-wide land plan involving all agencies holding responsibility is critical if this caribou herd is to be maintained at full strength. The two refuges alone would not do the job.

An ecological type protected nowhere in Alaska is the wet arctic terrain of marshes and lakes. A fine example, ideal for a wildlife refuge, is the coastal tundra just east of Point Barrow, in the Teshekpuk Lake–Cape Halkett region. Waterfowl biologist Jim King reports great nesting populations of Canada geese, black brant, and whistling swans, as well as an extensive moulting area for snow geese. Certain species of plants occur nowhere else.

The broad Yukon Flats near Ramparts, a vast, partially timbered but watery wilderness, needs protection. Once the site of a proposed high dam and still withdrawn for that purpose, these wetlands would make an admirable refuge. An outstanding waterfowl habitat, the Yukon Flats also support some of our largest populations of furbearing animals like beaver, mink, and otter.

Most human contact with the Far North will be along waterways. At least a half dozen of the major arctic rivers should be reserved under the Wild Rivers Act, with BLM jurisdiction. The finest river in the North is generally considered to be the Noatak. It is unique in that it flows across the tundra from east to west, between the two long arms of the western Brooks Range. No richer wildlife area can be found on the continent. The river lacks the severe rapids that block all of the northward-flowing arctic rivers as they cross moraines; it is ideal for small-boat travel. Almost pristine, it is America's wildest large river. Its tributaries, especially the Aniak and Cutler, should also be set aside.

Of the North Slope rivers, the Killik is most worthy of Wild River classification. Most of its upper section should be included within the proposed Gates of the Arctic National Park. The upper Killik flows through a spectacular valley of the northern Brooks Range, about which Lois Crisler has written so evocatively in *Arctic Wild*. The upper river is gentle, with many ponds and marshes rich in wildlife, and with sand flats for camping. Over the divide to the south lies the Alatna River. This gentle, meandering stream, flowing through what some consider the most beautiful valley in the Brooks Range, is an ideal float trip. It too should be included in the park. Another westward-flowing river, the Kobuk, should be preserved upstream from the Bornite copper mines. The upper river alternates canyons with open stretches in a country of large lakes, muskegs, and low rugged hills in its forested country. Part of the Sheenjek River lies within the Arctic Wildlife Range, but many leagues of unprotected river flow through a lovely valley of meadows and wooded benches, rich in wildlife. The entire river should be preserved. The East Fork of the Chandalar, which runs southwest from the Arctic Wildlife Range, is a worthy candidate, along with part of its tributary, the Wind River. Nowhere else in America can we reserve almost untouched waterways negotiable for most of their lengths by boatsmen of ordinary ability, in settings often resembling subalpine meadows farther south.

A number of the larger scenic lakes that speckle the Brooks Range on both its north and south edges should have their shorelines and immediate valleys closed to resource exploitation. Walker and Chandler lakes are best known, but many of the smaller lakes are equally beautiful and even more wild. The two Kurupa lakes and Shainin Lake, all three at the north edge of the Brooks Range and all within the boundaries of a national park proposed for the central Brooks Range, rank among the loveliest in all Alaska.

In January 1969, outgoing Interior Secretary Stewart Udall sought President Johnson's signature on a proclamation withdrawing a large area in northern Alaska as a national monument called the Gates of the Arctic. The name derives from two rugged mountains, Boreal Mountain and Frigid Peak, that rise out of the southern foothills near Mount Doonerak and face each other across the North Fork of the Koyukuk. They were called the Gates of the Arctic by Robert Marshall. Interior Committee Chairman Aspinall reportedly assured the President that he would hold prompt hearings if the proposal were submitted to Congress. Representative Saylor promptly introduced a bill to implement Udall's proposal. It has been gathering dust in Aspinall's files.

Interior Secretary Morton, as well as the Alaskan Congressional delegation, should know that many Alaskans support this proposal, as well as the national conservation organizations. The Alaska Conservation Society and the Alaska Chapter of the Sierra Club propose that Congress authorize a two-unit Gates of the Arctic National Park, with boundaries worked out by Alaskan conservationists. The park would include both north (arctic) and south slopes of the central Brooks Range, within the Baird and Schwatka Mountains. The west (Alatna) unit of approximately 7200 square miles would include a major river drainage and a series of highly scenic lakes where the northern forest abuts the mountains. The east (Doonerak)

unit would include about 2900 square miles of high, rugged peaks and deep, glacier-scoured canyons. The Doonerak unit as now proposed has been expanded to include lands proposed by George Marshall, based on the explorations of his brother Robert. Both units would extend across the Arctic Slope of the Brooks Range, taking in a number of fragile tundra lakes. The total size of about 10,000 square miles would greatly exceed any present U.S. park, but Canadians have established park tracts of comparable or larger size in four different regions. It's the biggest country we have and will require the biggest parks.

The north slope segment of the Alaskan conservationists' proposal greatly expands the Park Service concept of a south slope reserve. We consider the ecology of the arctic tundra north of the Divide to be as worthy of representation as the alpine tundra and subarctic forest to the south. We wish to provide a much larger sanctuary for presently persecuted wolves and grizzlies on the open tundra. The sharp and dramatic north face of the Range would be represented, with the large lakes at its edge. Simply put, an arctic park ought to include some of the true Arctic.

This park, like all national parks and monuments, would be closed to hunting and trapping, except that Natives would continue to hunt for subsistence. The entire area would remain subject to Native land claims. This preserve would be the first Park Service unit, and only the second area of any kind in northern Alaska, reserved for its natural features. It would remove from hunting only 3 per cent of northern Alaska; the remaining 97 per cent, including the Arctic Wildlife Range, would still be open to hunting. The recent state land selections for oil development are about the same size as the proposed park. Presently, the entire area lies within unclassified BLM public domain.

In addition to the designation of reserves, a number of other things must be accomplished soon in Arctic Alaska. Of the most immediate priority is a fair settlement of the Native land claims. The claims bill passed by the U.S. Senate awards the Natives a large cash grant, mineral royalties, and 2½ per cent of Alaska's land. The bill is presently being stalled in the House Interior Committee. The only alternative to prompt fair settlement is deep bitterness and possible violence as well as interminable court action by the Eskimos, Indians, and Aleuts. And chaos in resource management.

An important though little recognized need is adequate inventorying and mapping. The U.S. Geological Survey, under Dr. Pecora, is able and objective. Its excellent permafrost studies and Pecora's insistence on solving permafrost problems before approval of any pipeline permit, give evidence of this. The USGS could reasonably do the overall mapping, and key studies where urgently required, and general mineral surveying. The State's Division of Mines and Geology is equipped to do pinpoint surveys in detail on the more promising areas. They have begun extensive aeromagnetic surveys this summer in the central Brooks Range. Planned government surveys would be much less disruptive than random private exploration.

Research is essential on human disturbance of land surfaces, especially tundra. An early goal should be to identify those specific activities that cause the most serious ecological problems, determine what combinations of circumstances to avoid, and what means provide best remedial action. An excellent example of such useful research is Jerry Hok's work for BLM in Pet. 4, to determine what soils, degrees of soil moisture, and slope incurred the most severe damage from vehicles during the earlier exploration for oil. This knowledge will allow more precise regulations as to surface types to be avoided in the future.

Legislation is needed requiring planning and classification of state and federal land *before* sales, leases, or construction are permitted. Only by such a restriction can sane development be effected. The State does have a series of land classifications on the books, but up to now, they have been used mainly to facilitate rapid development, not to augment wise planning. No offshore oil leases should be permitted in the Arctic Ocean. Petroleum Reserve Number 4 should remain an oil reserve until such time, if ever, the oil there is truly needed. Caribou calving grounds should be given special protection, with disturbance by surface vehicles prohibited. At present, the Fish and Game Department has limited authority, and only over anadromous fish streams (those in which fish move up from salt water to spawn). This authority should be strengthened, and extended to all waters. Of particular concern is the location and method of gathering gravel. Alaska's Natural Resources Department recently adopted regulations for surface exploration and development, but these were watered down from the original proposals, and they apply only prior to leasing. They should be revised to apply after leasing as well, since that is when much of the damage is done. The BLM has sensible guidelines for industry, but they are merely recommendations, and not binding. As a result, effective control is lacking on federal lands. These guidelines should be strengthened, and made into regulations with enforcement powers. Both state and federal permits presently contain such language as "except as absolutely necessary." Such equivocal language will have to be pared away.

At present, any prospector may file a claim anywhere on the public lands, including most national park lands, national forests and refuges, in Alaska, without regard for other values. He need report neither his claim nor his activities to the agency managing the land. If he keeps up his assessment work, he may gain full title to the land. This bizarre state of affairs is permitted by the unchanged Mining Law of 1872. In shocking disregard of the public interest, the Public Land Law Review Commission has recommended retaining this antiquated law, albeit with revisions. If the Mining Law remains unchallenged, orderly management of the Brooks Range will be highly doubtful. Each agency should have the authority to regulate mining, or to exclude it after public hearings, from tracts with other overriding values.

Above all, we need coordinated planning. The winter haul road over the ice to Prudhoe Bay (the Hickel Highway) becomes an eroding morass, in part a canal, each summer. Need it have been built when, how, and where it is? The agencies managing Alaska's land need to agree where the resources are, and where the most suitable transportation corridors lie. No such agreement was reached before the haul road was built. It is a permanent monument, in any event, to our recent governor. Rumor now has it that Alaska's transportation commission is studying a railroad route up the North Fork of the Koyukuk. Though this route might be technically feasible, such intrusion into the Doonerak wilderness would be disastrous to Park Service plans for a Gates of the Arctic reserve. It marks a failure of coordination in planning. Unless conservationists work toward coordination, all talk of coordination will remain just that.

An essential goal is dialogue between all interested parties. Conservationists are now in a strong position to achieve their purposes. They should sit down with Native leaders, representatives of industry, state and federal bureaucrats, and politicians. Joint meetings with Canadians should be called. The public should be encouraged to participate, however painful for some bureaucrats.

But the foregoing considerations have been details of the larger question: What does the world wish to see happen to a last great wilderness of the only great planet? The question has not been answered because the world's people do not yet know it has been asked, or that it is a transcendent question.

Juneau, Alaska   RICHARD J. GORDON
September 1970

Author's Note

This book tells two stories. One is the account of a trip two friends and I took across the Brooks Range of Alaska; the story of the Range We Saw. The other story is the Range we didn't see. It is an account of things that are not apparent to a traveler in those mountains, but which exist in libraries—a brief history of the Brooks Range and its arctic slope, of its landforms, of the animals that have come and gone, and of the men.

Neither story comes close to describing the Range That Is. In our five-week transect we saw a very narrow corridor of the Romanzof Mountains, which are considerably less extensive than the Philip Smith Mountains, or the Endicott Mountains, or the Baird and Schwatka Mountains, or the Davidson Mountains, or the several other mountain ranges that combine to make the great length of the Brooks Range. We crossed the province of open tundra at its very narrowest point. The tundra plains we felt lost in were cramped compared to the vast expanses that lay to the west of us. In that direction the tundra is sometimes two hundred miles in breadth. What those plains are like I am not able to say.

The Brooks Range in the libraries is an incomplete one, too. Reports of explorers and scientists are few and paltry. Great areas of the mountains remain unexplored and unknown. True, there are no more blank spaces on the map like those that drew Robert Marshall to the Range, but the contour intervals are still wide. (Besides, the knowledge that aerial mapmakers have is poor, shared with too many, and hard to take pride in the way Marshall did in his hand-drawn maps of country his own legs had walked in.) What secrets do the Franklin Mountains of the Brooks Range hide? No one knows.

Many of the animals of the Range remain mysterious to us. For all their numbers, the endless caribou herds— *La Foule*, as French explorers called them, "The Throng," the living stream so mind-bending and numbing to those men who have seen it at full tide—elude us in winter. We have an imperfect idea even of where the caribou are for that longest season of the year, in large part simply because we can't see them. In their high home latitudes caribou are eclipsed by the winter night. For most of their lives the Earth's axis cants them away from the sun. When, with the approach of each winter's cold, the caribou pass into the southern slopes of the Range, they also pass into darkness.

The few scientific reports from the Brooks Range read like apologies for subjects and areas left unilluminated.

Almost all of them betray a note of excitement about all the work that remains to be done. One preliminary report, an appraisal of the Baird and Schwatka Mountains by biologist Fred Dean, is matter-of-fact until the very end, then concludes with: "The possibilities are endless."

One of the uncomfortable lessons the library held was the Lesson of the Lemmings. No one who considers the Arctic fails to be impressed by it. In the simplified arctic ecosystem, with its less diverse and efficient web of checks on population, the microtines (lemmings and voles) regularly boom and crash. The crash is a grim system for controlling numbers—it involves more animal pain, for the microtines and for their predators, than do more balanced systems. We are uneasy at the films of lemmings throwing themselves into the sea, perhaps because their suicide is truly unnatural. If Nature works toward anything, it is to fill niches and build the diversity and stability that makes such measures unnecessary. If man works toward anything, it is the opposite. Thus the observation that we are crowding subways, or the banks of the Ganges, like lemmings is the less interesting part of the lesson lemmings have for us. As we with our oil development preempt the lemmings' terrain, we delete the lessons—the warnings—against such preemption, and lose the alternatives to it; we cut away at our possibilities with a double-bladed instrument.

But it may be that in remembering and reading of the Arctic—a sparse and lonely land, one of the ends of the Earth—it is too easy to think about termination. It is natural enough, though. Uncertainty is the main note sounded there. The animals all walk a finer line, and the men too. Running through most Eskimo poetry is a sharp sense of extremity. One Eskimo song, by a man named Kingmerut who lived on the Ellis River, east of the Brooks Range, has stayed with me. "Fear was about me in my little house," Kingmerut begins, recalling a time when he was starving. "Remaining was intolerable." Kingmerut sets off, staggering inland, mumbling magic words. He passes lakes and rivers where no fish bite for him.

> I did so wish to see
> Swimming caribou or fish in a lake.
> That joy was my one wish.
>
> My thought ended in nothing.
> It was like a line
> That all runs out.

The purpose of this book is to urge that the possibilities remain endless; that the line never all runs out.

—K.B.

Chena

I first saw the Arctic at Fort Ord, California, on a dune above the ocean. I was kneeling and watching as my bunkmate, Private Paul Brown, an Eskimo whose native name was Atongen but whose grandfather called him "Buttocks" and whose mother called him "Whale," drew his home country in the Pacific sand. He showed me how the old bed of the river curved around White Mountain, Alaska, and then showed where the present river flowed. He drew the Island, or what had been the Island and was now a sandy, willow-covered hill in the dry channel, and he made rectangles to show where the village, the school, and the small airfield were. He sketched carefully, telling stories, and as I listened the map became real territory.

Several weeks before, Brown and I had stood at parade rest in a field of new soldiers, watching our sergeant's moving mouth. Brown was three ranks from me. I noticed him for the first time. His hair was at least sixteen inches long and blew wildly in the cold sea wind. Long hair was not popular then, and it made me wonder what Brown was. A Japanese, I guessed, or a Korean of some strange sect. Then he passed from my awareness. He would have passed forever, except that Brown and I both turned up, our heads shaved, in the same platoon.

Brown was one of five Eskimos in the company. The others were Fox, Smart, Mike and Patrick. All five Eskimos got faint from the typhoid shots, and each of them sat down suddenly as he walked from the dispensary. The rest of us Zuñis, Mexicans, Navajos, Iraqis, Blacks and Whites, our civilized veins accustomed to needles and artificial antibodies, marched off to the next series of injections. We left the five sitting in a row with their chins on their chests as the medics had instructed them.

Later Brown and I became friends, and we helped each other in small ways. Brown, with his Eskimo's mechanical skill, could help me assemble my M-1, and I could translate for him the orders of a sergeant from Watts or Brooklyn. Brown came to me once with one of the forms we had to fill out. It required him under "race" to check either Caucasian, Oriental, Negro, or American Indian, and Brown asked which he was. It was a hard question. I knew that if on entering a camp of his ancestors, in dark

of night, Brown had identified himself loudly as an American Indian, there would have been repercussions, but I did not want to explain this sort of subtlety to our sergeant. We decided that Brown was an American Indian.

Brown and I spoke very little. I was interested in Eskimo life, but Brown answered my questions only when he chose to. When he did not want to answer, he appeared not to hear, and went about his business, polishing his boots with rapid, tight circles of his cloth, or peering down the bore of his rifle, or writing, in his perfect, missionary-school handscript, long letters home. We were squad leaders, and with the platoon's other two squad leaders we shared a room of our own. We were together much of the time, in silence. But sometimes Brown would look up, regard me for a moment, and clear his throat.

"Boy, you sure are lucky you don't have to shoot dogs," he said one time. I asked him what he meant. He told me that before he enlisted he had to shoot three of his dogs. I asked why. Some were sick, he said. Some were old. Nobody to take care of them. Were they sled dogs? I asked. Yes, Brown said. Well, couldn't his father have taken care of them? There was no answer. Brown had said all he wanted to, and we went back to polishing our boots.

"It's squirrel hunting time back home," Brown said another time, turning away from the barracks window.

About this time of year, he said, the folks were moving to where the squirrels were. They were making a summer camp. They were catching the squirrels with traps. Sometimes they shot them.

Brown paused in the squirrel story and turned back to the window. I thought he was through, but in a moment he continued.

"The folks back home are funny. It must be some kinda custom or something, but when they cook squirrels they push the legs up through the mouth. Then they have to break all this (Brown ran his hands up and down his own rib cage, to illustrate.) When you eat the squirrel you must be careful every rib is broken. My mother told me something. I don't know if it's true. She says one time a man was eating a squirrel and he said 'pooh, pooh, I won't break these ribs.' So he ate the squirrel and that night a big squirrel that was nothing but ribs came and ate him up.''

I asked Brown if he thought it was true. He answered thoughtfully, ''No, I don't think it is.''

There was another thing he did not believe, I discovered later. The old folks—the grandmothers—used to warn children that if they were bad the northern lights would come and carry their heads away.

Brown and I were close, but never really knew each other, I think. No important secrets were exchanged. I entered our room once and found Brown alone at the open window, trilling to the birds on the lawn outside. We were not allowed out of the barracks, so Brown was talking to the birds, trying to draw them closer to the window. When he heard my step, he stopped and did not resume. But we did have the mountains in common. Brown was twenty and I was eighteen, and we both had had our best times in wild country.

On the day Brown drew the sand map of his home, the platoon was on one of the beach rifle ranges, taking a smoke break. We rested on a low hill of mesembryanthemum, in a sandy, fenced-in rest area, in the sea wind. The day had begun too early. The sky was blue, but not warm. Our shoulders still felt the recoil of the M-1 rifles, and our ears the concussion. Now it was quiet. There were two smells: the army smell of sweat drying on dun helmet liners, and the smell of kelp blowing in from the ocean. We had never seen the surf, for there was a ridge of dunes between us and the beach—a dangerous and impassable ridge, with rows of targets on its leeward side. There was no way in the world we could get over and down to the shore. Brown and I stood together in the wild smell of the invisible sea, and even the cigarettes the platoon was smoking smelled good. Neither of us smoked.

Brown knelt in the sand and began to draw the map.

''Here is White Mountain,'' he said. He showed me how the river had once curved around it, and drew the willow-covered island that had become a hill when the river changed course. He told me that White Mountain once was called Look Out, because when the river was there men beached their boats at the base of the mountain and climbed to the top, then looked north and south for enemy. In the old days the people fought at White Mountain continually. ''My mom used to find skulls and arrows,'' Brown said.

''What do the people do there?'' asked a soldier named Dillon, who was sitting nearby and overheard.

''They just live. They fish. Gather berries and hunt a bit. There's moose, bear, cranes, wolverines. Or some-times the folks go downriver for brants. And muskrats. Or they go to the ocean every summer for salmon.''

''What's the weather like?'' Dillon asked.

''This last month, March, the winds blow the snow hard. Now, April, it gets warmer. The people get lazy. By June the place is dead, all the folks are gone to fishing camps.'' Brown might have said more, but just then the order came to fall in. Dillon field-stripped his cigarette, and the three of us fell into formation.

Four years later, Brown had been to Korea, then Vietnam, and then I lost track of him. I was above the Arctic Circle. Two friends and I were going to walk across the Brooks Range in order to photograph it, and we had met in Fairbanks.

John Milton, Steve Pearson, and I spent our last three civilized nights in a rooming house. The small rooms were $5.00 a night for a single person and $7.50 for two. It was our first experience of Alaskan prices, and it seemed unreasonably high for what we got. Each room had two short beds with single army blankets. The management turned off the heat at night—more accurately at 9:00 P.M., for it was summer and it never got dark—and turned it on in the mornings. The rooms were cold at night and very hot in the mornings, especially hot when we came in from the cool Alaskan day. There was a handwritten sign on the wall of each room that read:

NO DRINKING
NO PARTYING
NO WOMEN IN MEN'S ROOMS

Two Athabascan girls from upstairs were always on the phone in the hallway. They were sisters. One of them, the prettier one, spent most of her time telling her boyfriend not to call her there.

On our second night John and I walked into town. We crossed the bridge over the Chena and looked down at the fast but calmly flowing gray river. There were swifts hunting the surface of the water. We watched them skim eddies and riffles that betrayed the river's speed, then walked on. Two blocks from the river was Second Avenue, where all the bars were. First we went to a nightclub named the Chena, after the river. The go-go girls at the Chena were pretty. For the most part they were better looking than the girls in Seattle, we agreed. But only one of them could really dance. She was an Indian girl who did the Philly Skate as if she had been in the big city, around black people, at some time in her life. When she sat down she was replaced by a very fat girl, employed as a curiosity it seemed, who danced a sort of hula.

The two Athabascan girls from the rooming house came in, looking for someone to buy them drinks. They invited us to join them at the Redwood Club, which they said was livelier than the Chena. The Redwood Club was jammed with people. There were a few soldiers in civilian clothes and the rest were Indians. John danced with the prettier Athabascan sister. The other sister had disappeared, so I sat at the bar and drank beer.

I decided I had never seen any group as drunk as the Indians at the Redwood Club. No one was gaily intoxicated, and many were out on their feet. The Indians set out to get drunk with deliberation. I tried to remember if anyone was really happily drunk in bars back home. I watched for a long time, drinking beers. I was a little sour, because John was dancing with the pretty sister, and I could not see the other one. An Eskimo woman made her way toward the bar stool next to mine. As she neared it, a man spilled his beer on her. She did not feel the wetness until she sat down. Then she spun off the stool and stood against me, looking blackly down at the stool as if the stool had got her wet. "Son of a bitch," she said. "Somebody spill his drink on me." She looked at me for corroboration. I agreed that somebody had.

The woman sat down. She was in her late thirties, wore glasses and a white blouse with a ruffle at the neck. She looked prim and schoolmatronly, in spite of her drunkenness. She drank for a while, then began shouting requests to the bandleader.

The music was not pleasant. The place was too thick with Indians and smoke, and, as I began to imagine, with a dignified, inarticulate despair. I was not sober. The evening already seemed old.

I went outside. It was good to be out in the northern air, and in the empty streets. It was past midnight, but there were pink clouds over the distant mountains and the peaks stood in perfect definition. I walked, and after a few blocks the little bar district gave way to the residential. It was a respectable part of town, without the trailers, corrugated roofs, and gravel that make up the outskirts of Fairbanks. The houses were neat and compact. The streets lay in an early-morning light, but no one was beginning his paper route or cooking an early breakfast. It would be hours before those things happened. The town was in repose, time suspended, everyone inside asleep.

I walked back. There was a fight back on Second Avenue outside an all-night restaurant. Two men were on the ground wrestling ineffectually until the man on top raised himself enough to give the other three quick blows. "Had enough old man?" he shouted twice. He looked like a soldier on pass. His voice was trembling with excitement. The man below conceded, and they both stood up. I saw that the loser really was an old man. He was at least forty

years older than the winner. "You won," the old man said. "You beat me. No hard feelings." He shook the younger man's hand, and they put arms around each other's shoulders. The young man was then remorseful at what he had done, and repeatedly asked the old man if he was all right. The old man, bleeding from an abrasion above his eye, became irritated at the young man's attentions. He shook himself free and went into the restaurant.

I was hungry. I found a quieter restaurant, went in, and had raisin pie a la mode. I would have eaten more than that, but the prices were too high. To cash my traveler's check I had to follow the waiter through a back room where old Alaskans in suspenders and cigars were playing poker with yellow chips and no conversation. The waiter asked me where I was from. I said Oakland—Oakland and Berkeley. He grimaced, in a friendly way, and said you could have either of them. He didn't like those towns. Too many colored people there for him.

Back at the Redwood Club things had slowed down. The band was gone. John was sitting at a table with his Athabascan girl, the girl's sister, and a bus driver. I joined them and we drank and danced for a long time. John's girl, Fannie, was very drunk; she would alternately collapse on his shoulder and drag him to his feet to dance. The bus driver was the worst dancer I had ever seen. He thought the point of discotheque dancing was to look primitive, and he hopped around like a caveman on hot ground. We had last drinks before the place closed. Outside, through the open door, the sky was getting brighter without ever having gotten dark. That seemed wonderful. We were past fatigue. We decided to find a club that was still open.

And then it was much later. Many things had happened that I couldn't remember. It was four in the morning at another club, the name of which I can't remember. The bus driver was gone. John was asleep against the wall of the booth and Fannie was asleep on his shoulder. I was talking with the sister, whose name was Anice.

Anice told me that her father was Irish and her mother Athabascan and a bit French. She had brothers and sisters back in her village whom she had never seen. They had been born after she left. One of her older brothers was here in the nightclub, and she pointed him out to me. This brother had married an Indian woman from the States, Anice said, a mean woman whom Anice had tried her best to get along with, but just couldn't. I asked what tribe her sister-in-law was, and Anice said, "You know—Navajo. They are all mean, that tribe." Anice and I talked for a long time, and found we liked each other well enough.

Then, from the darkness of the booth, Anice said she wished she was dead.

It surprised me and I asked why. She was pretty and intelligent, I said, and she was young. She knew she was intelligent and pretty, didn't she? No she did not, she said. She could see that the death talk had disturbed me, so she wished again that she was dead. It was an interesting idea, all of a sudden. She had a doctor's appointment the next day, she told me—possible cancer—but she didn't think she would go. I urged her to go, though I didn't believe she had an appointment.

It was five in the morning and the place was closing. With much shaking we woke John, but Fannie refused to move. John, still half asleep, watched as I lifted Fannie under the arms and carried her to the door. It was bright daylight outside. Fannie pulled free, sleepily angry, her eyes hurting in the sunlight, and tried to get back inside. I blocked her path. John watched, amused. Finally Fannie gave up trying to get past me, and John began walking her around. Anice and I went to call a cab. When we came back we saw John, alone, beckoning to us from a shed behind the nightclub. Fannie was inside, asleep on an old sprung sofa that lay at an angle on a junk heap. We were all tired of Fannie. Her skirt was dusty. I brushed her off and carried her outside.

Later, in the cab, I asked Anice why she had never gone back to her village. "Ah," she said, "there was nothing there." It was a simple question for her to answer.

The next day we were flying north. We were high above the great north country. The detail of the spruce forest and the intricate geometry of frost polygon was lost in the endless green stretch of the land. We passed over the Yukon, flowing at different speeds through its many channels, its wide brown waters far below us and finally behind as we droned northward. Our gear was jammed into the Cessna cabin and it was impossible to get comfortable. We were one hundred pounds overweight. Because I was the heaviest I sat in the front to balance the load—facing backward because of the way our things were stacked. I had to look over my shoulder to see where we were going. I turned once and there was the Brooks Range.

First the mountains were just white irregularities on the horizon. Then they were prickling with movement, it appeared, advancing on me like Birnam Wood, jumping bigger and bigger each time I turned to look. I was going in the opposite direction from Anice. I was traveling backward, but the right way. Then we were in the foothills and the Sheenjek was shining below us, running down from the mountains at the top of the world.

BOB WALDROP: *Arrigetch Peaks*

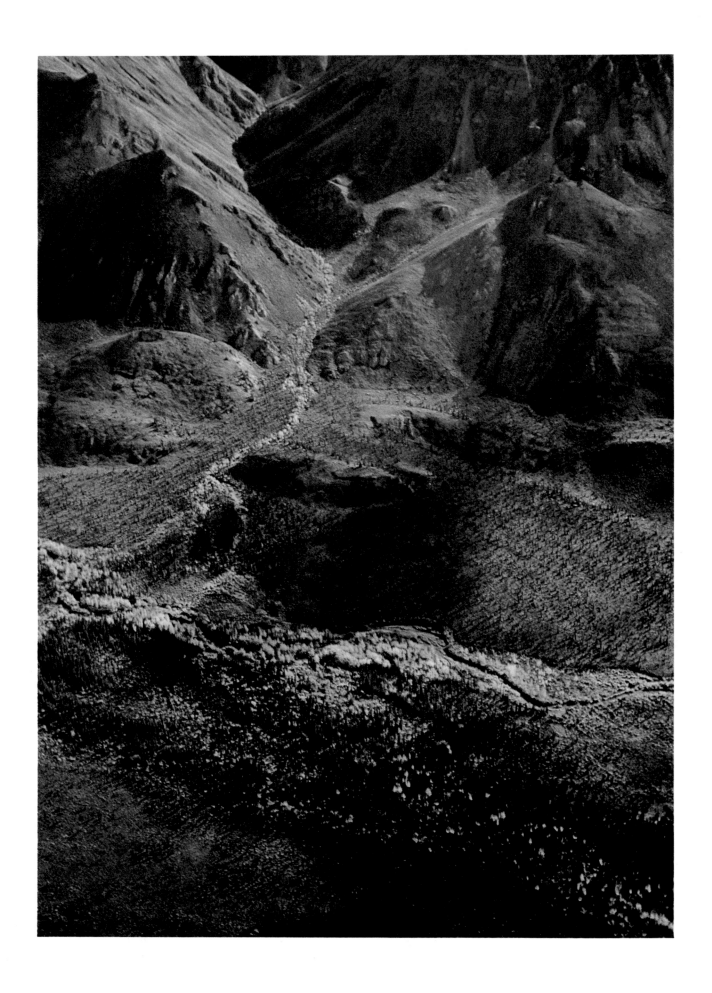

1. LANDFORMS

"A long time ago, they tell us, there was nothing here but water—no land at all. Raven, he fell to worrying about this and then he saw some stumps of bunch grass floating by and he got in his kayak and chased them. He paddled close to one and he hit it with his spear and he put the line around it and pulled it back to shore where he packed it down tight. Then he got in his kayak and went hunting again and he kept spearing grass roots and packing them down next to the first one and then there was land—and then there was land all around. . . ."

When I attempted cautiously to learn where Raven had stood when he first stepped into his kayak, and how he could paddle to shore before land existed, and where the people were when he called them and said land was ready, the old man simply returned his pipe to his mouth and said between his teeth; "We don't know about that. We only know what they tell us."

—J. L. GIDDINGS

ONE HUNDRED and fifty million years ago, they tell us, the Brooks Range lay under ocean. It was a range-to-be then, just the level floor of a seaway between "Arctica," a continent to the north, and the American continent. For 200 million years before that time, the floor of the seaway had gathered sediments washed down from Arctica and from the ancestral American mainland. Then, in the Jurassic Period of 155 to 130 million years ago, uplift began and a mild Brooks Range raised itself. The mountain-building continued gently until the middle of the Cretaceous Period, when with strong folding and faulting the first modest Brooks Range became truly mountainous. The deformity was especially severe at the center of the Range, where some peaks were pushed above the snowline, and some glaciation began. The mountains continued to rise until the mid-Tertiary, then eroded to mild hills again.

It was only recently, in the last 20 million years, that the present Brooks Range came into being. Uplift in the Miocene and Pliocene, and glaciation in the Pleistocene, gave the Range its present height and shape. The glaciers left the mountains with those characteristics typical of glaciated regions: sharp divides, deep U-shaped valleys with steep walls and parallel sides, and cirques, jagged ridges, and moraines.

The tundra vegetation of the early post-glacial Brooks Range was herbaceous, an association of sedges, grasses, composites, and small amounts of willow and birch. A rise of birch to prominence followed, with herbs and willows decreasing. Then came a replacement of birch by alder, and the influx of spruce that continues today. There are still few trees in the Range, even in the taiga zones of its southern slopes. The Baird and Schwatka mountains at the southwestern end of the Range have a subarctic continental climate, with dense alder swamps, a varied fern flora, and a mesophytic vegetation, but most of the Brooks Range is bare of tall growth and the mountains show what they are made of. The spine of the Brooks Range is of quartzite, limestone, and metamorphic rock 300 to 380 million years old. The younger rock of lower elevations is of sandstone, shale, and conglomerate, 70 to 220 million years old.

It is more dream-like and supernatural than a combination of
earthly features . . . It is a landscape such as Milton or
Dante might imagine,—inorganic, desolate, mysterious.
—ELISHA KENT KANE, 1855

Wide and far on either side, before and behind us, spread the arctic land, unlike anything else we had ever seen. Cones, ridges, rounded rock outcroppings rose dark from the tan tundra below. All smooth-looking, all rounded. "Bland!" I thought in surprise. "That's the word for the Arctic." But the blandness was eerie, for it was one face of danger; one never quite forgot winter.

—Lois Crisler

There is, to be sure, a kind of biotic riot in the summer outburst of color, scent, and sound . . . But always the season's opposite haunts you: *what about the winter? What must that be like?*

—David Roberts

These arctic mountains are distinguished by an everpresent mood of darkness, cold, and snow. Winter is a constant, though usually hidden companion during the short arctic summer; the quickness of the summer only intensifies an awareness that warmth here is only a brief respite from cold, that light will soon be followed by a deep and much longer-lasting darkness. This mood dominates the land and every living thing in it.

—John P. Milton

Staring out over the limitless expanse I at first saw only a rolling world of faded brown, shot through with streaks and whorls of yellow greens, for when I tried to see it all, the individual colors merged into anonymity. It *was* a barren sight, and yet that desert face concealed a beauty that rose from a thousand sources, under the white sun. . . . Even on the shattered ridges that are given over to the rocks, the creeping lichens suffused the gray stone with a wash of pastel tints ranging from scarlet through the spectrum into velvet rosettes of perfect black. There was no lack of color rising from living things— but it is only that the eye beholds too much in this land that has no roof and no containing walls. The colors flow together and are lost in distance that the eye cannot embrace.

—FARLEY MOWAT

Sheenjek

As the plane set down on Last Lake it frightened two moose from the edge of the water. From the plane window the scale of the country was so hard to understand, and the black spruces of that latitude were so stunted, that the moose looked larger than life. We were being set down among the giant beasts of the kind of lost continent that Arthur Conan Doyle imagined. The moose watched us unalarmed until the pontoons hit the water, then ran heavily off. We taxied to the tussock-grass shore of the lake, unloaded our things and paid the pilot, counting the bills into his hand. He was a Korea veteran who had played bush pilot well, I thought, reading a magazine most of the flight, looking up only occasionally. He had identified the moose as caribou, either to have fun with us or because he didn't know. He took off with an impres-

sive roar, for a Cessna pilot, and dipped his wings as he turned back over the lake and headed homeward. The plane was dramatic somehow; slow moving, for a long while remaining a point among the foothills, a human point above the great face of the land. Then it disappeared and we were alone in the middle of the country.

From the plane on our approach we had seen a cache a short distance from the lake. The small platform of dead white branches had stood out clearly against the living black spruces. We had been disappointed then at seeing signs of man, but now the cache became as curious to us as a stranger would have been. Steve Pearson, John Milton, the cache, and I were the only man-made things for many leagues around. We walked over to meet the cache.

*   *   *

Steve Pearson was twenty-seven, of medium height, with sturdy walking legs. He had grown up in New York. As a boy in that crowded city he had begun to think there was nothing in the world he liked. Then, on a train trip to the Middle West, he looked out the window and saw the great plains. He suddenly had discovered space, and could not believe his good fortune. When he grew up he became a wanderer. In the Army he was stationed in Korea and California, then traveled everywhere, preferring warm countries like Italy and Australia. He had hated Korea's cold. Most recently he had served as a press photographer in Vietnam, but he came to hate the war and left. Steve

never felt comfortable staying anyplace long. He was more than anything else an emigrant.

John Milton was twenty-eight. He had grown up in New Jersey, where as a boy he had read, and been much influenced by, Lewis and Clark. As a student at the University of Michigan, and later as an ecologist for the Conservation Foundation, he had traveled all over Latin America. He had gone to school in Mexico City, researched his master's thesis in Costa Rica, been pursued by Indians in the Oriente of Peru. His work had taken him to the Azores, the West Indies, the Canadian Arctic, and Europe. He and I had spent three months together in the Galapagos Islands off Ecuador's coast.

*   *   *

The heavy branches of the cache platform were all cut to a uniform length and nailed in place halfway up two spruces that grew closely together. The ground under the trees was littered with things that the ravens or wolverines had pulled from the cache. There was a teapot, some pans, a page from an Indian bible, an assortment of weathered funny papers, a letter to someone named Ambrose William, and a Selective Service card in Ambrose William's name. Above us, a pair of faded jeans was just visible over the edge of the cache platform. The jeans were full of something. We climbed a little uneasily, expecting I don't know what—a burial platform? But on top there was more of the same. There was the remainder of the Athabascan language bible, an Athabascan book of prayers, a child's English reader, several good unrusted traps, some Calpec in a blue bottle, some aspirin, some Turpin Hydrate Elixir, and some medicinal powders, the remains of a parka, and a pair of ragged blue jeans, stuffed with old shirts. There was a model 1895 Winchester with a lever action too rusted to open. The rifle apparently had fed from a clip, but this item was so rusted that it was impossible to tell. There was a knife with a wooden handle. There were several USGS maps of the Gulf of Alaska and other areas far to the south, and a map drawn in pencil on blue-lined paper, with no place names on it, no clue at all to what land the map represented, just an X beside one of the hand-drawn lakes.

That was all there was. It may seem a lot, taking up as much room as it does in the paragraph, but it did not take up much room in the Sheenjek Valley. It was the only mark of man we would see for many weeks, the only human sign in all that arctic country.

In the next days we camped at Last Lake and wandered around. I fished for grayling in the lake and in the small stream that ran from it, and John and Steve explored the

hills to the east. I waited to feel at home in the country, but the feeling did not come. I wondered what was wrong. I was not understanding the rhythm and resonance of the place, or its whatever; its mood, spirit, idiosyncrasy. Fishing, I watched the grayling—they tasted like trout but had great dorsal fins that they spread under the water—and I wondered what was missing from the country.

The Arctic had no smell. The summer snow did have a faint odor, and the smoke from our willow fires had a fragrance, and the black soil had a cold earth-smell when you dug a hand in it, but the wind brought no messages. The wind came raw and untinged, like the breath of an ice age. There was nothing like the resinous smell of the Sierra Nevada or the wet green growing smell of the Washington Cascades. Could a country be simply too big, too severe, to have a smell? I realized how important smell was to me. I remembered that the lynx of this country had a poor olfactory sense—maybe smell was not part of the scheme here? I wondered if I was just catching a cold.

Another thing about the Arctic was that you could not lie around in it. There were no warm rocks to lie shirtless on. The Arctic was cool even in summer, and there was surface wetness everywhere because permafrost prevented drainage. I wanted, perhaps because I am nearsighted, to bring everything to my nose, but I couldn't. There was no rolling around in this country. A certain contact with the land was missing; that might be the trouble.

John took to the Sheenjek country more easily. Every night he was busy writing in one of the journals, bound in red plastic, in which he keeps records of all his travels. He noted bog violets near the lake, small flowers that, in order to make up for lack of nitrogen in boggy soils, trap insects in their basal rosettes. He noted the red squirrels around the lake, and wondered why they were so silent. Was it, he asked his journal, a consequence of the scarcity of cover in this northern environment? He noted an "overwhelming sense of great distances, mysterious valleys, and an indefinable light air . . ." He noted the pair of arctic loons (*Gavia arctica pacifica*) that swam, calling now and again, far out on the lake. "How well," he wrote, "their lonely cry suits this solitary land." I myself was not sure yet about the solitary land, or how well the loon's cry suited it. The cry fitted the country well enough, I supposed. Steve kept no journal and I did not know how he felt about it.

To the south of Last Lake was a small field of *aufeis*. In warmer summers the field may have been a lake, but this summer only a thin crescent of blue water stood free of ice. Several surface streams ran over the ice, and a central stream had cut a channel through it. The channel's blue fissure bisected the field. The white of the frozen lake, with its blue tracery, was set against the green hills of tussock grass beyond, and the shadowed peaks, and the gray sky. Stopping by the frozen lake, I began to understand the country. The green hills, lying between severities of ice and sky, were somber. The green was a true rich green, but was clearly temporary. I understood as if someone had whispered it that arctic summer was brief and sad. Arctic summer was a false reprieve, a lie.

I climbed down into the ice fissure. The landward end of the fissure was floored by round stones. They made a narrow, cobbled beach that was dry for ten yards before dipping under the surface of the water. I crawled beneath an undercut wall of ice, lay on the cobbles, and looked up at the blue light that filtered through the ice overhang. I rested, listening to the multitudinous drip of the melting walls of the fissure. The noise was not loud, but was ear filling. There were myriad drippings, and echoes of drippings, from far turns of the channel out of sight around the corner. The drops imparted a just-perceptible chop to the water. There was a steady musical tinkling from the slivers of ice that floated in the channel water. The sound was like a reminder.

The everpresence of winter was the first fact of the Arctic that came home to us. It was a practical fact, in that inches below the soil was perennially frozen ground, but it was more than that. It was the truth of this country, as Steve would later say. Still, it was the only truth that the country allowed us for some time, and we began to tire of Last Lake.

I was anxious to be moving. The Arctic would mean more, I knew, once we were moving through it. We had discussed our route and decided that the best way was up the Sheenjek, across the Divide, and out to that margin of the Arctic Ocean called the Beaufort Sea. It would take five weeks, with side trips, and we needed to be underway, but John was sick and we delayed our start. John had a bad cough that persisted and kept him from sleeping. We liked to think that he had gotten the cough from Fannie, the Athabascan girl in Fairbanks. She had been coughing that night, we remembered. It was the Indians' revenge. As a last resort John climbed up into Ambrose William's cache and found the bottle of Turpin Hydrate Elixir. We had no idea what the elixir was for, but it smelled like cough medicine. John tasted it cautiously, standing under the cache, then swallowed a spoonful. He looked at us thoughtfully. He did not tumble over. After a while he said he felt better. It was poetic, we thought, treating the Athabascan malady with an Athabascan elixir. We waited for John to get stronger.

It was while waiting, and after a day's wandering around the country, that I had the first dream.

I walked up a river valley east of Last Lake and climbed the small slate butte that dominated the country to the northeast. The mosquitos were bad that morning until I gained some altitude. Wandering tattlers announced my progress from the very tops of spruce trees, the place those birds always choose to watch from. I came to a place where a grizzly had torn up some sod in digging for a ground squirrel, and I took small note of it, but then I came to where the bear had gone after a squirrel seriously. It was an excavation. The tremendous power of the bear was evident, and I was uneasy. I was glad I had my rifle.

Then, heading home, I dreamed. As I was walking down through a grove of spruce, I imagined myself stopping for a rest. I imagined a wolf. The wolf trotted through the forest toward me, unaware of my presence. He came very close. "Hello brother wolf," I said, surprising myself. It was not a natural thing for me to say. I am not good at conversing with animals, but I have a brother who is, and I spoke mostly for him. I also wanted to say something before the wolf came too close. The wolf looked up, startled, and turned to run off, but paused for an instant. He must have been held by some quality of my voice. There was something in his attitude, in that instant of arrested motion, that struck me.

"Reincarnation?" I said aloud. It may have been the wrong word. I was not sure that reincarnation was what I had seen. I spoke partly because I was a little scared of the wolf—just whistling in the dark—and partly because I wanted to say something more to him before he ran off.

The wolf froze and looked back at me. "Life is more beautiful than you'd think," he said, as if admonishing me, and he trotted off into the trees.

The dream was over so quickly that at first I thought little about it. It had possessed a real life, independent of me. I had no control over it once it started, and the ending had surprised me, and I was not at all sure what the wolf's answer meant, but I did not find these things remarkable that day. I did not break my stride, but continued down through the spruces. I might have forgotten the dream entirely, if we had not later met Averill Thayer. Four days after the dream, Thayer, who managed the Arctic Wildlife Range for the government, dropped in on us, landing his small plane on the lake. He knew we were planning to cross the range and wanted to see how we were doing. He was a man of few words. He spoke carefully, pronouncing all his articles distinctly, as if he had been alone in the Arctic so long that he didn't trust himself to get them out correctly. Pointing in the direction of the spruce forest where I had dreamed earlier, he told a story. He had been photographing there one day, he said, and had used up the film in his camera. He was walking back to the lake when a large black wolf came trotting out of the woods, not seeing him. "He kept coming until he was not, well, ten feet from me. Still didn't see me, until I guess I said something, and he looked up at me and ran off. First he hid behind a tree some ways off. He looked back from behind the tree and then he ran the rest of the way."

The day after Thayer left, we broke camp and departed. John was not yet strong enough to carry a full load, and Steve and I began with more than ninety pounds each. It seemed an incredible weight. It was a task just getting our packs to our shoulders, but we set out, walking through intermittent rain and wind, and as we moved through the country it began talking to us. The sky was gray and turbulent above and the land was green, yellow, and orange under our feet. The green was dominant, a soft wet green, luminous under the somber sky. Equisetum grew in fragile sprays, like a green mist over the ground. The yellow was mostly in the willows that bordered the streams and it showed up here and there in the tussock grass. The rarest color was the orange of a lichen that grew on certain rocks. It was a solitary orange. There was seldom more than one lichen-covered rock in sight at any one time. The rocks occurred as points of intensity—quintessence of orange, painfully orange—amidst green fields of tussock grass.

There was a duller orange in the moss at the edges of streams. Every fourth stream or so, for reasons we could not guess, was bordered entirely by orange moss. The other streams were bordered entirely by green. The moss grew in gentle hummocks by the streamside. The hummocks were full of water and delicate, easily disrupted by our feet. The entire country was full of water. Streams ran everywhere and the tussocks held water like sponges. The tussock hillsides were bright under the dark northern sky, as if in the absence of the sun their duty was to illuminate the world. It was not with an inward light that they glowed, precisely, but with a real light nonetheless, a refracted light better than the original source.

Walking under the weather I relearned all my mountain lessons. I looked up into the rain—no reason to be afraid of it—and the rain beat my face. I made myself comfortable in the cold, and at ease in the storm. These are ways of living I have to remember each time I go to the mountains. I was now relearning in my own right all the

things my father had learned, and relearned, in his time in the mountains. Mountains were the most important thing in my father's youth, and as a young man he had taken me into them, and to a considerable extent he and the mountains were, and are now, inextricable. The farther I walked, the more of my father's good lessons were substantiated. We stopped and rested. My green poncho, reaching to my knees in front, was pulled back over my pack to keep the pack dry, and it made the kind of tent that a table and blanket make for children. Sitting in the slanting rain and arctic wind, I ducked my head inside the tent. I was alone in there with my hands. I watched my hands, which resemble my father's. They were folded in my lap, pale in the undersea light beneath the poncho. I thought about the gifts of my father. The light inside was steady and green, though outside the poncho snapped in the wind.

Moving again. Under the weight of the packs it was most comfortable to watch the ground at our feet, but from time to time we looked up from the tussocks and arctic flowers to the peaks on either side of the valley. Mist and cloud were playing about the mountains, wreathing the cols, spilling out of high cirques and down the slopes. Above the mists was the ridgeline of peaks, a black lace of rock against white snow (or, if you wished, a white lace of snow against black rock) and above the ridgeline, sometimes obscuring it, was the gray sky, full of the promise of snow, or of rain at least—so heavy with promise that the gray verged on blue. The sky set off the lacework of rock, making the snow whiter and the rock blacker, making the ridgeline sharp, high, cold, and uninhabitable. For me high ridges, like the stars, have always been symbols of the severity of the universe. The ridges don't care about us. As I walked under the Sheenjek peaks I felt a renewed conviction about the impartiality of God. I wondered if the holy men who sat in Asian mountains usually came to the same conclusion. Or did holy men only go to the mountains in cartoons?

Storm after storm was blowing out of the north. In this weather the ridge looked like all the other alpine ridges in the world, but was very beautiful.

We came to a beaver pond. It was the northernmost beaver pond in the Sheenjek Valley, we guessed, for a few miles ahead the spruces gave out. Nothing but willow and dwarf birch grew between that final stunted treeline and the shore of the Arctic Ocean, and beyond that shore, to the Pole, there was nothing but ice. It may have been the northernmost beaver pond in the entire Brooks Range, and perhaps the entire planet, unless somewhere there were Siberian beaver more adventurous. The two north-

ernmost beaver who lived in the pond were not adventurers, in truth, but drudges who paid with hard work for their distinction. Their great pond was the work of generations and dynasties of beavers—a complex of four dams and four ponds that completely enclosed, as if by a moat, what once had been a steep hill and was now an island. We pitched camp across from the island. The larger beaver, the male of the pair, we assumed, swam up and regarded us with what John described in his journal as "suspicious old maid's eyes." It was not an unfair description, I think. In his journal John mapped the pond, and it made for an impressive blueprint, but like the human engineering feats that call attention to themselves—the longest spans and highest towers—the northernmost pond was unbeautiful. There were snags of drowned trees visible under the water, and the country around looked altered and drab. When we woke by the pond the next morning the beavers were nowhere in sight. A solitary duck landed on the water, ate a plant or two from the bottom of the pond, and flew on south.

We continued north. The Sheenjek Valley widened and the river made a great turn across the valley floor. We could look miles across to a low place in the far valley wall and see beyond to the drainage of the Kongagak, a river that flowed north into the Arctic Ocean. Ahead the Sheenjek became an impressive river. It flowed in many channels over the wide gravel floor of the valley. The water was the same gray as the gravel, reflecting as it did the gray sky, and walking close to the river we could see the channels only as differences in texture, as streams of motion among the river bars. The river slipped along at different speeds, in eddies and countercurrents, but always against us. We were walking against the stream, toward the source.

In the next days we walked along the river whenever we could. Above the flat gravel floor of the valley, the long slopes were cobbled with tussock grass, and the tussock hummocks made for bad walking. We could not relax when traveling on them because we were always making decisions; whether to step on this one, which looked likely to tip us off, or to step in the interstice between one hummock and the next, and have to pull a boot free. The gravel shore of the river was better going, though then it was necessary to cross and recross the channels, and to fight through occasional clumps of river willows. At first I unslung my rifle as we entered the willows, in case we surprised a bear in the closeness of the trees, but after a day or two I thought no more about it.

When the rain stopped the mosquitos came. Sometimes they arrived in such numbers that we stopped and put on our headnets. The headnets were uncomfortable, but they had a virtue. When the rain returned and we took the netting off, the world came back in all its color. It was like pushing back the hood of your parka and hearing the sound of the air again. It was like what happens when you turn a corner in the mountains, cutting yourself off from the others in your party, and find yourself suddenly alone on the land.

Walking through the rain, our route took us away from the river, out of sound but seldom out of sight. It rained for days, and rain beat our tents through the night, quickening all the streams in the Sheenjek country. Rivulets ran everywhere. Some larger streams had cut down to bedrock, but most streams were new and wandered over the land as they chose. The grass beneath the surfaces of these itinerant streams was flattened somewhat, but looked perfectly healthy down there. The new streams were inviting. They elicited from me a kind of dog's response, strangely reversed. Instead of peeing at every post I drank at every stream. The streams tasted as good and cold as the high ridges they flowed down from. When the streams were fast we linked arms and forded, six legs working against the current. I felt us moving toward the heart of the country.

Once we came to a stream too fast to wade, and we searched up and downstream until we found a spruce log spanning it. Crossing, I dropped my hat, and it was carried quickly out of sight. It was a green tyrolean hat that my parents had bought in Salzburg for my little brother. It was headed for the Sheenjek, and then, if nothing snagged it, for the Yukon, and then for the Bering Sea. I wondered if the Austrian hatmaker would be pleased. It seemed a noble end for the hat, lost in the unexplored wastes of northern America.

Back to the river. There the valley floor was flat, and the larger streams joining the river had lost the speed they gained on the gradient of the hillside, so that our crossings were easier. The smaller streams running down to the Sheenjek had disappeared completely under the gravel before they joined the river. We made good time. There were tracks everywhere on the river bars—wolf, bear, Dall sheep, caribou—and we left our tracks too. It was clear from the tracks that a great volume of life passed through this valley. We saw little of it—a porcupine and two ptarmigan in the morning, an eagle in the afternoon. We were not seeing the country as it really was. If we could somehow pass through this valley invisible and odorless, we agreed, it would be a different valley.

2. FIRST FAUNAS

They poured over the hills, flowed up the valleys, running to a new patch of green vegetation, then stopping to feed while those behind ran to fresher vegetation ahead. They came to a little lake east of camp—some waded out and began to drink, others started around the edges, both sides. This caused them to bunch up and many began to wade and swim across. They came on toward me, stopping when downwind. These moved upwind around me, but there were always more coming on. They came to within 30 yards of me, all around, except downwind.

The clacking of their hoofs, the constant blatting of the fawns, the grunting of the females, the constant coughing and wheezing all made a roar that was deafening. Then some bolted from my scent; the movement spread to about 1,000 and the ground fairly shook with the pounding hoofs, the roar increased. Each stampede only affected a thousand or so, then sort of petered out.

—WILLIAM O. PRUITT

DURING the glacial and interglacial interludes of the Pleistocene, great migrations crossed the Alaskan straits. Mammoths, big-horn sheep, mountain goats, pikas, musk oxen, caribou, moose, and giant bison, among other creatures, crossed from Siberia to North America, and from America camels, horses, and mastodons traveled to Siberia. Some stopped in the Brooks Range and stayed. Lions, elephants, mastodons, horses, camels, antelope, yaks, giant elk, giant beaver, and groundsloths all lived and died in great numbers under Brooks Range peaks.

It was a very different Arctic then. Saber-toothed cats ranged the foothills, stalking beneath the prismatic sparkling of parhelias in the October sky, or eager on the trail of game in winter snow, breath hissing as the moisture in it froze. The cats were larger than any modern lion or tiger.

They were muscular and stocky, more powerful than *Felis atrox*, the contemporary American lion that was the largest of all prehistory's lions. The canines of the saber-toothed cat were like scimitars, eight inches long sometimes, laterally compressed like blades, with the back edges serrated. The cats may have killed by striking, as a snake does. The saber teeth seem designed for jugular veins, and some paleontologists speculate that the cats fed less on meat than on blood. One of the last and most impressive of the saber-tooth line was named, with an irony a little sinister, *Smilodon*.

Dire wolves roamed the Arctic. They were larger than modern wolves, but otherwise very similar. They may have had the intelligent eyes of modern wolves, and may have practiced all the social courtesies that wolves now practice. Their bones don't tell. They may have been as

limber of spine, and able to make the same observation jumps, the same backwards or sideways joy leaps, the same dances of greeting. They may have been as fond of play, and of gathering together to howl—harmonizing always, never singing in unison, one wolf moving off his note if he heard another wolf voice it. They may have had the same varied language of howls, the same wide range of personality and striking delineation of character. But perhaps they did not. The Pleistocene was a grosser age, and the dire wolf may have been a creature closer to the wolf of our myths. Time seems to have brought refinement to arctic predators. As the Pleistocene passed, the brute strength of the saber-toothed cat and of *Felis atrox*, the atrocious lion, gave way to the grace of the lynx. The American cats became more feline. Similarly perhaps, as dire wolves passed the wolf strain became more lupine. But whatever their state of grace was, dire wolves were here. Dire wolves hunted, brutally or intelligently, among the mirages of the Arctic Plain. Dire wolves ran, ravenously or otherwise, under the crimson auroras of the winter night.

The animals that have inherited the Brooks Range from the camel and lion are all made for the cold. For the last 15,000 years, the Range has had a succession of cold climates. The weather now is comparatively mild. The Range was much colder 9000 years ago—it is likely that the Arctic Ocean was frozen over then. The bears, wolves, foxes, wolverines, lynxes, caribou, moose, musk oxen, beaver, porcupines, ground squirrels, voles, and lemmings that now inhabit the mountains live comfortably within the range of temperatures their various species can handle. The fifty degrees below zero common in present winters is considerably warmer than what their ancestors knew.

The animals of the present fauna must use the short season of warmth well, and they all do so, but their aptitude at this is corollary to their aptitude for frigid temperatures. It is the cold that beats the drum all Brooks Range animals march to.

The arctic animals that have the most difficulty with the cold are those with small bodies. Of these, only snowshoe hares travel about in winter, and at fifty below the hares themselves usually retreat to the caves made by alders when bent into curves by the weight of their snow loads. At fifty or sixty below, a squirrel would not survive more than a few minutes on the surface of the snow; a vole even less. The insulation of the snow is what makes heat retention—and life—possible. The October freeze-up, therefore, in those weeks before much snow has fallen, is a bad time for the small animals that do not hibernate. Tundra voles foraging in October avoid exposure to the heat sink of the darkening sky. When they can they stick to the cover of rocks and hanging vegetation. For the voles, and for all arctic animals in winter, outer space dips closer to Earth. The infinite cold of an impartial firmament sucks the warmth from any body that is not deeply furred or feathered. For tundra voles, a view of the stars—so silent, large, and bright in arctic winter—is a premonition of death.

When a safe thickness of snow has fallen, the voles tunneling beneath it are secure from heat loss to the sky. They still avoid the "snow shadows" cast by spruces, for the snow is thin there and the cold penetrates, but they have begun the pattern of life that will occupy most of their year. Their problems have not ended with deep snow, however. The snow, in keeping the ground temperature just above freezing, allows slow bacterial decay. Decomposing grass and leaves produce carbon dioxide, a heavy gas which, prevented from rising by its weight and the compacted snow above, flows into all the low places in the network of vole tunnels. The gas makes the voles nervous and stimulates intense activity. The voles tunnel ventilator shafts to the surface of their snow drifts, and steam escapes there in tiny clouds. The shafts ease the gas problem, but the frenzied tunneling exacerbates territorial disputes among the voles, who are solitary and antisocial animals. Occasionally a vole is displaced. He runs over the surface of the snow, but never for long, for if he does not find a way back down quickly, he is overtaken by the silent rush of an owl, or the reflexes and the extraordinary hearing of a lynx, or by the cold.

Snow is among the best of natural insulators. The temperatures below the snow surface are in the twenties when the temperature above is forty below, so voles do their winter tunneling in comfort. They tunnel through the summer moss, under logs, among roots, around fragile pillars of depth hoar (the lattice of ice crystals that forms between the underside of the snow cover and the earth). In years when the vole population booms, the network of tunnels grows and every taiga hillside becomes a labyrinth. The voles run about their labyrinthine business on carpets of moss. Their tunnels are pitch black sometimes, as the passages turn inside a log or under it, or within the skull of a caribou; then they open out into high, domed chambers, buttressed by stalactites of depth hoar, and lit by the dimmest blue light from above—moonlight, or the glow of the spring sun returning. The winter silence would bring a security as deep, were it not for the monsters that sometimes course along the tunnels on the scent of voles—weasels and ermine—sinewy, quick, and to a vole unbelievably huge.

The great booms in the populations of lemmings, voles,

and hares—cyclical booms that are peculiar to simplified arctic ecosystems—begin to build under the winter snow. For the hares the pressure of their own numbers triggers something. A heavy snowfall sets the hares to bounding—whole hillsides of drifted snow suddenly animated. The hares jump to reestablish their network of trails, but recklessly, without the caution that marks their normal lives. They leap in a hollow exuberance of overpopulation, and become easy prey for fox, lynx, or owl. The populations of predators grow spectacularly after boom years, to crash when the rodent population crashes. In the Arctic, lack of diversity makes for instability and uncertainty: winter for the predators is a time of plenty or privation.

The white and silent smoothness of drifted hills and plains belies, then, the exigent and uncertain life below. If all the voles in a given spruce copse are happy, then some weasel is not. The only animals truly serene are those that hibernate, risking everything on how well they can do in the abbreviated seasons of warmth—the vestigial spring, summer, and fall of the Arctic. They sleep in their dens free from pinched stomachs, and from the specter of an unexpected dark shape filling the passageway, glittering eyes, and sudden overpowering smell of weasel.

The resident birds do well in the cold. They watch the last of the geese and ducks fly south, and continue about their business. The grouse, its crop full of spruce buds, prepares for each winter night by diving from a branch into a snow drift, beating its way down several feet, then turning on itself as a dog does in lying down, making a snowcave. The ptarmigan changes to winter white, and forages among the willows. The owl hunts and the raven scavenges.

The cold has least terror for animals of bulk. The moose browses in temperatures that turn him gray—the cold so profound that each of his long guard-hairs is tipped by frost. The squeak of his footfall in the snow carries for great distances at such temperatures, and his exhaled breath freezes. But the cold establishes its authority in one way or another, even with the larger animals. Moose are vulnerable to attack by wolves only in the cold season, when hampered by deep snow, and Dall sheep are forced down from the safety of high elevations by their winter search for food. In the foothills the sheep must be vigilant for wolves, and their winter forage is less nutritious. The unseasonal snows that sometimes cover their food are survived only by the most vigorous sheep. For Dall sheep the cold season is the test.

The same exacting cold shapes the caribou. No animal, except perhaps for the musk ox of the barren islands to the northeast, is born in more bitter circumstances. The wind of the North Slope calving grounds often bowls a caribou fawn over before it takes its first step. But the fawn rises, and stands on hoofs that splay widely to support him on tussocks or snow. (When the caribou has grown the outline of his hoof will be larger than that of a man's hand with the fingers extended.) The hoofs are good paddles for swimming and good snow shovels for uncovering lichen. Shoveling, the caribou strikes out with his foreleg and hoof in a smooth, very fast, circular motion, and in a few moments exposes enough ground for a bite or two, then steps ahead to shovel again.

Like other herd animals, caribou are under strong pressures to conform. An independent intelligence is not something that shines out in them. Their faces are, in truth, a little stupid. It may be that a certain racial resignation is necessary in animals at the base of a food chain in their country, on whom so many others depend. But caribou run beautifully in concert. There is a flawless coordination among the animals of the racing herd, each caribou holding his position perfectly. No animal in the Arctic is faster. Rhythm and speed serve the species better than any tendency toward individual genius.

The two great caribou herds of the Brooks Range winter in the low taiga forests south of the mountains, protected by the Arctic Divide from polar winds and blizzards, but even in that calmer climate, from habit or for security, they seek out frozen lakes and other open places. (Caribou have good noses, but very poor vision, especially for motionless objects, and a comfortable margin of white around allows them some forewarning of enemies.) So, even in country where it might be otherwise, the caribou remains a creature of barren, windswept places.

Like the caribou with whom they are so intimately related, arctic wolves are cold-weather creatures. They too seek open spaces, preferring frozen lakes to spruce forest. They are made for the cold, with large feet to support them on snow, and thick winter fur that stays nearly frost free. If in following the caribou herd a wolf is caught in the open by a blizzard, he simply curls his tail around his nose for warmth and sleeps through the storm, digging himself out in the morning.

Wolves hunt Dall sheep, hares, squirrels, and even moose when the conditions are right, but the wolf's meat is caribou.

The arctic wolf is the choreographer of the flight of the caribou herd. Wolves have an eye for the coordination among the fleeing animals, and they insist on its perfection. The wolf's most common strategy in the midst of a caribou migration is to start random groups of caribou galloping, to see how they run. At three-quarters speed the wolf chases first one group, then another, running at them as indifferently as a fisherman before his strike. Only when one caribou starts slowly or lags behind does the wolf's intention crystallize. Any healthy caribou, even a fawn a week old, can outrun a wolf, so the wolf does not waste time with them. He watches for deviation, and seeing it, instantly becomes a hunter. Wolves are the enforcers. If the middling sameness of the caribou spirit is awful, then wolves are terrible. Wolves are the winnowers of the herd. They ask of the caribou, "Give us your lame and your weary."

The caribou in turn asks of the injured or failing wolf, "Try and catch me." For if the cold is the primary shaper of arctic forms, then next important for wolves and caribou is each other. The Robinson Jeffers question, "What but the wolf's tooth whittled so fine/ the fleet limbs of the antelope?" could have been asked the other way, had the cadence been better: "What but the fleet limbs of the antelope sharpened so fine/ the teeth of the wolf?"

As the Brooks Range cold increases, animal after animal drops from sight. Extreme cold is the great separator; first the arctic hare seeks shelter beneath bent alders, then the fox seeks his den. Finally, when the temperature snaps to

seventy-five below, as it does only in interior regions where the taiga is cut off by mountains from the moderating effects of the sea, there are only two animals about. One is the lynx. His poor sense of smell is not a liability now, for at seventy-five below his prey gives off no molecular emanations, and the air carries no clues. Smell has no bearing. Sound travels well in the winter silence, however, and the extraordinary ears of the lynx come into play. The lynx makes his rounds while his competition waits out the cold. He thinks of hares. The arctic hare is to the lynx what the caribou is to the wolf; the huge lynx feet are made to pursue the hare through drifted snow, and the lynx instincts and reflexes are tuned to cutting inside the long bounds of the hare's escape flight; so now in the deepest cold the lynx listens for hares.

The other animal still afield is the raven. For a race of later immigrants to the Arctic, the Eskimos, Raven was often the creator in origin myths. It is not hard to guess why the raven became Raven. Big and raucous among bare branches, and black against the white snow, the raven in coldest weather is visible where the lynx is not. He is the single living thing moving on a lifeless landscape. Inexplicably immune to the cold, he seems not to belong, a being from somewhere else. A loud antibird ingenious enough to cross over from a contiguous anti-universe. The raven roams about in temperatures at which steel becomes brittle and human lungs frost themselves when they draw too deeply. He is not arctic white, like the hare huddling now beneath the alders, nor deeply piled with fur, like the grizzly hibernating in its den, but he is outdoors. If any creature is an embodiment of the Arctic, it is, unfortunately and unlikely as it may seem, the raven.

Sometimes the caribou migration in June is so enormous that, according to what the people say, the animals are three days in passing a village; the whole country is alive, and one can see neither the beginning of them nor the end—the whole earth seems to be moving.

—KNUD RASMUSSEN

From our vantage point all of this achromatic world lay somberly below us as we waited for the coming of the deer. We had not long to wait. Franz caught my arm and pointed to the convoluted slopes of the distant southern hills, and I could just discern a line of motion. It seemed to me that the slopes were sliding gently downward to the bay, as if the innumerable boulders that protruded from the hills had suddenly been set adrift to roll, in slow motion, down upon the ice. I watched intently, not certain whether the sun's glare had begun to affect my eyes so that they played fool tricks on me. Then the slow avalanches reached the far shore and debouched over the bay. I tried to count the little dots. Ten, fifty, a hundred, three hundred—and I gave up. In broken twisted lines, in bunched and beaded ropes, the deer streamed out onto the ice until they were moving north across a front of several miles.

From that distance they barely seemed to move, and yet in a few minutes they had reached the center of the bay and had begun to take on shape. I had binoculars, but in my preoccupation with the spectacle below I had not thought to use them. Now I lifted the glasses to my eyes. The long skeins dissolved at once into endless rows of deer, each following upon the footsteps of the animals ahead. Here and there along the lines a yearling kept its place beside a mother who was swollen with the new fawn she carried. There were no bucks. All these animals were does, all pregnant, all driving inexorably towards the north and the flat plains where they would soon give birth.

The leaders reached our shore and began the ascent, but across the bay the avalanche continued and grew heavier. The surface of the bay, for six miles east and west, had become one undulating mass of animals, and still they came. . . .

The herds were swelling past our lookout now. Ten paces from us, five, then we were forced to stand and wave our arms to avoid being trampled on. The does gazed briefly and incuriously at us, swung a few feet away and passed on to the north without altering their gait.

Hours passed like minutes. The flow continued at an unbroken level until the sun stood poised on the horizon's rim. And I became slowly conscious of a great apathy. Life, my life and that of Franz, of all living things I knew, seemed to have become meaningless. For here was life on such a scale that it was beyond all comprehension.

—FARLEY MOWAT

It was a spectacle like none other left on Earth now. It had power over the spirit. The power lay not only in what you saw—this slender column driving onward into wilderness. It lay also in what you knew. Arctic night and hunger coming. In-gathering far away somewhere of individuals into this traveling column, driven by the great seasons. Knowledge of danger and darkness and fear, built into their tissues by the centuries. Life and the cold Arctic before you for a moment in one silent sweep of land and moving animals.

· · ·

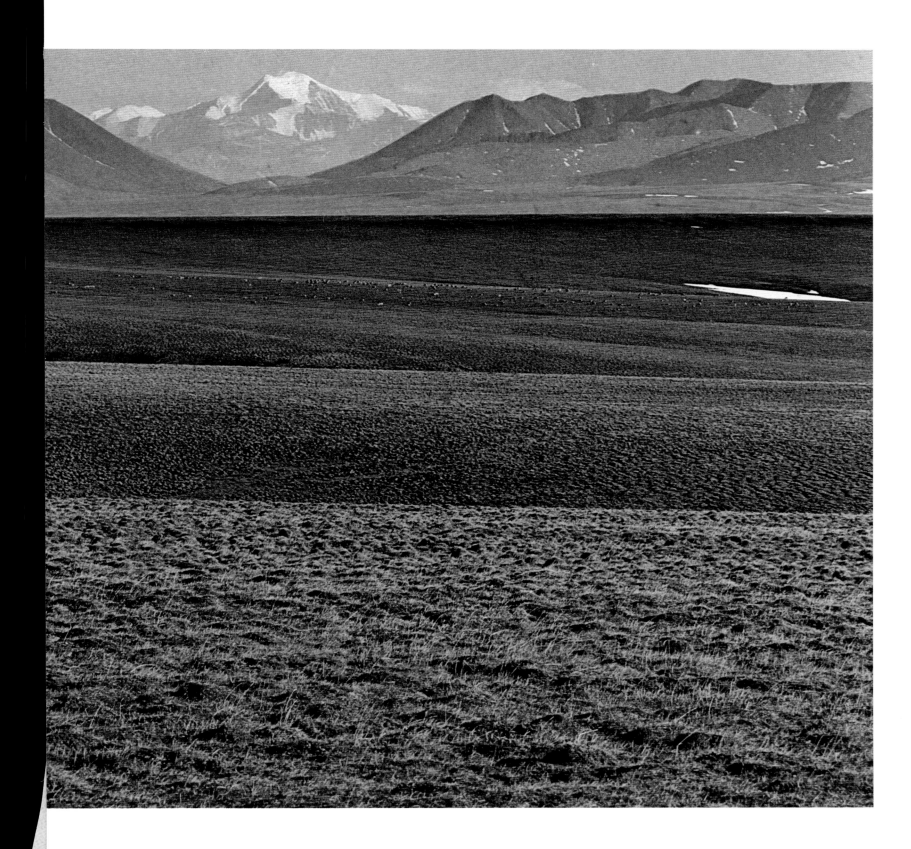

The bulls were coming not en masse but in waves, a few to a hundred or so in each wave. They crested on the long low skyline to the east, passed camp, crested again to the west. On the skylines they looked, as Cris said, like a row of cairns.

There was an odd effect between waves, an effect that was the epitome of wilderness, where there is no past and no future, nothing but what is before your eyes. The effect now was deadness. The land looked dead, forlorn and utterly deserted. My heart sank when Cris took his camera and went eastward to find a rock where he could shoot down through the heat waves—even snow in a crotch of rock looked like a rushing torrent because of heat waves. I thought of the slender thread he traced on foot, and of the vastness, illimitable, empty. How could he hope to find the caribou?

Then the next time I looked, there would be that choppiness on the eastern horizon again, another wave coming. But always the unknowing: some wave had to be the last.

. . .

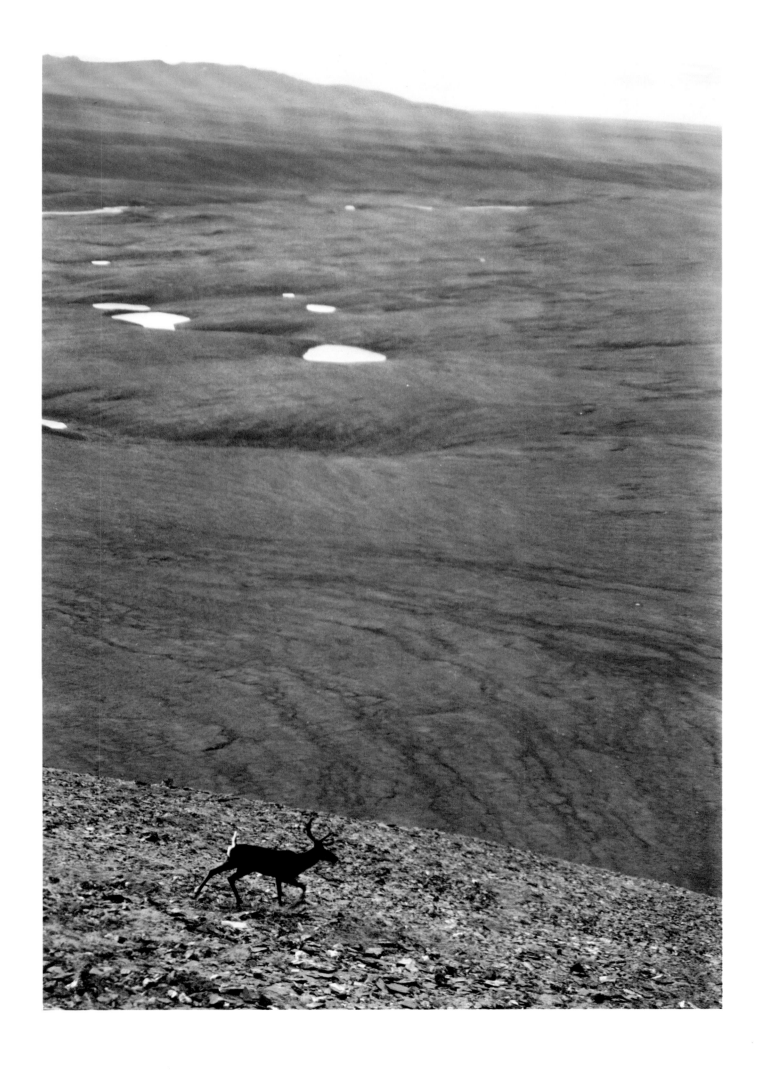

From the other side of my knoll came the crush-crush of hoofs on frozen grass, the deep, reedy, quiet "Mah!" of a fawn—a pleasing sound, like part of the wind and the tundra. Around the knoll came the living, suède-soft gray bodies, personal, beautiful, each coated a little differently. An alert fawn prancing after its mother suddenly dived at her for milk. Two bulls had dazzling white antlers, dipped in water, then frozen. Others, cows too, had blood-red antlers. Some had tatters of velvet flying in the wind, blowing ahead of them, for the caribou were coming with the wind. . . .

Each caribou had its individual problems. None could help another. Each must solve its own problem or perish. A cow favored a leg. A big bull, almost white, held his mouth open panting; he closed it and went on. A big heavy bull walked at one side of the column. A cow drew to the side; her calf nursed. The bulls, the cows, the calves passed her. She pulled herself away from her calf and at once was trotting. The calf paused an instant shaking its head, then was trotting too. A big bull trotted past the trotting calf—two speeds. He was a mole-colored bull with silvery belly stripe and snowy underhang or dewlap of fur; his antlers were high. He was limber power itself. His body flowed along. One sensed the reserve and depth of strength, the lightness and pleasure in control and in working far inside his strength.

. . .

The fawn got itself somehow down the steep bank and onto the lake. It crossed the flat whiteness, now hurrying, now seeming very tired and standing still. But it drove itself on. I thought it would lose the migration direction. But on the far side of the lake it turned southeast-ward again. A dot of life struggling onward in the white vastness, toiling alone up toward the pass, trying to catch up.

—Lois Crisler

WILBUR MILLS: *Newborn fawn, Camden Bay*

Aichilik

Early one afternoon we left the Sheenjek Valley and turned up a tributary valley. According to our map the new valley would lead to an even smaller canyon, that would lead to a pass, that would take us over the Arctic Divide. We followed the tributary stream for a mile, until it dropped into a gorge and we were forced to climb above it. From our height above the stream we had a last look back at the Sheenjek, running far below us. Ahead of us were far turns of the tributary valley, unexplored, as far as we knew. On either side were the small mountains, symmetrical and covered with fine talus, two thousand feet from base to summit, that contained the valley. It was high, bare moorland that reminded Steve of Scotland. We were a thousand feet above the new stream, at a point opposite the middle elevations of the facing mountain. We were on a level with the mountain's center of mass and it seemed at arm's length from us, in friendly proximity.

I would have said, if I did not know better, that when we reached a certain altitude the mountain began talking to us. It is the same sort of thing that happens when, in planning a photograph or painting, you frame the subject in a certain way and the composition clicks at you as it jumps into inevitability. Mountains don't talk, of course, as Coleridge knew, and he called this sort of notion pathetic fallacy. I have an intuition, though, that if Coleridge had walked alone for two weeks through the Brooks Range, or any other wild mountains, he would have discovered the fallacy in pathetic fallacy. We now had been walking long enough ourselves that the mountains had begun stirring, in a motionless way.

We camped at the head of the valley, beneath our pass. The sky cleared and we had an evening of alpenglow on the peaks to the north. The midnight sun was no longer in effect. The nights were getting darker—too dark now to read comfortably at night—and we slept well.

When Steve and I woke the next morning, it was as bright as daylight inside our white tent. There was a ground squirrel outside on the sunny side of the tent, scratching at the canvas. His shadow was projected on the dazzling tent wall beside my head, and I could see his every detail, even whiskers. I banged him through the tent, and he scurried off. The tent wall was now blank. I poked my head outside. The skies were cloudless and the morning was not so cool as the previous mornings. The sun stood above the horizon in a saddle between two peaks, and was blinding. Waking was an event in the mountains.

We rose and ate, and decided to take our first day of rest after five days of walking. It was to be our last day in the known country south of the Arctic Divide. Each of us set off in his own direction. I walked toward the jumbled moraine that filled the head of the valley, planning to climb from there to the glacier, just visible from our tent door, that occupied part of a cirque high above camp. It was good to be alone and without a pack. My feet felt very light, and unencumbered by my pack I was able to enjoy the tundra detail underfoot. There were arctic poppies and lupine, red moss and green moss, and the mixed grasses and sedges of the highland tussocks. There was an occasional red mushroom of a sort I had not noticed before when laboring under the weight of the pack. I walked along the moraine ridge with the bare, rocky walls of the narrowing valley on either side of me. There were nearly continuous rockfalls on the steep walls. I squinted but could not discern the Dall sheep that must have been making them. At the end of the moraine, in a depression in the jumbled rock, lay a green tarn, just large enough for the wind to start miniature waves on its surface and a small lapping sound. From the tarn I crossed and began climbing the chute that led to the glacier.

The main stream from the glacier ran down the center of the chute, too fast to be beautiful. It tasted of glacial milk. I stayed away from it, climbing the drier rocks to the side. I heard small trickles running everywhere beneath the rocks, with the bass sound that all water has, no matter how thinly flowing, when it runs under talus. Rarely, a creek would surface and run for a few feet over the moss before going down again. The water in the small creeks was good and I drank at every one.

I left the chute for the terminal moraine above it, climbed over the moraine and onto the glacier. I was on a small, steep field separated from the main glacier field by a crumbling comb of rock that crowned the slope of ice above me and marked the Arctic Divide. I carefully skirted the main crevasse in the center of the field. Walking less carefully on the far side of the field I fell into another crevasse. I went to my armpits in the snow that had hidden the fissure. My feet dangled free, over an abyss of unknown dimensions. My rifle lay on the snow inches from my face. I saw the beads of snow water on the blue steel. I was

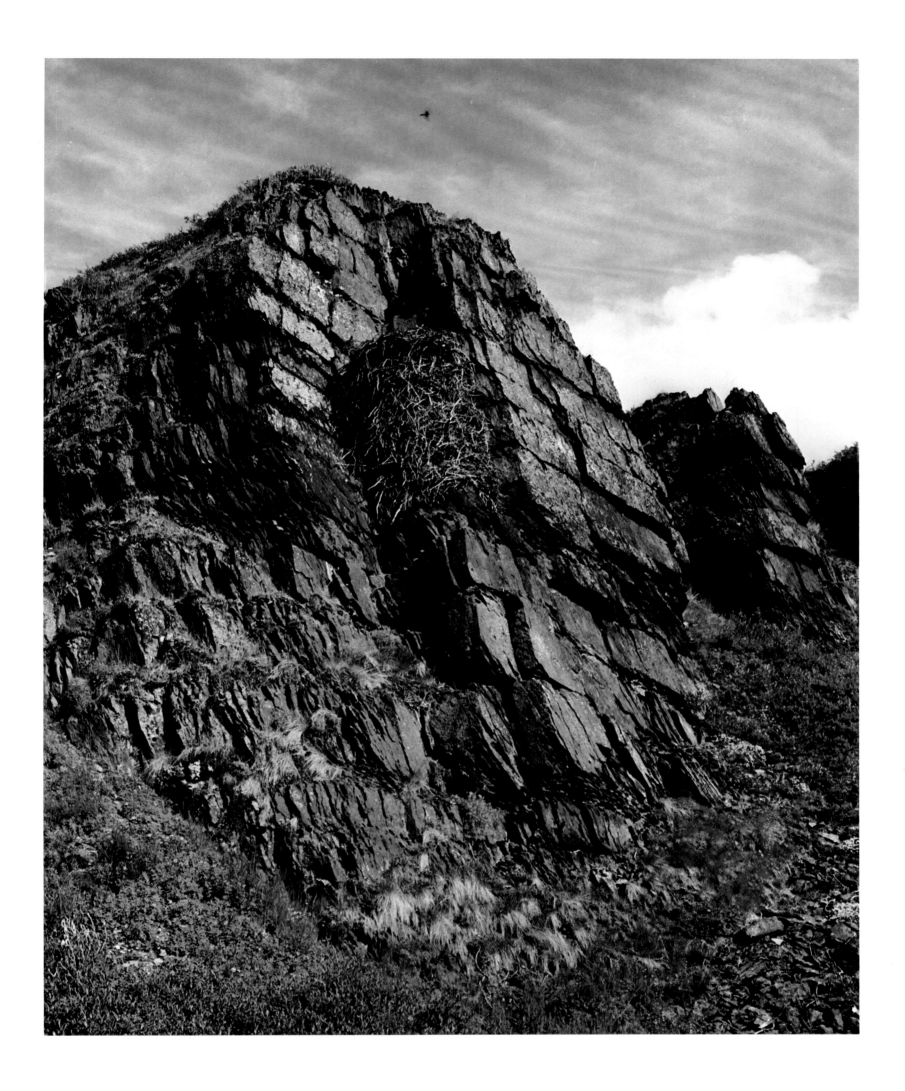

careful not to move. I guessed that the crevasse was a small one, but I was not at all sure. I thought sadly of loved ones. I imagined my body coursing along through dark subglacial tunnels. I imagined it banging around subglacial corners, in an icy stream, lodging somewhere never to be recovered. Then I waved my foot gently about, and found that I was in a small crevasse after all, two feet wide at the surface and narrowing rapidly—easy to chimney out of had I fallen entirely in. I maneuvered myself flat on the snow and worked my way to my feet. I was embarrassed at my carelessness and I decided not to tell anyone about it.

I climbed the ridge and looked down for the first time at the main field of the glacier. It was a great hanging glacier and it drained north to the Beaufort Sea. The smaller field that I had imaginarily died in and become a feature of, now at my back, drained south to the Yukon. I fired four joy shots, feeling each time the sharp kick of the rifle and watching the noise, like thunder, peal around the circle of mountain faces below me. Then I descended the ridge and dropped into a southward-running valley that would lead back to camp. I slalomed down the gravel-dune shoulders of the decomposing mountains, floating quickly down below the level of the glacier that had scared me earlier, stopping only to empty my boots of gravel.

By now the day was longer than I had wanted it. It was one of those days too long to remember what happened at the beginning of. I remembered the tarn, and the bass trickling of the water under the talus, a syncopated, hypnotizing rhythm from under the rocks that seemed paced by an intelligence. I remembered certain patterns of lichen. On the way home I saw a set of ram's horns, one horn imbedded upright in the moss and filled with rainwater like a flagon, and I would remember that. But other details were going, and have now gone. As far as I know, much of that day's high country no longer has existence in any human consciousness. I entered our valley at a point several miles below camp. I smelled the smoke from our small fire long before I saw our tents. The trace of willow smoke was strong in the odor void of the valley. When I finally saw the tents they were distant specks in the immensity of the valley, inconsequential in it, although for this country the valley was a fairly small one. I rejoined my friends, we went to sleep, and that was how our last day on the south slope of the Brooks Range ended.

As we climbed slowly toward the pass the next day, I began to chafe at the pace. I had been the strongest walker, and the frequent rests and curtailment of my pace was tiring me. I sat on a rock and waited for John and Steve to get far ahead, then took off after them. I let my legs out

and did not rest until the top. My lungs were working like engines and I had to tie a bandana around my head to keep the sweat out of my eyes, but I felt less tired at the top than when I began. I had passed the others and left them far behind. I thought of myself as the young man from Madras. "There was a young man from Madras/Whose balls were made out of brass/In stormy weather/They'd knock together/And lightning shot out of his ass."

From the saddle above the tributary valley we had a last look at the south slope of the Brooks Range. It was a vast country of rolling arctic moors and mild bare mountains, dappled by sunlight through cloud, and it seemed to slope away forever.

Then, as we reached the narrow canyon that led to our pass and prepared to camp, the cold set in. The weather change was sudden. Our hands were too cold to work efficiently in untieing knots and setting up camp. The forty-nine-cent gloves we had bought in Fairbanks were poor protection. I no longer felt like the young man from Madras. A cold fog was streaming out of the canyon, the very canyon we had chosen to ascend and none of the others, pouring down from the Divide as from a leak in a dam. We worried for the first time about the weather we might find beyond the Divide, where no last buffering range of mountains obstructed the winds blowing down from the Pole. We were higher now than the last willows, and lacking willow branches for fuel, we cooked inside the tent on the Svea stove.

The next afternoon we climbed the pass and stood on the Arctic Divide, looking northward. The northern slopes, of which we saw snatches through the mist, were more precipitous than the southern slopes we knew. The new country was broken up, scarred, and hard to read. John and Steve called the terrain below us Mordor Valley, after a fabulous country in a book by Tolkien. The two agreed that it was exactly as they had imagined Mordor. It struck me as remarkable that they both should think so. I had not read Tolkien but I knew he was British. Perhaps, I thought, the Scottish highlands had been the wildest land Tolkien had known, and had served him as the peneplain on which he carved his imaginary relief. These arctic mountains were just exaggerated Scotland I knew, for I had now walked in both terrains. Perhaps Tolkien's flight of imagination had been a controlled flight, with the low mountains of Scotland as model and matrix. Perhaps it was this that allowed John and Steve to find the same metaphor. I wondered if Tolkien knew about the Brooks Range. Would coming here now be redundant for him?

We began to drop down to the headwaters of the Aichilik River, the drainage of which we had now crossed into,

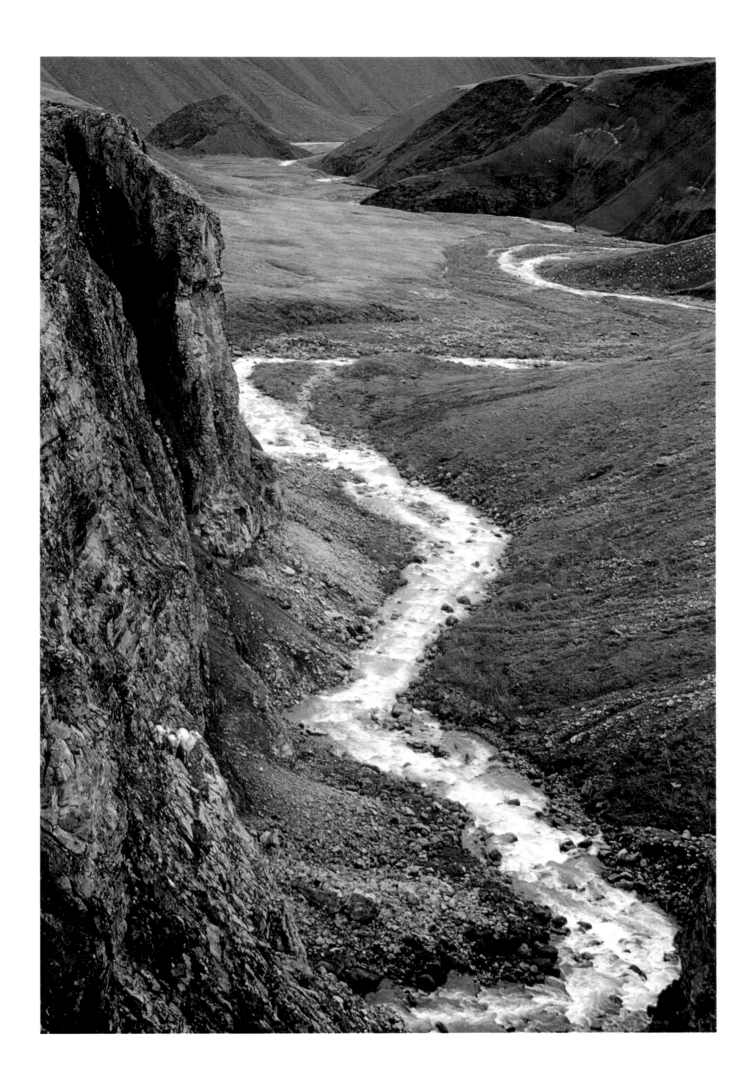

but the going was difficult. The slopes were composed of small, loose talus and they looked too steep for men with packs. We followed narrow game trails and made precarious progress. From time to time one of us, along with the patch of slope he stood on, would slide several feet downhill. We contoured the slopes as the sheep and caribou had, trusting their judgment.

A cold wind was blowing from the north. When I wasn't using my hands to steady myself, I walked with arms folded across my chest to keep them warm. Small flakes of snow began to fall. The cold was demoralizing. Hours passed and we seemed destined to spend our lives contouring an unending precipitousness.

It was strange, the state of mind a day of cold and exposed climbing brought. Yesterday I had thought I was into the rhythm of the mountains. All dreams of home and comfort had left me then, and I suspected they had gone for good. But today, as the going got steeper and colder, my mind wandered away. I began by wondering if I would ever get out alive. This was a mild wonder, not nearly as serious as the kind of speculating I had done as a small boy in the mountains. I knew from experience that I would not die, so instead I began to wish that I could get out soon. My mind left the mountains. I imagined my return home, imagined myself in my girl's arms again, and the better apartment I would get, and all the food I would buy. I thought about all the work I would do when I got back—the novel I had to finish, or begin, actually—and I planned how I would arrange my time to do all the things I wanted to do. I thought about the basketball I would play, the weights I would lift, the biceps I would grow. I would spend more time with loved ones. I would take better advantage of the urban life, the galleries, nightclubs, conversations, slums, libraries. It would be a more gentlemanly life. I would do a more professional job on the manuscripts I edited, getting them really right. But at the same time I would use California better—explore more of the Sierra and the Big Sur coast, and get up to the redwoods more often. I would move to San Francisco. Why was I living in Oakland, anyway, when one of the world's great cities was just across the bay? I imagined my San Francisco apartment. It would be several Victorian rooms with high ceilings, and as I walked along I painted and decorated it in my head, designing it around my grandmother's high brass bed, which I would resurrect from my father's garage.

The snow began coming down harder. We worked our way down to the stream—one of the headwaters of the Aichilik—and walked along it until we found a spot flat enough to pitch our tents. It snowed steadily and things

were getting a white look. If this was the way things would be, we decided, from here to the Arctic coast, then the next weeks would be bitter.

The next morning it was still snowing lightly, but enough sun shone through to have melted most of the night's snowfall. As in past cold mornings, we lay in our sleeping bags for hours after waking, fitfully drowsing and dreaming. I had done this wakeful dreaming earlier, but now, beyond the Divide, the dreaming would begin to dominate my days and for the first time I made a note of it in my journal. More asleep than awake that morning I dreamed about the apartment house I had left behind in Oakland. The house, built in 1894 and now a facade of chipped paint and eroded, turn-of-the-century ornament, is owned by the Temescal Rug Company, which maintains an office on the street level. The second floor of the main building is connected by a flimsy wooden bridge to a windowless, barnlike annex that was once a gym ("Athletic Club" in large letters, painted over once, is now visible again through the paint, which has faded). Max Baer may have trained there, for all I know, in the days when Oakland was a fight town. The lofty room that held the ring is now used for cleaning rugs. My apartment was at the end of the wooden bridge, in what probably once were the gym offices but have been remodeled to hold a shower and a stove. I dreamed that in coming home I startled a walrus (arctic images appeared often in my Oakland dreams) on the back stairs and it ran ponderously across the bridge toward my door. His way was blocked by a large black dog that belonged to my neighbor, Bob. The walrus tried chesting his way around Bob's dog, but the dog sat on his haunches and refused to move. The walrus opened his mouth, and the mouth became as large as a hippopotamus's mouth, and it closed in slow motion, crushingly, on the dog's head. The dog made no effort to get away. When the walrus opened his mouth again, the dog's body fell over like a sack. Bob, my neighbor, his face expressionless, as his personal, Staggerlee sense of pride told him it should be, approached the walrus that had killed his dog, not wanting to fight, but compelled by the sense of pride. He leaned against the walrus's neck, straining to push it back. Inevitably the mouth opened again and closed in slow motion on Bob's head. Bob made no effort to escape. His sister was standing beside me, and I caught her as her knees buckled and she started to faint.

"I got to get you upstairs to lie down," I said, "and get my 30-30!" (Another arctic image—I had no 30-30 at home, but a borrowed rifle lay beside me in the Brooks Range as I dreamed.) Bob's sister looked at me contemptuously. "Bob's got enough trouble on his hands," she said.

When I was fully awake that morning I tried to read, but after a few pages my interest lagged and I set the book down. I made up stories of my own with the book closed before me. The best of the stories were those meant for Chris and Gina, the little girls who lived next door in Oakland.

In one story Chris and Gina become fabulously wealthy following their discovery of treasure near the Temescal Rug Company in a vacant lot where the buildings have been razed for the freeway. (I would work out the details of the discovery when I got home.) The girls buy their daddy an El Dorado and their mother a fine house. They are rich girls now, but still the same girls at heart. Window shopping one day, they enter a musty old store. They buy a book from the musty and mysterious old proprietor, and inside the book is a map. The girls decide to leave their new-found wealth for the adventure of following the map. They depart. To a certain point the map is true to the terrain, but then the two topographies fail to correspond and the girls, crossing a pass, find themselves in a strange country.

I lay in the tent, planning and dreaming, until I got sick of it. Earlier, I had passed time capturing mosquitos from the roof of the tent, looking especially for those that had stolen some of my blood, and then flattening them between the pages of my journal. It would give the journal verisimilitude, I thought, and make it interesting for my grandchildren to discover in the attic. Now the mosquitos were gone. There was nothing to do but think. When I reached the point at which the anticipated cold outside balanced, and then became less disagreeable than, the surfeit of revery inside, I got up. I put six shells in the rifle and six in my pocket, and in a light snowfall started down the Aichilik Valley. For some reason I was not compelled, as usual, to round every turn in the canyon and see what was beyond every corner. I found I liked traveling at leisure. I appreciated the things you miss when pushing fast through the country. I stopped for long periods and let the country sink in. Sitting high on a hillside I looked down the valley and saw the subtle greens and yellows of arctic summer, the colors subdued by the powdering of snow. There was some red, too, for the abbreviated arctic summer had almost ended and an abbreviated arctic autumn was about to begin. As I watched, sleet materialized out of the red and green of the far hillsides and blew at me. It seemed to originate in the far slope and not in the cloud above. My poncho kept me dry and fairly warm, and I sat on the hillside as still as a stone. The sleet that did not strike me blew on past and up the valley. I was not thinking much. I ate half a meat bar, then moved around to the other side of the hill, where I ate the other half, in an uncomplicated sort of ritual. My mind was working, but not so feverishly as it had in the tent. I was no longer thinking fondly of people or of home as I had before. I guessed that was a stage I had completed. I was thinking more abstractly. Sitting on the tundra hillside, I worked out an idea that pleased me. It was a modification of the geography of hope idea evolved by Aldo Leopold and other wilderness writers. For Leopold, the best part of a map was its blank spaces; they were an unknown geography that he might hope to set foot in one day, and they were valuable to him as such. As the sleet blew past, I proposed to myself a corollary concept—the geography of distaste. The Brooks Range, in this weather at least, was a geography that the average man would hope never to set foot in, a severity that he would want no part of. It was valuable as such. Its existence made San Francisco or Boston cozier, in the same way that you feel cozy under a good roof with the rain beating on the pane.

The snow began falling more thickly, and the ceiling of cloud that had obscured the tops of the valley walls lowered. The wind came up, suddenly much louder. The howling seemed to have no effect on the speed of the falling snow, and that made me uneasy. From the sound of it, a real storm was coming from the north, its approach masked by this mild one. I headed back to camp, stopping now and then to sit still and watch things. No storm came. Stopping and watching, I found I was seeing the country without emotion. That was a relief after all the tent-generated activity of my imagination. I made a game of it. With no effort I made my mind perfectly blank. I watched the country as if I had been there forever or never there at all. The snow was falling softly and thickly and the whiteness had closed in, reducing the world to very little. I felt no more sentient than a stone.

When I rose, however, no lichen had grown on me. I suppose I had been more sentient than I thought. I had imagined that I had rested my imagination, but when I stood up from it I felt stranger than before.

Shortly after the snow cloud engulfed me, sitting to the north almost as still as a stone, the cloud closed in on John, who unknown to me was walking south up one of the Aichilik's headwater gorges. As he walked in the closeness of the cloud, he had the persistent feeling that he was being watched. It was the kind of intuition that yetis are made of. He turned from time to time to look, but saw nothing. Once he thought he heard something beyond the curtain of the cloud dislodge some talus, but otherwise his walk was soundless. Deciding to turn back, he sat on a stone and looked back the way he had come. The mist thinned somewhat, and above the line of his tracks, on the opposite side of the stream from them, he saw a neat set of tracks paralleling his own. A bear or sheep, he decided, or a curious wolf.

Steve and John were daydreaming too. In the kind of dreaming predictable on a trip like ours—dreams of home and plans for our return there—the three of us were very much alike. Steve planned the South American trip he wanted to take after the Brooks Range, and he thought about Australia, the country he felt most at home in. He pondered going back to Vietnam, to the north this time, where he would photograph the other side of the Vietnamese story. John thought about getting his doctorate, about his work, about getting married. He promised himself that when he got back he would budget better and invest more. He would get a new apartment. He could not sleep for thinking about it all. His sleeplessness disturbed him a little. Was it, he debated with himself, a result of leaks in his tent and the permeating dampness, or was the fault in himself? Was his imagination like a battery, charging with anticipation during the day and discharging in the calm of night?

This kind of homesick dream is common enough, after all. Traveling salesmen must have them in hotel rooms. Dreams in the mountains are probably a little stronger and better, however. Revery has an intensity in the mountains. It can have the pure emotion of a sleeping dream, whether through some effect of the thinness of the air, or because in the absence of a certain kind of stimulation the mind turns inward with a special force. Once, as a small boy in the Sierra Nevada, I dreamed for days about getting a chihuahua. The chihuahua was advertised in the comic book I had, which told you on the back page how to send in for one. You could actually carry it around in your pocket. And another time a roll of wire mesh discarded at Cascade Pass started me planning a cage for guinea pigs. The cage began simply but became a palace of mesh as the days of walking passed.

But the three of us were embarking on another dream also, I think. It was an older dream, the kind of dream at the quick of the native religion of this country. It was the Tundra Dream, for want of a better name, though tundra is surely only one of the terrains it can happen on, and though "dream" may be the wrong word. For me, the wolf fantasy on the Sheenjek was the beginning of it. I don't know when it began for the others, but in John's journal, in an entry made as we were nearing the Divide, is evidence that it did begin.

"While walking in the grassy, nearly hummock-free upper valley, I was followed constantly by a shrill piping squeak or whistle coming from the grass. The sounds had a strange effect—it was almost impossible to locate their origin with any precision. Usually they came from in front or behind, beyond that I could not tell. After several miles of nearly continuous vocal accompaniment, I surmised there was not just one swift and invisible beast but many small ones hidden in the grass."

John, the scientist, went on to identify the cause of the noise, "a small vole (Alaska singing vole, *Microtus miurus*)? dashing from one small tussock where he'd just tuned up to another hiding spot." But what is more interesting I think, and what gives John away, is the swift and invisible beast. I'm glad that John heard his step too, and felt his presence. The swift and invisible beast was animating everything around us. He was more than just a metaphor that jumped accidentally to John's mind. The Arctic was making shamans of us. The mountains were no longer just talking to us occasionally, but all the time.

Our days in the upper Aichilik were harsh. As we walked into the wind, the cold and sleet abused our northern exposures. Our beards gathered snow and our faces were red with cold. Cradling the rifle, I walked with my hands in my armpits to keep them warm. My nose was running—just an annoyance, for in the germ void of the Arctic it was hard to catch a cold. After a while I no longer bothered to wipe, but, I'm embarrassed to say, just licked. At the beginning of the day the walking was fine. You felt tough to be out in spite of the elements. You were the young man from Madras. But then the cold began to work. Toward the end of the day, after crossing and recrossing the stream, the leather uppers of our shoepacs had lost their impermeability and our feet were wet and cold. When we stopped to make camp, our faces were too numb to talk right, and our fingers so cold that we could untie knots only slowly, with intense concentration.

Each day as the cold began to win over us, the dreams returned. I thought a lot about food. Our Brooks Range meals had been scanty and repetitious, and I made up for them in my imagination as I walked. In my sleep one night I dreamed I was in a huge South American dining hall, running from table to table and, as surreptitiously as I could, stealing and eating desserts of all kinds. The Latin cooks and waitresses noticed me from time to time, and admonished me in a way that was unpredictably friendly or serious.

But as we left the upper Aichilik the weather changed for the better. The cold spell had killed the mosquitos.

The sun came out occasionally and we were able to dry our things. The Aichilik Valley opened out and became very beautiful. The peaks of the mountains, simple pyramids patterned with new snow, dropped away in the long, green, treeless planes of the lower slopes and alluvial fans, and these ended in the flat gravel floor of the valley, over which we walked. The floor of the valley was a lithic river of water-worn stone that contained the smaller, liquid river. As we walked northward both Aichiliks, stone and water, became impressive rivers. Each time a large stream joined the Aichilik, the valley widened. Twice, in passing the points of confluence, we looked back to see great triangular mountain fortresses dividing the new stream from the stream we had traveled down. The fortresses had not been remarkable when we passed under them from the south, but their northern exposures were massive and distance gave them symmetry. We could still look up the streams to their origins in the high peaks of the Divide, now solidly white and Himalayan.

BOB WALDROP: Himalaya-like Mountains

We made good time on the cobbled river bars of the widening valley floor. In places the bars grew to become minor deserts of small stone. Walking on the deserts, we were sometimes out of sight of the river. In the expanses of stone there were patches of sand with tracks of bear, wolf, and caribou, the sand smelling strangely of the sea.

When we tired of the cobbles we sometimes climbed above to walk the caribou trails on the tundra slopes. We never strayed far from the lithic river, but followed its tussock banks, and the river was always with us. Walking above the river, I frightened a baby bird. He panicked unwisely, for I was not near the nest, and he fled down the caribou trail. He refused to depart the straightness of the trail, and I was able to run him down without taking off my pack. He was a nondescript baby bird, and to my uneducated eye he could have grown up to be almost anything avian, but he was handsome. I smelled him and tested his warmth against my cheek. He smelled good, the way a young bird should, and he was warm, as I had known he would be. He was an animated spark of the country that we had struck off in our passage. His mother came up tardily and went into her broken-wing act, so I let him go.

On August 11, John made an entry in his journal. He described a covey of ptarmigan we flushed that morning: "When they burst from before our feet in whirring balls of brown and white, I could see the hunter's instinct light in Ken's eyes; he waited about five minutes in silence while we all continued walking down the riverbed—then announced suddenly: 'John, I'm going back to see if I can get one. I'll catch up with you and Steve later.' And he was off, unzipping his weighty 30-30 from its case and striding into the willows. 'But Ken,' Steve yelled, 'you'll only blow it apart if you hit it with that gun.'

"'I'll aim carefully and blow its head off,' Ken yelled back over his shoulder. Then he was gone. He needs some justification, I suppose, for carrying that gun two hundred miles through the wilderness."

They were laughing at me, I realized at the time, and perhaps were a bit annoyed, for we had planned to cross the range without killing anything and so far had been successful. They did not know, because I had not told them, that it was not any need to justify the rifle, or lust for the ptarmigan's life that moved me, or any hunger for the meat. I did not care if I blew the ptarmigan apart. I only wanted the feathers.

I had watched in admiration as the eight ptarmigan stalled at the apex of their short flight and settled into the willows, and I had suddenly seen, in a flash of arctic inspiration, how perfectly ptarmigan feathers would decorate the hood of my parka. The big feathers were reddish brown to match my beard, with white tips for grace, and with meat at the other end to justify killing the bird before whomever it is you feel guilty in shooting animals. Before the last ptarmigan had landed in the willows I was arranging the feathers in my imagination. After walking several miles down the Aichilik, I knew exactly how they would go. The design had simplified itself. It was partly Plains Indian, and a bit Norse perhaps, but mostly my own. The ptarmigan had disappeared, unfortunately. My totem went unevoked, though it troubled my brain for several days, during which I thought of little else. Finally the idea began to go stale. My determination to have the feathers wavered, then departed.

3. INUIT

He was squatting in the darkness.

He was quite alone on earth, when suddenly he became conscious and discovered himself. He had no idea where he was. Nor did he know how he had come there. But he breathed and there was life in him. He lived!

But who was he? A being—something living. More than that he could not comprehend. All about him was dark, and he could see nothing.

Then he groped about with his hands. His fingers brushed over clay wherever he felt. The earth was clay; everything about him was lifeless clay.

He let his fingers glide over himself. He knew nothing of how he looked, but he found his face and felt that he had a nose, eyes, and mouth, arms and legs and limbs. He was a human being—a man!

—APAGKAQ

THE FIRST MEN came to the Brooks Range after its glaciers had receded. They were consummate flintworkers, and are now called the Denbigh flint people. If there were earlier men to sight the Range, a sea folk, perhaps, who saw the cordillera under ice from coastal settlements at the edge of its thawing north slope, then the rising sea has obliterated any record of them. The sea has not risen since the arrival of the Denbigh people, and their artifacts, found only at sites on the North Bering Sea and at certain Brooks Range passes, are the first that we know.

The Denbigh culture had its origins at least 5000 years ago on the Bering Sea, at places like Capes Denbigh and Krusenstern. From there the flint forms and ideas moved northeastward, deeper into the New World, and westward, back into the Old World of Siberia. The Denbigh ideas flourished in those places long after they had died out on the west coast of Alaska.

The Denbigh flintworkers were the first of the race later to be called variously the People of the Shadow, the People of the Twilight, the Polar Eskimos, the Inuit. Their first names for themselves were writ in water—or chiseled in ice—and are forgotten. It is reasonable to guess that whatever the first name was, it meant "The People," as it did for the *Inuit*, the most recent of the Eskimo peoples, and for so many other American tribes. The Denbigh people were hunters competent in the boreal forest, on the arctic plains, and on the sea. Their great talent was in making microblades. The blades are similar to blades found at Neolithic sites in the forests of Siberia and on the Mongolian steppes, but they are finer. Denbigh burin spalls, used by the flintworkers for grooving and splitting antler and ivory, are sometimes as fine as spruce needles, and today bear fossil witness to a great and meticulous skill that was lost to succeeding cultures. The oval foundations of Denbigh houses, still just under the moss at Cape Krusenstern (for arctic moss grows slowly) are much like the foundations of the low skin huts still erected by caribou hunters on Brooks Range passes.

The next people to know the Brooks Range were whalers. The Old Whalers left few bones of caribou or other land animals in their refuse piles. They were seamen who lived almost entirely on seals and whales. The mountains of the Brooks Range and the tundra plains cannot have had much practical meaning for the whalers. They probably visited those regions only occasionally. Perhaps hunters went, weary of the taste of sea mammals and seeking caribou. Religious men may have gone, seeking the mountains. But such pursuits were incidental to their real business—a business of great antiquity in arctic waters. Men have been hunting whales off arctic coasts for four thousand years.

If the Old Whalers were anything like recent Eskimos who pursued whales, the gravity of their enterprise was unparalleled by any other event in their lives. The whale hunt stood at the very center of life, an essential drama, like birth or death. The six paddlers, the single helmsman, and the harpooner prepared themselves at a ceremonial house, avoiding their wives, fasting sometimes, never eating much, and standing continuous watch together by the sea. They were confident in the knowledge that the whale's great desire was to be captured by them, and the knowledge that the women at home were living by strict magical rules that attracted whales. Once on the sea and in pursuit, the crew's method was to race the whale to the place he was expected to surface next. When they saw his great shape rising from below, the paddlers positioned the boat, the harpooner set himself and struck. The harpoon head, piercing the thick skin and penetrating the blubber, detached itself from the wooden spear shaft (which floated and was retrieved later) and turned to form a toggle in the whale's flesh. If the hunters were successful, the whale tired himself pulling the boat and the inflated sealskins that were attached to the line. When the whale was exhausted, the paddlers drew up, singing magic songs. The helmsman beached the boat against the whale's head and the harpooner took up his killing lance, striking the whale again and again in the head. Then the crew secured the whale, and headed back from wherever the whale in his great strength had taken them.

The mountains then, for the Old Whalers who lived near them, were distant abstractions that stood at their backs through the long hungry days in which they watched the sea; then receded behind them, unseen, as chanting they paddled seaward; and finally stood ahead of them as in success or failure they paddled home.

The next people in the Brooks Range lived in large oval houses covered with earth and entered through the skylight. They are now called the Choris people and they had established their new culture a thousand years before Christ. Like all Eskimo peoples, the things they left in largest numbers were blades. They left spears, arrows, adzes, scrapers, knife blades of slate, as well as grooved stones for smoothing shafts, stone hammers for flaking flint, and special stones for sharpening implements of ivory and antler. They left barbed dart heads for sealing like those used by recent Eskimos.

They threw their assortment of weapons at whales and seals, and at caribou and bears too, for they had learned to live on the land again, a talent their predecessors the Old Whalers had forgotten. The first of the Choris people to enter the mountains must have felt like discoverers. There

must have been a great deal of pleasure in finding that they, the Eskimos, were intuitive cartographers; in relearning how to find each other in the midst of great expanses of featureless tundra, a miraculous Inuit ability that had gone rusty in a thousand years of whaling. It all must have made for a heroic era.

> A wonderful occupation
> Hunting caribou!
> But all too rarely we
> Excel at it
> So that we stand
> Like a bright flame
> Over the plain.

The Choris people cooked their meat in small clay pots. They made considerable use of antler for tools, and their needles of bird bone were so fine that only the thinnest sinew strand could pass through the eyes. They were artists, and did their best work in ivory. They practiced scapulimancy—the art of divining by scapulae. The shoulder blades of caribou were engraved and then cracked by fire. The cracks were read and interpreted by shamans.

The Choris people left a puzzle. Among the varied bones uncovered at their campsites are the bones of a very small caribou. It was a caribou smaller than any caribou race known before or since. It stood only as high as a modern reindeer. Could it indeed have been a reindeer? Were the Choris people herdsmen who brought hobbled reindeer across from the Chukchi Peninsula—from Asia— to the New World? Modern Eskimos have made poor

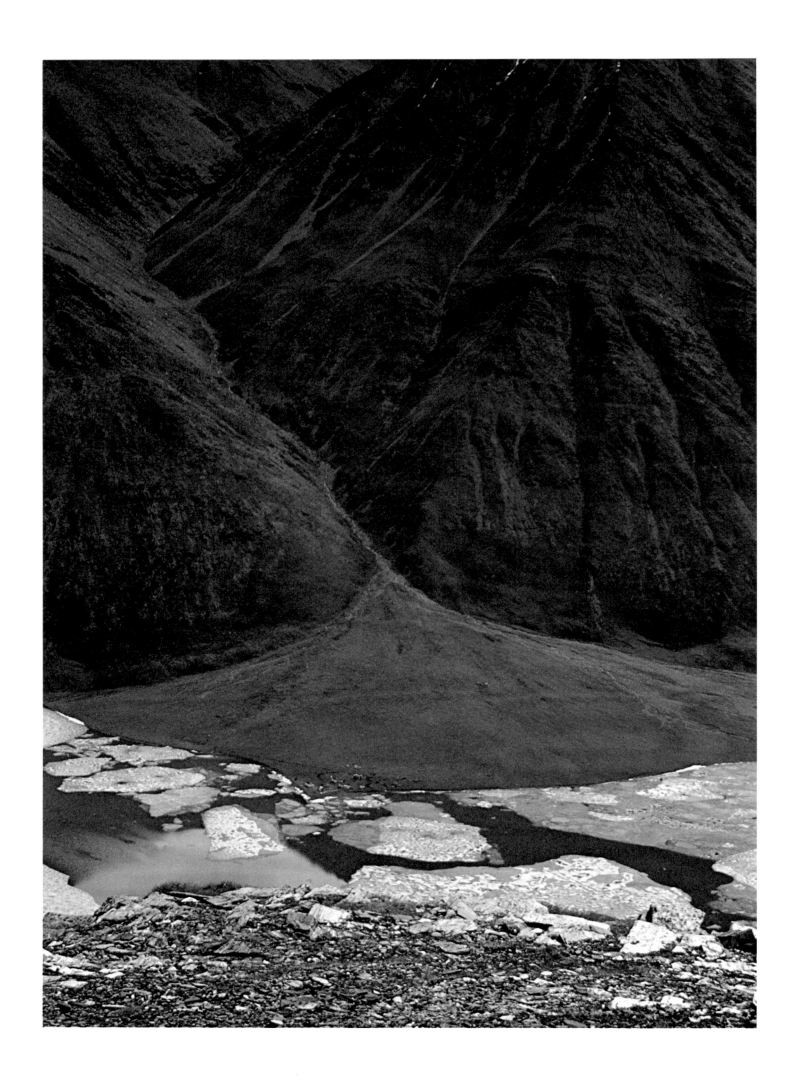

herdsmen, and there was no precedent for such a vocation in earlier cultures, but it may have been. Perhaps herdsmen once sought lost reindeer in Brooks Range valleys. Perhaps the tundra once sounded to a deerherd's calming songs.

The next people, like the Choris people, had much in common with modern Eskimos. They were the Norton people and were at home both on sea and land. They wore labrets, artificial teeth of ivory thrust through slits in the lower lip, of the kind that recent Eskimos often wore. They must have been a frightening people to encounter for the first time.

The next people in the Brooks Range were an aberrant people. Something happened in the Arctic that made them different. The Ipiutak people, as they have been called, were little like the practical men who preceded and followed them.

One of the first Ipiutak artifacts to see the light of modern day was a skull, with eyeballs carved from ivory and inset with pupils of jet, that stared up at its discoverors. It eyed the twentieth century with an unblinking Ipiutak gaze, and made the archaeologists uneasy. More Ipiutak sites were uncovered, and more of the same came to light. The Ipiutak people, it became clear, put an extraordinary emphasis on preparation of the dead. Their conception of an afterlife seems to have been more elaborate than that held by other Eskimo peoples. Weapons and tools were buried with the dead, but also buried, as one archaeologist noted, were "grotesque objects of no conceivable practical use." There were "travesties of utilitarian objects," like arrowheads of antler with some of the barbs pointing in the wrong direction. There were small death's heads that fit over the tips of the fingers, and "skeletonized" carvings with the ribs and joints emphasized.

An unusual amount of energy went into Ipiutak art. Practical craftsmanship languished. Ipiutak men found time to fashion elaborate swords and knives, with side blades inserted in a manner peculiar to their culture, but found no time to make pottery, as their predecessors had, and their successors would. There are few clues to why the Ipiutak people broke with tradition. Some Ipiutak figurines resemble carvings from western Siberia—perhaps the new tradition came from there. Or perhaps from somewhere else.

The current that flows north from the Pacific through the Bering Strait has for centuries carried palm wood, coconuts, Japanese fishing floats, and such things, and has deposited them on arctic beaches. This detritus must have seemed as alien to arctic tribes as meteors do to us. There were some barren-ground Inuit, even in recent times, who saw trees only as driftwood and who speculated that wood grew in forests under the sea. They believed that the undersea groves were uprooted in storms and driven ashore. What could these people have made of Japanese characters inscribed on glass floats? Perhaps the germ for the Ipiutak idea, in one form or another, simply washed ashore.

Or perhaps it was a single man, with a black vision, who changed the course of Inuit history. Perhaps the man had the hypnotic power that later shamans would have, but of a messianic intensity that swayed the entire race. The boreal deserts of the North, like the xeritic deserts of the Old World, are a terrain prolific of visions. It may have been that the Ipiutak vision came at high altitude, for there is evidence that the Ipiutak people were the first to spend much of their time away from the sea, hunting caribou in the Brooks Range. Perhaps, while the dark shaman was alone in the mountains, a boreal satan appeared before him in the wilderness, and this time was convincing.

Or perhaps the Ipiutak culture was a manifestation of something that had been building in Eskimos for some time. Perhaps it was a shuddering of the race, in the middle of its history, at the severity of the existence it had endured so long—a lapse of durability in a succession of sturdy peoples.

Ipiutak death's head

The next people to know the Brooks Range, the Thule people, were predecessors of recent Eskimos. Their way of life was not very different from that of the people who met the first Europeans. In winter the Thule people lived in permanent houses by the sea. The walls of the houses were often built of whalebone, of skulls especially, and the roofs of whale jaws. Clearly they were a formidable people —they swallowed whales. In summer they lived inland in conical tents. In village middens at places like Barter Island they left dog sleds, kayaks, women's boats, and snow knives. They left bolas weighted with ivory balls that opened in the air like spokes of a wheel when thrown into rising flocks of sea birds. They left wound plugs and wound pins for preserving the blood of harpooned seals. They left snow goggles, seal-oil lamps of stone, the broad knives of women, and ivory ornamental combs with engraved handles.

The Eskimos of the nineteenth and early twentieth Christian centuries drew on the sixty centuries of Inuit ingenuity that had preceded them. Faithful to their tradition, they were an inventive people. They made use of a number of technologies to survive. There was a man's technology and a woman's technology, and technologies for each season and each kind of game.

In autumn, a man pulled on his caribou parka, and over that his transparent rain parka, sewn from strips of seal intestine. He walked down to the sea and pushed his kayak into the water. Floating there, he fastened his rain parka to the kayak hatch and tightened his sleeves at the wrist, making himself watertight. He could now capsize his kayak, do a complete roll, and come up dry. He was now part of his boat. With alternate strokes of his double paddle, he set out. As he neared game, he secured the double paddle at the ivory guards on his deck, and moved stealthily ahead with a single-bladed paddle. Then he reached for his bow or lance.

In spring, it was a toggle-headed harpoon that the hunter reached for. Most often it was a seal that he threw it at. On impact with the seal the harpoon head detached itself from the shaft. Angled barbs drove the head in a curve through the seal's flesh so that the point ended at right angles to its angle of entry, unshakably fixed there. The harpooned seal, dragging the inflated seal-bladder floats attached to the harpoon line, tried violently to escape. The hunter retrieved his floating shaft. He worked his way to the spring ice, where with the ice pick at the end of the shaft he dug a hole, planted the shaft, and used it for leverage as he fought the tiring seal, playing the seal as a fisherman would his fish.

In winter the hunter stood on the sea ice above the breathing hole of a seal, or he knelt on land in ambush behind blocks of snow. He could wait motionless for hours, kept warm by undergarments of fawn skin, with the hair turned in, by a parka of heavy caribou skin, trousers of dog skin, and thick fur stockings inside his winter boots.

In winter while the man was hunting, the woman was building or repairing her ptarmigan fences, and tending her line of rabbit snares in the willows. In summer the woman hunted eggs and the root caches of mice. She built salmon weirs in the river or speared fish with leisters. In autumn she collected blueberries, cranberries, crowberries, bearberries, cloudberries, and lingenberries, and froze them in her ice cellar. In all seasons she was busy making and mending clothes. She made summer boots with soles of unbleached bearded-seal hide and uppers of scraped ringed-seal hide, with an intricate double stitch for waterproofing. The sinew threads of the stitching

swelled when they got wet, so no water could get through the stitches. She rubbed the summer boots with seal oil, and, because they became stiff when dry, she scraped and chewed them daily to soften them for use. She made winter boots with soles of bleached bearded-seal hide and leggings of ringed-seal skin or caribou skin with the fur left on. In winter she hung the damp boots out to freeze at night, then beat them with a stick in the morning to knock the ice out. When her family's clothes were in order, she turned to making wooden buckets, tool bags of wolverine hide, and the like.

There were few men strong enough, or skillful enough at the woman's technology, to survive without some woman toiling to keep him equipped. A woman was more vital to a hunter's success than his harpoon or bow. (The murder of a husband in order to kidnap his wife was the standard Inuit melodrama.) A woman's sturdiness was tested by the Arctic as exactingly as the man's. She endured better, if anything. When starvation came, as it often did, she was commonly the only member of her family to survive. She ate her children's bodies, then her husband's, then was rescued.

> *Need has compelled many people to eat human flesh; they had to do it to save their lives when their long sufferings had affected them so much that they had almost lost their senses. Hunger holds terrors; hunger is always accompanied by dreams and visions that may destroy even the strongest man and make him do things he would otherwise detest. So we never condemn those who have eaten human flesh; we have only pity for them. So many in our tribe have eaten it that even our taboo rules provide specially for them. In particular, we take strict care that such people never eat the meat of bears or ravens. That meat is like human meat, and we fear that the memory of their misery will drive them mad.*

The coastal Eskimos who lived at the edge of the North Slope called themselves the Tareumiut. Tareumiut men wore parkas that were belted at the waist and reached below the thigh. They wore pants of dog, caribou, or seal skin, with caribou-skin stockings. The soles of their boots were of polar-bear skin, and for insoles they used grass or baleen shavings. They wore caribou cloaks, and in very cold weather they pulled on polar-bear mittens. The Tareumiut women wore parkas that reached below the knee, with rounded front and rear flaps that were split almost to the hip. Their parkas were more elaborate than the men's, with decorative panels in front and behind. Wolverine feet hung from the panels at intervals. The

woman's trousers differed from the man's in that her boots were sewn onto them.

The Tareumiut were traders, and by trading were able to vary their clothing materials. Caribou parkas were most common, but Siberian reindeer skin was also used, and the skin of hoary marmots, mink, muskrats, and birds. (Feather parkas were light and warm, but not durable, and were worn only by poor people.) The Tareumiut traded at Barter Island, a small island at the edge of the North Slope, sixty miles from the Brooks Range. All of Alaska's most northern tribes assembled there. From the Tareumiut provinces came walrus skins for umiaks—the large Eskimo open boats—and for rawhide rope; bearded-seal skins for kayaks, boot soles, and light rope; walrus ivory, whalebone, and other products of the arctic seas. From the interior of the Brooks Range came caribou skins and wolverine fur for trimming. From the Kobuk River to the west came jade adze blades and whetstones. From the Canadian Arctic came soapstone lamps and copper knife blades.

By the 1850's, the Tareumiut were coming to Barter Island from the west with Russian tobacco and metal goods and exchanging them with Canadian Eskimos for Hudson's Bay Company trade goods. Most Tareumiut, and other Eskimos, saw Russian and English trade goods before they saw Russians and Englishmen.

The Tareumiut hunter of the 1850's carried a recurved bow made of spruce driftwood that had been carried from the Canadian interior by the Mackenzie River, and then washed westward by coastal currents. In his lifetime it was not likely that the hunter would see wood except in windrows along narrow arctic beaches, and he made careful use of what he found. The driftwood bow was backed by a cable of braided sinew, which the hunter adjusted to the moisture in the air by twisting at the middle with an ivory tool, usually engraved, that he carried in his belt. An antler quiver was at his back, filled with blunt arrows for stunning small birds and rabbits, and with barbed arrows for waterfowl and caribou. On his forearm was an engraved ivory bowstring guard. His face was framed by the wolverine or wolfskin ruff of his parka hood.

The Tareumiut archer was only occasionally accurate at seventy-five yards, and relied more on his stalking ability than his marksmanship. The real work of his life was with harpoon and spear. He went after polar bears with a spear, usually stalking the bear as it slept after eating. The Tareumiut believed that polar bears were left-handed, and approached and speared the bears from the left side. The Tareumiut man took part in cooperative hunts of bowhead whales. He was a fisherman also, though

to his taste fish was a poor substitute for meat. He fished for tomcod in January through holes in the ice, spreading the caught fish in a circle around the hole, their noses pointing inward—a design conceived to attract more cod. He fished for crabs through the ice, lowering a small net stretched over a baleen frame and baited with a seal's nose, leaving it near the bottom, then pulling it up in half an hour.

But most of all he hunted seals.

The Tareumiut man trapped seals with wide-meshed, weighted nets spread under breathing holes in the ice. The seal, rising slowly, was not hindered by the net, but in diving it became entangled and drowned. The Tareumiut crawled up to seals sleeping beside breathing holes that were exposed by the spring sun. The seal would wake from time to time and look about, so the hunter had to proceed slowly. When the seal became suspicious, the hunter pretended he was a seal, making noises like a seal and moving in a sealish way—things he had learned in years of close observation of seals. When he got close enough he jumped up and harpooned the seal before it could slide into its hole. Tareumiut stalkers used a variation of this method in hunting bearded seals. A number of hunters would crawl toward the sunning seal, then suddenly jump up shouting and running toward it. The bearded seal was stupefied by fear, and forgot the safety it easily could have found in the waters of its hole.

In spring, when the leads first opened in the ice and the seals left their breathing holes for the freedom of traveling along the leads, the Tareumiut followed them. A seal hunter selected a narrow lead and built a snow house over it. The house was made of thick snow blocks, for it was important that the interior be as dark as possible. The length of lead that lay within the darkened house was then covered with a piece of ice, in which an artificial breathing hole had been chipped. The artificial holes had a fascination for the seals—perhaps they missed their own holes and the familiarity of their private territories, lately abandoned for a rootless life spent cruising the leads. Rising to breathe at the holes, the seals were harpooned.

Most of the time—because most of the time was winter —the Tareumiut hunted seals through breathing holes in the winter ice. With a dog on a leash, the hunter sniffed out a hole. It was almost impossible to find the holes by eye, for they were covered by a thin dome of ice, with snow covering the dome. When his dog had found the hole, the hunter removed the snow over it with his snow knife, exposing the ice dome. With the ice pick at the end of his harpoon he opened the dome, then scooped the ice from the opening with a special implement of musk-ox horn. He inserted his prober—a curving length of caribou antler—and with it felt out the submarine shape of the hole. When he could see in his mind's eye exactly where and how the seal would rise, and knew how he would thrust his harpoon, the hunter withdrew his prober. He covered everything with snow again. Then, at the angle he would drive his harpoon, he sank a hole through the snow aligned with his hole in the ice dome. He placed his seal indicator in the hole. The indicator was one of several designs, made either of swansdown and sinew, or of horn. It was designed to move when the rising seal's head brushed it, or when the disturbance of the water that preceded the seal rocked it, telegraphing the seal's arrival. When the indicator was in place, the hunter spread out his skin breathing-hole protector and stood on it. The protector was to keep snow out of the hole in stormy weather, and to keep the hunter's feet warm, and to deaden sound. With harpoon in hand the hunter waited—five hours, six hours, two days sometimes—watching the seal indicator. If a seal did rise to breathe there, and if the hunter's calculations were correct and his aim true, the fight was short. The hunter clubbed the harpooned seal and hauled it up onto the ice, crying out from his diaphragm each time he heaved.

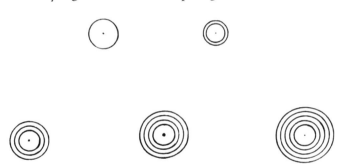

The Tareumiut were a people whose horizons were straight as arrows. The most common motif of Tareumiut art was a dot with a compass-drawn circle around it. It is easy to guess why that design, and its simplicity, had appeal for them. They, the Tareumiut, were the dot in the center of a featureless terrain, encircled by plains of ice and seas of tussock grass. When the Tareumiut separated, each man to his seal hole, each woman to her berrying, then that Eskimo became the dot, in the middle of a circle that curved on as uncompromisingly as before, or more so.

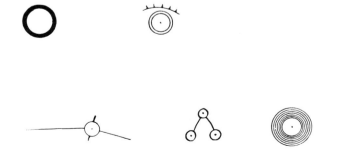

The mountain Eskimos who inhabited the Brooks Range called themselves Nunamiut. Nunamiut hunters adapted the methods of coastal tribes living a more traditional Eskimo life to their own inland life. They learned to pursue the animals of the mountains as resourcefully as the Tareumiut pursued the animals of the sea. The Nunamiut skill with the kayak in fresh water, their maneuvering in pursuit of caribou crossing fast-flowing Brooks Range rivers, was an art entirely different from that of handling the same boat in the sea, and it dumbfounded the Tareumiut who observed it.

(The Inuit receptivity to ideas, like the idea of a kayak, and their skill at modifying them, is indicated by the quickness with which ideas traveled, through new forms, between Inuit tribes. The Arviligjuarmiut, a barren-ground people to the east of the Brooks Range, in the absence of driftwood made their sleds from seal skins, folded in the shape of runners and ties and frozen. In the spring the sleds thawed and the dogs ate them. At that point the form ceased to exist, done in by the rays of an ascending sun and the sled dogs' hunger, but the idea persisted in the sledmaker's head, to be incarnated again in the next long night of winter, and passed along if necessary. In a similar way the Netsilingmiut, a tribe of the Canadian Arctic who lacked driftwood for harpoon shafts, fashioned shafts from caribou antler straightened in hot water. Through adaptations like these, from the earliest Denbigh times, ideas traveled like electricity and in no time were nearly circumpolar.)

The Nunamiut were caribou Eskimos. They knew the caribou migration patterns and knew the best times and places to wait for the herds, both in summer when the herds migrated north, and fall when they returned south. They ambushed caribou at river crossings, or organized cooperative hunts on land. One cooperative method was to build two converging lines of cairns along a migration route, with each cairn built to look like a man. The hunters hid themselves at the narrow end of the cairn funnel. The caribou were uneasy at seeing the cairns, and they slowed as the funnel narrowed. Driven by the urge to cover ground and by the pressure of numbers behind them, they continued nervously. Suddenly women and children appeared behind the herd and among the cairns, shouting and making noise, and the caribou stampeded toward the hidden men and their snares, bows, and spears.

Other animals were hunted. The mutton of Dall sheep was considered the best of foods, and sheep were hunted with dedication when the caribou migrations had passed. Grizzlies, approached carefully, with the greatest respect for their intelligence and strength, were speared and bou, by its conversion of the lichen of its poor range to fat, allowed the Nunamiut to live in mountains that would otherwise have been uninhabitable.

Many great Nunamiut hunters, then, must have begun the enterprise that would occupy their lives as small boys hiding behind cairns. The boy watched, or listened perhaps, his face pressed to the tussocks, as the herd approached. He heard the growing noise, the clicking hooves and soft gruntings building to a din, the ground shaking, the overwhelming odor of the herd. There was a moment of alarm, perhaps, as his senses panicked under the weight of the great life of the passing herd. But then triumph as he jumped up shouting with his companions, to see the herd thunder away from him toward the waiting spearmen. Afterwards, as his elders labored through the butchering, he could talk endlessly about how it had been, for Eskimos were extraordinarily indulgent parents.

The Nunamiut were not overly careful about the neatness of their houses, but were very concerned with personal appearance. They experimented continually with the design of clothes, and competed in it. They wore hats of beaver, otter, marten, and mink, and belts fashioned from wolverine claws.

Nunamiut women did not use patterns in making clothes. In planning a parka, the woman looked very carefully at the person she was making it for, often without his knowing it. As a girl she had spent years watching her mother sew, and had considerable experience assisting in the work before she was required to make a parka herself. She made her calculations.

In preparing the skin, she first removed the inner membrane and any particles of fat adhering to the skin. She let the skin dry for two days, then rubbed a paste of boiled brains or liver into it, and worked it with a scraper. She put the moistened hide under her sleeping skins for two nights, then worked it again with the scraper. Often she scraped it five or six times, and with each scraping it became softer and more pliable. When she wanted a fine finish she used river sand as a friction agent. When the skin was ready, she set to work with needles of caribou bone or walrus ivory, thread of caribou sinew, and a thimble of bearded-seal hide.

When the men were not hunting, they were making and repairing equipment. They made dog sleds, the most difficult job of all. They made snowshoes—pointed snowshoes for hunting in open country, because hunters could run faster in that kind, and rounded snowshoes for use in brush-filled country. They made rounded snowshoes for women also, because the pointed ones caught in the woman's long knee-length parka. Men experimented with

snared. Musk oxen were hounded by dogs until they formed their defensive circle, and then were speared to death. Wolves were killed with spring traps—eight-inch willow stakes sharpened at both ends, bent or coiled and bound with sinew, then covered with blood or meat, frozen, and left in a place frequented by wolves. The wolf wolfed the frozen meat, it thawed in his stomach, the sinew digested and parted, and the trap sprang open. Foxes were trapped with deadfalls made of ice blocks. Ducks and geese were taken on their way to North Slope breeding grounds, and on their return south. The women snared ptarmigan. Using gill nets, willow traps, hooks, and leisters, the women took grayling, lake trout, char, whitefish, ling cod, and herring. The flesh of all these creatures was welcomed, especially when the caribou migration, following some unknown alternate route, did not appear.

But the Nunamiut bread was caribou. Caribou meant everything to them that buffalo meant to the Plains Indians, that cattle mean to the Masai, or that seals meant to the Tareumiut.

From the neck, spine, and from the backs of the caribou's legs, the Nunamiut got sinew for sewing. From the bone and antler they fashioned utensils, tools, and weapons; from the hides they made tents, bags, and kayaks. The caribou's skin was perfect for winter clothing. It was light, flexible, and good insulation. It was nearly impervious to wind, but at the same time allowed water vapor to escape—an essential virtue, because sweat freezing inside clothing could be fatal in the Brooks Range winter. Caribou skin warmed the Nunamiut outside, and caribou fat warmed them inside. Fat is necessary for generating body heat in a cold climate, and a caribou bull often carried as much as forty pounds of back fat alone. The carisnowshoe design the way women experimented with clothes, varying the number of crosspieces and the length. The men made snowshoe netting from cow-caribou rawhide. They made heavy cord from bull-caribou hide, and rope from moose or bearded-seal hide.

The children watched and learned, and played. They played a kind of stick ball. They played football with a sealskin stuffed with caribou hair or grass. They played wolves and caribou. The girls played dolls and the boys arm-wrestled and practiced archery. Both boys and girls played house. They skipped rope, spun tops, and played string games. They gathered in a circle, with everyone's lips tightly closed—the first one to laugh given a funny name for the rest of the day. They played king of the mountain.

Adults joined in most of the games. They competed with the children in seeing who could walk farthest with a breathing-hole indicator balanced on his forefinger. They played roulette by spinning a drinking bowl of musk-ox horn, the handle of which when it came to rest pointed at the winner, who collected the bets.

Eskimos are rough-and-tumble people, and Nunamiut play was usually abrasive. The Nunamiut fought rock fights, with those hit considered "dead" and forced out of the game. They played games of keep-away in which the whole village participated, with no-holds-barred and anything-goes, at a pace that sometimes didn't slacken for hours. There was a game in which several players sat in a row. Whoever was "it" walked along the row kicking the others in the sole of the foot, then walked over their toes, then their shins, and then ran away, the others trying to catch him. There were trials of strength—Indian wrestling with crooked middle fingers, or two-man tug of war, with seated opponents trying to pull each other over by a short length of cord with wooden handles at either end. There was a game in which opponents took turns hitting each other in the chest or face, testing one another's ability to dish it out and take it. *Tudlutijuk*, the boxing game, was deadly serious. Men traveled great distances for a chance to be champion, and sometimes died in the effort.

The Nunamiut games, besides being fun and keeping people happy, developed the toughness and dexterity of the children and kept grown Eskimos fit when game was scarce. Practical applications were obvious in the archery competition or in the Nunamiut version of cup-and-ball, in which a bone was drilled with holes and tied by a short length of cord to a toy spear of bone, then the holed bone thrown up to be speared. The applications were subtler in the Nunamiut construction games. In one of these a large pile of seal flipper bones was set between the players, who

on signal dove for them, each grabbing as many as he could. Knowledge of seal anatomy then came into play, each player laying out his bones in the order they occur in the flipper, the winner being the one who assembled the most nearly complete flipper. In a small way the game tested powers of observation and knowledge of the natural world—things that needed testing in people who would spend their lives stalking game.

(The Nunamiut, and other Eskimos, were zoologists by profession, but by avocation also, out of pure curiosity. Their classifications system had a category called "that which is about to be food," and included most of the animals in their world, but they knew about inedible animals too. Children knew the birds in their area. Show a child the eggs and he could describe the bird, not by color as children should, but by form and behavior as an ornithologist would.

(The Nunamiut were paleontologists too, with theories about past warm periods in which giant elk, bear, and shrews lived in the Brooks Range. The fossil history that the Nunamiut claimed for the Brooks Range was richer than anything our own scientists have discovered, and included giant flying whales. The warm period in which giant life proliferated was ended, according to the Nunamiut, by an earthquake followed by a rise in the waters of the North Slope rivers. There was a great flood, and all the Nunamiut gathered on the bluffs near Umiat. Then the waters subsided. The land drained, leaving fish in inland lakes, where fish are still found today. Large sea animals crawling down from the mountains to the sea cut the upper channels of the Colville and other northward-flowing rivers.)

In winter, the Nunamiut games moved indoors. Winter was a period of much visiting, if the summer hunting had been successful and there was plenty to eat, and was a time of intense sexual activity. It was also a time of black depression, as the lightless winter dragged on, and of hysteria, rage, and sometimes murder.

* * *

A peculiarity of Eskimo technology was that it did not intervene between the men who practiced it and their world. It did not shut a man off, but brought him closer. It confronted him with universal realities. For a Nunamiut man, his tribal knowledge of the herds, and his driftwood bow, and in winter his snowshoes, all worked to bring him within seventy yards of the grazing caribou, and still nearer to the bear, sheep, and geese that inhabited his mountains. For a Tareumiut man, all his ingenuity, and all the labors of his wives, and all the wisdom and inventions of generations of his ancestors, went to place him alone on the ice. It left him standing or kneeling above the breathing hole of a seal. There were other things he did, but this was the main thing. He was dressed to wait and watch through almost any extreme of weather. Often in his life he had been caught on the ice in a blizzard and had slept through it with no other protection than his clothes. The ruff of his parka hood was of wolverine fur, which some ancestor had discovered to be the fur that stayed most free of frost. The wolverine ruff was trimmed the proper distance from his face. Later, when white explorers would try to improve the hood by enlarging the ruff to cover more of the face, they would find that the wearer's breath froze on the hairs near his nose and mouth, and the ruff became an ice mask. The Eskimo design was correct. The Tareumiut hood, the parka, the thick caribou trousers, the fur underwear, and the winter boots, allowed him to stand and watch for hours a harsh beauty that would have numbed and driven anyone else indoors. No southern hunter ever stared as unblinkingly at the elemental simplicities. No other way of life could have been more symbolic of man's position in an inhospitable universe. No hunting ever had the drama of the wait at the seal hole, where the two sea mammals—seal and Tareumiut sealer—came together. The universe under the ice, with its currents, cold upwellings, and swimming life, met the universe above the ice, and its winds, cold rains, and running life, at that violent point. The holes were necessary for the seal, to breathe at or drown, and each seal had a number in its territory that it visited at intervals. But men breathed at the holes too, or survived at them. *"Sometimes in winter snow we can't find breathing holes."* The Tareumiut killed at them or starved.

The skill of Eskimos at hunting the animals of their country was not accompanied by arrogance. Perhaps it was because the Eskimo's weapons gave him an insufficient edge over polar bear, wolf, and bearded seal to make him proud, or perhaps it was his religion, which did not insist on a special creation for humans, that made him thoughtful about the animals he pursued. (Caribou and grizzly bears often traveled about in human form, he believed, just as shamans were in the habit of turning into animals.) Or perhaps his weaponry, ingenious yet ingenuous, neither devilish nor apocalyptic, worked on the religion, allowing it to develop doctrines free of false pride. Whatever the reason, when a seal was killed the Tareumiut sealer gave it the drink of fresh water he believed it had been seeking. When butchering a caribou on the Canadian barren grounds, an Umingmaktôrmiut hunter was careful not to cut the skin around the eyes or the head of the penis. That would shame the caribou's spirit and cause the hunter bad luck next time. When her son had killed his first caribou, an Umingmaktôrmiut mother pretended to weep and fight her son for it—to assure the caribou's spirit that the Umingmaktôrmiut were sorry.

The technology that brought the Eskimo hunter within a harpoon or arrow flight of game did not erect any barriers to sympathy. The hunter's religion didn't deny the game its soul, and his classification system didn't insist on its inferiority. The hunter, in sighting along his shaft at seal, musk ox, or bear, found himself regarding a being of whom anything was possible.

If the Eskimo's technology brought him closer to this world, it brought him just as surely to the threshold of the other world.

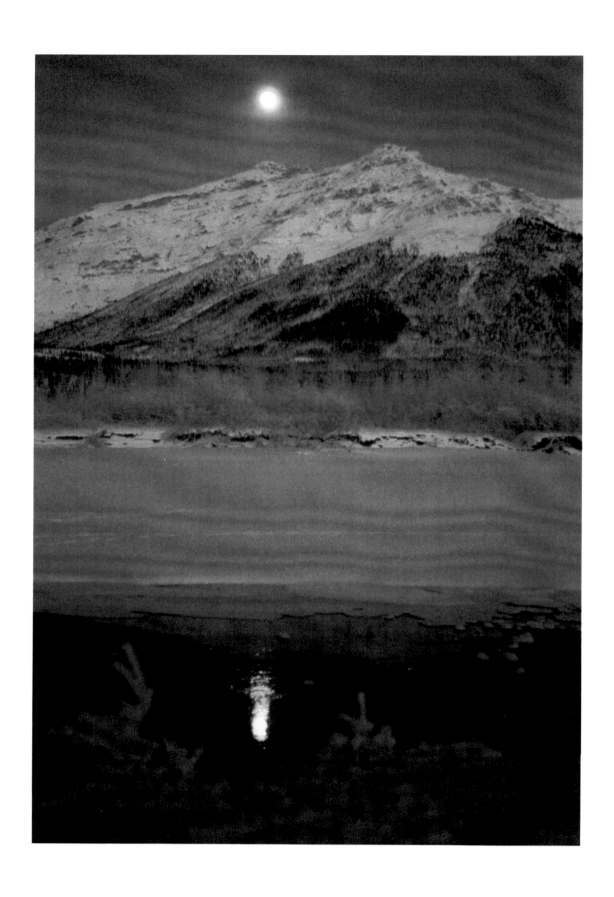

The Tareumiut man knelt on the ice, watching through the hours for a movement of his seal indicator. He turned away for an instant, pinched off one nostril and blew his nose, then turned quickly back to his vigil. He was the dot in the center of the circle. There was no sound, except perhaps for that of the wind scurrying over the ice. The broad winter sky stood blackly above, unless the northern lights were dancing there, or the winter moon rising:

He was standing by a breathing hole waiting to catch a seal. It was a fine day in mid-winter, no wind, and the moon at the full. And while he stood there at night waiting for seal, with his face turned directly towards the moon, the moon suddenly seemed to come nearer. He gazed at it steadily, and yes! the full moon was really coming nearer and nearer. At last it was as if it were right over the snow on the ice and he saw the phantom of a team of dogs, a sledge and a man. There were four dogs spanned to the sledge, while a fifth came along loose. As the dogs approached Kûkiaq the moon had difficulty in making them obey, so eager were they to come right up to him. At last he stopped them and made signs with his arms, indicating that Kûkiaq was to go to him. Kûkiaq ran over to him. The moon, a big, angry man, stood with his back to him by the side of his sledge, which was made of four whale jawbones tied together.

"Close your eyes and sit up on my sledge," said the man, and Kûkiaq did so. At once the sledge began to move; Kûkiaq could feel the swish and the wind of its speed round him; it was sweeping along. Kûkiaq wanted to see where they were driving to, and would only peep through his eyelids without actually opening his eyes. Then he looked into a tremendous abyss and almost fell off the sledge. The man became thoroughly scared, and Kûkiaq made haste to close his eyes tightly again. They drove on, and it could be heard from the resounding noise of the sledge that they were on new ice that was bare of snow. Shortly afterwards the sledge stopped and Kûkiaq could open his eyes. He saw before him a large village, many houses and numbers of people playing about; two of his friends who had just died came running over to him and struck him on the shoulders with their fists so that it really hurt. He was in the Land of the Dead up in the sky.

The moon wanted to take him into his house, which had bright, beaming windows, and they walked to the entrance together. In the passage lay a big dog barring the way, so they had to step on it in order to get through. It growled, but otherwise did nothing. The inside of the house was moving out and in, almost like tent walls flapping in the wind; the walls of the passage expanded and contracted like a mouth chewing, but Kûkiaq got through safely. The house had two rooms, and in one half sat a young, pretty woman with a child in her amaut; her lamp was burning with such a big flame that Kûkiaq's neck-band became scorched simply because he glanced at her. It was the sun. She waved at Kûkiaq and made room for him on her platform, but he was afraid he would forget to go home again, and therefore hurried away, letting himself slide down from the house of the moon towards the earth itself. He fell in such a manner that he came to stand at his breathing hole on the very spot where he had been waiting for seal when the moon came and carried him away.

Kûkiaq is the last of our shamans who has been up with the sun and the moon.

—KUVDLUITSOQ

It is not hard to understand how undeviating horizons, encircling an inventive people, turned minds inward with a special force. The solitude of the sea ice inevitably made for shamans. Uninterrupted polar distances made for spirit flights to the heavens, or to the bottom of the sea, where the shamans conversed with the deep-voiced spirits who controlled the migrations of fish and cetaceans. The great spaces in their emptiness made a fecundity. In the absence of someone to talk to, sometimes without even a dead snag or a boulder for companionship, Eskimo hunters populated their terrain with spirits. Like the Eskimo carvers who turned ivory or soapstone over in their hands for hours, looking for the forms imprisoned in the grain, Eskimo storytellers turned the land over in their minds, feeling the weight of it, and finding the spirits there.

The whole world is full of spirits, some small as bees, others as big and frightful as small mountains. The shamans used them as helping spirits, but people who were not shamans were afraid of them.

—ANGUSINAQ

There were mountain spirits who hid in crevices and were almost exactly like men, except for something peculiar about their eyes. They were also much faster than humans. They winked sideways, and were able to run down caribou and capture them alive.

There was a tribe of spirits who were gluttons. They had big bellies, but were fast enough to run down caribou. Before beginning the chase, they laced their stomachs in with thongs, and thus corseted had no trouble with their wind. Each glutton-spirit was able to eat a caribou and her calf at a sitting. When he finished he dug a hole in the tundra to accommodate his distended belly, and lay there comfortably while his meal digested. He was irritable at this stage. If someone appeared in the distance the glutton shouted at him to go away, for glutton-spirits prized their bellies and were afraid that the sound of footsteps would burst them.

There was a tribe of spirits called the Shining People. They were called this because the fires in the windows of their snow houses could be seen shining at a great distance. They were like humans except that the rims of their eyes were very narrow, and they never slept. The Shining People once adopted a human child, but each time the child wanted to sleep they raised him up and shook him. They were unfamiliar with sleep and thought the child was going to die. The Shining People would not let him sleep, and finally he did die, of fatigue.

There was a shadow race of spirits who were just like men, but invisible. Men saw their snow houses and their tracks in the snow, but never saw them alive. The spirits materialized only as they died. A woman once married an invisible man, lived with him, conversed with him, and loved him, but despaired at being unable to see him. One day, in frustration, she stabbed the air where her husband sat, to see a young man fall, handsome enough as it turned out, but dead at her feet. After the murder the invisible men gathered at the woman's village to avenge their tribesman's death. Nothing could be seen but bows bending as invisible arms drew them back. The Eskimos of the village did not know how to fight back. When the invisible men saw that the Eskimos were unable to defend themselves, they broke off the attack, unwilling to kill defenseless men.

There was a tribe of spirits called the Fidgety Ones. They were harmless except that they liked to tickle the people they met. They were like humans except for their incurable restlessness. They were able to disappear into river stones.

There was a tribe of spirits called seal-men, who were part human and part seal. It was thought that this hybrid race began when an Eskimo woman, to avenge the murder of her husband, laced her newborn son into the skin of a newborn seal cub and taught him to swim. The boy became as easy in the water as a seal. When he had grown up he lured his father's killers far out to sea, where they were drowned in a storm. The descendants of this first seal-boy were incomparable breathing-hole hunters. When they found hunting above the ice to be unfruitful, they dove through the hole to pursue seals underwater.

There was a solitary, dangerous spirit who inhabited string figures. He attacked women, sometimes carrying away those who were too eager to play at string games.

There was a giant woman who smelled of seaweed and stole children.

There was an insane race of calfless men who crept about unable to walk. They ate their own families if they had the chance, or anyone else who fell in with them.

There was a giant named Inugpasugssuk, who was so big his lice were the size of lemmings. He waded far out into the ocean to catch seals, clubbing them with a tree. Once he harpooned his own penis, which had bobbed up so far away that he thought it was a seal. The pain made him sit down suddenly, causing a great wave to rise and inundate the land. Great numbers of fish were washed ashore, and that is why fossil fish are found far inland today.

There were giant bears too huge for men to hunt. There were Chinless Ones, dangerous spirits, and there was a spirit with a single eye in the side of his head. There was even a spirit with no eye at all.

Inuit storytellers even populated the moon. A shaman returning from a spirit flight there reported that,

> *The man in the moon said that last year the caribou-hunt had not been very good in the moon, but this year it was much better; the caribou in the moon this year were fatter than usual, which was no doubt due to the fact that the summer had been cool and there had not been very many mosquitoes.*

The shadow creatures imagined by the Inuit are part of the inventory of the tundra province. The terrain engendered its spirit fauna just as it engendered its mammoths and dire wolves. The endless plains of tussock grass required spirit tribes and races, just as they required tundra voles, so spirits came into being. They quickened and multiplied almost exactly as tundra voles do, except that they were dreams in human heads instead of a Creator's.

With the mammoths, lions, and saber-toothed cats that once roamed here, the spirits are now ghosts of the country. They are part of its arctic texture and must be reckoned with.

The old Tareumiut provinces are full of ghosts—or the ghosts of ghosts. There are polar bears with ten legs, seals with human faces and hair, walrus dogs with long scaly tails that kill with a single blow, ice shrews who inhabit the pack ice, shy and harmless giants, and dwarfs a foot tall but quick, and so strong that if a dwarf should seize an Eskimo that man is a prisoner until it decides to let him go.

The Kobuk River country at the western edge of the Brooks Range is the home of a giant named Kayaklua-guniktuu. The child of ordinary parents, he ran away from home when his father tried to kill him. He grew into a giant and spent his life at good deeds. He taught animals to defecate, cut an extra joint in the caribou's leg so that it could run faster, and taught women to bear children without dying.

The Mackenzie Delta at the eastern edge of the Brooks Range is the home of invisible men called Ijerqan:

In the early infancy of man, people were never alone, whether they lived in a settlement or were travelling on long journeys.

They were surrounded by a spirit people, Ijerqan, who lived as human beings and were in fact human beings—except they were invisible.

Their bodies were not for our eyes, or their voices for our ears. And when people travelled and pitched camp and began to build their snow huts, one might see round about the snow-drifts that the snow blocks began to move, being lifted out of the drifts in cubic form and piled together into a snow house which seemed to grow of itself. Occasionally one might see the glitter of a copper knife—that was all!

They were clever people, these Ijerqan, and they did not mind people coming into their houses, which were arranged just as those of human beings.

All their belongings were visible, and people could trade with them very profitably. If one wished to buy something, all that was necessary was to point to it and at the same show what one was prepared to give for it.

If the spirit people agreed, the object required lifted itself up and moved toward the man who wanted it. But if they declined the bargain, the object remained where it was.

So people were never alone; they always had small silent and invisible spirits around them!

But one day it happened that during a halt a man seized his knife and cried:

"What do we want with these people who are always right on our heels?"

Saying this he flourished his knife in the air and thrust it in the direction of the snow huts that had made themselves. Not a sound was heard, but the knife was covered with blood!

From that moment the spirits went away. Never again did anyone see the wondrous sight of snowdrifts forming themselves into snow huts when one made camp, and for ever the people lost their silent, invisible guardian spirits.

It was said that they had gone to live inside the mountains in order to hide from man, who had mocked and wounded their feelings.

That is why to this day one can see the mountains smoking from the enormous cooking fires flaming inside them.

—AUNARAITSAIQ

In each Eskimo story about spirits there is a moment, if you watch for it, in which you can feel how the straightness of the horizon sometimes came around at The People to pierce them like an arrow. It was a moment in which the precariousness of life filled The People suddenly, fear flowered, and minds snapped into madness. In that moment the Inuit heard the spirits' step and felt their breath. *"What do we want with these people who are always right on our heels?"* the Mackenzie man screamed, seizing his knife. The Tareumiut caribou hunter endured the moment when he felt himself in the grasp of the dwarf, a grasp inescapable as long as the dwarf willed it to be. The seal hunter froze in the grip of the moment when he felt the touch of the ice shrew against his leg. The ice shrew, the Tareumiut believed, entered a man's clothing through the toe of his boot. If the man did not move, the shrew would crawl all over his body and leave through the toe it had entered. If the man moved, even slightly, the ice shrew would burrow into his heart.

Giants, the Tareumiut believed, were normal people who had become lost and had grown in solitude to giant stature. It's easy to see the moment in this belief too. It must have had its origins in the experience of hunting men or berrying women who, lost or alone on sea ice or on a tundra without scale, with nothing to measure themselves against, felt themselves gain size.

Hysteria, like the larger dose of cosmic radiation that the Inuit received, was a price paid for living on the northernmost margins of the planet. The Inuit allowed for it. Much ingenuity went into the games and celebrations designed to make winter pass quickly. Sometimes, when gifted comics were on hand, or when an especially large and varied group had gathered to spend the dark months, that winter was remembered as a happy time. But sometimes things went wrong, and the Inuit allowed for that also. Crimes committed in winter were considered mitigated by their season.

Ivigtarssuaq (a spirit) came to Tarraijuk, it is said, while he was out alone hunting caribou, and so violently did the spirit possess his body that it took several men to hold him; he struck out so furiously and raged so violently against his surroundings.

*   *   *

In describing the Netsilingmiut, John Ross, one of the earliest explorers, wrote, "Here if any where, we ought to find how the human mind is developed under the narrowest education, in what manner the 'light of nature' as it is termed, operates on the moral character and conduct, and how far human reason can proceed, under the smallest possible quantity of materials to act on, and under a very narrow range of application. If also there are peculiarities of character, whether for good or evil, the moralist and metaphysician may here speculate on what belongs to the original mental constitution of these people, and what is derived from their narrow and limited intercourse with their own species, in a society so restricted in numbers . . . where there is nothing beyond themselves to see, and no one to imitate."

It is not hard to imagine what the Brooks Range meant to people with nothing beyond themselves to imitate. For the Nunamiut, the mountains were the place they lived—commonplace—but for the Tareumiut who lived within sight of them, they must have meant relief from the flatness that lay unbroken in all other directions. For the Tareumiut tribes that lived out of sight but within knowledge of it, the Brooks Range must have been a geography of hope. For these tribes, traveling to the mountains, feeling the ground rise strangely underfoot, leaving the summer fogs of the North Slope behind, up into the brighter, thinner air, all must have been as good as watching the sun rise for the first time after the dark months, or like the taste of caribou after a winter of seals.

There are few straight lines in Eskimo art. There was more than enough straightness for the Inuit in their natural world. The curve dominates Eskimo engraving and sculpture. The Eskimo artist must then have found new and welcome forms in the Brooks Range, just as the Eskimo storyteller, needing something the size of a small mountain to compare a spirit to, found metaphor. For a young boy who would become an artist, a journey to the mountains, where he could see in the very land forms a modeling that he had known before only in human faces, or in the limbs of animals, or in the wind-sculpted forms of the pack ice, must have been a revelation.

The best Eskimo art came from west of the Mackenzie. The implements of more eastern Eskimos were often unadorned, but with the western Eskimos who lived in the shadow of the Brooks Range and on the Bering Sea coast, nothing went unengraved. Perhaps the mountains in a small way had something to do with this.

For the *angatkuk*, the shamans, the mountains were a source of things to be discovered and power.

Shamans in some tribes were initiated at birth into their profession, as were certain infants of the Musk Ox people, who called the children *tarakut ihilgit*, "those who have eyes in the dark"; some shamans evinced their special powers later, by their talent for remembering events from their prenatal lives, in which they had traveled about as free spirits; some men were made shamans by unusual events, like the man who, walking alone on the ice, felt a sky-lemming fall from among the stars and land on his back; but in practicing their art all shamans used solitude and the

visions it allowed. For Eskimos, as for so many of the world's peoples, visions came vividly at high elevation.

> *I wanted to become a magician, and go up to the hills, far into the hills and rocks, very far, and sleep up there. Up there I see two spirits, two there were, two great hill spirits, tall, as tall as a tent.*
>
> *They sang drum-songs, they went on singing drum-songs, the two great hill spirits. I did not utter one word; I kept silence while they sang drum-songs; I was ashamed and did not dare to speak to them.*
>
> *The day after I went home; and then I was a little of a magician, only a very little of a magician.*
>
> *But to the many I said nothing of it; I was ashamed to speak of it, because I was still only a very little of a magician.*
>
> —OTAQ

BOB WALDROP: *Sheenjek Valley, storm*

For the girl who would become a shaman—and women made some of the most powerful shamans—whether she was initiated by being held up newborn and made to look through her own afterbirth, thus receiving second sight, or whether she felt her calling later, as a young girl sitting in a seance, her mother seated behind her with hands pressed over her eyes, not to be opened on pain of death, the two of them listening to the voice of the shaman, who had been bound and left in the center of the floor—listening as the shaman's voice rose slowly up through the smokehole on a spirit flight, the voice fainter and fainter and finally disappearing, and then the long half-hour wait through the tension and full silence, her mother's warmth behind her, her eyes tightly closed while the shaman at some great distance conducted his supernatural business; and then the shaman's voice from far away as he returned; and whether it was in this way that she came to feel the

spirits (or whether, more cynically, it was because she was curious and brave enough to peek)—however it was that she became a magician—the mountains, and the mountain mists, and moonshine on distant hanging glaciers, and the jagged immense silhouettes of peaks that shut off the stars, must all have been useful to her.

Shamans, some Inuit tribes believed, were seen by the spirits of the air as shining figures, and the spirits were attracted to them. Normal people were like houses with the lamps extinguished. We can only guess how many shamanesses, through the centuries, wandered shining through Brooks Range mountains.

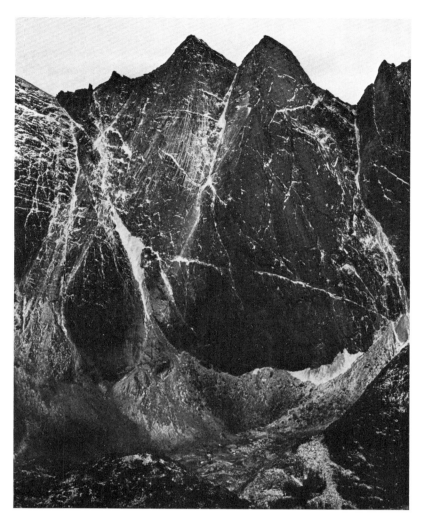

*   *   *

The various tribes of Inuit—the Nunamiut, Tareumiut, Nuvungmiut, Qordlortôrmiut, Kangerjuatjiarmiut, Ahungahungarmiut, Nagjuqtôrmiut, Agiarmiut, Kiluhigtôrmiut, Umingmagtôrmiut, Eqalugtôrmiut, Ahiarmiut, Netsilingmiut, Iglulingmiut, Kégdlingujarmiut, Kigdlinermiut, Kûngmiut, Pâdlimiut, Utkuhighalmingmiut, Nagssugtôrmiut, and Takamiut among them, inhabited a coastline thousands of miles long. The six-hundred-mile stretch of the Brooks Range coast was just a fragment of what they knew. There were vast differences among the tribes, but remarkable similarities too, for a people who wandered the entire width of a continent and more. A Nunamiut Eskimo from the western Brooks Range could understand much of the dialect of an Eskimo from Greenland.

The Inuit were a cosmopolitan people who crossed the Bering Strait to Asia in a single day. They were trading with the Eskimos of Siberia for Russian tobacco before Russians had reached the New World. At the same time they were a narrow and insular people, telling pornographic jokes about other peoples and inventing racist mythologies. (Indians, several Inuit tribes believed, were the offspring of an Inuit woman and a dog—"humans, no doubt, but not like us in habits." Indians sniffed the air like dogs and carried meat in their mouths. Their women came into heat like bitches, flung their hair out, and ran about the village to have men fight over them like dogs and copulate with them. And white men, a large number of Inuit tribes believed, had minds like small children.) One band of Inuit, living in the far north of Greenland, was so isolated from other men that its members believed they were the only people in the world.

Inuit languages were among the most complicated and difficult to learn in the world. Their system of justice was ill-organized and sometimes non-existent. The Inuit loved and were fascinated by children. They believed that newborn children were reincarnated souls, and respected children for their clearer memory of previous life. They listened to children. What the child said and did might seem foolish, but in truth the child was wiser, the Inuit knew, than an adult could ever understand. For many Inuit the chief pleasure in life was watching small children play. The Inuit were sometimes kind to strangers, and sometimes cruel. They were extraordinarily protective of one another, but kindness was not a simple proposition in the North. Infanticide was an Inuit kindness, as was the practice of leading off aging men and women who requested death, and leaving them to die alone.

The Inuit had undimming memories for historical

events. People and unusual happenings were so few and far between that everything was remembered. There were Inuit in the 1920's who told stories about the John Ross expedition of 1829, and knew the names of the expedition members, the first white men the tribe had seen. Among Ross's men was Agulgaq (he who takes long strides), Iggiararssuk (little throat), Aglituktoq (the one who is unclean before the spirits), Ingnagssanajuk (the half-old). The memories of these white men surely lived longer in the Arctic than in their own homelands. The Inuit lived lives without salt, for they disliked the taste of it. The Inuit enjoyed touching one another. If something blew into someone's eye, an Inuit companion held the patient's head and fished it out with his tongue. The Inuit made no alcoholic beverages. They were poets, carvers, and singers. They were excellent boxers. They were good-humored in the face of a taboo system that should have been overwhelming.

They were an earthy people. Human manure left at campsites where the Inuit awaited the caribou made for a lusher vegetation in those places. The Inuit, in a number of real ways, were a part of their country.

An Inuit child came into the world. His mother gave birth on her knees, aided by friends. Sometimes, as with the Netsilingmiut, the baby slid directly into a hollow dug in the snow of the sleeping platform. His first breaths condensed in the cold air of the snow house. He was wiped with the forehead skin of a caribou, or the skin of a long-tailed duck or great northern diver. An amulet carved from a good, straight willow was fastened to his parka to make him grow fast. If he grew up, he lived a life full of uncertainty, bravery, mystery, hardship, and laughter. When he made arrangements to meet friends at some future time and place, he sometimes finished by saying, *"If we still live."* Among some tribes, he died alone in a small house built for that purpose. Among others, the people of his village gathered around to watch him for as long as they could before he left.

BOB WALDROP: Lake in storm

First thing I remember, I was at Nagokigina gamiut. I was sitting on my mother's lap, sucking at her breast. My mother told me we were going to a sealing camp. She took me out, put me on a sled. Then I forgot.

When I remembered next, I was in the entranceway. Some woman I didn't know led me into the kazigi. The men pulled me up (through the floor entrance) and put me on the log (at the edge of the men's sleeping places). I saw two men lying on the bench. One was Aiyaqsaq. I knew him. I didn't know the other man. Then I forgot.

Next time I remembered, I was on sand dunes beside a pond. My father was making the bow of an umiak from driftwood. I asked my father to make me a little kayak. I don't remember whether I got the kayak.

—Daniel

In spring we moved to Kanikhligamiut. We did not get many seals. Pukhta oGokh got only one. Late in the spring, my family moved to Chikogaligamiut, hunting walrus and mukluk. Before we moved from spring camp, my uncle killed one caribou. After he got the caribou, he piled the meat and left some of it because he had no sled. White fox came around. My uncle hid behind a block of snow; when the foxes came to eat the meat, he shot them. I stayed alone with my mother when the men went to Chikogaligamiut. I took my new kayak out on the ground when the snow was melting and practiced paddling it on the ground.

In the summer we moved to fish camp. I always followed my father when he went fishing. . . . My father made a small net for puffins. When autumn came, we moved to Chaqawagamiut with nets and walrus-hide ropes. I think summer and fall were long when I was a boy. Now they are short.

—Daniel

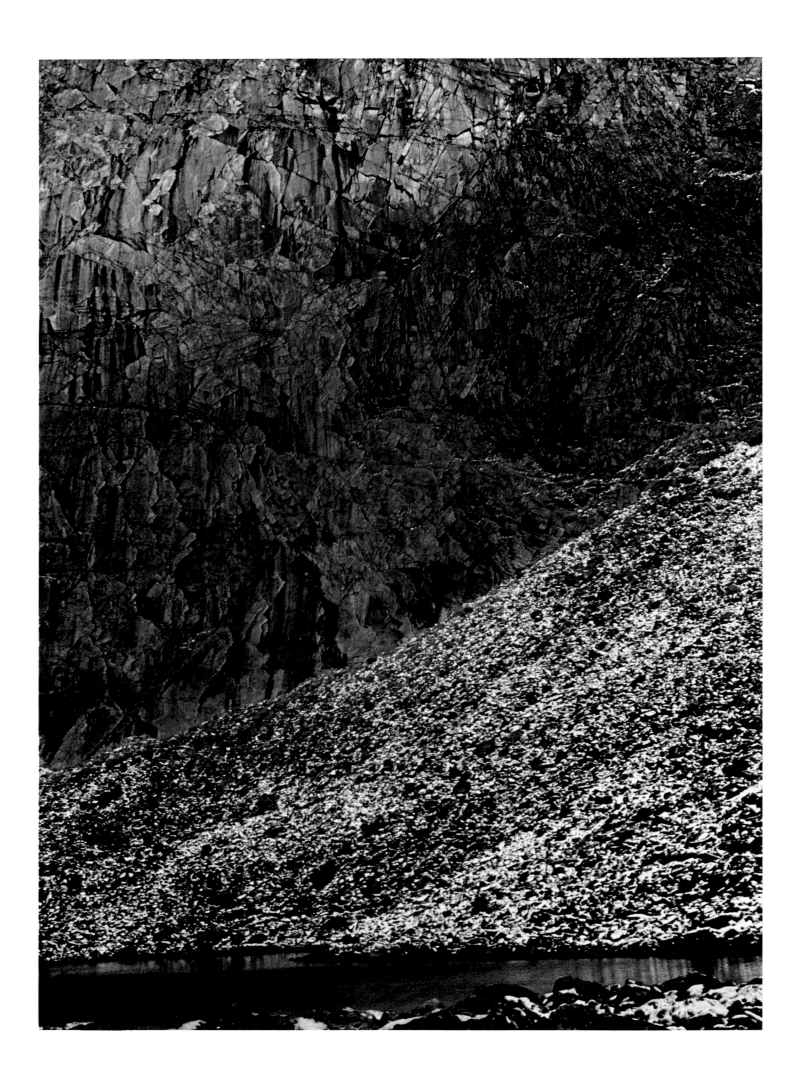

Then we heard a noise. We could not make out what it was; sometimes it sounded like a dying animal in pain, and then again like human voices in the distance. As we came nearer, we could hear human words, but could not at first make out the meaning, for the voice seemed to come from a great way off. Words that did not sound like real words, and a voice that was powerless and cracked. We listened, and kept on listening, trying to make out one word from another, and at last we understood what it was that was being said. The voice broke down between words, but what it was trying to say was this:

"I am not one who can live any longer among my fellows; for I have eaten my nearest of kin."

Now we knew that there should properly be no one else in this part of the country but ourselves, but all the same we could distinctly hear that this was a woman speaking, and we looked at each other, and it was as if we hardly dared speak out loud, and we whispered:

"An eater of men! What is this we have come upon here!"

We looked about us, and at last caught sight of a little shelter, built of snow with a piece of a skin rug. It lay half hidden in a drift, and was hardly to be noticed in the snow all round, which was why we had not made it out before. And now that we could see where it was the voice came from, it sounded more distinctly, but still went on in the same broken fashion. We went slowly up to the spot, and when we looked in, there lay a human skull with the flesh gnawed from the bones. Yes, we came to that shelter, and looking in, we saw a human being squatting down inside, a poor woman, her face turned piteously towards us. Her eyes were all bloodshot, from weeping, so greatly had she suffered.

. . .

"Kivkaq," she said (literally, "you my gnawed bone," which was her pet name for Padloq, whom we knew well) "Kivkaq, I have eaten my elder brother and my children." "My elder brother" was her pet name for her husband. Padloq and I looked at each other, and could not understand that she was still alive and breathing. There was nothing of her but bones and dry skin, there seemed indeed hardly to be a drop of blood in all her body, and she had not even much clothing left, having eaten a great deal of that, both the sleeves and all the lower part of her outer furs. Padloq bent down quite close, to hear better, and Ataguvtaluk —for we knew her now, and could see who it was—said once more:

"Kivkaq, I have eaten your fellow-singer from the feasting, him with whom you used to sing when we were gathered in the great house at a feast."

My husband was so moved at the sight of this living skeleton, which had once been a young woman, that it was long before he knew what to answer. At last he said:

"You had the will to live, therefore you live."

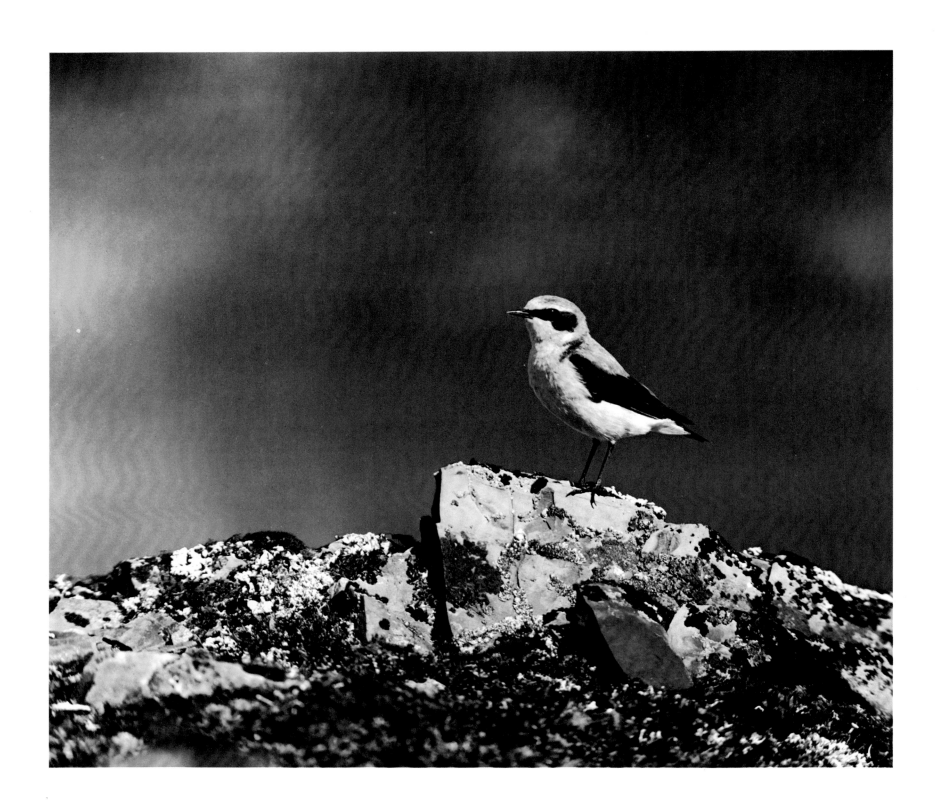

"I am just an ordinary woman, knowing nothing from myself. I have never been ill and seldom dream. So I have never seen visions. When I sometimes go up country to gather fuel I am only happy in feeling the heat of the sun, and many are the memories that rush over me from the parts I see again and where I have wandered ever since I was a little girl. I experience nothing but that when I am alone, I have to be content to listen when others tell.

—NALUNGIAQ

There is fear in
Turning the mind away,
Longing for loneliness,
Amid the joyous
People's throng.
     Iyaiya—ya—ya.

There is joy in
Feeling the warmth
Come to the great world
And seeing the sun
Follow its old footprints
In the summer night.
     Iyaiya—ya—ya.

There is fear in
Feeling the cold
Come to the great world
And seeing the moon
—Now new moon, now full moon—
Follow its old footprints
In the winter night.
     Iyaiya—ya—ya.

Where does it all go?
I long for the east!
And yet, no more shall I see my uncle,
To whom my mind would fain be revealed.
         —TATILGAK

Do you know yourself?
So little you know yourself.
Feeble I lie here on my bench
And only my memories are strong!
      Unaya—unaya.

Beasts of the hunt! Big game!
Often the fleeing quarry I chased!
Let me live it again and remember,
Forgetting my weakness.
      Unaya—unaya.

Let me recall the great white
Polar bear,
High up its back body,
Snout in the snow, it came!
He really believed
He alone was a male
And ran toward me.
      Unaya—unaya.

It threw me down
Again and again,
Then breathless departed
And lay down to rest,
Hid by a mound on a floe.
Heedless it was, and unknowing
That I was to be its fate.
Deluding itself
That he alone was a male,
And unthinking
That I too was a man!

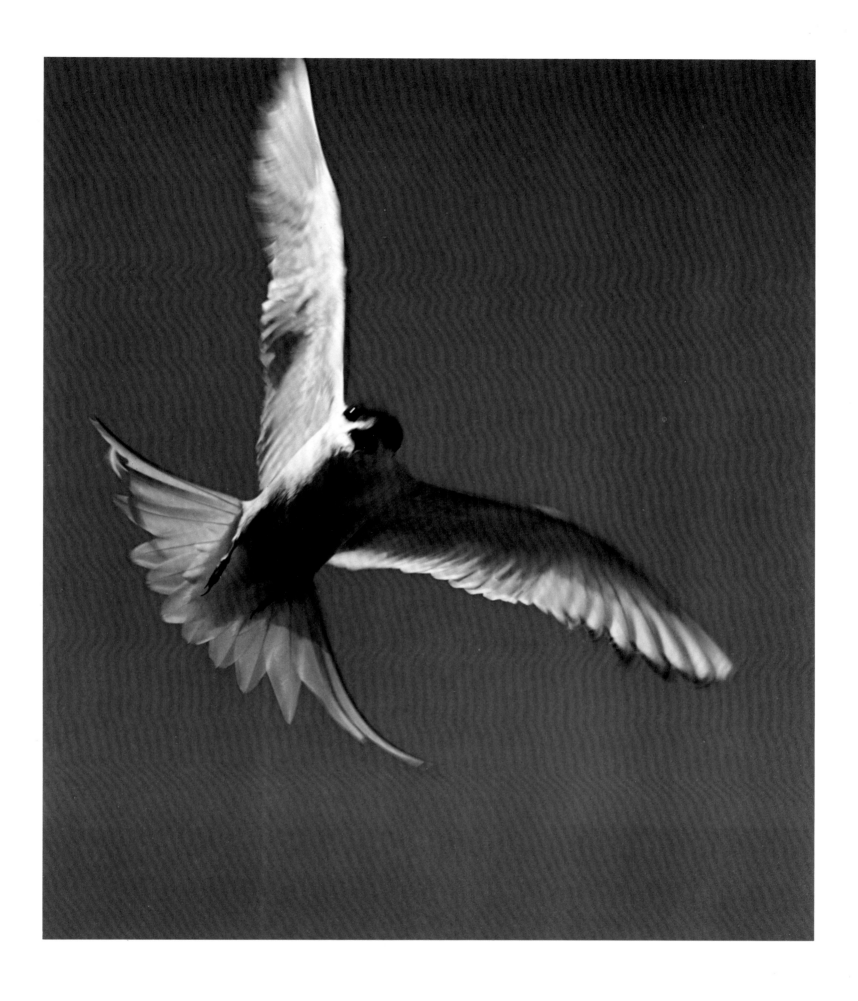

The woman hunts around. She picks out one. "That is one we can use." The man comes along behind and cuts it down. They are going to use those poles to stick down in the mud on the bottom of the river. After two or three days they have enough trees. They work hard, start early in the morning and work until dark until they think they have enough poles. Both of them start to haul the poles down. The man takes the big end and the woman the small end, and they take those poles to the river. If one is too heavy, they drag it, but they want to carry those trees if they can so the limbs will stay on. The man packs the trees out on the ice to where he left the willow markers. Nobody else ever takes a place marked out like that—they never butt in.

Well, they push those trees down through holes in the ice and make a fence. They leave one hole at the end of the fence where the trap is going. Now they finish that fence to the bank, and they finish making the wing that turns upstream, so they have a funnel to the hole in the fence. Now they are ready to put down the trap net.

That woman looks down through the ice where the trap is going, and she sees fish going down already. She tells her husband, "Fish are going down already!" Pretty proud of her man. "We are going to be all right this winter." They get happy when the trap is going to be finished—everybody is working, even the little boy and girl are dragging trees to the holes. Hard work, you know! No right kind of tools, just caribou horn ice pick—but happy just the same.

. . .

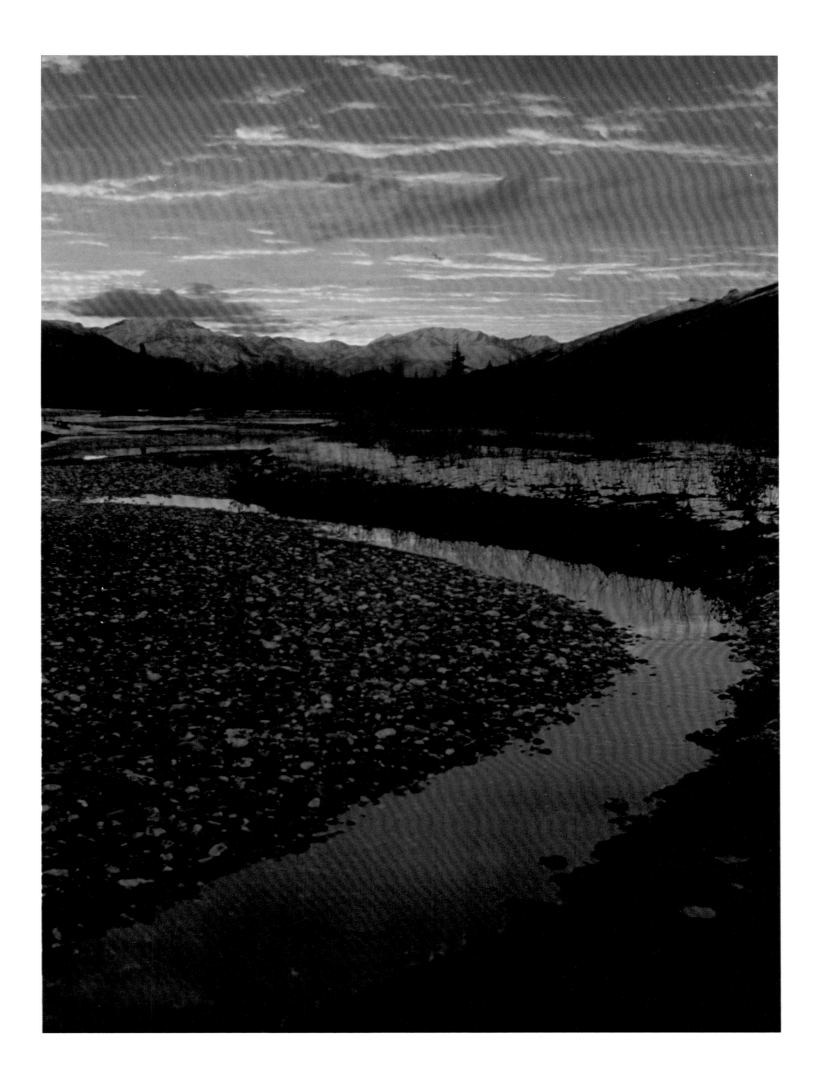

They put two fish on a stick—two or three sticks standing around the fire, one end stuck in the ground. They watch it good—tip it now and then—turn it—one side to the fire is cooked, starts to drip down fat—kids start to lick it with fingers—turn it around—catch it good, turn it around, watch it cook. When the fish are cooked, everybody in the house is eating, eating that fish, just nothing but those fish. And a couple of hours after that the man says, "Bring something else in—we are going to eat more." He calls his wife and tells her to bring some food. They eat every little while that night. Maybe some old man comes in and tells old-time stories, and they have a good time.

When it gets dark those nights, they have a stone lamp with fish oil to burn—a little moss alongside. They light the moss. Just a little bit of light, but they are satisfied all the same. Good light! No electric light in those days.

Late at night they begin to get sleepy. Everybody starts going outdoors. If it is clear, they look at the stars. Did you ever see a little bunch of stars (Pleiades) they are watching? Then it is bedtime—that is their only time at night—moon and sun and stars are the only time they have. They see that little bunch of stars over there somewhere, and they say, "Bedtime—we got to get up early in the morning."

—KOBUK RIVER MAN

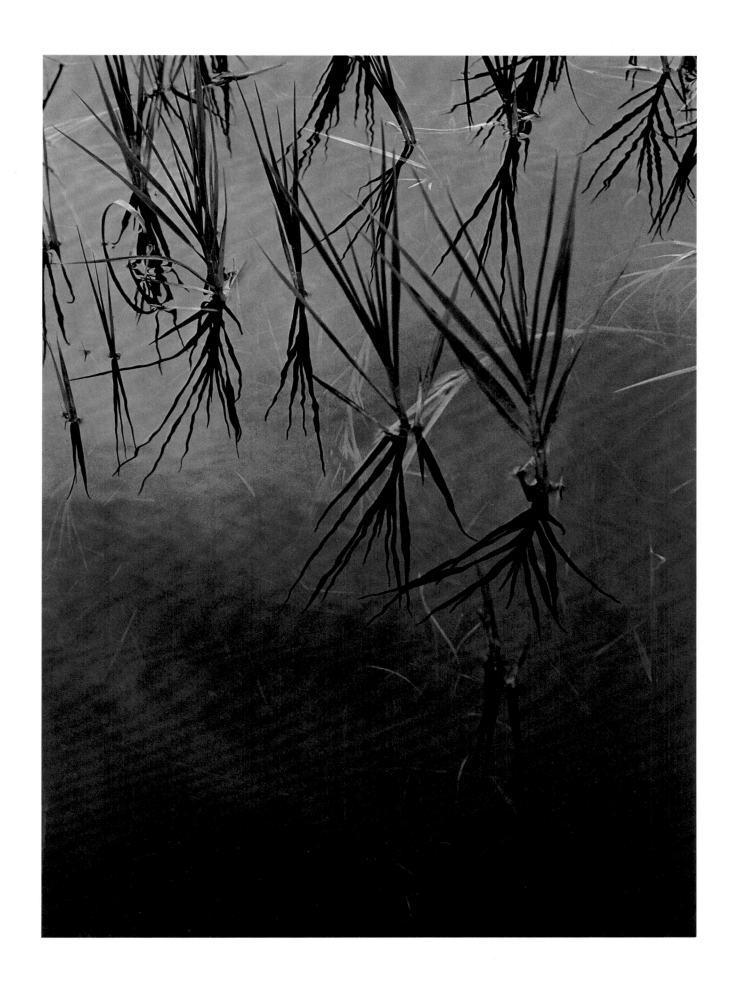

Jago

We followed the Aichilik down to where the mountains ended. As the river flowed northward the Brooks Range diminished in height until the river, and we alongside it, were moving through foothills. There was no longer much stone in the summits around us. The summits were rounded and grassy, but still high enough, a few of them, to be patterned with new snow. The valley had widened further in the gentler country, and the gravel bar, smelling more strongly now of the sea, was half a mile wide.

North of us the river flowed between two final hills, as through a gate, and then into the sea of the open tundra. In the gap between the hills we could see a little flatness. The bit of level horizon was a fascination for us after the weeks in which our horizons had been jagged.

A short distance ahead of us the Aichilik Valley met a westward-running valley in a great crossroads of lithic rivers. As we approached the crossroads, the low sun broke through for a moment and shone obliquely out of the westward-running valley, as if through a crack in a door, illuminating with its crepuscular ray a thin band of bright, subarctic green across the more somber arctic greenness of the Aichilik Valley. Then the light subsided. We left the Aichilik and turned left up the westward-running valley. The new valley would take us over a pass in the foothills, then down into the valley of the Jago River.

A narrow canyon led from the westward-running valley to the pass, and the next morning we turned up it. Shortly above camp the character of this canyon changed. The canyon, through some circumstance of its configuration or mineral accident, became lush. It was a pocket of varied life in the close-cropped sameness of the tussock foothills. The poplars grew larger than any we had seen north of the Divide. In places they were high and numerous enough to be called trees. A Dall ram watched us from above, and there were ptarmigan in the poplars and plover along the shallow stream. The stream itself was embroidered. There were streamers of algae beneath the surface and a number of fish swimming there, for the first time in our experience some species other than grayling. A baby plover sprinted ahead of us, frightened, but running very competently, its tail held steady as it ran. The tail inscribed a straight line against the sandy background of the stream bed, but bobbed twice each time the bird stopped, apparently to accommodate a lag in the momentum of the bird's neck. As I watched it, Steve called from ahead and pointed with his walking stick to some tall willows. A moose was browsing there, a cow, cropping leaves above her head. She was the first moose we had seen since Last Lake on the Sheenjek. She was in caribou country, hundreds of miles north of the moose sphere of influence. It seemed a lonely and circumscribed existence, but there may have been similar valleys that we did not stumble on, and other moose.

The canyon was beautiful but there was something unexplained about it. There was the mysterious fecundity. We were not unhappy to leave it. The spare hills were reassuring when we were in them again—they were the world the way it was supposed to be. We walked toward the pass. The sky closed in on us and snow began blowing horizontally, hard but not cold, into our faces. The greenness of the hills on either side was obliterated, almost, by the lowering whiteness. We walked with heads down, receiving the snow on eyelashes and watching the ground.

The gentle pass was in cloud and covered by snow, but as we descended its northern side we left that local climate behind. As we had in crossing our pass on the Arctic Divide, we now found ourselves in a new terrain. The sky to the north was, at last, blue. The sun was low, and we walked in a perpetual morning light. The usually long and regular slopes of the green tundra hills were now slightly tumbled. They had a shape and shadow we had not seen before.

We walked west, paralleling the northern edge of the Brooks Range. We followed the shoreline of the tundra sea as one would follow a Pacific or Atlantic shoreline, walking the coastal hills a few miles inland, catching an occasional glimpse of a featureless horizon. In places the sea intruded in estuaries of level tundra. Above the straight horizon of one of these estuaries we saw the top of Marie Mountain, a final peak of the range. Marie Mountain stood like a Gibraltar above the tundra plain, and from its base we planned to embark on our last leg across the tundra. We altered course for the mountain.

The tussocks of the estuary were patterned with new snow, in which we set a single line of footprints, walking single file. We labored in a large silence, for the wind had stopped and the mosquitos were long gone. We walked westward into a low sun. The angle of the light was so oblique that the balls of bog cotton were illuminated dazzlingly and everything below them reduced to blackness. We traveled through constellations of cotton balls burning against a dark plain. Steve walked ahead, a silhouette moving in the center of a sunburst. I could look at him only for an instant. It was less painful to watch his feet than his head, which moved in the very center of the sun. The glare caught the powder of snow he kicked up with each step, a bright rhythmic cloud at his feet.

From the estuary we climbed into hills again, walked through them a while, and then, topping a rise, we looked down on a great bay of level tundra below. The bay was shut off from the greater tundra sea by two peninsulas of low hills that curved out from the Brooks Range, almost meeting and enclosing the field of the bay, but not quite, leaving a narrow gateway.

The analogy to a bay, like the other marine analogies suggested by the tundra, was inescapable, except perhaps to someone who had never left Kansas. If I had been transported to the hillside asleep and suddenly awakened, I would have thought it a bay. It was shaped by littoral and liquid principles, not terrestrial. It was calm, perfectly flat, and dark green, its tussocks textured like waves on a day of light conflicting winds. As we watched, fog spilled through the gate and slowly filled the northern expanses of the bay. It was so much like a transliteration of the San Francisco Bay I had grown up above—that temperate bay translated to arctic terms—that it was like a dream.

We camped above the bay in order to spend the sunset hours there, planning to move on to the Jago River the next morning. When we had pitched our tents we sat at the doorways and looked north. The open tundra beyond the bay was a solid sea of fog that rolled against the bay's barriers of hills, found the small gap in them and flowed through, filling more of the bay's northern edge. The sun slid along the horizon. The sun was low, the hills were low, and the sea of fog, though it stretched forever horizontally, occupied only a vertical degree or two. The world was concentrated at the horizon, and the eye did not stray above a few degrees of the horizon line. If the fog within the bay had drifted to its southern shores, the world would have widened vertically, but it did not. The northern horizon held a thin line of fog as if by magnetism. The world was stratified.

The sky above us was pale blue and immense, but void. Only at the horizon, where it stretched in a rose-colored band, and above that in a band of blue-green, was the sky significant. The strata of light were unworldly. It was as if we were so near the edge of the planet that the colors partook more of space than of this Earth. They were extraterrestrial pastels—more like the rainbow in the rings of Saturn, if there is such a rainbow, or like shades of an aurora over a martian pole. They were hues of another planet farther from the sun.

The next morning John reached outside his tent and put the orange juice in the sun to thaw. I noticed this in time and moved the plastic bottle back into the shade, so that when we rose and ate there was a slush of ice in the juice and it was very good. It had been 23° that night, but soon it was 60° in the sun.

As we finished our tea Steve spotted two caribou bulls on a snowy hillside south of us. They were the first caribou we had seen. They lay in the snow facing in our direction. The caribou, with their wide antlers, were very proud, unmoved, and graceful. They looked to me like Sioux horsemen in winter cradling long rifles. They weren't like deer. As I watched them, a couplet from a Robinson Jeffers' poem leapt to my mind as if it had been my own creation: "Which failure cannot cast down/Nor success make proud." Jeffers had intended that the line describe a hawk on a rock, but it worked for the caribou too.

John and Steve walked over to have a closer look, and the caribou saw them. The animals rose, and as they did much of their nobility left them. They stood on splayed hind legs—we were later to understand that this was a caribou characteristic—and then ran about aimlessly for a while, apparently unable to decide which way to go. Reaching a decision finally, they ran straight past our tents, passing within thirty feet. They ran with their chins up and their heads tipped back. It was a posture that suggested panic, and I expected their eyes to be white with fear, but as they passed by I saw that the eyes were calm. It was just the way caribou ran, and it may have had something to do with the weight of their antlers. Once past the tents, the caribou continued their running back and forth, sometimes swinging closer to look at us curiously, but generally swinging away, steadily working farther off, smaller and smaller, until somewhere in the middle distances of the tundra bay they were lost to sight.

We broke camp and continued west. We walked for three hours across a level plateau of tussock grass that, misled by the deceptive scale of the country, we had planned to cover in an hour. Then the plateau dropped away under our feet into the Jago Valley. The valley was wide, and like the other Brooks Range valleys north of the Divide, it was simplified. Here the scale of the simplicity forced contemplation. The world had just four elements. There was the gravel bar and its braided river; the long, green, concave slopes of the valley walls; the snowy granite peaks; the sky. There were no trees, no adornments of any kind to vitiate the pure sweep and strength of the landforms. We descended, crossed the Jago, and pitched camp.

North of us the Jago Valley widened into the tundra plain. Once past the last hills, the fan of the river spread

out infinitely, like a mythological source. It looked as if the whole tundra province were a delta of the Jago. Our tents stood at the edge of the open tundra. There were few foothills where we had camped and the Range ended abruptly there, with the tundra beginning suddenly at the base of the escarpment of high peaks. The boundary between the two provinces was accentuated by the recent snow. The snowline followed the 3000-foot contour almost without deviation—flawless white snow on one side of the line, flawless green on the other. Looking south we saw the towering white cordillera of the Brooks Range; rotating our heads one hundred and eighty degrees we saw great plains. "Nebraska!" Steve said. He couldn't get over the discrepancy. It made a little boy out of him, and he swiveled his head back and forth between the two extremes.

That night we were all conscious of our insides for the first time in the trip, and we felt strange the next day. We were smitten nearly simultaneously, so we assumed that it was something we had eaten or drunk. John thought it was the river. The Jago had been running milky with glacial silt the previous afternoon, and John remembered from someplace that it was bad to drink glacial silt.

I felt lightheaded, but strong. As I lay in the tent my mind raced, as it had every morning since the Sheenjek, but now it raced differently. Instead of circling around problems, it ran through them, obliterating each one. I found that I had perfect confidence in myself. I saw exactly what I would do. I knew with a total liberation from doubt that all my best-laid plans would succeed. The assurance, instead of passing through me like a flush and departing, stayed. It began to scare me. I wondered what I had ingested and whether it was affecting the others in the same way. I worried about where my old self was.

The time had come to get meat, so I set out hunting. For the first five minutes of walking I felt very strong, then suddenly all my strength left me. It was as if in midstep someone had cut my strings, or jerked a plug and let my afflatus out. I felt drugged. I was weak but my mind was working clearly, and there was considerable relief in knowing that the new self had been artificial and temporary. I had a slight tremor, as from nervousness. It was like the shakiness that comes when blood-sugar levels are low. Walking was the strangest sensation. I was not tired, precisely, but I could not make my legs move faster. I didn't know what part of myself to call on, what reserve to muster, in order to speed my step. I thought about going back but I continued on, resting often. At one of my rests I ate a meat bar, and that seemed to help. I could not guess

what was wrong with me. (My opinion now, after reading arctic accounts of a similar lethargy, is that we suffered from fat deprivation.)

Some time later, walking slowly on an earthswell in the tundra north of Marie Mountain, in a pleasant warm wind, I heard an animal noise. I saw a shape far off, walked toward it, and saw the shape resolve itself into a caribou. When I was a hundred yards from it I lay on the tussocks and fired. There was the report at my ear, a long instant, and then the thud that meant meat, a full stomach, success.

I come from a family for whom animal lives are sacred. Just a year earlier in South America, I had discovered that when food was short I liked hunting, and admitted it to them. They had trouble understanding, and wondered how such strange seed had come among them. I was now above the Arctic Circle, thousands of miles from any brother or sister, but I felt their disapproval. I jumped up and followed the caribou, who was trying to run away.

The curve of the tundra swell was so attenuated that you could have mistaken it for the curvature of the Earth. Every point you stood on seemed the highest point. As we ran along it, the earthswell presented the caribou and me to the sky. I was unmindful in a strange way of the caribou. I watched him only out of the corner of my eye, knowing that I had him, remembering to watch my footing in tussocks and careful not to run so fast that when I stopped my aim would be unsteady. I am not a hunter and it was all foreign to me. I heard the sound of my breathing and of my feet in the tussocks. I had shifted into another state of mind, or mindlessness, whether through some hunter's atavism, or through some new effect of whatever it was we had drunk. It seemed that I was not supposed to look the caribou in the eye. I felt myself running through a ritual that no one had ever taught me, but that I was nevertheless doing all right in. I was sorry for the caribou, shot through the lungs, but that sympathy was lost in the nameless emotion. It was lost the way a tern's fear of altitude might be lost, I imagine, in the mindless enterprise of navigation by the stars.

I caught up with the caribou and killed him. I took his quarters, then his liver, heart, and kidneys, which I tied up in my T-shirt. When I had finished butchering I walked off to the north a ways. I wiped the blood from my hands with some tussock grass. The tundra swell presented me to the sky. I felt the way the Little Prince must have felt—the tall landmark and central feature of a very small planet. Over my left shoulder, just visible over the swell, was the distant edge of mountains to the west, a host of peaks, a snowy prickling just above the curve of the earth. The

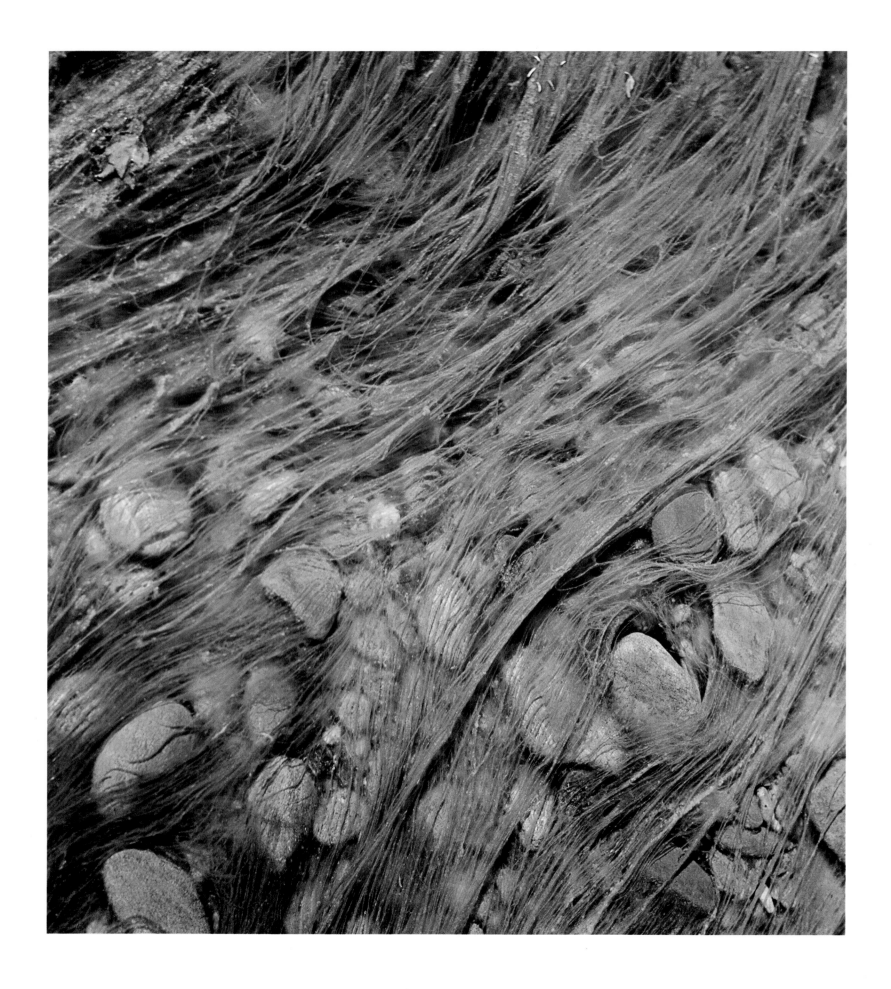

warm wind was blowing from the south and the sky was big and gray, except for the thin orange band at the horizon.

Returning to camp under the weight of the meat, I felt my weakness come back. I ceased to feel like the salt of the Earth. It took forever to cover the very small stretch of earth between me and the Jago. I rested so often that my trip became an epic journey. When I got back the others were in camp, feeling just as weak and strange as I.

That evening as we cooked the caribou we debated what was wrong with us. We dismissed the idea of the glacial milk. We talked instead about the lush valley, with its single moose, that we had passed through three mornings before. We remembered the streamers of algae beneath the surface of the stream. Something unusual had nourished that growth, we theorized, and nourished the other exaggerated growths of the valley. We remembered the fish, of a species we had never seen before. It was a strange place and we had drunk from the stream that flowed through the center of the strangeness. We sat around the fire remembering peculiar things about the valley.

If an outsider could have heard us he would have been alarmed, I think, at the way we assembled our case against the valley. We were three more or less educated men, and we spoke in language that sounded scientific, but I realize now that a dark current of the wildest superstition ran underneath. The rivers of stone we followed were leading us back into an Age of that material. We were not heading simply north, but in more directions than we had planned. We were not disturbed by our own conversation, which sounded perfectly natural at the time. If someone from the twentieth century had parachuted in on us, however, and listened carefully to our diagnoses, I believe he would have pitched his tent a considerable distance from ours. Steve finally said he thought the valley had a spell. He said so only half-seriously, but it was what we all meant. When he said "spell" the conversation ended, as if he had hit on the word we were looking for.

That night we saw our first northern lights. Earlier John had described the displays he had seen on his earlier trip to the Mackenzie Mountains, and we had watched the sky, hoping that the nights would get dark enough to see some before we left the Arctic. Glancing at the sky to the south that night, I thought I saw something. It was a ghost cloud, so faint I thought it was my imagination. It moved perpendicularly for a moment against the direction of the wind, then disappeared. I saw it again, and tried without success to get the others to see it. Then came a more noticeable pillar of light, and the others saw it. Rapidly as the sky darkened the aurora brightened, snak-

ing, shifting, slipping in long columns across the sky, the prismatic colors just perceptible. It is impossible to convey how strangely the aurora borealis strikes someone new to it. Steve and I watched until the cold drove us into our tent.

The next day an eerie ground storm came up in the south. The clouds above the Jago Valley stood motionless and calm, but a strong south wind blew down the river bars. The wind raised a yellow cloud upriver that moved toward us, following the turns of the river. We could not tell whether the cloud was dust or vapor or a combination of both, even when it was upon us. It was warm and there was a graininess to it that suggested at least some admixture of sand or dust. When we were in the midst of it the cloud obscured the eastern mountains from which we had come. It was not a single cloud, we saw when it arrived, but a number of smaller storms blowing down each of the river's channels, like a host of minor furies.

As the storm was passing I had an intuition.

For the past three days at the same time each afternoon we had seen a vapor trail very high in the sky. The contrails were the first signs of man we had seen since the beginning of our walk. We had assumed that they were commercial airliners on a polar route, or Strategic Air Command bombers on contingency runs beyond the Pole and back. Now, after our sickness, and after the odd ground storm, I remembered the single white scratch against the high blue sky and I had another idea. The planes were bombers all right, but they were not going to turn back. They would fly beyond the Siberian Arctic and drop the last bombs of a world war that was already over. Our sickness was radiation sickness. The warm ground wind and the strange vapor cloud that blew from the south were epiphenomena of some distant fire storm. We would arrive at Barter Island, and its Defensive Early Warning installation, to find nothing there. Vaporized. We would stand at the arctic shore and look out across a frigid and inanimate polar sea, having reached the end of the trail a little later than our civilization had, but just as inevitably. We would huddle on the shore that night and the northern lights would dance over us.

For a moment I knew it was true. Then I thought again, and realized that the war might be—probably was—my imagination. I found that John had run through the same fantasy. Talking with him about it made it seem less likely, but we didn't pretend to laugh at ourselves. There might have been other people surviving on the Earth, but just as easily not. There was no evidence either way, nothing but an endless tundra to check the two possibilities against. There was no way that we could know.

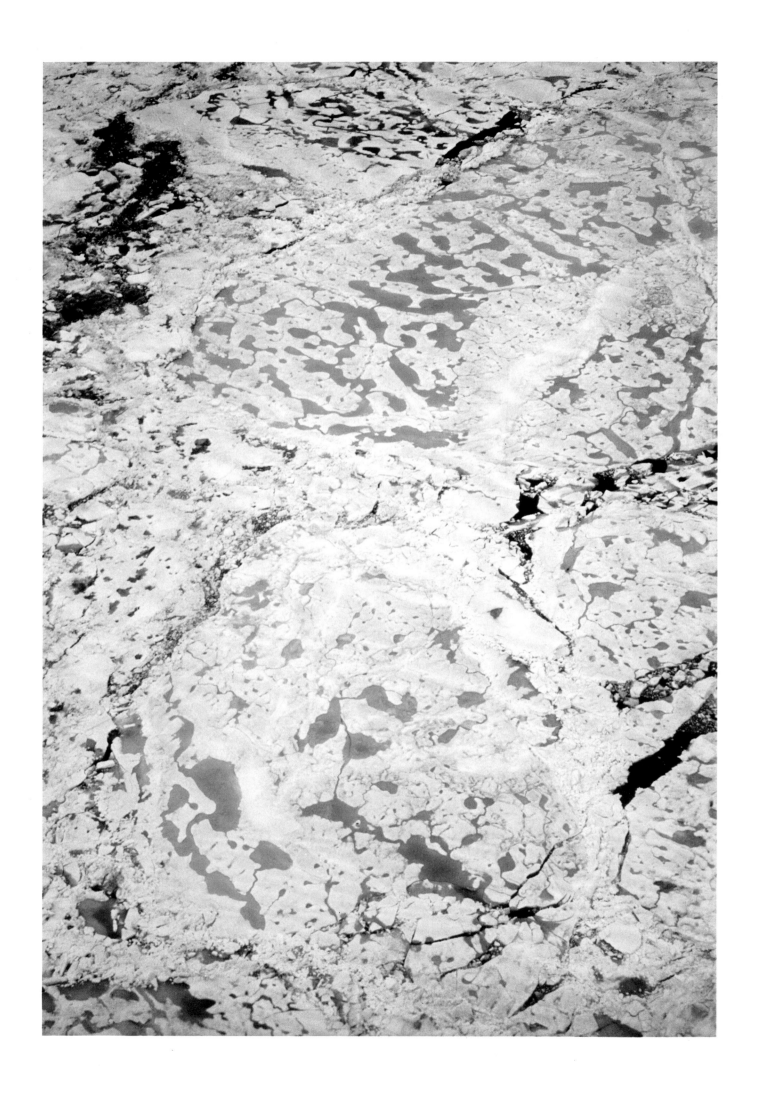

But of the land on the other side of the bald men none can give any trustworthy account because it is shut off by a separating wall of lofty trackless mountains, which no man can cross. But these bald men say—which, however, I do not believe—that men with goat's feet live on the mountains, and on the other side of them other men who sleep six months at a time . . . The whole of the country which I have been speaking of has so hard and severe a winter, that there prevails there for eight months an altogether unsupportable cold . . . even the sea freezes . . .

—HERODOTUS
45th Chapter of the 4th Book.
(c. 430 B.C.*)*

4. *EXPLORERS*

They first pointed to the ships, eagerly asking, what great creatures those were. Do they come from the sun or the moon? Do they give us light by night or by day? Sacheuse told them that he was a man, that he had a father and mother like themselves; and pointing to the south, said that he came from a distant country in that direction. To this they answered, "That cannot be, there is nothing but ice there."

—JOHN ROSS
An Account of the Discovery
of the Polar Eskimo. London, 1819

WITH THE explorations of the Norsemen, and those of Columbus, Frobisher, Hudson, Baffin, and Cook, the new world known to Europeans expanded northward and westward. The Brooks Range, on the farthest northern corner of the continent, waited until the very last to become known. In 1648, a Cossack trader named Simeon Deshnev came close to the Range. Deshnev was one of the descendants of a band of Cossacks who in fleeing the Czar had established themselves in western Siberia in 1557, and then had moved eastward. In his travels along the arctic coast of Siberia, Deshnev saw the first American Eskimos (probably from the Diomede Islands) ever seen by white men. In the next century Vitus Bering came still closer. "On February 5, 1725," Bering wrote, "I received from Her Imperial Majesty the Empress Catherine Alexeyevna, of illustrious

and immortal memory, the instructions drawn up by the hand of his Imperial Majesty Peter the Great, of deserving and eternal fame, a copy of which follows:

'1. Build in Kamchatka or in some other place in that region one or two decked boats.

'2. Sail on these boats along the shore which bears northernly and which (since the limits are unknown) seems to be part of America.

'3. Determine where it joins America . . .'"

In 1789, Alexander Mackenzie traveled down the great river that would be named after him, getting very close. Then, in July of 1837, Thomas Simpson, P. W. Dease, and their twelve men sailed in a whaleboat westward from the mouth of the Mackenzie River to Point Barrow, surveying the previously unknown stretch of coast that ran most of the length of the Brooks Range.

Approaching the mountains from the southwest, a Russian naval lieutenant named Zagoskin traveled up the Koyukuk River, causing the first rumors of white men to circulate among the Nunamiut Eskimos.

But the first white explorers to become a part of the Brooks Range—a part of the scheme of the mountains in the way that Eskimos were a part—were the ethnologists who went there to study Eskimo life. The ethnologists were white men only in a loose way. The logistics of early northern travel required so many months of unbroken companionship with Eskimos, and the austerity of the land forced a way of life so nearly like the Eskimo life, that the Europe in the ethnologists departed. It rubbed off, as if against the elbows of Eskimo companions in tight snow houses. It froze and peeled away like skin on frostbitten cheeks. The Eskimos, for a number of good reasons, often refused to believe that the ethnologists were the white men they had heard about. They laughed at the suggestion. The white men in turn, Diamond Jenness especially, slipped into the habit of using "we" when writing of Eskimos. But the ethnologists did keep notebooks and rifles among their caribou skins. When they returned from the North, time and amenities made fairly good white men of them again.

Vilhjálmur Stefansson, who traveled the Arctic Slope at the turn of the century, was one of the first ethnologists to know the Brooks Range. Stefansson was perhaps the only arctic explorer unimpressed by the Eskimo talent for survival in the Arctic. He considered himself equal to most Eskimos in his ability to handle the environment, and he probably was. He was a strong and competent man, if sometimes an unpleasant companion. (When something went wrong in the Arctic, in Stefansson's account of things, the fault always lay in someone, or some agency, besides himself. When his companion Martin Anderson went snowblind, it was because Anderson had carelessly gone without snow glasses; but when Stefansson himself went lame, it was because of a carelessly made sock.) Stefansson was the kind of man who is forever in competition. In the North his competition was with Eskimos. It seems a strange compulsion for an ethnologist, but when Stefansson arrived in a Native village the first thing he did was show the people how far his rifle would shoot.

On one of these occasions Stefansson missed his target. He told the villagers he would try again. The Eskimos were frightened by the noise, and protested that another loud report would scare the seals away. "It seemed to me imperative, however," Stefansson wrote, "to show them I could keep my word and perforate the stick at two hundred yards, and in spite of their protests I got ready to shoot again." Stefansson hit this time, but to his bewilderment the villagers were unimpressed. The noise of the rifle caused a greater stir than its accuracy. Stefansson patiently explained that with the rifle he could kill a caribou or polar bear at twice that distance, if he wanted. The villagers nodded at this, and asked if Stefansson could kill a caribou on the other side of the mountain. He admitted that he could not. The rifle was no great thing then, the villagers informed him, for a shaman of a neighboring tribe had a magic arrow with which he could kill a caribou on the far side of the tallest mountain.

"When I showed them later my binoculars that made far-away things seem near and clear, they were of course interested; when I looked to the south or east and saw bands of caribou that were to them invisible, they applauded, and then followed the suggestion: 'Now that you have looked for the caribou that are here to-day and found them, will you not also look for the caribou that are coming to-morrow, so that we can tell where to lie in ambush for them?' When they heard that my glasses could not see into the future, they were disappointed and naturally the reverse of well impressed with our powers, for they knew that their own medicine-men had charms and magic paraphernalia that enabled them to see things the morrow was to bring forth.

"At another time, in describing to them the skill of our surgeons, I told that they could put a man to sleep and while he slept take out a section of his intestines or one of his kidneys, and the man when he woke up would not even know what had been done to him, except as he was told and as he could see the sewed-up opening through which the part had been removed. Our doctors could even transplant the organs of one man into the body of another. These things I had actually never seen done, but that they were done was a matter of common knowledge in my country. It was similar in their country, one of my listeners told me. He himself had a friend who suffered continually from backache until a great medicine-man undertook to treat him. The next night, while the patient slept, the medicine-man removed the entire spinal column, which had become diseased, and replaced it with a complete new set of vertebrae, and—what was most wonderful—there was not a scratch on the patient's skin or anything to show that the exchange had been made."

Although Stefansson saw the humor in his situation, and although he became accustomed to the way his higher knowledge was invariably received, still he could not avoid the temptation to be impressive.

"One day when I was explaining to my Eskimo that

there were mountains on the moon and going into details of the moon's physical characteristics, the account I gave did not coincide with the opinion held by my Eskimo listeners, and they asked me how I knew these things were so. I explained that we had telescopes as long as the masts of ships and that through them we could see the things on the moon's surface. 'But had any white man ever been to the moon?' I was asked, and when I replied that no one ever had, they said that while they did not have any telescopes as long as ship's masts, yet they did have men, and truthful men, too, that had been to the moon, walked about there and seen everything, and they had come back and told them about it. With all deference to the ingenuity of white men, they thought that under the circumstances the Eskimo ought to be better informed than the white men as to the facts regarding the moon.

"One of the local shamans had for a familiar spirit the spirit of a white man, and in séances spoke 'white men's language.' We were present at one of these séances; and when I said that I was unable to understand anything of what the white man's spirit said through the mouth of the woman whom he possessed, it was considered a very surprising thing, and apparently inclined some of the people to doubt that I was really a white man as I represented myself to be. . . ."

Stefansson was often irritated and frustrated by the Eskimos he traveled with, but he was just as often amused and sympathetic. He loved white men in the North less. He was delighted by the failure of the white explorers who were trying to improve the design of the Eskimo hood, and he was angry when he saw missionaries at Point Barrow encourage Eskimos to live in wooden houses. The Barrow Eskimos had lived for centuries in cold-proof, thick-walled sod houses comfortably heated by one or two seal-oil lamps, ventilated through the long tunnel entrance and the smokehole, and perfectly suited to the northern winter. In a generation, in their half-successful attempt to keep the wooden houses warm, the Barrow Eskimos burned up what had once seemed a limitless supply of driftwood, and tuberculosis was rampant among them. Stefansson disliked missionaries. He was untainted by the missionary instinct, and was glad he had never felt it. He was delighted at the way Eskimo belief in spirits persisted in Eskimos who had converted to Christianity:

"There are also in every community Eskimos who are in the habit of visiting heaven and conferring there with Christ Himself, with Saint Peter and others, quite in the manner in which they used to visit the moon while still heathen and have discussions with the man in the moon. The man in the moon used to teach the shamans songs and spells, and now St. Peter teaches the deacons of the Eskimo church hymns and chants (which are, curiously enough, generally in the jargon language which the whalers use in dealing with the Eskimo).

"There are also frequent and weighty revelations in the matter of doctrine. If the missionary should learn of any of these things and should disagree with them (but he is not likely to learn, for the Eskimo have found out that the missionaries do not approve of present-day revelation, and therefore keep it secret as much as possible), they might be respectful and polite about it to his face, as they always are, but among themselves they would say that while they had no doubt that the Lord spoke unto Moses, neither did they doubt that he also spoke unto this and that countryman of theirs; and if what God said to the Hebrews seems to disagree with what He has said more recently, then evidently it is only reasonable to accept the later version."

*   *   *

Stefansson, like the explorers who followed him, was caught up in the strangeness of his life. He strove to be a practical man in driving his dogs or securing meat, and as a writer he made a great effort to dispel the mystique of survival in the North and encourage settlement there, but in spite of all that, he daily faced the improbability of his existence, and wondered at it. There was a ritual common among the Eskimos Stefansson met from the Coronation Gulf to Alaska that no number of repetitions can have prepared him for. On seeing Stefansson or any stranger for the first time, the Eskimos of that country leapt to their feet and instantly "began a monotonous noise which is not a chant nor is it words—it is merely an effort to ward off dumbness, for if a man who is in the presence of a spirit does not make at least one sound each time he draws his breath, he will be stricken permanently dumb."

The strangeness was in the Eskimo greeting that Stefansson commonly received: *"We are as we seem."* It was in mirages on the arctic plains that Stefansson traveled, and in the way distance distorted size: Marmots appeared to be polar bears, and lemmings looked like musk oxen. If you were looking for the polar bear, Stefansson wrote, you would see it in the lemming. On the tundra a man, shaman or not, saw what he wanted to.

For Vilhjálmur Stefansson, the strangeness came home most strongly in the unknown tribe that he stumbled upon and brought to the attention of the world.

From a Danish trapper named Klinkenberg, Stefansson heard the first rumor of an Eskimo people unlike any other Eskimos. Klinkenberg, sailing a schooner near Herschel Island in 1905, had been blown eastward to Vic-

toria Island, from where he returned a year later with a story about a people who spoke Eskimo but looked like Scandinavians. In 1908, Stefansson launched a four-year expedition, one of its goals to find the new people.

South of Victoria Island, Stefansson's party fell in with a tribe of Eskimos who, strangely, were unable to perceive that Stefansson was not an Eskimo. Stefansson wondered why they could not see he was white, and he questioned the people. "Couldn't you tell by my blue eyes and the color of my beard?" he asked. "But we didn't know," they answered, "what sort of complexions the white men have. Besides, our next neighbors north have eyes and beards like yours." Following the directions of the villagers, Stefansson traveled to Victoria Island, and there found himself face to face with the fair tribesmen.

"We had been told by our guide that we should find the Victoria Islanders of a light complexion, with fair beards, but still we were not prepared for what we saw—we had believed what we had been told, but we had not realized it. Natkusiak kept saying, "These are not Eskimo; they merely dress and talk and act like Eskimo." And so it seemed to me.

"It is hard, looking back over a gap of years, to call to memory even the intense feelings with which we meet a crisis in life. That morning, when the nine men and boys of the village stood before me in line on the ice in front of their huts of snow and skins, I knew I was standing face to face with an important scientific discovery. From childhood I had been familiar with the literature of the North; I knew that here a thousand and there a hundred men of Scandinavia and of England had disappeared into the Northern mists, to be hid by them forever from the eyes of Europe; and when I saw before me these men who looked like Europeans in spite of their garb of furs, I knew that I had come upon either the last chapter and solution of one of the historical tragedies of the past, or else that I had added a new mystery for the future to solve: the mystery of why these men are like Europeans if they be not of European descent."

Stefansson was face to face with more than just an important scientific discovery, of course. He was facing the sudden realization that history was more wonderful and complicated than he had thought, that men were brothers in a way he had not guessed before, that arctic currents moved humans as unpredictably as they moved coconuts and Japanese floats. And it was more than just a puzzle for the future. It was, in Stefansson's words, a crisis in his own life. Stefansson, the wanderer, the proud, brave, irascible, solitary man who felt most at home among an alien people, was face to face with himself.

Blond Eskimo (of the Umingmaktormiut)

WILBUR MILLS: Driftwood, Camden Bay

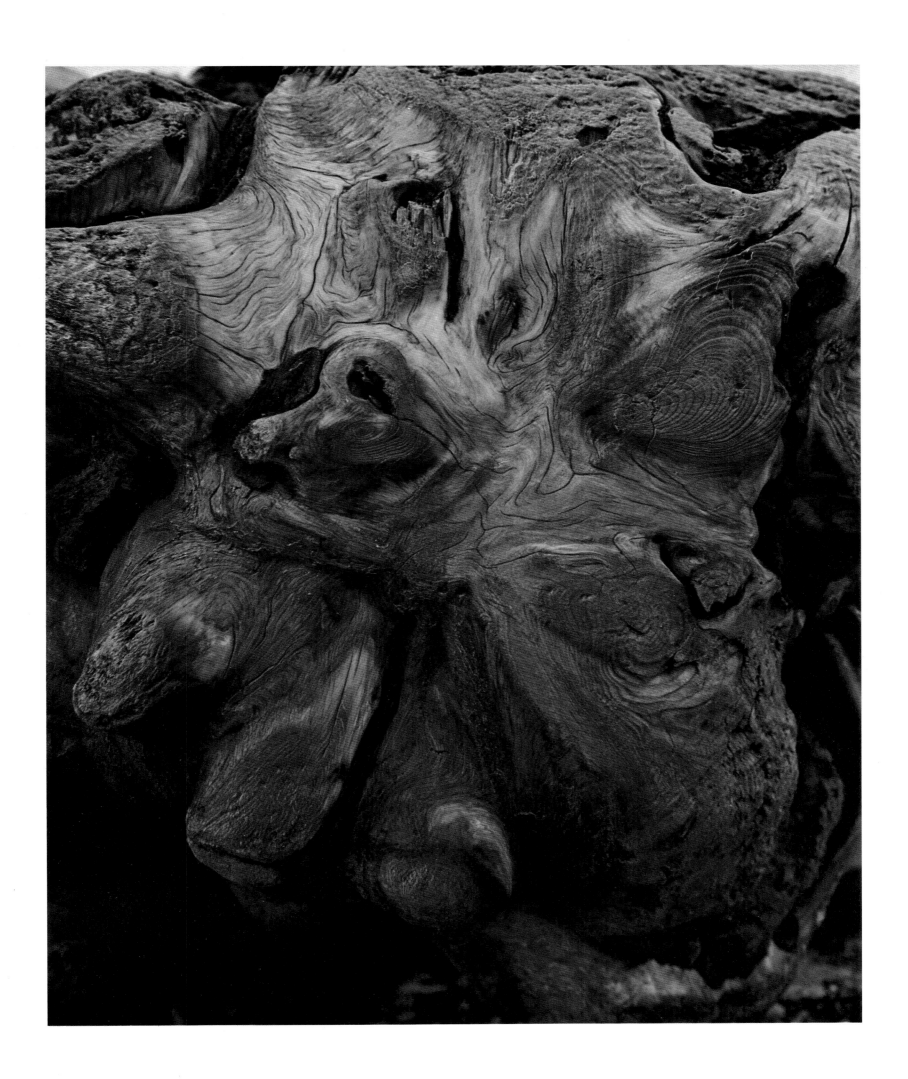

The greatest chronicler of the Eskimo life was the Danish ethnologist Knud Rasmussen. Rasmussen was a circumpolar man. He traveled by sled among Eskimo tribes from Greenland to Alaska, recording legends, beliefs, taboos, customs, games, poems, stories, and vocabularies, and collecting clothing, implements, amulets, drawings, and carvings, from all of that nearly interminable length of coast. Rasmussen's method of assuring an accurate census of the lands he visited was to take the names of everyone he met, and the name of anyone who might be away hunting at the time. At each village of new people, Rasmussen recorded names. ''The people in the area between Ogden Bay and Bathhurst Inlet are distributed as follows: At Kegdlingujaq; *Anulalik* (the one who brings a piece of skin to be softened with the teeth), his wife *Qulaihuk* (the one who wishes to shoot over the target), his other wife *Qunualuk* (the smiling one), daughter *Augpalugtaq* (the red fox), and foster son *Tuatina* (the willowy one) . . .'' and so on, for the people of the Queen Maud Sea, Victoria Land, Cambridge Bay, Ukatlit, Kulgajuk, Kuk, Malerisiorfik, and other frozen places. In this way Rasmussen's moving pen worked its way along thousands of miles of arctic coastline, sketching out a cartography of lives. If any single man grasped who the Inuit were, it was Rasmussen. He was part Greenland Eskimo himself, and he was taken for an Eskimo by most of the people he fell in with. His ear for Eskimo poetry and his talent for conveying the mood and resonance of Eskimo life were unequaled. The volume of the ethnological work he produced in the years following the First World War was heroic, and he rightly became a Danish national hero. He is remembered today by Nunamiut Eskimos, who liked him and recall that his Greenlandic dialect was easy to understand.

Rasmussen received his first schooling as a boy in Greenland. His teacher was his mother's sister, Helga, a half-Eskimo woman. The young Knud Rasmussen cut up constantly and was impossible to teach. His brother and sister imitated him, and his Aunt Helga despaired. One day she could endure the children no longer. She jumped up on a rock outside the house, and shouted that if they continued to misbehave, she was going to the mountains to become a mountain phantom. Knud was thunderstruck. He begged her not to do it. Later he remembered it as the worst day of his childhood. But in fear of the mountain phantom his education began, to be completed not very brilliantly in Denmark.

The man who knew Rasmussen the explorer best was Peter Freuchen, his companion through fourteen years of arctic travel. The only conflict the two men had in all their years of traveling together was over Rasmussen's belief that tea should be boiled. That seemed an incredible practice to Freuchen. Still, it was not much of a disagreement, though it happened every morning. Freuchen was a large man, and Rasmussen was short; Freuchen was solid and sensible, and Rasmussen was something else, but the two men got along, and in their differences they delineated one another. The things about Rasmussen that most puzzled Freuchen are the most illuminating about him. Freuchen was unable to teach Rasmussen navigation. Knud refused to learn how to secure the hour angle, making up his mind at the beginning that he could never master it. Freuchen couldn't understand Rasmussen's stubbornness. He tried to teach Rasmussen with such determination that both men got angry. Then they laughed at themselves. Rasmussen announced that he was giving up astronomy on the spot, and he celebrated his decision with boiled tea and pudding.

On another occasion Rasmussen decided that he would no longer shoot bears. He made himself a lance with which to fight the bears when his dogs had cornered them. This was the kind of enterprise that mystified Freuchen. He simply reported it, in his account of their life together, as one of the inexplicable Rasmussen phenomena. Surely Freuchen would have understood better if he had not been so aware, polar explorer that he was, of the dangers of the bear. It is not so hard to guess what Knud Rasmussen—the incorrigible boy, the daydreaming student, the quarter-Eskimo—was up to.

Rasmussen and Freuchen, like Vilhjálmur Stefansson, were caught up in the unearthliness of their lives.

The two men stood together one February 22 and watched the sun rise above the horizon for the first time since the dark months of winter had begun. Following the example of their Eskimo companions, they pushed back their parka hoods, removed their mittens and faced the new light. The ritual was intended by the Eskimos to assure that they live at least until the sun disappeared again the next winter; for the white men the meaning was vaguer. But it must have been a full and strange moment for all of them.

Once Freuchen and Rasmussen lay together in the remains of an iceberg that had just exploded. They had ignored the taboo against butchering animals on top of an iceberg—it does seem one of the more irrational Eskimo prohibitions—and they had dressed out a polar bear there. The bear's warm blood, flowing into a crack, had altered the interior balance of the iceberg—a balance achieved under great pressure in the icecap—and the iceberg had re-

adjusted violently. They looked at each other across the fragments of ice, and the world must have seemed strange indeed. As they picked themselves up and dusted off, they must have been more aware than usual how much there was in the world unknown to them.

Peter Freuchen accepted the improbability of his life uneasily. He married an Eskimo woman, Navarana, and fathered half-Eskimo children, and settled into an Eskimo life, but the course his history had taken never ceased to amaze him. Of his first child he wrote:

"The boy himself was a healthy specimen. One of his eyes had a slight cast, but everyone knew that this misfortune was only to assure us that he was really old Mequsaq—Navarana's one-eyed grandfather—reborn. He also possessed a blue Mongolian spot at the base of his spine, as does every Eskimo child. This would fade by the time he was three or four years old. But in addition, there was another birthmark farther up on his back, near his kidney. This would seem to indicate that he was also to be named "Avatak." A boy of that name who had lived up north had just been shot by his uncle in a fit of hysteria. The bullet had entered the body at the same spot as the mark on our son. Thus the boy entered the world with names already provided."

When his children had grown a bit, Freuchen brought them two motherless bear cubs for pets. "The bears were good wrestlers," he wrote, "but eventually they grew too big and strong. The children cried once, and said that the bears had beaten them in their games." Little could Freuchen's own father have guessed the lands his son would travel in, or the games his grandchildren would play.

After Navarana died, Freuchen visited Denmark for only the second time in many years. There is a photograph of him, a large bearded man in ill-fitting pants, standing on the dock with his two children—small Greenlanders—in either hand. He was still solid and sensible, but was a marked and altered man. He must have looked foreign to his countrymen, and felt foreign to himself.

Knud Rasmussen accepted the improbability of his life happily. Facing the new spring sun with his hood back and his cold hands bare, or kneeling in wet snow on the sea ice, in a circle of companions, eating in ritual the raw liver of a freshly killed seal, Rasmussen felt himself return to another kind of consciousness, and he liked it.

Rasmussen had an eye for the small strangenesses of polar life, and was haunted by them. He was traveling once in bad weather with a storyteller named Netsit. At the end of the stormy day the two men built a snow house. Resting inside, Rasmussen felt it a special occasion, and

he took out two cigarettes, offering one to Netsit. To his surprise Netsit did not light his cigarette, but wrapped it in a rag. The next day, as they were passing a black rock island in the middle of a fiord, Netsit asked Rasmussen to stop the dogs. Then the Eskimo set about propitiating the spirits of the weather. "I can just make out what it is he is doing," Rasmussen wrote, in the present tense, as if trying to remember and describe a dream. "I see him go down on his knees and with his knife cut a small hollow in the snow. With most careful hands he lays in that hollow the cigarette and two matches, and then covers the hole again with snow. Then through the gale I hear him murmur a number of formulae, ending with his drawing attention, in a voice full of pathos, to the rare gift he has made." The next morning the weather had indeed cleared. Rasmussen drove his dogs on, but now even the cigarettes in his pocket were charged with a new life.

Rasmussen listened to Eskimos carefully, and was haunted by what he heard. "The most awful experience I ever had was what happened to Nagfaq, the mother of Inugssak," an Eskimo told Rasmussen. "Once when there was a famine she gave birth to a child, while people lay around about her dying of hunger. *What did that little child want here?*"

An old woman approached Rasmussen once, and said:

My name is Arnagliaq (the one who was made a woman). I am so old that I have nothing to pay with, and yet I am a woman and need both sewing needle and thimble. If you give me these things I can only repay you with a wish. And that is: May you live long! But if I were to add another wish to these words, a wish that comes from the experience that my age gives me, it is this: May you never be as old as I am!

*   *   *

In the years after the First World War the Nunamiut Eskimos left the Brooks Range. They settled near towns where they could find jobs. The Eskimos of the North Slope did the same, leaving their many coastal villages and gathering at one or two spots along the arctic shore. The ethnologists, who depended on Eskimo the way wolves depend on caribou, followed. The scientists ceased to be nomads, and a good measure of the romance went out of their lives.

The next travelers in the Brooks Range mountains found themselves alone. Where their predecessors had been preoccupied with the Inuit, these new men saw the land. The Inuit had called attention to themselves irresistibly: George Swinton writes of Eskimo sculpture that, "among the remarkable features of Eskimo carved heads are their expressiveness and serenity, which are charac-

teristic of Eskimo existence. Although this may sound platitudinous and emotional, Eskimo faces, as a group, appear more expressive, profound, and interesting to me than those of most groups. God's love and wrath—or Nature's—seem to have been etched permanently into them.''

There were no such faces now, just the face of the land.

The first of the new explorers—the prospectors and trappers who wandered the southern foothills of the Brooks Range in the first half of the twentieth century—did not figure in the history of the mountains. They were inarticulate men who left no record of what they saw. We know much more about the Eskimos and Indians of the country than we know of them. There were among them men who led lives more solitary than any shaman's, but their visions went unrevealed and their philosophies untaught. The bits of information we have about them were recorded by other men. A trapper named Ernie Johnson, for example, told Robert Marshall his reason for living in the Brooks Range, and Marshall noted it:

> I can make better money as a carpenter, but I am staying out here because I like it among these ruggedy mountains better than anywhere else in the world.

Robert Marshall, who traveled widely in the central Brooks Range in the 1930's, did tell about what he saw. Marshall was the staunchest advocate of the Arctic since Vilhjálmur Stefansson. Stefansson had called for opening the North to development; Marshall called for closing it. He wanted to see all arctic Alaska perpetuated as wilderness.

Marshall's pretext for exploring the Brooks Range was the gathering of data on tree growth at the northern timberline. He admitted readily that this, and his other scientific excuses, were just that—that he really explored because as a boy he had read Lewis and Clark, and had always wanted to be an explorer. Blank spaces on a map moved him as nothing else did. The blank spaces continued to hold him even when he was grown—if indeed he ever grew. There is evidence that he never did. His adventures in the Brooks Range were a boy's adventures. In his book there is a photograph of him, with a one-armed sourdough to his right, a pipe-smoking Eskimo to his left, Marshall in the middle, holding his friends around the shoulders as if to make sure they don't get away, grinning what clearly is, in spite of his heavy beard, a boyish grin.

Thirty years after Robert Marshall left the Brooks Range, David Roberts entered. Climbing the granite peaks of the Arrigetch Mountains in the middle of the Range, Roberts found the land as wild as it had been for Marshall. But because the Brooks Range wilderness, like any other, contains infinite possibilities, Roberts saw the mountains differently:

Igikpak and the Arrigetch

It is the mildest, gentlest wilderness I have ever seen.

It is the loneliest, emptiest wilderness I have ever been in.

I am writing not about two different parts of the map, but about a single paradoxical place: the western Brooks Range.

For instance: on August 8, 1968, my wife Sharon and I took a walk from our base camp, three miles west of the range's highest mountain (Igikpak), down the Reed River, which was only a boulder-hopping creek in the treeless headwaters where we were camped. The flowers were still in bloom, but most of the mosquitoes had died. It was a fragrant, warm day, the temperature pushing 70°. In a little pool where I had caught trout we stopped to bathe. The water was too cold to stay in very long, but after our dip we lay naked in perfect comfort in the tundra grass beside the stream, listening to the birds and insects, catching glimpses of the frowning black cliffs on Igikpak, 6000 feet above us.

Exactly a year later, on August 8, 1969, Art Bacon and I

took a walk up a side-fork of Arrigetch Creek, in the middle of the Brooks Range's most spectacular pocket of granite peaks. We were thirty miles east of our 1968 base camp, at the same latitude, at a slightly lower altitude.

The flowers, like the mosquitoes, were gone for the year; even the berries were over-ripe, and already the willow leaves showed tinges of red. In the chilly mist that was descending on us, we clambered over boulders cushioned with a dank red moss. At the foot of a 75°, 2000-foot wall on a nameless peak, we fooled around making twenty-foot starts on a route. Soon, however, the cold chased us off. The gloomy chasm we had hiked into seemed preternaturally dark. Except for our talk and the ragged whisper of wind up high, it was an utterly soundless place. When we turned to head back we saw, as if they had been cut off by the mist from the solid world below, the sharp tops of the "Maidens," wet black granite slabs starting to coat with a layer of new snow and verglas. The sight made us want to hurry back to camp and hide in our tents.

The contrast was, to an extent, a seasonal oddity: the August of 1968 was one of the driest and warmest in local memory, the same month in 1969 beset by cold and early snowstorms. On top of Igikpak we loafed in our T-shirts; in the Arrigetch we climbed with numb fingers and rested in down jackets. But the paradox—the uncanny blend of gentleness and loneliness in the range—does not depend on quixotic seasons.

It can be glimpsed from any summit. Around you, the moss and lichens abound, painting the rocks thousands of feet above the last bushes and tens of miles north of the last trees. You may hear swallows or finches, see bees and butterflies. But in the distance, instead of familiar valleys or a coherent ridge crest, instead of trails leading down to roads leading down to towns, there is a monotonous expanse of barren black peaks, lumps, most of them, with here and there a gloomy spire. The valleys are small, crooked, aimless—like the peaks, they all look the same. In the whole sweep of land that you can see—and especially to the west—there may not be another human being.

The paradox can be sensed, too, in camp. The meadow under your feet is a luxurious carpet of reindeer moss; but you know that only inches beneath is the permafrost. Ground squirrels and conies scurry through the weeds near you, but there is something furtive about their existence—you cannot pretend, as you might in a temperate forest, that these little animals are playful companions. At night the air may stay warm, and the half-dark is full of a comfortable coziness: nothing seems too big or too far away. But in the middle of the night you may be awakened by pelting rain and the old rumble of thunder: it will be darker now, except in those stark moments when the nylon walls of your tent flash alive in the glare of the lightning.

You may, as we did in 1968, sense the paradox as you sniff a smog-like air and smell the faint sweetness of burning spruce—and realize that what is for you an atmospheric condition is, fifty miles south, a raging forest fire, and that there is nobody there fighting it and nothing to do about it but let it burn itself out. You may apprehend the contrast, as we did in 1969, floating down a river like the Alatna on some sunny afternoon, some day full of soft wind in the birch leaves and glimpses of grayling in the green water under your boat—and have the sun set suddenly behind jagged, nameless hills, while you float on southward into the twilight, in which, somewhere miles ahead on a river bar, a lone wolf is moaning, filling the valley with a cry too alien to call despair.

You may find, in this gentle wilderness, a sense of scale and balance that seem not inimical to man. You will be often reminded of other, less northerly places: of Colorado, of Wisconsin, of New England or even Virginia. But these are deceptive intimations. There is, to be sure, a kind of biotic riot in the summer outburst of color, scent, and sound, into which you, like so many visitors to the Brooks Range, have intruded. But always the season's absent opposite haunts you: *what about the winter? What must that be like?*

Winter in the Brooks Range is twice as long as summer. There are really only those two seasons, climaxed by June days of perpetual light and their December counterparts of darkness, marked off by those two events most basic to the arctic year: freeze-up and break-up. On the big rivers the freeze-up comes around the middle of October, the break-up not until the end of May. In the meantime the arctic is a frozen world, a world no man could feel lazy or at home in. Yet the animals, whose tracks in the snow cross every valley, whose cries occasionally echo in a windless silence, manage to survive. Every summer the weeds, and the leaves of the deciduous trees, and then the flowers, and last the berries, come back to life. Perhaps that is what you sense, in the middle of the bug-thick heat of summer: that for all the pandemonium of life and growth around you, it is a guarded and careful blooming, as if each plant knew exactly what space it owned, and what inner things it had to save against the winter. The summer's is a ragged lushness: bushes grow thick, but not tall, the trees keep to a cautious size, each year the berries go to waste by the millions, but they grow small and close to the ground. And the water—no ecology that I know of seems to use its water more cleverly. There is none of the violence of desert erosion—yet, in terms of rainfall, the range is almost a desert. You sense that things grow slowly, and that every wound in the landscape shows its scar for a long time. Nothing conveys the sense of the land's carefulness like the reindeer moss, that strange quilt of interlocking, apparently rootless cushion that surfaces the treeless tundra everywhere. When there is plenty of water, the reindeer moss soaks it up like a sponge; walking on patches of it is indeed like walking on a vast sponge. When it is dry, the moss shrivels and contracts; walking on it, you feel it crumbling and hear it crackling, and you might well think it had died, but for the fact that the next rain brings it back to spongy life.

It is the rivers, in the last analysis (as may be true anywhere), that are the soul of this land. Between those two events—break-up and freeze-up—the rivers offer man the only natural avenues into this labyrinthine wild. In 1969, in the higher creeks, ice was beginning to form by early August: too soon, for at that rate the freeze-up would come about three weeks early. Each morning, as we walked up the valleys, we could hear the ice creaking and melting, as if it had only been joking; but each night a little more would form. By the end of the month, the highest lakes were frozen over, and the snow on the peaks was there to stay. We glimpsed in these headwater valleys the impending winter. We anticipated the freeze-up, but made it in our boats down the Alatna well before it really came.

So I have never seen it, that event that marks the end of river travel for the next eight months. I have never stayed for the winter, and never, in this age of airplanes, been really dependent on the rivers. I sense what this summer tourism at the convenience of airplanes means: I sense what I have lost—the freedom of dependence, of "doing it for real." Looking down the Noatak in 1968, knowing abstractly about its 400-mile odyssey through agoraphobic lowlands and Pleistocene canyons, I could only envy Philip Smith, who in 1911 had taken the first white man's boats down the length of what was, for him, a rumored link with the Arctic Sea. Drifting down the Alatna the next year, in boats our pilot had flown in and would pick up when we were done, I was jealous of the Helmericks, who as late as 1944 had lined their overloaded boat two hundred miles up a river known not by USGS map, but only by the bends and landmarks catalogued in aging Eskimo minds. I longed for an age when the mountains in which we received pinpoint airdrops had been blank spaces on hand-drawn charts between the great valleys that men traveled by, knowing full well that in that earlier age, I would not have dared or wanted to climb the mountains. Serious as our climbing might be, it was only a wilderness game, a game played by overgrown children still trying to get lost in the woods. The woods, as we knew, are no longer big enough—nobody gets lost any more. And the airplane is responsible for that.

"In the time before steamships . . ." Melville begins *Billy Budd*. Only on third or fourth reading did I see the point: not a date, not an event, but an age, a time when the world was different because there were no steamships. A better time? Probably not—but there is no denying Melville's nostalgia for it. So much of what we learn about the Handsome Sailor comes, in that skillful and deliberate book, third-hand, inaccurately, ambiguously, in pieces: from a hazy memory of a chat with a Baltimore Negro forty years before, in a slanted and white-washed naval chronicle, between the lines of a sentimental anonymous ballad.

"In the time before airplanes . . ." I might have begun this narrative. But for me that vanished age is even more remote than the engineless seas were for Melville, because I was not born yet when the airplane took the *incognita* from this *terra borealis*. My intuitions of that lost age are, like Melville's, at best indirect, unreliable, tantalizingly ambiguous. I can read, in the dry prose of a geologic report or the inarticulate effusions of a once-popular book, about where some of the first explorers went, and approximately why; but the more basic empathy—the "what was it like?" and the "what really happened?"—escapes me, except in fugitive visions. Like Melville's sources, the ones I have dug up defeat the truth, and I find myself looking not so much to written record as to those weak links from man to man, preserved only in memory and rumor, that stretch back into the Brooks Range past as far as the near edge of that once-upon-a-time when the only people to whom the place was ever home lived there, those bands of nomads almost as alien to our thinking as wild animals: the Eskimo.

The links stretch back—but they end abruptly, or they miss each other. The Helmericks, on the Alatna in 1944, make no mention of Robert Marshall's 1931 trip, just as Marshall seems scarcely aware of the Murie brothers' 1922 winter dog-sled journey. The men with the greatest sense of continuity are probably the old-timers, the miners and trappers who have stayed in the arctic, and thus, by definition, the least likely to write about it. It is the "experts"—the geologists, the glaciologists, the foresters, the naturalists, the mountain climbers: in a word, the outsiders—who feel the urge to announce their discoveries to the world, as if in fear they might evaporate in captivity.

One of the views into the past that, for me, did not defeat the truth, a single hour more eloquent to me than the whole rambling book that Connie Helmericks wrote about their adventure, came when I found, near the end of our 1969 expedition, the cabin opposite Kutuk Creek that she and her husband Bud had abandoned in the spring

of 1945. The sense of a personal, special place, which all of Connie's bland enthusiasm about their little home in the wilderness could not transmit, sprang vividly to life in that solitary hour I spent poking through the cabin: the windows gone, a big hole in the roof, but the hand-made chairs still sitting there as if left the week before, the tacky little shelves as serviceable as ever, a jar with old tea bags in it resting on one of them. On the back of the door I found a pencilled note they had left on their departure. It began:

—Welcome—

This cabin was built by Bud and Connie Helmericks September, 1944. We spent a very happy and comfortable year here. Left June 1, 1945 for Alatna.

You are welcome to use this cabin as long as you like and anything in or about it. Freeze-up came October 15. Break-up came May 29

Bud & Connie

Visitors may sign below.

The first visitor was a man named Walt Leslie, who had stopped in August, 1947, and who listed his home as Nome, Alaska. The next entry read:

Connie & Bud   *October 15-17, '47. Age 29 now. Fairbanks, Ala. Just built our home at Takahula Lake—30 mi. Communications Outside via our plane, the* Arctic Tern.

In that second entry, as bland as ever, there was no sense of loss: but surely they felt it. To be able simply to fly up and land at the doorstep of the cabin they had hauled a thousand pounds of gear up-river to build, and in which, during an airplaneless winter, they had nearly starved, knowing that only they could save themselves; to have replaced the last idyllic "in-ness" possible in the Brooks Range with "Communications Outside"!

I signed the note, only the fourth visitor (but for Bud and Connie themselves) to find it in the quarter-century it had hung, fragile and yellowing, on the back of their door.

Another hour eloquent for me in its evocation of the past came a week before our Arrigetch expedition, when Sharon and I met Adolph Murie in McKinley Park. An old man now, over seventy, he was still spending his summers watching wild game in the Park. He spoke softly, and only after deliberation, but his eyes and voice were as bold and alive as the trips he had taken in his youth. His brother Olaus had been dead now for six years, but when I asked Adolph to talk about the old days, and especially about that amazing 1922 circuit of the Brooks Range, the pain of the loss—not only of his brother, but of the past, of the time before airplanes—was in his words.

If there was a single great exploration in the western Brooks Range, however, if one had to choose its Lewis and Clark, it would have to be the 1911 expedition of the USGS geologist Philip Smith. In three summer months, his party ascended the Koyukuk to the Alatna, up the length of that river by canoe (even sailing on some of the slower stretches), across Portage Creek Pass to the headwaters of the Noatak, which they descended in the month of August, beating the freeze-up as smoothly as if they had known from the beginning exactly how long the whole trip would take. In search of an Eskimo-reported pass to the west, Smith, on July 16, 1911, was the first white man to enter the Arrigetch Valley itself. He took a pair of photos of the glaciers and granite walls near the head of Arrigetch Creek, but found no pass. "This divide is so nearly unscalable," he wrote, "that almost any other route would be preferable." In 1962, a glaciologist named Tom Hamilton went up Arrigetch Creek to duplicate Smith's photos. It was a kind of thrill for us, seven years later, to find both cairns that Hamilton had built, marking the spots from which Smith had taken the photos; they were the only signs we found in the Arrigetch of previous human visitors. And we discovered the pass that Smith had given up on, a steep, rotten headwall between two peaks that we named "Xanadu" and "Ariel," a climb that bordered often on the technical, but which, it was obvious, scores of sheep, bobcats, even bears had made year after year. We were perhaps the first men to cross the pass—unless the Eskimo who had informed Smith had known, after all (as was entirely likely), what they were talking about.

Another link with the past had to do with a human settlement near the middle of the Alatna called "Rapid City." In the gold rush of 1898, when miners swarmed into the major valleys of the Brooks Range, one group got stuck, apparently, by the freeze-up, at a camp on the Alatna beside the only rapids in the whole river. They built a few cabins on the spot and settled in for the winter. Only thirteen years later, passing the spot, Smith referred to the "fast-disappearing evidence of the old camp." Two decades after Smith, Marshall stopped at the site. The ruins prompted in him the following speculation:

"A few miles above the Iniakuk River . . . were the crumbling remains of four cabins. They had been built in the autumn of 1898 when an early freeze-up caught a group of tenderfoot stampeders on this lonesome river

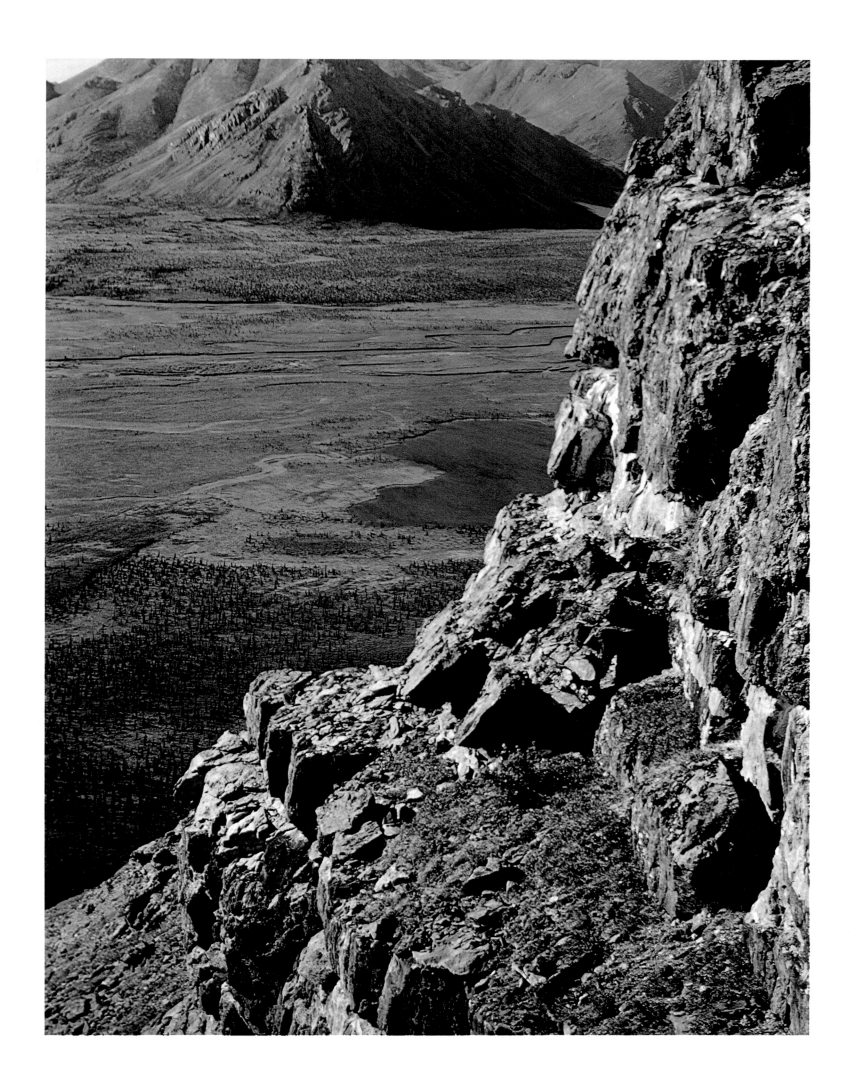

and cut them off from the rest of humanity. One can imagine the horror of these people, probably already discouraged in their quest for gold, wishing they had never left their secure farms or cities where they had lived in safety and relative comfort, thinking that in a day or two they would start down the river in their boats safely ahead of the freeze-up, but wanting to prospect just once more in the hope of still finding a bonanza which would free them from a life of constant labor. Then suddenly, waking up one early October morning, weeks before the date of the freeze-up even in the coldest regions to which they were accustomed, they found the Alatna covered over and escape locked up until distant spring.

"So they built these cabins which they ironically christened Rapid City. After thirty-three years the roofs had fallen in as well as most of the walls. We entered one of the cabins in best repair. It measured 12 by 12 feet. . . . It gave me a queer feeling to see this simple equipment slowly rotting under the timelessness of nature, probably unseen by human eyes for many years, completely disassociated from that part of the earth and its processes which is human, and yet to realize that for one endless winter it constituted the most intimate reality in the life of one lonesome person. It was easy to imagine this futile prospector lying on his back in the hard bunk as he had lain for many nights before, seeing the pegs in the wall, the chinked logs, and the cold ceiling, wondering why in the world he had ever left the comforts of a reasonable civilization, hating the misery to which the quest for gold had led him, wishing for only one thing in the world—that he might get away where life was safe and gregarious. But it was also easy to imagine that in later years when this same man was living the desired safe and gregarious life of ordinary America, where the codes of society and the proprieties of civilization had killed the spontaneity of the frontier, where days and years were filled with the routine fight for a living, that he must have often thought of the great adventure of his lonesome winter."

Aware of the place and its visitors, I hoped, as we approached it on our trip down the Alatna, to add another, seventy-one-year footnote. Surely, I thought, there would be some trace of the cabins left. It was a cloudy, placid day, near the end of August, as we floated down the lonely river, escaped from the mountains at last. Ahead of us, out of sight, I heard the roaring of the rapids, and knew that it must be the place. But all the while we had been smelling the faint odor of ash and soot, like a recent campfire. That June had been a record month for forest fires in Alaska; although they were all extinguished by now, we knew, from sighting the vast black scars on the flight in, that the

forests on the south slope of the Brooks Range had been hit particularly hard. At the rapids, Sharon and I got out of our boat. On the left bank, where Rapid City should have been, the fire had burnt everything but the biggest trees to the ground. The burn stopped at the river—the forest on the other bank was still growing, and even the weeds on the sand bar were alive. But any vestige of Rapid City was gone for good.

When Smith had come up the river, he knew that at least three survey parties had preceded him. The earliest of them, that of Stoney in 1886, had ascended the Alatna as far as either Kutuk or Unakserak Creek, a few miles above Arrigetch Creek. In 1911, Smith had found no Eskimo in either the Alatna or the Noatak, except for summer fishing camps on the lower reaches of both rivers. But through Stoney, Smith had a link with the Edenic time when these valleys had been, in every sense, the home of the inland Eskimo. Stoney had found, about twenty miles up either Kutuk or Unakserak Creek (his geography being so poor that Smith could not tell which), a permanent, occupied settlement whose name he reported as Nimiuk ("cottonwood"). Similarly McLenegan, the first white man to explore the upper Noatak, had found in 1885 a few winter settlements, from which the Eskimo would wander up and down the river in the summertime, hunting and fishing.

But in the last decade of the nineteenth century, the herds of caribou, on which the people were utterly dependent, began to dwindle mysteriously. Forced by starvation down to the coast, where they could live by trade off the whaling ships that had just begun to penetrate the Arctic Sea, the Eskimo exchanged a nomadic life of their own for a stationary, parasitic one, in which they discovered the delights of tea, tobacco, and Christianity and the horrors of drunkenness, measles, influenza and syphilis. In twenty years, according to Diamond Jenness, their population had diminished to one-fifth of their previous numbers.

Even Smith's journey, in 1911, seems remote from the Eskimo, as if he had already entered a modern age. For us, fifty-seven years beyond his "time before airplanes," the Eskimo were only ghosts in an empty landscape. But ghosts whose remains, when we came upon them, were the most suggestive of all. The series of little cairns, seven of them, in a geometrical pattern whose meaning was lost on us, that we found on the upper Reed, a mile above what was to be our Igikpak base camp—what were they for? for hunting, navigation, or just because the place "needed" them? The fortress-like overlooks that Vin and Grace Hoeman found, at the end of the same expedition, on

their ascent of Mount Papiok—on what Noatak herds or invaders had men secretively peered in those days before there was a single piece of metal in Alaska? Ambiguous, frustrating, unreadable by us, these signs: but we could only be grateful, all the same, for having stumbled upon them, for their testimony to a way of life that even its acculturated descendants had lost, except as a dim memory in fading legends.

*　　*　　*

What man does in the wilderness is so easy to do—and so hard to write about. Those of us who love the wild regard it as sacred—nothing poses a more blasphemous threat than a new road, an oil rig, a snowmobile, or even the possibility that somebody else might go where we have been. Surely this is, in some sense, a perverse attitude. Few men who really live in the wilderness—not just for a month in the summer, but all the time—treat it as sacred.

In writing about it, the easiest pose to fall into, and the one of which we should be the most suspicious, is that of Thoreau. It is easy, in comfortable retrospect from an armchair or an office, to treat each blade of grass as a miracle. But when you were there, did you? Perhaps you did, for an intellectual moment or two, probably because you had read Thoreau. But not day by day.

The hardest thing to capture about the wilderness—the quality most absent from writing about it—is its ordinariness. There are, certainly, beautiful eccentricities within it: exotic spears of granite in the Arrigetch, delightful pools and waterfalls in a valley we named "Aquarius," a mountain full of quartz crystals above the Noatak. But on the whole and on the average, all wilderness is dreary, monotonous, ragged—the same, mile after mile. Men who live in it know it: we who can only visit it recognize it implicitly, in the way we come to know and grow bored by the surroundings of our camps ("same old boulder, same old skyline")—but we feel guilty for this discovery, as if somehow, when afflicted by that "same-old" feeling, we were not appreciating the wilderness fully enough: as if the hours spent in the tent reading or playing cards were hours of irreverence to a Deity of Nature.

It is mainly the Romantics, and among them, especially Thoreau, who have poisoned our perceptions of the wilderness. To them everything had to be sacred, special, revealing of a higher Presence—and it is their bad habits, whether or not we think of ourselves as literary, that we fall into when we look at nature. Their dogma has pervaded our culture, filtered into National Park postcards, license-plate slogans, even cigarette ads.

It is refreshing occasionally to read a description of the wilderness written before 1750. It does not often occur to the earlier travellers (some of whom, of course, made the bravest voyages possible on the surface of the earth) that all those trees, all that water, or all those mountains are beautiful. When Cárdenas blundered onto the Grand Canyon in the 16th century, he cursed it for blocking his way. Bound as the earlier expeditioneers were by fear, by worldly ambition, by a Christian ideal of the civilized place, they managed sometimes to see the wilderness with fresher, more honest eyes than did the Romantics. They saw, sometimes, what was there.

It is, paradoxically, its ordinariness that makes the wilderness so special. In the raggedness of a forest or the chaos of a mountain range we can see, if we purge our minds of Romantic habits, the essential alienness of a world not only pre-existent to man, but utterly without concern for him. There is a kind of Design in the superbly adapted interaction, for instance, of alga and fungus in a lichen: but beyond the Design, there is a Randomness. In the wilderness, given iconoclastic eyes, we can see the emptiness of space, itself a miracle, but not, so far as our frightened minds can judge, a sensible one. There are so many alternatives, says the wilderness, to what we have always taken for granted. This is its specialness: whatever else it may be, the wilderness is not, like a city, a book, or a symphony, an imitation of human order. It is just there. We could not have made it ourselves, because it is too different from us to have predicted.

*　　*　　*

Stoney and McLenegan were government explorers. Smith, also a government employee, was a surveyor and geologist. The Murie brothers were naturalists, paid to make a study of the Dall sheep and caribou in the Brooks Range. Marshall was a forestry expert: one of his excuses for wandering up the Alatna was to look for a single, special tree, reported by an Eskimo woman to have cottonwood bark and spruce needles (Marshall thought it might be a Douglas fir, but never found it). Tom Hamilton was a glaciologist. We, like the 1964 party that was based in the next valley south of Arrigetch Creek, were mountain climbers. And there were all those nameless miners and trappers. Only the Helmericks seemed to have no professional excuse—but she became a writer of sorts, he a bush pilot and big game guide.

Why did all of us have to have official reasons for going there? In part, for some, it was a question of money. But I suspect it was also partly internal: we needed, each of us, a proof that what we were doing was, in some sense, "important": not simply self-indulgence, a waste of time. Or perhaps it sprang, subconsciously, from an awareness of the alienness of which I have just spoken: in such a

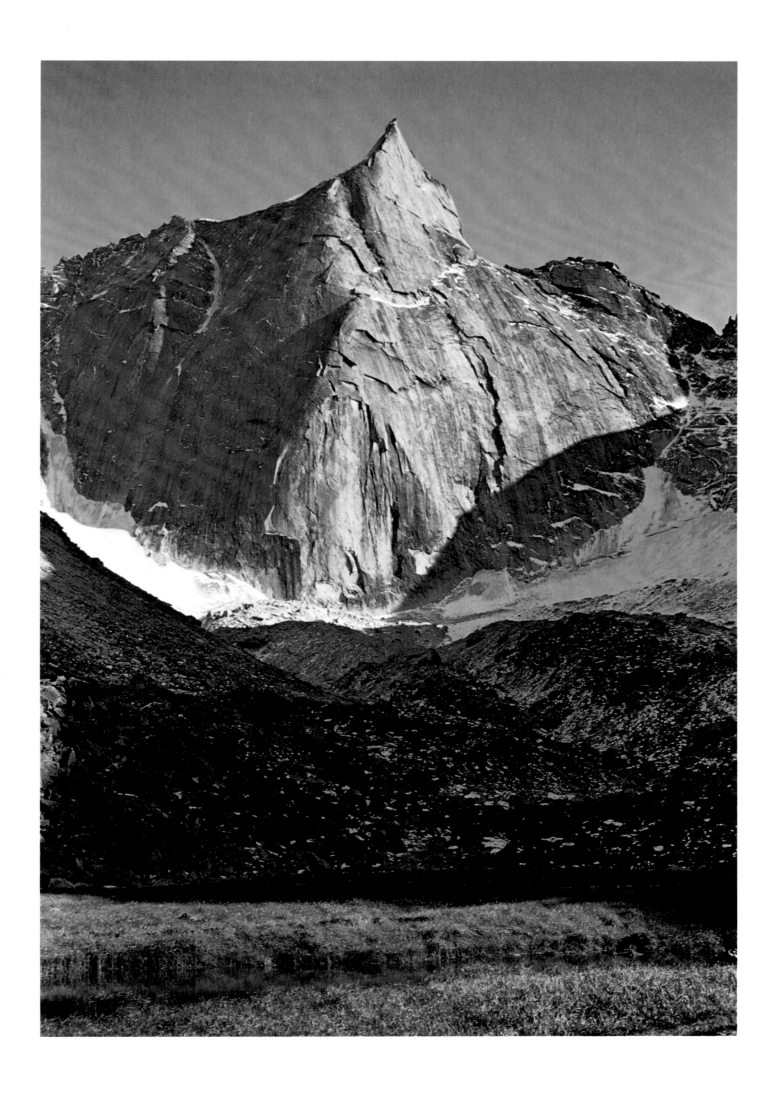

purposeless place, we had to make some imposition of purpose to define our being there. Faced with the vertiginous question, "What shall I do now?", it is helpful to be able to remind yourself, "Find that strange tree," "Explore the headwaters," "Figure out the stratigraphy," or "Climb the highest peak."

As a mountain climber, I felt most sensitive to the rock itself: especially to its texture, both under the hand and in the eye. Good climbers tend to be dabblers in most varieties of rock, but connoisseurs of granite. I was no exception, and the whole reason for my being there was the knowledge that, in two small outbursts in the Brooks Range, one might find prongs of granite instead of the usual hills of schist.

The play of sunlight on granite has always been, to me, evocative of all sorts of urges and fears. A trio of pinnacles on the southwest flank of Igikpak—we called them "gargoyles"—provided for us in 1968 a whole theater of hallucinations. Sometimes the gargoyles looked like monks and nuns, hooded but harboring grace; sometimes like great Jurassic birds, perched predatorily over our narrow valley; they could dance in a sunny sky, or brood somberly in a rainstorm. In 1969 we traced patterns on a "Mosaic Wall" above the biggest lake in Aquarius Valley, or watched the play of wind as it wrote ambiguous warnings in snow and ice on the huge north faces of the Maidens.

But the tactile sense, for the climber, is the most articulate. Accustomed to granite, we could enjoy, if only for the sake of variety, the weird gray swirls of limestone on "Ariel," or the limestone slabs that clinked under our boots, like broken china, on a gentle hike up the "Breadloaf"; or the prosaic lumps of schist west of Igikpak; or a golden vein of crumbly rock, almost like sandstone, in the headwall above the glacier that fed Arrigetch Creek. But to be serious, we had to be on granite. A climber's hands are as sensitive to the grain of granite as are a composer's ears to key: I can remember, long after having forgotten the visual shape of given blocks and slabs, what they felt like. Rocks, like music, seem to send us messages we cannot translate into words. We convert them, often, into warnings or reassurances: the rotten granite shingles on "Tupik Tower" warned me against overhangs and loose boulders, just as the hollowness of "Caliban" gave me hints where not to put my feet. On Igikpak I indulged in the warm roughness of dry, clean granite in the sun on the south side of its summit ridge, but moved warily in the eternal shadow twenty feet away, over its northern, ice-hung edge. But these signals, invaluable as they are to the climber who wants to get back in one piece, obscure the more lyrical speech buried in the rock. My hands did homage to it; my fingers questioned it here, listened there, and obeyed it implicitly on a few special ledges; my fingernails hoarded its grains for days after the climbs were memory; but my brain could not descend to my nerve endings—instead it remained where it ought to, aloof, calculating, deciding.

Only in my brain did that imaginary, impelling abstraction exist: the route. The route is, at best, a barely solvable maze. If the maze is full of dead ends and wrong turns, but still has one true path in it, and if the brain can find and the body follow that path, then it is a good route. Caliban was an adequate route, but an obvious one. On a peak we called "Parabola" we found a hard route, but one that mocked us by showing us, near the top, a trivial alternative. On Tupik Tower we found only dead ends, nasty ones, because we were never sure, thanks to that rotten, shingled rock, that they really were dead ends.

Only Igikpak came close to being the perfect route, and that because, for one thing, it was the highest peak in our whole wilderness, and for another, it was a maze that grew more difficult, step by step, as we drew near the goal. In plain terms, it ended with a 200-foot pillar of superb granite, topped by a thirty-foot overhang, climbable only by circling the pillar, using direct aid in just-sufficient cracks, and finishing with a totally committed pull-up over the edge of the top itself.

On the summit we felt divorced from the world below, at the center of our labyrinth, legitimized by our quest. But there was, as we could have guessed, nothing there, nothing but a summit, a few loose rocks on the flat top of the highest peak in the western Brooks Range.

In the Greek myths about labyrinths, there is always something dreadful or wonderful at the center. But what if Daedalus had never thought of wings? What if Theseus had found no Minotaur? Could they have found something else at the empty center? Could they have borne the coming out, the rolling up of the ball of yarn, with half the happiness we felt on our long descent, that August day, into an arctic dusk?

DAVID ROBERTS

BOB WALDROP:
Cairn, Arrigetch Peaks

J. L. Giddings was another of those who went to the Arctic after the Inuit had moved. Giddings did not find it a lonely land. Because he was an archaeologist, the Inuit were always with him: their presence was as impossible for him to ignore as it had been for Rasmussen or Jenness. His profession made him sensitive to arctic ghosts. Giddings probably saw the land in a truer light than did Robert Marshall, for whom an imagined freedom from human associations and the imagined opportunity to walk where no one had walked before, made the Brooks Range shine so bright. Giddings knew that the tundra under his feet had been walked for thousands of years.

His occupation was full of the kind of monotony that filled Eskimo lives. His troweling was not much different from repairing nets, hafting harpoons, or chewing skins to make them soft, and it allowed the same kind of meditation.

Troweling and pondering, in the sea wind, Giddings could imagine the Denbigh life. He saw the Denbigh hunter sitting on his domed roof, repairing equipment or carving ivory, scanning the sea for beluga while he worked. (Coastal Eskimos stored and discarded much on their roofs, and among the buried remains of collapsed roofs Giddings found most of what he was to find.) A chip fell from the hunter's hand and Giddings picked it up, five thousand years later. His life was spent in this kind of connection with vanished peoples, and it must have made for a rare understanding.

Giddings found buried sites by a method he did not himself understand. Each time he began to search, he asked himself where the People would have stayed. He knew all there was to know about the ancient Inuit, from a career of reading studies and monographs, and more directly, from his own excavations and from what he knew of the modern Inuit who assisted him. He set out. His method required much walking. He wandered the old beach ridges far inland, following his feet. Ceaseless movement is characteristic of all arctic animals; caribou, wolves, lemmings, and archaeologists too, apparently. As Giddings walked, letting his feet and his unconscious take him where they would, he watched for irregularities in the tundra that might mark buried houses.

Giddings admired Knud Rasmussen's work. It is clear that he considered Rasmussen a poet and himself something less. In his less flamboyant way, though, Giddings was as good as Rasmussen at conveying the resonance of Eskimo life. He could not converse with Eskimos in their native tongue, as Rasmussen did, in part because Eskimos no longer spoke it much, but he did have an ear for their pidgin, and he had a feeling for the drama of their exist-

ence. Traveling on the Kobuk River one summer, Giddings fell in with a gray-haired old man named Kahkik.

"We learned that Kahkik, though a native of the upper part of the river, was equally at home at Kotzebue, Selawik or wherever he happened to be on the banks of one of the rivers flowing into Kotzebue Sound. Once, when asked where he lived, Kahkik answered, in the rather difficult semi-pidgin that some old Eskimos still affect, 'Me no live; me all same ptarmigan!'

"We should hardly have become tired of his endless droll stories, river gossip, and more serious accounts if he had chosen to remain with us all summer. At the end of three days, however, Kahkik was anxious to be on his way. We offered him a supply of food, all but a few small items of which he refused on the grounds that he preferred to travel light. He shook hands again, stepped into his kayak, and without looking back, disappeared around the bend of the river.

"We failed to see Kahkik again in 1947, although his friends assured us that he was still travelling along the river. His trips were becoming fewer, however, and he was said to talk childishly at times."

Kahkik told a story about a great man named Mauneluk, an arctic prophet and iconoclast, and Giddings remembered. Kahkik spoke:

"When I was maybe twelve years old, there was a man—Mauneluk—he talked about what to do for the people, and from that time on what that man said has happened. Those people, they had rules about things to do. And that Mauneluk saw that when a girl got to be about sixteen years old, those people said she was *kongok* and had to stay out of the village by herself. And that Mauneluk when he got together with people, he went right up to one of those girls and said he wanted to drink from her bucket of water. That girl didn't want to give him water, but after a while she gave it to him, and he drank it, and after that she won't be any more *kongok*. And Mauneluk said to those people, when a woman was going to make baby, she would not have to go away from the village to make baby, and those girls would not have to go away from the village when they first started to make blood.

"That Mauneluk lived at the mouth of Ambler River for a long time. And he got a wife from Noatak women, and they raised two kids, one girl and one boy, and then that man left his wife and took the two kids with him and raised them. And that man said later to those people, 'White men are strong—after a while they are coming by in a big boat in the air.'

"Mauneluk was always looking for rules to break . . . Some time ago, that Mauneluk went down to Shesualek

because he heard those people never used berries or leaves when they cut white whale, and he took his two kids along with him, and that man, when he got down there after a while those people they caught white whale, and all the people got busy down at the edge of the water, and Mauneluk went out and picked wild rhubarb leaves, and he came back and cooked those leaves, and he went down to the people on the beach and he asked them for a piece of blubber to eat with those leaves. And those people were scared. After a while they gave him a little piece of blubber. He ate that blubber and those leaves, and he never got sick. Before that time even if little kids broke off little leaves while the people were hunting white whale, all the people got sick, but after Mauneluk did that nobody ever got sick any more when they ate leaves with blubber.

"And now winter comes, and in winter time the moon gets dark, and things go wrong. When the moon gets dark those people, if they forget and leave food out on the cache, they have to throw it away. They must put ashes over food so the moon won't come down and take it away. And when that moon starts to get dark, those people tell Mauneluk, and he went home, and they don't know what he is going to do. After a while Mauneluk came out with his gun, and he pointed that gun at the moon and shot many times. And Mauneluk had lots of food outside without ashes on it and nothing happened. And after a while he went in his house, and he came out again, and he called up to that moon, 'Hello, Grandpa! I am glad my Grandpa has come. You come again some time!'

"And Mauneluk, the last thing he ever say—his last words, 'All the people—I don't know what they are going to do, all the people.'"

A young girl, when she is beginning to be a woman, she know it. She goes way behind the village and stays a whole year in a little house her family built for her. Nobody but her mother and little boys can go near. Her face is always covered by a hood that hangs down to her waist in front. On the front of that hood hangs beads. When that girl has her monthly, she has to stay inside that little house for four days—never go out. After that she looked around to see which was the highest mountain. She looks at that high mountain and says, "I want to see you forever!"
—PEGLIRUK (*as told to J. L. Giddings*)

There was a peculiar feeling about this mild and melting spring landscape that made an impression upon me and, without being able to explain why, I had ever the presentiment that I would meet something I had never before seen. Over the meadows there was the song of thousands of birds, one continuous tremulous tone of joy and life. I saw geese, ducks and eider ducks swimming about in all the lakes and every time I approached they rose noisy and cackling, only to drop into the next lake. The swamps were full of wading birds building their nests and laying eggs, and all these voices from thousands of birds joined into one great chorus singing that once again the earth lived.

—KNUD RASMUSSEN

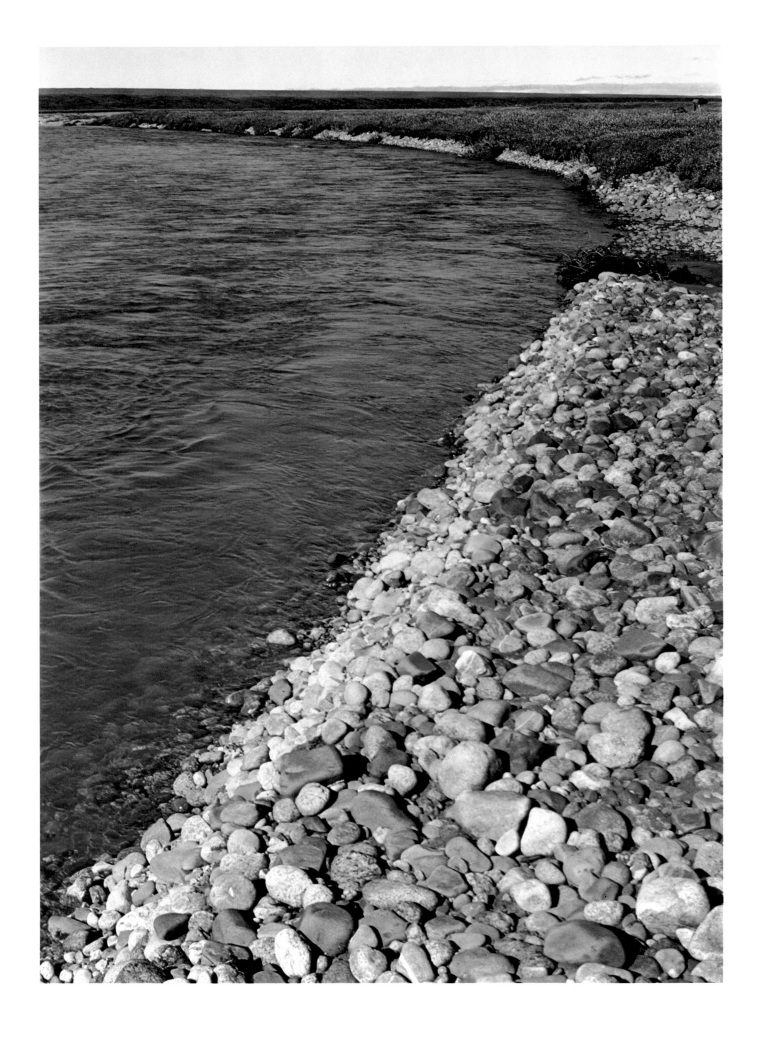

Continual sealing began to pall on the Eskimos when the safe disposition
of their blubber removed the last excuse for lingering on the sea-ice.
The long winter had come to an end, and the midnight sun was shining
over their heads. They forgot the monotonous hours of confinement
within the dimly lighted huts, when the blizzards raged outdoors and
the twilight of noon resembled night rather than day. The earth was
awakening to life again after its long sleep. Ducks and loons flew
overhead, the ptarmigan in the valleys were seeking out their mates, and
a faint tinge of green had crept into the brown tips of the low dwarf
willows that protruded above the snow. In the hills lay countless lakes
teeming with trout and salmon, and herds of caribou grazed on the
slopes and plains. Soon large pools would form around the margins of
the lakes, and the unlocked waters race in foaming torrents to the sea.
Everything beckoned us landward, to a joyous life in the open air. There
would still be a few more snow-storms, succeeded by fogs and rain;
later, dark clouds of mosquitoes would assail us night and day without
rest. But there would be many days, too, of mild, clear weather when we
could sleep beneath the open sky; and food was abundant everywhere,
so that we could roam where we pleased, as free and unfettered as the
caribou we hunted.

—Diamond Jenness

Next morning we were awakened by the sun shining through the tent. We rushed outside to find a crystal-clear day. There was not a cloud in the sky. Every mountain was covered with snow, every peak showed a clean white edge set against pure blue. Almost everything in life seems to be at least somewhat blurred and misty around the edges and so little is ever absolute that we felt a genuine exultation in seeing the flawless white of those summits and the flawless blue of the sky, and the razor-edge sharpness with which the two came together.

—ROBERT MARSHALL

Okpilak

One day on the Jago River the caribou appeared. The day before the tundra had been empty; then suddenly the deer were there, not the great herd that arctic travelers sometimes see, but scattered individuals moving with a purpose through the country. When they saw us they stopped to look us over, and now and again they would run for no apparent reason a few hundred yards counter to the direction of their migration, but they otherwise dallied very little, as if mindful that the assembly point was far ahead and they were behind schedule. They hastened east along the edge of the mountains in the direction we had come.

And one night on the Jago autumn came to the tundra. Overnight, or rather over two nights, the low plants of the tundra carpet turned from green to scarlet. We woke one morning to a red landscape. The bearberry leaves, which earlier had gone quietly from green to the color of dried blood, suddenly were as bright as blood from an artery. The blueberry leaves were suddenly red-purple and the dwarf birch scarlet. The alluvial fans were no longer green wedges in the sides of the mountains, but red, and they called attention to themselves like new terrain. The autumn tundra glowed now under the gray skies, in magic independence of light from above.

The color change was completed on our last day in the Brooks Range. On that day I climbed Marie Mountain, the last peak in the range. I scrambled up a talus chute and into the cloud that enclosed the summit, and walked in fog along the summit ridgeline. The fog reduced visibility to a circle two hundred feet in diameter, and it forced my attention to the ground. Underfoot was a mosaic of thin flakes of rock, covered with a brittle black lichen. Here and there in the mosaic were white bits of caribou bone and antler. It was a surface unlike anything I had seen in the Range, and except for scattered patches of

moss, it entirely composed the Marie Mountain summit ridge. I followed caribou trails—narrow gray paths where caribou hoofs had worn the black lichen from the rocks. The trails would peter out, and for a while I would walk undirected over unmarked rock, but another trail would appear in the mist. The new trail would be a little to the side, a little lower on the ridgeline perhaps, but going in my direction.

The fog cut off all sound, except for the clink of the brittle slabs under my feet, and I walked in the deepest silence I had known in the Brooks Range. I followed the ridgeline to what I thought was the summit. My intuition told me it was the highest point on the mountain, but in the fog I had no points of reference and could not be sure. I found a patch of moss and lay down on it, wrapping myself in my poncho and waiting for the fog to clear. I was hoping for a view of the Arctic Ocean. It was warm at first and I almost slept, then the temperature dropped and I had to move on to keep warm.

I was a short distance below the summit when the fog began to clear. I saw that it really had been the summit. The cloud banks withdrew rapidly, with tendrils of mist retreating everywhere, streaming off the shoulders of Marie Mountain, streaming out of the Jago Valley below me, streaming off the open tundra, drawn inexorably to the north as if by the power of a spell reversed. I saw the near tundra in its new red cast—with its oranges, rusts, and lavenders—and the far tundra, blue with shadow and distance. To the north I saw the Arctic Ocean. From Marie Mountain the ocean was greatly foreshortened, and it appeared as simply a bright, final margin to the tundra sea. The tundra below we had cleared, but the sky above was an arch of high gray cloud that stretched from horizon to horizon, almost meeting the ocean, but not quite, leaving a narrow band of orange to mark clear sky. There were rainstorms at the edge of the ocean, falling as purple curtains against the band of orange light.

From Marie Mountain the country looked larger than life. It was as if without noticing it we had changed globes, and were on a much larger planet than before, a planet with a longer curve to its surface. The landforms were correspondingly enlarged. The ridgelines were attenuated and summits heightened. I could look down and see the small stretch of tundra I had labored across with the caribou meat on my shoulder. I saw how pitifully short a distance it truly was in the sweep and reach of the country. If we were not near the end of our journey as we imagined, but beginning a Jonathan Swift or Frank Baum sort of journey, then it might have explained the size of the country. It was such big country.

Early one afternoon, in an arctic fog, we pushed off into the open tundra. Marie Mountain loomed behind us, then vanished, and we were walking without landmark on the tundra sea. We fell immediately into a tundra rhythm.

The next days of walking were indistinguishable from one another. The fog limited our vision to concentric circles. Perception of color was in a circle close about us, perception of shape in a larger circle. The fog shut each of us off and made for privacy. The circles of our perceived worlds overlapped, for we had to walk within sight of each other, but this did not infringe on the privacy. As I walked along I discovered a game I thought I could play forever. I would let my mind wander to thoughts of home, plans, imaginings; then whenever I wanted I would think back to what I was doing. I was walking under my pack. I was listening to sounds muted by the fog. There was the rhythmic tearing sound the grass of the tussocks made as

you stepped on them, and the sucking noise your boots made in occasional counterpoint as they pulled free of the mud between tussocks. In the closeness of the fog the sounds seemed to be happening inside your own head. All sound was altered by the fog and pleasant to listen to, because it was private. I listened intently but without effort. The sound was everything. The rhythm was everything. There was a timelessness. Steve's figure was moving ahead, walking forever.

We walked in the center of a circular patch of tundra that did not change from day to day. We could not be sure that progress wasn't an illusion; that we weren't just leaning in the direction of our march like three standing waves in a river, going nowhere. If we were indeed traveling through the tundra, it was the way an ocean wave travels through water, imparting motion to it for a moment, but leaving featureless fluid expanses behind, rolling toward similar expanses ahead. The fog walk was not entirely a pleasure. It reminded John of a sensory-deprivation experiment he had volunteered for as a student, except that here there was no experimenter to let you out when you yelled.

Our sense of direction was baffled by the fog. We guided ourselves by the sound of the Jago on our right, and checked our direction from time to time by compass. When we left the Jago for the Okpilak, crossing the landmarkless tundra between the two rivers, we navigated with the compass alone. There was a strain in trusting the little instrument and mistrusting our own good senses. The compass began to have the fascination that the pistol has in Russian roulette. John, who held it, became irritable. He grinned broadly, very relieved, when we finally heard the roar of the Okpilak through the fog.

When the fog withdrew we saw that the tundra was not

perfectly monotonous. Here and there a stone sphinx stood above the tundra desert, but these were for the most part behind us, and ahead the world was an endless succession of long undulating groundswells. Because the land undulated as it ran north, the horizon was always close at hand. From the crest of each swell there was another swell immediately beyond. Each tundra wave was so nearly like the one before that even with the fog gone we walked a tundra treadmill and made dubious progress. Slight irregularities on our horizons became significant. Grass sixteen inches high along a streamcourse looked as tall as cattails. The banks of small streams became as interesting as river bluffs.

Then somewhere on the tundra the country stopped talking to us. We had been walking too long in the Arctic, and the terrain had ceased changing. We were familiar with the terrain's every remark before the remark was delivered. We could anticipate it as you would your wife across the breakfast table. We nodded and smiled a little at the substantiation of what we knew we would hear, but were not really touched by it. We were committed to getting out. The tundra became just something to cross. Our minds had already crossed it, and were far ahead with plans for our return to human country. We lay in our tents in the morning with plans racing around in our heads, and as we walked the tundra, the plans ran around in circles. There was no way to carry them out, and a tension began to build. Our dreams were practical, possible dreams of the kind that is no fun unless there's a chance to implement them. We slept badly.

It was not the right way to say good-bye to the Brooks Range. In the Sierra Nevada leaving the mountains is a proper climax to a walk through them. In the Sierra, the last day is often the best day. Descending the East Side of the Sierra, by way of McGee Creek Pass for example, you drop down in a day from the snow and granite and thin alpine air of the High Sierra to the sage desert of the Owens Valley. In your descent the country becomes less steep and wild. It's transitional country, first with aspen by the stream, then signs of cattle in the sagebrush, then the first fences. You are not supposed to appreciate it as much, but you find that you are appreciating it as much as the high country. The day becomes warmer. The wind no longer smells of lupine or snow, but of sage, and of possible human history and habitation. Soon milkshakes, a bath, clean sheets, but not quite yet. You are on your way home and there is a singing in your heart.

Our leaving the tundra was different. There were too many miles of grass and it was taking too long. It would have better been a single day's experience. Every morning

there were more tussocks ahead of us, and the same horizon. The same tussock seascape lay at all points of the compass, green in the middle of the day, then glowing red through the long hours when the sun was low, but otherwise unchanging. Crossing the tundra had all the disadvantages of a prolonged farewell.

The caribou meat was gone and we were on short rations again. My dreaming shifted from people and projects to food. I would go to more restaurants when I got home, I decided. I would go to good places in San Francisco, but to seedy places also. I would be democratic. I thought about the cheap Italian restaurants in north Oakland near where I lived, and the Chinese cafe around the corner. I thought about Jenkins barbeque in west Oakland. It seemed to me, as I thought about it, that Oakland was more cosmopolitan, Byzantine even, than I had ever realized. I remembered the open door of Las Palmas bar, with loud Mexican music blaring into the street. I thought about Housewives Market in west Oakland. It was a market for the whole world. Mexicans, Indians, country people from the South, and people of indeterminate origin all shopped there. There were hog maws, chitlins, mountain oysters, tongues, tripe, brains, necks, catfish, fish with names you never heard before, grains and flours you never saw, vegetables you could not imagine how to cook. The market, and its smells, belonged more in Morocco or Ecuador, and in California should have been illegal or underground. I would shop at Housewives and learn to cook the things you buy there. I would learn how to really cook. No more pan-fried Swiss steaks and frozen vegetables.

As I walked I played my game. I would let my mind wander away until I felt it had strayed far enough, then I would shift back to the Arctic. I would listen to the sound of my feet in the grass, and watch the ground pass under. Delicate yellow grasses passed below as if they were telephone poles and I were a plane flying over. Deep purple bushes passed, a drop of dew in each of the myriad leaves. The dwarf birch of a dwarf autumn passed beneath. Green, yellow, orange, red; all the colors of tundra autumn were passing under, but more was ahead, and the same thing after that.

As we stepped through dwarf birch and the other boot-high shrubs of the tundra, the wet rubber toes of our boots came away patterned with miniature roundish leaves of all colors. The patterns were like leaf patterns in Japanese paper, except that here the designs were wet and fresh and their creation was continuous. A rearrangement, an aftertouch, came with each step through the brush of miniature branches. When we came to wet sedge that had

no dwarf birch or other leaves to add to us, the blades of grass and the pools of water between tussocks wiped our canvas clean, and the next composition began from scratch as soon as we hit dwarf birch again.

When I tired of arctic designs, I let my mind wander again; to food, friends, anything.

I thought most about breakfast. I imagined myself sloshing butter around in a large frying pan—from the long row of frying pans, of different sizes, that I would buy and keep above the stove—and then I imagined myself breaking three eggs into it. I would cook them over a low flame, as my grandfather had taught me when I was a small boy, then salt and pepper them just right. I would experiment with pancakes. I would make some of the sugar syrup my girlfriend's brothers made when they were boys.

I promised myself that I would never forget how my stomach felt in the Arctic. Whenever I got bored with food, I would remember how it was to be a little hungry all the time. Whenever I got tired of warmth and the hearth I would remember how cold and wet I had been.

*　　*　　*

One morning I woke at four and left the tent to piss. It was clear with a cold wind blowing, and the mountains were pink to the south. I put my feet in my boots, not bothering to lace them, and walked in bare legs some distance from the tents. It was not so cold as I had expected and I felt tough to be out with no pants on. The chill morning was beautiful, and I wondered why I had never got up this early before. The tundra was truly beautiful in this early light. It was a revelation. The tundra had been speaking to me all the time, but I had been in the tent too much, and hadn't heard. Then the wind began to wake me. I realized how numbingly cold I really was. I stumped back to the tent as fast as I could, trying to keep my unlaced boots on.

*　　*　　*

If we were tired of monotonous vistas, we were more tired of each other. The tundra magnified petty irritations, and as we walked across it we looked at the back of the man in front of us, arranging and adding to the long list of grudges against him. Every morning that promised rain each of us pulled a comrade's poncho back over his pack and tied it there, and then had the same thing done for us. At first it had been a pleasant-unpleasant intimacy, like zipping your mother's dress. Now the contact was disagreeable.

One of the things that bothered me about John was what I privately called his Lewis and Clark Syndrome. We were a lot like Lewis and Clark, he said as he contemplated the Okpilak River bluffs, which reminded him of the bluffs Lewis and Clark saw on the Missouri. We had seen the same grizzlies and the same great plains, he said, except that here the plains were tundra instead of buffalo grass and the herds were caribou instead of buffalo. John called our trip an expedition. He named everything we saw, and the names annoyed me. Gem Lake, Nameless Valley, Diamond Tarn, Tundra Gate, Emerald Valley, Lone Mountain. John wrote, or more accurately, lettered, daily in a large red journal. He filled it with diagrams and maps, and pressed arctic flowers between its pages. John wrote sometimes with insight, but often, it seemed to me, with a style formed by reading too many old travel writers. In John's journal misty rain clamped its clammy fingers over us, and silver mists wreathed rocky spires lovingly. John, I thought, lived second-hand emotions, and felt things he thought an explorer-naturalist was supposed to feel. He smoked a pipe just like Mark Trail.

John's apparent contentment with the Arctic annoyed me. I could not decide myself what I thought about the country, whether I loved or hated it. I thought that I perceived the mountains more fully than John, that I was better at certain mountain arts, like routefinding, but he appeared to like the mountains better. I was afraid that he really did love the Brooks Range in a simple and complete way. I suppose the thing I could not forgive John for happened back on the Sheenjek. John stopped as we walked along, he stooped, reached between two tussocks, his wrist well inside, and came out with a bird in his hand. I had missed it. I could not understand, and will never know, how his eye had caught the nest there.

There was less bile in my feelings about Steve. His cautiousness, and what I considered his overly long analysis of our possible routes and alternatives, sometimes bothered me. But his idiosyncracies were comic in a way that John's were not and were easier for me to live with. Steve deeply hated the cold, and in his drive to get warm he burned numerous holes in his gloves and singed all the mosquito netting off our tent. I called him the Moth. If it was warm, Steve would cradle it. I might have resented the loss of the mosquito netting and added that to the list of grudges, but Steve did not burn the netting until August, when the mosquitos were gone. I might have resented the way Steve venerated his single bottle of tabasco sauce, but he shared the bottle with us, and I venerated it too.

If the others resented me, and they surely did, I suppose it was for the brainless way I approached the mountains. I was not much help in rational discussion of problems. I wanted to let things happen to us. I was a bit younger than they. I wanted the trip to be a physical test, to see how much distance we could cover and how much country we could see. When my companions were hobbled by foot injuries, I chafed at our slow pace. I must have been obnoxious in my good health.

*   *   *

I went down to the river one evening to fill the water bottles. I knelt on the bank and held the first bottle under. In a minute my hand had lost sensation. I put the hand in my pocket to get warm and filled the second bottle with my left hand. The Okpilak ran somberly under heavy skies, very fast and silty. It was a powerful-looking river that coursed through a single channel. The sod along the banks was undercut and much of it had fallen into the current. Later, when we traveled farther from the mountains, the gradient of the North Slope would decrease and the river would slow. It would become less a torrent and more a deeply flowing, quiet, flatland river. Silt bars would begin to edge the water, and the ripple marks that patterned the bars would serve as graphs of the river's gentler undulation. The first sea birds would appear over the river, and as we moved north their numbers would increase. But for now, as I held the water bottle under it, the Okpilak was still a mountain river.

*   *   *

Most of all, on the tundra sea, each of us became tired of himself. We were deadly bored with our own minds. There was nothing on our horizons to stimulate new thoughts, so the same old thoughts went round and round. We wallowed in our reveries until we became sick of them. It was a visceral sickness, a sensation like having eaten too much cotton candy. Imagination was consuming itself. A lethargy came on us. We found it oppressive not to be moving, yet we spent long hours each morning lying in camp. It was better to be walking—then we had motion at least—yet somehow it took the strangest dreaming effort to get out of our bags and set our feet to walking. We could feel inertia assuming a force in us, like the power of sex or the will to live. Our problem was more than just coming to grips with wet socks after the warmth of the sleeping bag. It was more, but we could not say what. None of us had felt anything like it before. I thought of it as Tundra Sickness.

The tundra brought us an equality, and we all remarked on that. We seemed reduced to a dead-level sameness of wit, intelligence, and aptitude. We had been walking single-file or three-abreast across an unvarying landscape, and the universe was bringing identical forces to bear on each of us. We felt similar emotions at the same time, and continually found ourselves voicing thoughts that were at that moment rising to the lips of a companion, or hearing

JOHN MILTON: *Hills and Arctic Ocean fog*

our own thoughts expressed by him. That we were so much alike should have been disturbing, for we did not then have high opinions of each other, but in our tundra lethargy we were not disturbable.

We all seasoned our food heavily. It was as if with tabasco sauce and pepper we were trying to combat the drabness of our lives. None of us was able to read. I began *The Proud Tower*, a paperback Steve had brought along, but its tale of the insanity of all human enterprise in the years before the First World War depressed me. No lives could have been so empty as the author made them out to be, I thought. Why would an author push a thesis like that? I wanted a book that celebrated fullness in the world.

From time to time jaegers cried out from the mist above our heads. Occasionally one of the gulls would materialize, look impartially down at us, unsurprised by our presence, then disappear. They reminded both John and me of the frigate birds we had seen in the Galapagos Islands. They were not like gulls. The gulls I had known before were serene watchers from pier pilings, graceful enough in the air, loud and insistent spirits sometimes, but scavengers after all. The jaegers were different. They were birds flying in the shape of gulls but with the animus of hawks. Was there a corollary to Bergmann's Rule, I wondered, or should there be one, to explain jaegers? Could it be that the farther north an animal ranged, the fiercer it became? The birds appeared, sudden distillations of the arctic sky, transformed by latitude. They dipped close to earth, like hunting cries incarnated but momentarily silent. They looked through us with predatory eyes, saw nothing there of interest, and dipped away into the fog, to cry distantly beyond it.

One day we saw three caribou. They looked at us curiously from across the Okpilak, then ran off.

Another day we saw a grizzly at a great distance to the north. He appeared to be nearly black with a silver mantle over his hump, but as we drew closer we saw that the mantle was an effect of distance or the shine of the sun on his coat. Up close he was just a brown bear, walking south as we walked north. Unmindful of us, but with our gratitude, he crossed to the far side of the river. Through the binoculars I saw him shake the water off. When he was across from us on the far bank he saw us, and rose quickly on his hind feet for a better look. He moved as nimbly as a monkey would have in standing, and that suddenly made him seem a much smaller animal. He was not a small animal, we had to remember, but the most powerful predator on the American, or any other, continent. It seemed unfair, and disquieting, that an animal so strong and capable of such speed should also have such reflexes. He passed to the south of us, rising on his heels now and again to peer in our direction and sniff the light north wind. Then, in the middle of one such observation, he caught our scent, dropped to all fours and ran off, not stopping for as long as we watched him.

There had been times, back on the Sheenjek and the Aichilik, when I had reproached myself. Here I was, I thought, with my eyes scanning the mountains and tundra at the northern edge of the world, on a far corner of the map, where few other men have been, in Alaska, in the Arctic, with nothing but wolves and caribou and northern lights around me, and the subdued colors of arctic sum-

mer, and the severity; and I was not at that moment drawing any lessons from it, not appreciating what my eyes were surveying, not taking away any photographs, mental or otherwise. Then quickly I convinced myself that this was fine, that the Indians and Eskimos took no pictures, that the beneficial effects of weather, space, and distance were not immediate, or always readily apparent. By the time we reached the Jago, I no longer felt obligated to say "Just think, here I am in the Arctic." Now on the Okpilak I forgot that I had ever felt the need to say that. It was entirely normal to be in the North. The tundra rhythm was the only rhythm I remembered.

Then the trip was almost over and we were nearing Barter Island. We walked toward the two towers of the island's installation that were now visible through the clearing fog. We had seen the two structures in clear weather for the last sixty miles, and they had appeared in the distance to be towers or silos, but now we were close enough to see that they were radar screens or reflectors of some sort. As I walked I looked up frequently to the screens, and they filled my attention. Then I turned to look at the mountains behind us, and when I looked north again I had trouble finding the screens. I realized how very little of our horizon they truly occupied. For someone less near the end of his journey, they would not have been

JOHN MILTON: *River, Arctic Plain*

landmarks. As a game I panned the horizon as a cameraman would have, traversing it slowly with my eyes. From east to west was the Brooks Range, a hundred-mile front of peaks, like a distant army halted. The peaks were of the pale, difficult blue that snowy mountains get when you look into the sun at them. The sun was an arctic sun, low in an immense, pale-blue arctic sky. I followed the line of mountains down to where the westernmost peaks were lost in the distance. From that point of imperceptible relief, the curve of the tundra horizon began. I followed the curve north, unavoidably speeding up a little, for there was nothing but horizon to see. I forced myself to slow down, but even so I panned right past the screens, and I had to flick back to them. They were inconsequential.

Now that we were about to leave it, I began to appreciate the country more. The tundra sea was not really so monotonous. There had been, I remembered, bright days when the fog cleared and Mounts Michelson and Chamberlain stood to the south of us—all glacier and white summit. On those days the Okpilak was beautiful, running blue across the tundra. On one such day the first herring gulls had appeared, first one, then others, big and white, steering gracefully inland over the strange landscape with their familiar sea cry.

And on foggy days there were things to see. Ptarmigan in the tussock grass, alas. Bears, and the three caribou across the river. Rainstorms slanting at the edge of the ocean, and last ducks flying south.

Now that the trip was nearly over, I remembered, too late to do much good, the wandering albatross. I recalled that the albatross sometimes spends a year at sea, never sighting land. The terrain of the sea, for those four seasons, must mean the world to the albatross. The things he reads in the waves, in the wind textures on the sea's surface, in the cold upwellings and crosscurrents, the things that warn him there, the things he can prophecy, satisfy all his need for new horizons, and that need in birds is at least as strong as it is in men. *Diomedea exulans*, the albatross was called—the homeless one who keeps God's counsels. I should have tried to read the tundra sea the way the albatross reads the roaring forties and the other ocean latitudes he wanders in. I would have done so, I decided, and the swells and dips in the tundra would have meant more to me, if we had not been walking so long. If we had begun on the tundra, instead of finishing, it would have been different. The country was beginning to whisper to me again. It's always that way—the import of wild country growing as you leave it. Once the mountains are safely in memory the lessons and symbols begin

to take shape. The country was whispering, but not very loudly yet.

As we neared the coast the land got wetter. The slight ridges of the frost polygons we began to encounter were the only dry ground. The polygon ridges were like a network of levees through rice paddies, and we followed them when we could, making geometric progress toward the coast. Soon we would top another rise or two, I knew, and there would be the sea, but as yet there was no emotion. I waited for some sense of approaching climax, but it did not come.

So what had the trip meant, then? For old explorers like Stefansson and Rasmussen, after the great arctic distances they left behind them, our trip might not even have been noteworthy. Our walk had not been an ordeal. It had been hard at times, however, and we had come through it well, and there was some pride in that. We had labored through some strange states of mind, but not much stranger than states we had known before. After a week in any range of wild mountains, a walker has rubbed elbows with most of the same specters. He may not have conversed so intimately with them, but he knows their names. Fear comes in the mountains, after all, because a chill universe dips closer to earth there. A broad night sky draws off assurance just as it draws off heat, but the same night sky stands over every part of the planet, once the electric lights are out. We had only been under the sky longer than most.

We had gained what, then? We had learned that the icy polar wind is not so cold. We had walked, and the mountains and tundra had stripped away our veneers, one by one, until we were starting from scratch, for whatever that was worth. And we now possessed the country in our heads. We had the arctic spaces, the glaciers and peaks we had been free to name, the rivers of stone and seas of grass. The arctic wind would always blow for us.

There were no cliffs where the land met the sea. The sod simply angled under the calm water. We could see grass beneath the surface, still healthy apparently. What recently had been tussock ocean was now Arctic Ocean. The diminished summer ice pack was in the far distance, almost out of sight. We stood stupidly on the shore. It was strange to feel so little. For days my mind had wandered ahead—to this coast I had assumed, to human territory—and I had expected to meet it there. Now I was not sure where my mind was. If the Jago River dream of world war had come true and Barter Island had been vaporized, or if someone in authority had requested us to go back the way we came, I would have turned on my heel without regret, I thought. Then we remembered to shake hands.

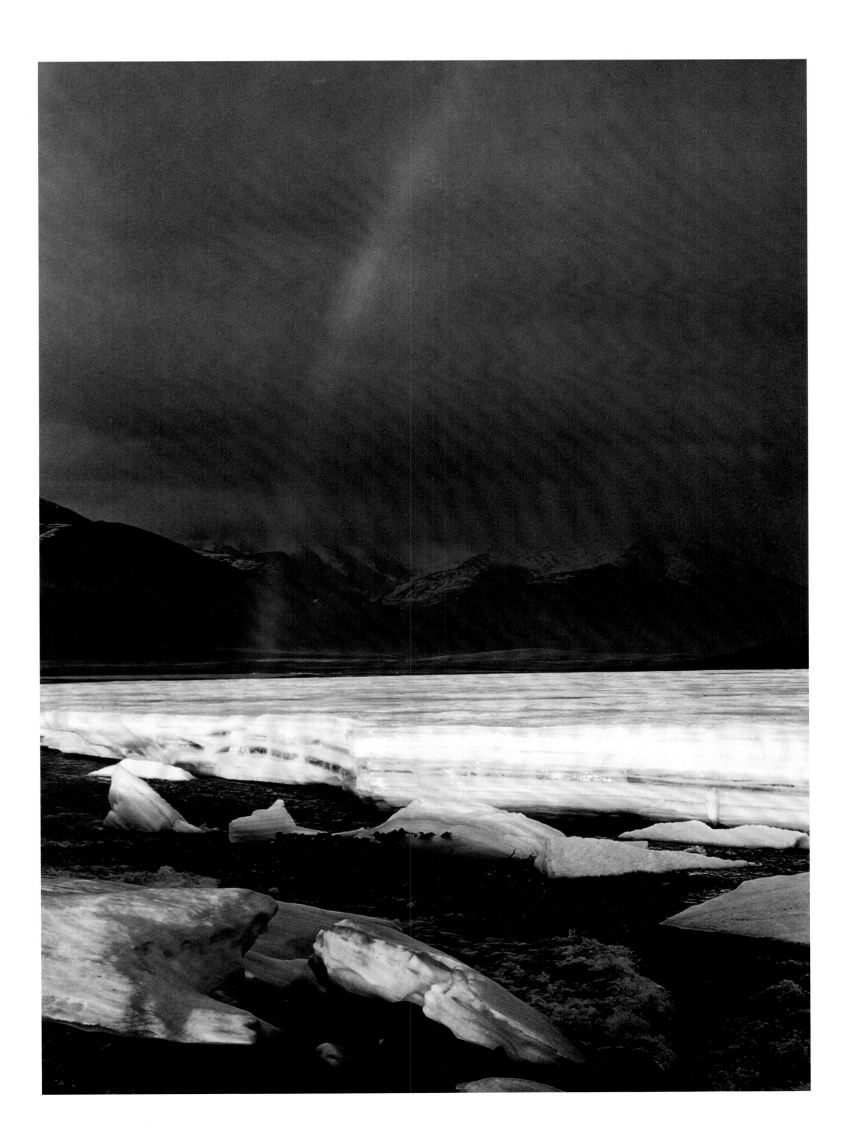

Then he called his dogs, harnessed them to his sledge, and bound his old rifle and his spears fast. "It has come to pass that a man starts on his travels!" he called abruptly in at the window: that is the Polar Eskimo's farewell.

—KNUD RASMUSSEN

Just after midnight, when the air was coolest and the snow had stiffened a little where there was no water underneath, we said goodbye to the village. All the men and women stood round our sledges and wished us luck on our journey. There the parting word is always:

"May you get to the place you are aiming for."

The sharp white light lay cold over the mountains, and we had to get out on to the sea ice before the heat of the sun drew the strength out of the dogs. We set our course straight across the great lake, with the last leavetakings of our friends ringing in our ears. Water and wet snow slushed in over the sledges and we were soon soaked through, for we had to get down on our knees and pull the sledges out of the mush every time they came to a standstill. We only had this bad going as long as we were up on the river. As soon as we got out on to the sea ice we were all right.

—Knud Rasmussen (June)

It was in the beginning of December, an unusually cold period when the thermometer was often down to 50° below zero. There was not much light, and we had to start out early in the morning, in moonlight, if we were to make any distance on our day journeys. A fresh nor'easter was blowing and sweeping the snow along, and it almost seemed as if it became colder as the darkness gave way to daylight. We no longer saw the sun itself, only its red glow penetrating the clouds in all its glory. However, with the wind against us we were not interested in the glow; we had enough to do to preserve our faces from frostbite. It was fire we inhaled, and the cold felt like sparks flying out of one's nose. . . .

As soon as twilight fell, and we had fixed upon a place to sleep, Qâvigarssuaq and I used to ignite large beacons of blubber to guide the two Netsiliks to us, as our sledge tracks on the bare ice were difficult to follow. In those dark evenings these bonfires glared with entrancing beauty; all around us was waste and gray, and when we stood still we could hear the grating moan of the ice out in the open sea, which was never very far away.

—Knud Rasmussen (December)

Once upon a time two men thought they would like to travel round the world, that they might be able to tell others what it was like.

That was in the days when there were still many people and all countries were inhabited. Now we are growing fewer and fewer. Accidents and sickness have come upon men. You see that I drag out my life without being able to stand on my legs.

The two who were anxious to set out on their travels had just taken wives and had as yet no children. They cut themselves drinking-cups from musk-ox horns, each of them one, cut from the same head, and then they set out, each in his own direction, to meet again some day. They set off with sledges and used to encamp when the summer came. It took them a long time to get round the world; they had children, they grew old, and the children themselves grew old; at length the parents were so old that they could not walk along, and the children guided them.

At last they met, and then there was nothing left of their drinking horns but the handles, so many times had they drunk on the way, and scraped the horns against the ground, as they poured into them.

"The world is very large," they said when they met.

They were young when they had set out; then they were old men who had to be led by their children.

Yes, the world is large!

—QILERNEQ

I will walk with leg muscles
Which are strong
As the sinews of the shins of the little caribou calf.
I will walk with leg muscles
Which are strong
As the sinews of the shins of the little hare.
I will take care not to go towards the dark.
I will go towards the day.

GILBERT STAENDER: *Sand bar and wolf tracks, Alatna River*

It took a dash of fortitude to crawl out of the warm bag and start the fire, but once it was going the tent speedily warmed. A couple of hours sufficed for us to cook and eat breakfast, break camp, pack the sleds, hitch up the dogs, and be on our way. The weather was perfect, the going was good, and we could observe the whole pageant of a mid-winter arctic morning growing out of a mid-winter arctic night. It was full starlight when we started, heading straight on the course toward Polaris. After half an hour the black sky began to turn gray, and the unbelievable arctic brightness of the stars slowly faded. The gray became faintly blue, and then a single snowy peak in the northwest showed a tip of pink. So gradually that you could hardly notice it advancing, the pink spread from peak to peak until all summits to the north and west were colored. The pink kept creeping down the slopes, changing imperceptibly in color, until all at once you noticed that it had vanished, and that the mountainsides were bathed in a golden spray—craggy peaks, snowfields, dark spruce timber, everything. Then suddenly, at high noon, after journeying a whole morning in the shadow, there was a wide bend in the river, and we drove out into the sunlight.

—ROBERT MARSHALL

GILBERT STAENDER: *Winter, Alatna River*

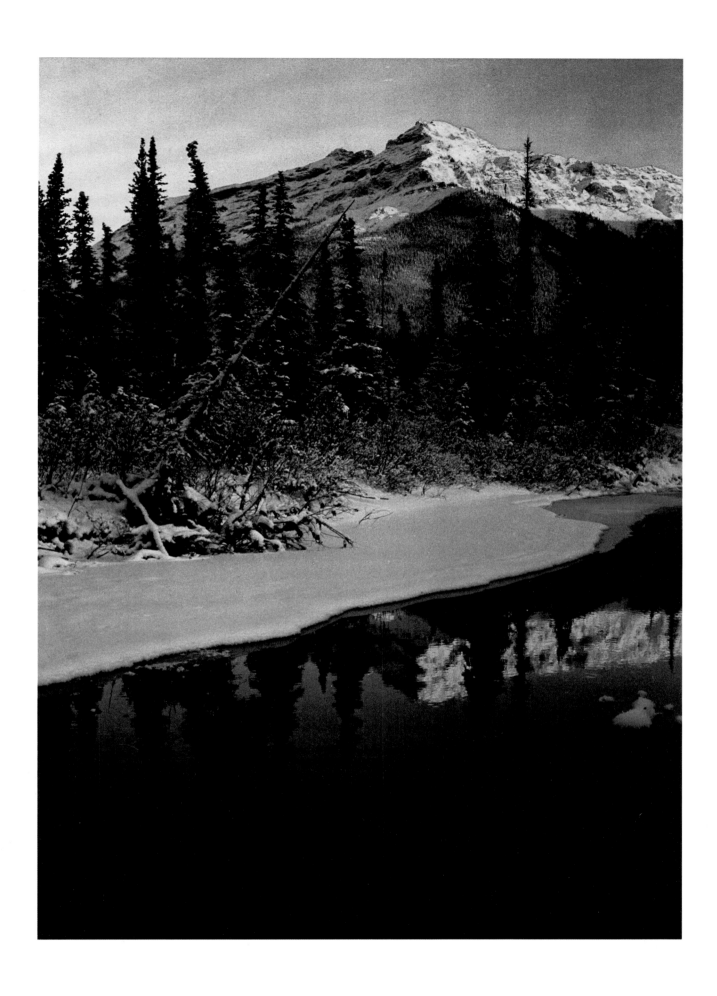

And I think over again
My small adventures
When with a shore wind I drifted out
In my kayak
And thought I was in danger.
My fears,
Those small ones
That I thought so big,
For all the vital things
I had to get and to reach.
And yet, there is only
One great thing,
The only thing:
To live to see in huts and on journeys
The great day that dawns,
And the light that fills the world.

5. PROSPECT

THE DANISH ethnologist Knud Rasmussen once spent a sleepless winter night conversing with an Eskimo named Ugpik. Rasmussen was the first white man Ugpik had met who spoke his language, and Ugpik was eager to learn all he could of European customs. In return he related to Rasmussen his own beliefs. "His philosophy of life," wrote Rasmussen, "was to the effect that we human beings know so very little of life and its controlling forces that we have an imperative duty, not only to ourselves but also to those we hold dear, to live as carefully as possible; that is why we are furnished with all the amulets that can assist us through the difficulties of life, and that is why we must bear in mind all the demands made upon us by the taboo rules."

The carefulness with which Rasmussen's companion approached his world is the indigenous approach in the Arctic, time-tested and true. A long history has proved it compatible with the Brooks Range and North Slope provinces. Our own approach is the opposite and that should give us pause.

The tundra ecosystem at the top of the world is the most fragile we know. A single caterpillar tractor, driven once across the tundra plain, can leave a track that deepens with time, becomes a ditch, and lasts for centuries. Consequences radiate disruptively from the ditch's eroding sides like cracks in ice or ripples in a pond. This tundra fragileness sometimes seems a fabulous fragileness, like Achilles' heel or Samson's hair. There is a fatal aura about it. We should see the warning, and be warned, just as those two almost-invulnerable ancients should have been. Perhaps the tundra will be the loose thread from which the world unravels. Perhaps the end won't come at the hands of some mad colonel who pushes a button, as we most often imagine, but at the hands of a lonely and drunken tractor driver who embarks on a long, straight drive across the tundra and into the arctic twilight.

There is a new literature coming out of Arctic Alaska. The old oral literature concerned itself with hunting, the seasons, the land and sea, and the anxieties and joys of life in the North:

> *The great sea*
> *Has set me adrift*
> *It moves me like the weed in a great river,*
> *Earth and the great weather*
> *Move me,*
> *Have carried me away*
> *And move my inward parts with joy.*

The new literature springs from a different view of life and the land, and of what things are valuable:

> *The North Slope of Alaska. The place we call the Arco Circle. It was the middle of nowhere until Atlantic Richfield made the first major oil strike on the North American continent in the last forty years.*
> *It's one of the coldest, most desolate, most inaccessible places on the face of the earth.*

But the North Slope of Alaska was not the middle of nowhere for its first inhabitants, the mastodons, elephants, saber-toothed cats, horses, camels, antelope, bison, groundsloths, yaks, giant beaver, giant elk, nor for the lions that once ran under northern lights; nor the dire wolves that ululated among the crenelated mirages of the Arctic Plain; nor for the animals that succeeded them and remain today, the wolverines, wolves, lynxes, foxes, sheep, moose, musk oxen, caribou, polar bears, grizzlies; nor for the peoples who came, the Denbigh Flintworkers, the Old Whalers, the Choris, Norton, Ipiutak, and Thule peoples—a succession of sea-going races that began whaling 4,000 years ago in the waters off the North Slope, a formidable people who lived often in houses made of whale jaws and left behind them a profusion of blades; nor was it nowhere for their descendants, called variously the People of the Twilight, the People of the Shadow, the Polar Eskimo, the Inuit—a race of hunters, inventors, and sculptors, the drama of whose lives is unequaled, perhaps, by that of any other people; a race of poets and religious men who created a mythology for the North Slope and peopled the country with shadow races—with spirits, who are as palpably a part of the terrain as the mastodons with their fossil presence; nor was it nowhere to the white explorers who followed the Inuit into their chosen extremes of latitude and weather, men like Smith, Rasmussen, Stefansson, and Marshall, who became part of the drama.

The North Slope, and the mountains of the Brooks Range from which it slopes, are not desolate to the great flocks of waterfowl that begin their lives there, nor to the eagles, gyrfalcons, jaegers, and owls that hunt above the peaks and plains, nor to the resident sourdough who said, "I like it among these ruggedy mountains better than any-where else in the world," nor to the Eskimos who still follow the caribou today. The North Slope is not cold in summer to the insects who inhabit tundra microclimates where the temperatures rise to above one hundred degrees Fahrenheit within inches of the ground, nor even in winter to the voles and other small mammals who go about their lives under the insulation of the snow, nor to the wolves that wrap tails around noses, sleep through blizzards, and dig themselves out in the morning.

The Brooks Range is the northernmost mountain range in the United States, and the tundra plains of the North Slope are the northernmost plains. These two ultimate provinces, mountain and plain, are the last great wilderness in the nation. It is a wilderness of endless distances and infinite detail, of great glaciers and peaks, cottongrass and arctic poppies; of lean austerity and seasonal release from austerity, green in spring and animated then by great herds of caribou, flocks of waterfowl, and fluctuating throngs of lemmings—the whole country moving northward in migration—then suddenly turning to reds, rusts, lavenders, and oranges in autumn, when the migration goes back the other way.

The Arctic Slope was somewhere before Atlantic Richfield. It was everywhere, the entire world, to the people who called themselves *Inuit*, the People. They left it unscarred and rich in human history and associations. We, the Oil People, who are only the latest in a succession of arctic peoples, must somewhere find the grace to leave the Arctic as we found it, adding our own legends and no more, for the next people to pass that way.

GILBERT STAENDER: *Ptarmigan tracks*

Kaktovik

The installation, with its antennae and radar domes and reflectors, rose improbably from the flatness of Barter Island. It looked like a moon station. Below the antennae were aluminum bungalows arranged in trains and supported by pilings above pads of gravel. The first man we saw as we reached the station was a sourdough who stood outside one of the bright metal bungalows in an old wool shirt. He was toothless and grizzled. He should have had a pan in his hand. He watched us uncomprehendingly as we walked up. When John told him where we had come from, he did not seem to understand. John repeated it, but the old man clearly failed to grasp the significance of what we had accomplished. He was shy and unaccustomed to talking. He indicated with a nod the building we should report to.

The small group of men standing outside the reception building watched us guardedly as we approached. The plane was not due for several days, and they must have wondered where we came from. They looked puzzled when we told them, and that was to be the pattern. Few of the station men we met regarded our long walk with admiration, or even comprehension. Most of them asked us, why? John became a little annoyed, but I was amused. Earlier, when we had looked back from our last North Slope camps toward the Brooks Range, the mountains were impressively distant. They would look, my companions thought, even more impressively distant to the men at Barter Island. I had disagreed, and had predicted the kind of reception we were getting. I now felt superior to any need for recognition, and watched my companions with a benign good humor. I felt unusually wise.

I played the detached and faintly amused observer until we got inside the building, and then I began to weaken. Inside, under a roof again, with new faces all around, my tongue loosened itself and I began to talk. The people at the station were as eager for new conversation as we were, and soon everyone was talking and listening furiously. I saw in a rush how wildly improbable the life at the station was. I knew I was a little crazy from my isolation in the mountains, but I saw that these men were all crazy too. The stories of the men, and the different reasons they had come here—as various and exotic it seemed to me as the reasons men joined the foreign legion—would have filled books, and I wanted to remember all the stories. We entered the dining hall just as one of the station shifts was eating dinner, and we joined them. I ate and ate, and there seemed to be no limit to my capacity. I ate until a sharp pain beneath my sternum made me stop. The blood rushed to my head and sweat broke out on my forehead. I was in food shock. I saw that John and Steve, who had eaten great quantities themselves, were watching me with concern. I stood up, walked around for five minutes, then resumed eating.

For the next thirty hours we scarcely slept. Steve slept a few hours, John slept a little less, and I slept not at all. I tried several times, but the pressure of food against my ribs made sleep impossible. I had actually eaten myself into a traumatic and sleepless condition! That was remarkable, I thought, as I lay with my eyes closed, listening to my heart beat furiously, pacing my insane new metabolism. I planned to remember it and note it. My eyes closed, I heard someone new come in off his shift—happy loud footsteps and a new voice—and heard another voice tell him, "That's one of these guys who walked across the mountains." I wanted to open my eyes and see what he looked like, but didn't.

The station men left their equipment in shifts all through the day and night, so there were always new faces. There was Otto, a simple man who donated all of his inflated salary to charity, and who was the butt of most of the surprisingly gentle practical jokes played at Barter Island. One time his friends convinced him that because

of a peculiarity of some polar time change he had bought drinks for everyone for a period twice as long as he thought he had. Then they gave him his money back. There was an eighteen-year-old dishwasher who wanted to be an actor. He talked to me about Shakespeare as if mine was the first ear on Barter Island available for that purpose, and he told me about his dilemma. Before coming to Alaska he had worked as an orderly in a mental hospital, and had witnessed the death of a patient. There was a suit over the death. Another orderly was charged with using unnecessary force, and the dishwasher had been asked to send a deposition. The accused orderly had been more violent than the rules permitted, the dishwasher believed, but not more violent than orderlies often were in practice. The dishwasher knew the pressures that had made the man act as he had, for the dishwasher had felt the pressures himself. Now, in Alaska, he felt the burden of the man's fate on his own shoulders, and it rode heavier every day. Wrestling with the burden occupied all his waking hours. There was nothing else to think about, no place to seek relief. He was alone with his conscience in the bare and soon-to-be-frozen North. The single-spaced pages of his deposition were piling up beside his typewriter as he tried to explain things to a distant court. It looked like a novel.

There was an engineer, an old man who when he heard that I recently had been in South America, invited me to his room. The small room was meticulously neat, and filled with mementos from a lifetime of work in foreign fields. For me, every item in the room seemed charged with a monumental end-of-lifetime loneliness. In its neatness and richness, in its redolence of pipe smoke, the room reminded me of my grandfather's house. The engineer had the same feeling for things made of polished hardwood that my grandfather had when he was alive. There was a large map of South America on the wall, and the engineer indicated with his pipestem the places in Brazil and Venezuela where he had worked. As I left he wrote his name and address on a card. I looked, and there was my grandfather's graceful and disciplined Old World handscript.

Through the sleepless hours we ate, talked, listened, and read desperately, as if at any moment someone might take it all away from us. Sports Illustrated! Time! Ebony! Popular Mechanics! I found myself reading only a paragraph or two from each article. I wanted to read more, but the distractions were infinite. New conversations, new magazines. Barter Island got its news from a teletype machine that would rap something out from time to time. I was forever jumping up to read the latest word.

Insights came in a rush, as they would to an observer who was seeing Western civilization for the first time. I wanted to remember everything and write it all down. It would make for a great literary record of a single period of wakefulness, I thought, but too many things happened and I now remember only snatches.

I remember walking down to the Eskimo village, Kaktovik, which stood a half mile from the installation. I remember the paths between houses—a network of odd boards and scraps of metal over the thawed and puddly ground. The children with runny noses playing outside. The sled dogs chained down by the water, their conversations and laments so continuous that soon we no longer heard them. The beached boats needing paint. I remember visiting people, going in and out of their houses, built of scavenged wood and corrugated metal. Most were like doll houses inside, built tight to retain warmth, with low ceilings and doorways, and with drying clothes hanging everywhere from low beams. Small children were underfoot, in shirt tails but no pants, and the old-ivory color of their legs and cheeks demonstrated how recently their race came from Asia.

I remember our conversation with Neil Allen, a Kaktovik Eskimo who was sixty-five but looked much younger. He was a strong and energetic man. He told us how his family had come from Point Barrow in skin boats in 1911. Life had been harder on this coast then, he said. The people went hungry often. He recalled times when his father returned from hunting too tired to speak. Neil had gone up to his father one of these times, with his nose running, and had asked his father to help him. His father turned toward him and said, "This is the way life is. I can't help you."

I remember looking up from my reflections, as we walked back to the early-warning station, to see standing unchained in the middle of the road a half or quarter wolf, golden against the gray gravel, poised in profile and perfectly motionless, like a symbol waiting for me to attach its meaning. It watched our approach, pretending not to notice us, and stepped aside at the last moment.

Back at the station, the pace of events did not abate. I remember fragments. I remember Steve's tic returning. The tic had departed in the quiet of the Sheenjek country; now suddenly there it was again—a muscle in Steve's face jumping. It was a chilling return, and I watched aghast for a moment; then something else came up and my attention turned elsewhere. I remember looking at myself in a latrine mirror. It was a strange confrontation—my new bearded self staring back. I took off my shirt, for the first time in weeks, and looked at myself. I had not lost more than eight pounds, but I looked immeasurably leaner. All

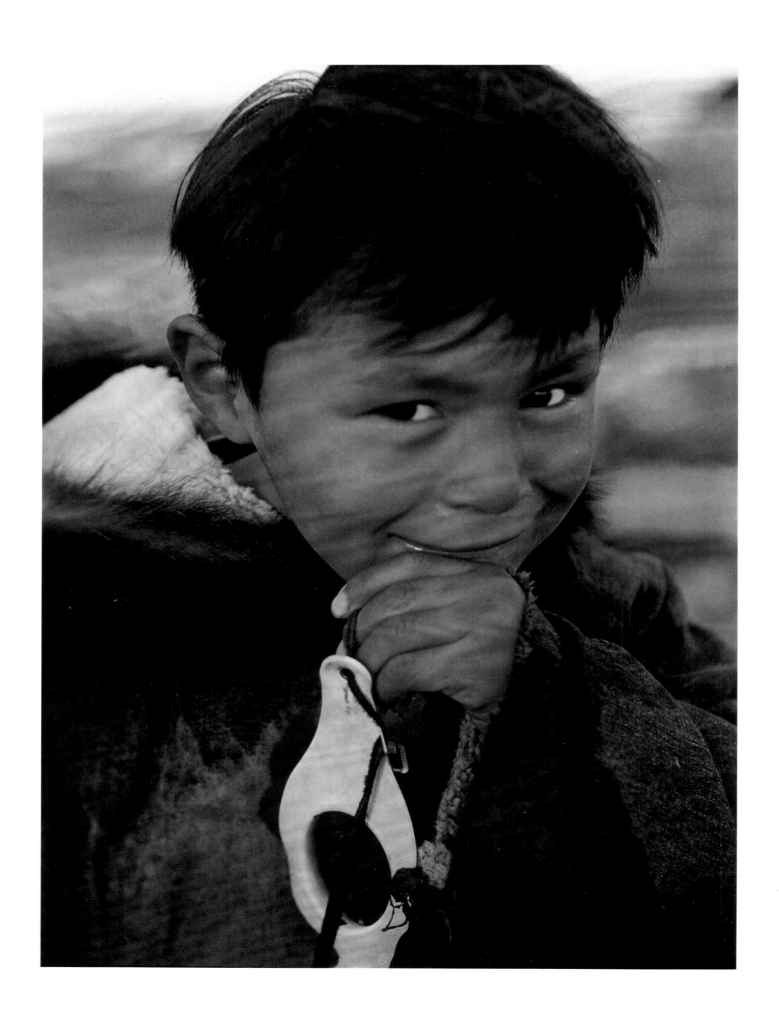

the muscles were clearly defined under the skin. I looked like one of those ectodermisless torsos illustrating an anatomy book. I looked good.

Then suddenly events did slow down. The security officer of the station saw us and made a fuss about us. We had no clearances. We were asked to leave. It was nothing personal, Otto said, very embarrassed—he knew we weren't spies—but regulations were regulations. The Eskimos would not mind if we camped at the edge of the village.

So the three of us were walking again. We three were under the sky once more, a sky not yet dark enough that evening for the aurora borealis to dance there, but soon to be. As we walked Steve bitterly cursed the Army mentality. There was no way he could escape it, it seemed.

John and I were disappointed. The station had been comfortable and exciting. Now our packs were on our backs once more. We were listening again to the sound of our feet in the gravel. We left the moon-station behind us, its metal domes shining silver-blue in the arctic twilight. We walked toward the wooden village, glowing a warm red in the light of the same low sun. Behind us at the station no human life was visible—everyone was inside working the equipment, apparently. Ahead we could see the figures of a few children still playing among the shacks. As we walked in exile toward the alien village, the irony was inescapable. But it really was not bitter at all, and John and I just looked at one another. Ahead we heard the voices of the dogs, and the sound of children laughing.

Friends of the Earth in the United States, and sister organizations of the same name in other countries, are working for the preservation, restoration, and more rational use of the earth. We urge people to make more intensive use of the branches of government that society has set up for itself. Within the limits of support given us, we try to represent the public's interest in the environment before administrative and legislative bodies and in court. We add to, and need, the diversity of the conservation front in its vital effort to build greater respect for the earth and its living resources, including man.

We lobby for this idea. We work closely with our sister organizations abroad, and with new and old conservation organizations here and abroad that have saved so much for all of us to work for.

We publish—books, like this, and in smaller format—because of our belief in the power of the book and also to help support ourselves. Our environmental newspaper is "Not Man Apart."

If the public press is the fourth estate, perhaps we are the fifth. We speak out for you; we invite your support.

Friends of the Earth Foundation, also in San Francisco, supports the work of Friends of the Earth and organizations like it with projects in litigation and in scientific research, literature, and education.

Publisher's Note: The book is set in Centaur and Arrighi by Mackenzie & Harris Inc., San Francisco. It was lithographed and bound by Arnoldo Mondadori Editore, Verona, on coated paper made by Cartiera Celdit and Bamberger Kaliko Fabrik. The design is by David Brower. The Layout is by Kenneth Brower.